The White Sands of Pasir Poetih

Frederik Bras

Published 2009 by arima publishing

www.arimapublishing.com

ISBN 978 1 84549 296 0

Printed and bound in the United Kingdom

Typeset in Garamond 11/14

Swirl is an imprint of arima publishing.

arima publishing
ASK House, Northgate Avenue
Bury St Edmunds, Suffolk IP32 6BB
t: (+44) 01284 700321

www.arimapublishing.com

Prologue; (Playroom)

The children cheered when the Indonesian servant clad in full Indonesian regalia, entered the room. His colourful headgear especially was very much admired by the children. With a smile he handed Lily a carafe filled with fresh fruit juice. After she bowed to thank him, Lily dressed in her paper royal costume, served.

Her face was set in the "I am of royal blood" expression, which suited the scene of the play. Three pairs of eyes, apart from her own, looked down with great anticipation at the glasses as she filled three.

"We have to do better," Lily said while she was filling the fourth glass for herself.

"Wong, the next time you must be more convincing as the dragon," she said disapprovingly. "When Mas slays you, you must fall down right away and not behave like a drunken sailor. And Lancelot on your wooden horse, you must look straight at me when you enter the stage because you are in love with me. Will you kindly do that next time?"

The four children were playing their version of the "Knights of the Round Table". The Regent, Mas' father and his Dutch wife looked on amusedly.

"They are so serious about their game," the Regent turned to his wife.

"You wonder what the future will hold for them don't you? They all are from different nationalities; nevertheless they are such good friends. Of course that is how it should be but there is more than just friendship between these four. This is something special between them. It has a magic hard to describe, intangible if you like."

"I certainly would also describe it as more than friendship, and indeed hard to define," his wife replied. "Isn't there an Indonesian belief that there is such a thing as a common soul? Richard is the only one who is Dutch really and although they are still children you can see that he is already keen on Lily, but she is only twelve and he is as old as Mas, just fifteen. And Lily is actually Hungarian by birth. That is, her parents are."

"How then did her father become an officer in the Dutch forces?"

"There is nothing to be surprised about. The Dutch forces are even more of a mixture than the French foreign legion. Just look at the names. Some names in the forces are even Arab names. Again any nationality is possible in this Indonesia of ours and nobody is different if you have been born and brought up here, which is what these children have been of course. And I have so much of my life lived here too, that I also feel Indonesian. And your children, our children are certainly Indonesian."

"That is only because they were brought up here of course. You could equally say that they are Dutch because you, their mother is Dutch. But in outlook all these children are Indonesian, you are right of course. What binds them is stronger than what divides them artificially. These children as you say have such an uncanny strong bond. Their friendship will last throughout their lives. You'll see." His wife nodded.

"You are absolutely right. I just hope that the thunderclouds along the horizon will not mar their lives. The Japanese are out to dominate Asia."

"Don't worry about that. That will never happen, America will not tolerate that," the Regent said with conviction.

"Let us hope that you are right," his wife said pensively.

Neither the Regent nor his wife had any idea that the thunderclouds were very real and that they eventually would influence the lives of everyone living in the Dutch East Indies at that time; including the lives of the four children, who were playing their game of: "The knights of the round table."

Chapter 1

The feeble rays of the watery yellow sun only just managed to pass through the window of his chauffeur driven limousine. It did nothing to warm his mood. All the trees, lining the road they were passing, had lost their leaves now and their bare branches showing only the first covering of snow, already melting in places, were the only features breaking the monotony of grey buildings, warehouses and chimneys of Tokyo's outskirts. Whole sections of unfinished building blocks of concrete were left haphazardly standing in between the warehouses. They only added to the already dismal scenery around him. There was nothing cheerful or colourful for him to see that could lift his spirits of doom!

In his hands he firmly clutched the papers revealing his plan for the attack on Pearl Harbour and the assault on Singapore. He on purpose had made no copy. A copy could fall into the hands of another person. The plan had to be top secret. No one else so far was to know about it. As long as there was nothing in writing except his own notes, which he kept carefully hidden, no person but he himself would know what he had planned. The keystone of success for his meticulously worked out campaign, depended on its absolute secrecy. But would this enterprise succeed? If it did not; he would be blamed not only by the Emperor and Tukagoshi the minister of war, but by the whole Japanese nation. The Emperor would lose face and the nation would never forgive him for it.

He had worked out the strategy to its finest detail; as much as it was possible to do so. Nothing was left to chance. Yet he knew that even in the most meticulous detail, there could still be an element which was overlooked and which could just be the one factor, which would result in a calamitous disaster, which could never have been foreseen by him. The reason was that the plan could not possibly be made watertight. There were too many factors, which depended on other unknown factors, which in turn depended on other still unknown ones again.

If one went wrong, all the others, since they depended for success on one another, could well collapse like a pack of playing cards around him and he would be left with a jumbled up heap of meaningless jig saw. He knew the consequences if that were to happen! A cold shiver passed the whole length of his spine. In that case the only way out for him would be Hara-kiri. But that would not be a honourable Hara-kiri; it would be a premature one. He would be committed to a Hara kiri out of shame for his failure. Not at all the Hara kiri he desired. His failure would call for atonement on his part, and he had to oblige: giving his life. It was the Japanese way. It would be expected of him. He could not hide anywhere! No: Yamamoto had a much more grandiose plan in his mind than just a simple suicide.

If he could succeed in dealing an effective blow to the American Navy in Pearl Harbor, to be followed by the conquest of Singapore from the British as well; his name would forever shine on the firmament of Japanese folklore. He held no illusion that Japan could win a war against America. He knew also that the other generals and admirals of the war counsel he was about to meet, did not hold the same view as he did. Neither did Tukagoshi the minister of war. As far as Yamamoto was concerned, they believed in fairy tales. And what would the Emperor think? He would have to believe what he was told.

He would listen to Tukagoshi's advice. Yamamoto knew that it would be the wrong advice. Wrong for Japan and equally wrong for him!

If he Yamamoto did succeed in dealing a heavy blow to the American Navy, it would only be a temporary victory. America would recover and the Americans would hunt him down. They would find out that he masterminded the attack on Pearl Harbor, he was sure. And they would kill him. They would never let him get away with it. But this at least would be a honourable Hara-kiri. One he could accept himself; a protracted one; a bushido's death, first having slain his enemy. If only.......

"We have arrived Sir," the driver announced, confronting Yamamoto with the reality of his situation. He had to cut off his train of thought. Anxiously he looked out the window. Was he ready for this ordeal? He had to be, like it or not! The car drove at 30 MPH through the gateway into the lane leading to the Emperor's Palace.

Joyously coloured flowers preciously cultivated, usually flanked the lane. Now they were all dead; their bare branches dripping wet from the melting snow. It was not a welcoming entry. The scene only reinforced the impending death feeling he felt deep down. The limousine reduced speed to twenty miles, then to ten, then five MPH, agonising moments, then stopped exactly in front of the side entrance to the palace, where two sentries in full military uniform including fixed bayonets, were posted.

The side entrance was chosen as a show of respect to the Emperor. One sentry stepped forward and opened the car door for Yamamoto. There was nothing else for it. He had to get out of the car and accept the cards dealt him by fate. With difficulty Yamamoto gathered his Samurai sword from the seat and climbed out. His heart pounded loudly in his chest. The sentries presented arms and shouted attention as Yamamoto brushed passed them, still struggling to hook the heavy Samurai sword in its place on his belt. It was a continual battle for Yamamoto, trying to wear the sword correctly. His nervous fingers refused to obey. The sword was too long, inherited from a tall ancestor. He had to have it on his belt before entering the palace. It was part of his uniform. It was a sign of respect to the Emperor.

Warily he climbed the red marble stairs in front of him. Soon he would be in the presence of the Emperor and the Council of war ministers: generals and admirals.

Yamamoto did not look forward to this meeting. He visualised the cool non-blinking eyes of the war minister Tukagoshi resting on him. Those eyes had a hypnotising quality and he had experienced their kind of influence before. They then had belonged to a rattlesnake when he was lying on the sand in the Mojave

Desert. One foot from his face the rattler had been ready to strike. It was only at the last minute that his presence of mind and his agility as an athlete, to be able to move quickly, that the strike had just missed him. But the memory was fresh in his mind. He recalled the fear he had felt then.

When he reached the top of the five red marble steps he had just climbed, he heard his name announced over the loudspeaker. The sound reverberated through the empty hallway; one wall bouncing his name forward to the next, then the next passing it on again and so forth. To Yamamoto, it was as though they did not want to have anything to do with his name.

The floor covered with luscious red carpets, did nothing to dampen the eerie tone. His anxious mind interpreted the sound like a litany of death; the sound of doom itself; a foreboding of things to come should his plan fail. Nobody then would want to know him. Even his wife would share in the shame.

At times like these, he wished that he had never reached the rank he now held: that of supreme commander to the forces. He then would not, nor need to have, these feelings of fear and inadequacy. But he had to ban those negative thoughts from his mind, get hold of himself. "Control your thoughts," he severely spoke to himself. He considered the main necessity for success the ability to do just that. It had given him the rank he once cherished and now was his, and he should be satisfied that he could die a brave war hero when the time came. To Yamamoto, this was the highest honour a soldier could desire. To die for the Emperor after acquiring victory first! It was the only way he could think. After all he was Japanese.

The large mahogany door in front of him was swung open by a lackey bowing low as Yamamoto started to enter the room. He filled the doorway; then paused, looking round, his gaze finally resting on the Emperor, a small figure sitting at the head of the table. Except for the Emperor, everybody stood up and bowed. Yamamoto also bowed, first in the direction of the Emperor, then at every one standing at the table in turn, starting with the war minister Tukagoshi standing like a statue to his left. Only then did he enter the room and accept the chair, which was drawn from the table by a geisha, who then busied herself to relieve him of his sword. Yamamoto's lips were dry. If only he could confide in someone; anyone, the reasons for his fears. But that was not possible. The war council would not want a compromise. It would only result in considering him a coward. Yamamoto knew of himself that he was far from being a coward. He had shown his courage on more than one occasion before. It wasn't cowardice that made him hesitate now. Long ago he had decided that war against America, the industrial Giant, was a mistake, worse; it was suicide, Japan's suicide as well as his own death. Of all the generals and admirals the Emperor had summoned to his Palace today; he, Yamamoto, was in the best position to know this.

His military studies in the USA, had brought him in close contact with influential American families. The wealth of those families had impressed him. This wealth had been brought about by industrial undertakings and top management, the total of which resulted in industrial power, the like of which Japan, no matter how hard the labour force toiled, could never match, not in the foreseeable future, maybe never, he thought. Wealth, synonymous with industrial power, America possessed in abundance. No, he did not want war with this formidable industrial giant.

Japan had planned for war, yes extensively so. Everybody knew it: the British, the Dutch, the French, also the Americans, but everybody chose to ignore it. Japan able to take on the United States? Impossible! They would not dare, the Allies had smugly declared, not wanting to face up to the all too clear ambition of Japan.

Yamamoto was involved in all the war plans. Naturally he was. Nevertheless, he preferred to negotiate if that were possible. However Japan needed oil for its developing industries and for the war in China. Having no natural resources of oil, oil needed to be imported and America effectively controlled the sale of this essential product.

The atrocities of the war in China were too well known and disapproved of by the Allied powers, which considered that the conflict in China against an inferior enemy was only a training ground for future more ambitious expansion, namely the conquest of Asia by Japan. This was the main reason that had resulted in the embargo on the flow of oil to Japan. And the Allied powers were absolutely correct. Japan was preparing for war and the conquest of Asia. But Britain, France, the United States and the Dutch East Indies apart from the oil restrictions and keeping a not too watchful eye on Japan, chose to do nothing to prevent it. Every one reasoned that Japan did not have the industrial means without which it could never win and realising that, Japan would never start a war, which would lead to its suicide!

All she did was sabre rattling. The apathy through arrogance to face the truth was total!

It was true that to a great extent Yamamoto was actively involved in the plans for war; he wanted expansion into Asia for Japan also, such as possession of the Dutch colonies full of oil. The list included Singapore and Malaysia, but he did not want to risk war with America, a war he knew Japan could not possibly win. But how could he keep America out of the conflict?

Any attempt by Japan at widening the war even with China and Southern Indo- China alone, would already be considered a dagger pointed at the heart of the Philippines and indirectly at the heart of the U.S.A by the Americans. That America might declare war on Japan, if that were to happen, was far from unlikely. Japan was too ambitious and becoming dangerous already, the Americans had decided.

There had been a glimmer of hope getting the oil it needed. Japan was flirting with the Dutch East Indies. In its expansion policy, the Japanese had encouraged Japanese women to marry Dutchmen living in the Dutch East Indies. A few lonely men, especially planters, had married Japanese women and found them to be good housewives, dutiful, obedient and above all loyal. Japan wanted in this way to get an entry into the oil from the rich oil fields the Dutch East Indies possessed. The subsequent Japanese delegation to Batavia, the capital of the Dutch East Indies, was met courteously. The Japanese stated their case forcibly; demanding delivery of oil, not in a subtle way, but even in a rather arrogant manner! At least so the Allies thought. In a way because of this, but mainly through the most powerful influence, namely that of the USA, the only real power Japan feared and the only one with muscle; the delegation came back empty-handed. It meant a severe slap in the face for Japan.

Yamamoto was now powerless. Oil was necessary. He now realised there were only two ways open for Japan. One was to scrap their extended Asia plan and Yamamoto knew full well that none of the warlords were going to give it up, or alternatively: an extended war, out of which Japan would come out the loser, there was no other way.

Yamamoto knew the mood. The warlords were arrogant. Japan had won the navy battle against Russia in 1910 and the Japanese considered themselves a superior race. They were also successful in their war against China. They could win a war against America too, so they thought. Moreover Hitler was winning. France was already beaten and there was every indication that Britain would fare no better. When that happened Germany would help beat the Americans. Germany was still smarting from America's involvement in the Great War of 1914-- 1918.

"Your Majesty," he addressed the Emperor, when it came to his time to speak: "I don't agree with the opinion of those of my comrades, who think that America will stand idly by when we further expand into French-Indo China to be followed by the conquest of the rest of Asia. I have listened to all the arguments. We will almost certainly risk war with America."

Expectantly he looked round the war council seated at the port wine coloured mahogany table, a masterpiece of carpentry. If only there was one of them who would support him now! One who would raise his voice and would see his point of view. One who would be mature enough to see that to risk war with the USA was suicide! No one moved. There was no indication that anyone shared his misgivings. His gaze finally came to rest on Tukagoshi the war minister.

At this moment, Yamamoto realised that the case for avoiding the war against America was lost. He had seen it coming. Tukagoshi's behaviour was all too plain to see. He wanted war.

Thus far, Tukagoshi had looked down in front of him at the tablecloth, which only barely managed to cover the cherry wood inlay of the table. The Japanese characters on the cherry wood inlay spoke of the brave exploits of the Bushido knights of the Empire. He did not need inspiration but if he had needed any; it was there, right in front of him!

Everyone seated around the table was in deep thought after Yamamoto's words. They waited for Tukagoshi to speak and give his opinion, as was the custom. It was up to him to create the correct atmosphere. Was it going to be a warlike address or a peaceful one?

Tukagoshi after the silence, which hung like a dead weight in the room, at last considered that the time had now come for him to speak. He was no longer going to be intimidated by the might of America like Yamamoto was. He got up and bowed in the direction of the Emperor. His inscrutable face behind the glasses he wore betrayed no emotion. Neither did the rest of his behaviour. Here was a statue speaking. Only his lips moved, not even his mouth. His gaze remained fixed in front of him. You could easily believe that he was looking into the future, getting information from some unseen source. It seemed as though Tukagoshi had heard nothing of what Yamamoto had said. He chose his words with care and lent weight to them by long pauses in between. "We take it," he started," that Yamamoto is not against war. Yet his reluctance to attack America is hard to understand. Is it," he hesitated again, "that his reluctance to wage war against America is influenced by the friends he has in that country? I understand," facing Yamamoto this time,"that you were intimately friendly with two boys; friends your age."

At this point he even managed a faint smile, which was totally out of character and which he immediately regretted. The smile almost instantaneously froze on his lips.

"And you boarded with that family, is that not so?" he resumed, stroking back the creases in his face produced by the careless smile. This time he had unmistakably turned to Yamamoto.

Yamamoto shivered when he saw the cold non- blinking eyes, without emotion resting on him. The whole experience of the rattlesnake in the desert came back in all its clarity. But this was the opportunity he had been waiting for. Now that the war council's mood preferred war, he would explain the extensive, and what other people later perhaps, would call: "clever" plan, to deal the Americans a heavy blow in Pearl Harbour.

He got up pushing his chair back, adjusting the papers on the table in front of him, which contained his plan for the attack on Pearl Harbour. The Emperor studied him intently through his myopic spectacles, realising that Yamamoto had something very important to say. The index finger of his right hand moved, pushing his glasses further up his nose so that he could see Yamamoto better. He had always admired the quality of this general and his prudence. What did he have to say now?

Yamamoto looked around the table to make sure that he had the attention of everyone in the war council, especially Tukagoshi's, then inhaled the air forcibly and deeply a few times before he spoke:

"I want it to be understood," he began pronouncing his words carefully, "that my allegiance first and foremost is to my Emperor and to Japan. My hesitation," he went on, "is caused by my awareness of the industrial power of the U.S.A. This power is simply awesome. I have seen it. If we are to win this war, we must strike a decisive blow to, and must destroy, the American fleet, or at least cripple it severely from the very beginning.

"I mean literally from day one! This is of the utmost importance." He paused and looked around the table letting his words sink in.

"How?" Tukagoshi almost whispered, coolly hypnotising Yamamoto, yet moving ever so slightly on his seat nearer to him, like a snake slowly approaching its prey.

"Surprise," Yamamoto said shaking himself bodily, to escape from the spell which Tukagoshi's eyes had produced. Again he paused.

"An attack on Pearl Harbour perhaps?" the Japanese admiral sitting on his left hissed.

"Yes!" Yamamoto confirmed. "When we declare war, the declaration must immediately, and I emphasise immediately, be followed by the attack on the American fleet with every possible might available to us. This means we must have our striking force, that is aeroplanes first and aeroplanes second and third, within easy striking distance, already in the air near PEARL HARBOUR when the war declaration is handed to the Americans. Before they even have had time to read the last line on the paper, our bombs will already be dropping on the American fleet. A daring plan yes, but again no time must be allowed to pass between the declaration of war and the actual annihilation of the American fleet. Time is of the utmost importance." Leaning over the table in the direction of Tukagoshi he continued:

"If we lose this important item, the surprise factor in the attack, the Americans will have time to avert the strike and the fleet will leave Pearl Harbour. In that case it will be much more difficult to deal a decisive blow." He rustled the papers on the table in front of him to win time and let his words sink in.

Tukagoshi now was fully sitting at the end of his seat, thereby betraying his only emotion so far. This was not what he had expected! He had totally misjudged the feelings he thought Yamamoto held for America. Yamamoto all the time had a plan worked out, and what a fantastic plan it was. Annihilation of the American fleet of all things! Nothing less! The impact of what Yamamoto had said was evident in the silence, which followed his words.

"Once the American fleet is out of commission or at least badly damaged," Yamamoto continued: "the rest of Asia can be conquered quickly. I see no difficulty ahead in that way." He was speaking confidently now. "This plan will succeed. You only have to do your bit. The total plan will not be exactly known to each one of you but only to me. This is for security sake," he added. "You must not question any of your parts in it but you must exactly do what you will be instructed to do; exactly what you have been told without fail." He looked round the table. "Am I clear?"

A long pause followed after Yamamoto sat down. The only sound came from the ticking of the clock on the wall. It was almost as if people had stopped breathing! The Japanese admiral blinked a few times before he got up to speak

"You mean to say that our fleet; that is aeroplane carriers and destroyers will have to travel a distance of about 3000 miles undetected to Pearl Harbour?"

"Correct, I am counting on the fact that you will do just that." Yamamoto confirmed coolly. "First you must sail north then east and only when you reach the longitude of Pearl Harbour turn south. Pearl Harbour must be approached from the north. Not from any other direction, otherwise the fleet will be detected and the Americans will be forewarned."

Admiral Nagushi sank back in his chair dabbing his forehead with his handkerchief.

Three thousand miles with a fleet of at least forty ships undetected to Pearl Harbour! Nothing less Yamamoto expected of him. How on earth could he do that even doing exactly what Yamamoto had suggested he should do? Yet Yamamoto with his daring self-confidence already considered it done!

"What about Singapore and what about the Philippines?" Tukagoshi, who in his mind through wishful thinking had already seen the American fleet destroyed and in flames, wanted to know. He was no longer standing like a statue but he was tugging at his coat sleeve. The emotion had finally become too strong even for him.

"I am coming to that," Yamamoto replied standing up again, stroking the creases out of the papers lying in front of him. He spoke easier now after his confidence had returned. In his mind he had carefully calculated that there were undoubtedly some points in Japan's favour. The Japanese war machine was already well oiled. They had had war experience in China for years.

Around Nangking their battleground experience was invaluable. He and his generals outstripped their inexperienced American counterparts in this respect. These American generals and commanders, he considered fashion boys wearing ridiculous uniforms and felt hats Their soldiers were not battle-hardened like his own soldiers; they were used to easy living, they could never live off the land like his could, and instead needed Coca cola, popcorn and doughnuts to feel satisfied. Moreover America's last battle, the Great War, was entered into when the war was at its last stages. The Germans were already nearly beaten then, but not this time!

"I'll explain Singapore first."

"The Philippines," Tukagoshi interrupted, "because that is American territory."

"Later," Yamamoto dismissed him, realising that Tukagoshi again wanted to refer to the friendship he at one time held for his friends in America.

"Singapore," he firmly resumed "The defence of that peninsula is altogether dependent on an attack from the sea. But we will not attack from that direction. No; instead we will land 150 miles north of Singapore. The beaches there are easily approachable from the sea. There are no coastal batteries to hold us up and the roads from Singapore are too primitive for the enemy to find us quickly. We can have all our troops, I reckon initially 10,000 men ashore, before the British know about our landing. We have excellent maps that were made by our secret services. The swampland between our landing area and Singapore is to our advantage; we can move quickly but the British cannot. Tanks and horses are useless in that terrain."

"Then how are you to move your troops?" General Suzuki butted in. "We will use bicycles," Yamamoto said calmly.

"Bicycles?" exclaimed Tukagoshi fumbling with his sleeves from excitement again. Was Yamamoto serious? Even the Emperor sat forward in his chair, almost forgetting his dignity. What on earth could Yamamoto mean? Did he really say bicycles?

"Yes bicycles, children bicycles," Yamamoto replied confidantly.

"We have experimented with these and calculated that we can travel an average of thirty miles per day even in swamp land. This means that in distance we can be in Singapore in five days after the landing. Of course it will take longer, it may take a month, two months at the most in my calculations. Opposition is weak, we have spies who speak Malay fluently and the natives will be on our side. They see us as liberators from their colonial oppressors.

The British will not expect this attack from the land and they will certainly underestimate our speed. As I said before; thanks to our bicycles, we can travel fast."

"You need tanks and horses," Suzuki the cavalry officer insisted. He scraped his throat, which he always did when he became nervous. His mother had tried to wean him of this nervous tic: "it is not becoming an officer of the Imperial Japanese Army," she said. But her words had failed totally. It soothed his nerves when he became nervous and that is why he persisted in this silly habit.

"How would you get them there so quickly?" Suzuki after loudly clearing his throat for the second time repeated his objection.

"We will," Yamamota spoke with confidence, "from Siam.

A small force of our army, will invade that country from the north at the same time that the fleet and air force attack Pearl harbour. There is no army to speak of, no resistance. We will force the prime minister of that country to sign a peace treaty with Japan. He must do that in name of the King who is too young. Not one shot will even be fired; he has to sign. I am counting on the fact that he is a wise man. There will be no difficulty. If he offers resistance, we will appoint somebody else in his government as temporary prime minister, who will sign the peace treaty and who will sign in name of the King instead. But the minister is a wise man," he said with confidence. "Moreover as I said before; the children bicycles are our tanks and horses initially; that we will prove."

The Emperor sat upright again

"I take it you are absolutely sure?"

"About this I am absolutely sure Your Majesty," Yamamota replied. "We can take Singapore in three weeks, maybe one month. We will by then have 30000-40000 troops available, for the invasion and capture of Singapore."

"But the enemy has 70,000 troops," Tukagoshi said referring to his information in front of him.

"In theory yes; but the British have hardly any planes. We depend on our success on Pearl harbour. I can't emphasise this too strongly. The only possible defeat lies there and only there," Yamamoto warned.

"Defeat?" the Emperor shifted in his seat, his heart missing a beat or two.

"Defeat?" exclaimed the other members around the table.

"I said possible defeat," Yamamoto reminded them.

"If we can isolate the Philippines, the Americans under the command of MacArthur will have to surrender, or be totally annihilated in three month. But if we fail in our objective at Pearl Harbour, MacArthur will be able to get reinforcements and will become a formidable opponent, whom I hate to have as an enemy then.

His reputation is well known and it was Roosevelt himself who has sent him for the defence of the Philippines. Our success is possible only by a short intensive attack on the American fleet and then a quick war, capturing Singapore shortly thereafter.

"Once we have captured the Philippines and Singapore, the Dutch East Indies will fall into our hands like a Sakura flower falling onto sacred earth. We then will have as much oil as is necessary to continue the war. The Dutch army is of no consequence and the navy is old-fashioned. There is only one modern battleship the "de Ruyter", but we have a navy thirty times numerically stronger.

After the fall of the Dutch East Indies, Singapore, and the Philippines, the whole of Asia is in our hands. America will have to negotiate a peace settlement.

"Imagine we will have: French Indo China, Siam, Malaysia, Singapore, the Dutch East Indies, and the Philippines, all the territories now occupied by the colonial powers. The peace settlement with America will be on our terms. We will then have so many prisoners of war to bargain with, that we can enforce this exchange. India will be taken care of by our Allies, Germany and Italy, and England will be totally isolated. We will arm local troops, who can keep law and order to unload the burden on our own troops"

"What about resistance?" General Yamashita asked, carefully, stroking his moustache back in place, which was disturbed by his irritated hand-movement when Yamamoto had used the word "defeat". And that in the presence of the Emperor! A Japanese soldier never entered the word defeat in his vocabulary.

Yet he was very much aware of Yamamoto's envious war record. He would not have warned of a possible defeat if that possibility had not been a real one. So real, that it had to be given the most careful consideration in order that it could be avoided. Yamashita considered that he too would give it the same attention. He was sure that Yamamoto had already carefully worked out the plan for the campaign in the Malaysian peninsula. Enough detail to know that it was going to be successful.

On previous campaigns, Yamamoto had left nothing to chance. His deservedly enviable success rate as a general, no doubt was a result of this careful attention to detail. Yamashita had therefore decided to bring up the subject of resistance, so that he also would be aware of all the pitfalls possible. Who knows; he might be the one chosen by Yamamoto for this part in the campaign.

"As you know," Yamamoto replied patiently, there are about 70,000 British troops for the defence in Singapore. Considering that we only have about 30,000 men: would seem that we are outnumbered two to one. In fact we have many more planes than the British. They need them for the European war. I am confident that the Singapore campaign will be successful."

At this point he deliberately sat down. He had said what there was to be said. His confidence was infectious. A silence fell after Yamamoto's last words.

The Emperor, recovering from the word "defeat" started to breath again. He observed Yamamoto closely. He was the obvious choice for such a daring plan. He looked from one to the other of his generals and admirals seated at the table. Yamamoto had the edge. They were all able, yes, but they did not have this special quality difficult to define. It had something to do with daring to take calculated risks. But only after having considered all the risks in detail first: thereafter carrying out the plan to perfection.

Tukagoshi the war minister had convinced the Emperor that they needed a leader, ruthless and determined. "Djenghis Khan and Alexander the Great were," he said to the Emperor "and look what they accomplished."

In his thinking Tukagoshi made a cardinal mistake. Djengis Khan and Alexander the Great had lost everything they had conquered eventually. That did not occur to him. The pleasure it gave him thinking of Yamamoto's war plan whetted his appetite and he became drunk, contemplating the glorious battles, which were to come. He liked confrontation; after all he was minister of war. Did he have any misgivings about the might of America? None!

He nodded a few times lest one nod did not convey enough agreement with the plan, which Yamamoto had enfolded. But Yamamoto himself was not under any illusion whatever. He would never get away with it, and Japan would ultimately lose the war. About this he was certain.

He was equally certain that none of the admirals and generals would agree with him to a peaceful settlement instead and that they would decide on war, with or without him. It was impossible for him to stem the tide.

The attack on the American fleet would be successful and Singapore would be taken in a short time. He had no doubt that the Japanese forces could accomplish this. But America the industrial giant would recover in time and then Japan would discover and feel what the might of America meant! In the meantime he would have his glory first! His accomplishments would be sung in war songs, having succeeded in the annihilation of the American fleet!

Thousands of Americans would die with one stroke. To top it all, the conquest of Singapore! He would be the most remembered Japanese hero of all times. The glory would be written in all Japanese annals of history forever! That he would die was certain, but what unique hero death. His Hara kiri would be momentous!

"We want to think about it," Yamashita thoughtfully remarked.

"No!" Yamamoto said. He stood up: dramatically, imposing the force of his personality on the others and turned to the Emperor. "The plan implies that nobody here leaves. No word must leak out from this meeting. We cannot go home and say good-bye to our families. The secrecy must be total: it is the way to success, I insist."

The Emperor was impressed with Yamamoto. It was as though his presence filled the room all by himself. Here was the totally confident warlord: standing apart from all the others, all by himself. Here was a warlord who did not need approval. Instead he dictated what he wanted. All the other warlords looked insignificant by comparison. Was he the Djenghis Kahn reincarnated he wondered. Could it be? He had heard of reincarnation. After all was he not a God himself? His people thought so.

It seemed to all the distinguished generals and admirals present at the table, that Yamamoto had done his homework. No one; not even for a moment, could have imagined that Yamamoto's heart was pounding from the release of adrenaline in his body. He took a sip of water from the glass in front of him to wet the dry mucosa of his lips and pharynx. When he took up his glass, the meaning of it was wrongly interpreted. The war council considered it a request for agreement to his plans and they congratulated him, for having studied his plans so thoroughly and carefully. They raised their glasses also. No one noticed that Yamamoto had spilled water from the rim of his glass due to the tremor of his hands. He was simply scared to death! A foreboding warned him that his plans would not go exactly as he wished.

Forty-eight hours after Yamamoto's meeting with the war council and with the Emperor of Japan, the attacking force of the Japanese navy in the shape of three aircraft carrier battleships and twenty destroyers, left Tokyo Bay. A Japanese fisherman, whose rowing boat was nearly capsized and swamped by the wake of the enormous wave caused by the last destroyer leaving, muttered to his mate:

"I wonder where this mighty fleet is going on manoeuvres and why all this secrecy; none of these ships carry any lights!"

When he said that; the industrial Giant across the Pacific was still slumbering. But not for much longer!

Would Yamamoto's plan succeed in total or only in parts of it? From the moment he was appointed supreme commander of the forces, Yamamoto realised that his fate was sealed. He could not refuse the post. Tukagoshi the war minister would have to tell the Emperor that he refused the post. It was unheard of that a mortal would question the Emperors judgement. It was considered that the Emperor had wanted to appoint Yamamoto, although in reality it was Tukagoshi who in name of the Emperor had done so. It was the highest honour that could have been bestowed on him. But Yamamoto from the beginning had realised that there was a negative side to the rank he was offered.

Japan was a warring nation. War against America, which denied oil to Japan, was already under consideration at the time of his appointment and Yamamoto knew that he could not change the mood of the warlords. Ultimately they would go to war, with or without him as they had done now. And by carrying out the war plan against the USA in the shape of the attack on Pearl Harbour, would mean that the Americans would hunt him down.

They would find out that he master- minded the attack. He could never escape the consequences of becoming supreme commander of the forces. The appointment had been forced upon him, and he could not have refused the honour.

Can anyone ever escape the consequences of a decision, even if forced upon one? Yamamoto realised he could not.

A feeble telegram by Dutch intelligence, reported the movement of the Japanese fleet with unknown destination. It was ignored! The general apathy on the Allied side was total. No one wanted to believe that an Eastern power could have the means and courage to lounge an unprovoked attack on America. Japan possessed both requirements and did. The prediction of Djojo Bojo in Java, centuries before, that a yellow Eastern race would occupy all the islands of the Dutch East Indies, which lay draped like a garland of emeralds around the equator, was taking shape. That Yamamoto's fate, because he could not refuse his appointment of supreme commander to the Japanese forces, would indirectly change Lily's life and mine forever, I could never have dreamt.

It was many years later that the Emperor of Japan looked at the setting of the sun. Half of it was lying below the horizon already. It was then that the thought struck him. What kind of persuasive power must Yamamoto have had to make him and the members of the War Council believe in the successful outcome of the daring plans he had enfolded to them so long ago. Looking at those plans now in the cold light of the day, the chance of success must have been very small. Yet Yamamoto had carried off all the promises he had made.

Suddenly another thought struck the Emperor. No one at the War Council had asked Yamamoto if Japan would win the war. This important essential question, which could have been answered either way, strangely enough was never asked. What would Yamamoto's answer have been? The Emperor realised that the hero he was thinking of and who had sacrificed his life for him, had not been an ordinary man. He bowed forward very deep towards the setting sun as a sign of respect. Just one name fell from his lips: "Yamamoto!"

Chapter 2

The silence following Doel's last words was deepening. It was as though it had independently acquired a life of its own: lying brooding in the corners of the hut, vibrant deep dark and sinister; like a wild creature waiting to pounce on its non-suspecting prey.

The shadows cast by the oil lamp, which was hanging on a rusty nail hammered haphazardly in the bamboo pole of the hut, were dancing on the billik matting of the walls. Menacing souls from the underworld stirred to life by the words Doel had used in his story?

The outside air coming through the open door of the fisherman's hut was cool on my brow and I gratefully accepted the slight breeze on my feverish forehead.

I could think straight again and got up from my cramped position behind the rottan table where my chest was pressed against it. I kicked the creaky chair away with my foot and felt immediately better. The blood was flowing back into my legs; the cramp disappeared. Was anything in the story he had told me plausible? It had been an extraordinary story.

As though by an inner instinct I wanted to turn the light from the oil lamp higher, so as to chase away the dancing menacing shadows on the billik matting of the hut. Then I realised that something heavy on my hand was trying to prevent me from doing so. I had to force the heaviness on my hand away and barely managed to turn up the light from the oil lamp.

The wick rose with difficulty, as though it was alive, resenting my interference at first, but then reluctantly accepted the increased light. Immediately the dancing shadows disappeared and the sinister darkness, which had accompanied them faded from the middle of the interior of the hut. But they remained in the far recesses, resenting the light that had so cruelly invaded their territory.

I paced up and down on the wooden floor of the hut, deep in thought. Absentmindedly I walked to the Chinese calendar on the bamboo wall, left by someone. I needed something to do and tore off the page of the day before.

The Chinese writing on the calendar advertised a brand of jasmine tea by a shop now long forgotten. The new calendar page read December 8th, the year 1941. The new date meant nothing to me. But equally nothing in the story had meant anything to me.

Yet Doel's story had captivated me. To a certain extent it had sounded like a fairy tale in the sense that it was believable, yet somehow impossible. In this particular story though, there had been something different. There was more to it than was just apparent, more than just lying superficially on the surface; it had a deeper meaning.

It was as though it stirred awake something: almost, but not totally, forgotten. It sounded more like a foreboding; a quality, which is not present in a fairy tale. Was this something of the nature an animal possesses? An instinct perhaps if you wanted to give it a name, warning you. An instinct no longer present in man, lost by civilisation?

I looked at my watch. It had taken Doel at least an hour to tell his story. "Djojo Bojo," I muttered to myself. The maize harvest. Could it be possible? There wasn't any evidence to corroborate the story. Nothing! A most unlikely prediction! And yet!

Of course there was a war on but the war was 8000 miles away, too far to even notice. Was the story ridiculous? Of course it was, I decided, although Doel believed it.

Everything was peaceful and quiet in this island Java, one of the islands of the Dutch East Indies. Multatuli in his book had compared them to a garland of emeralds entwining the equator, an apt description. Through the open door of the hut, I looked at the peace and quiet outside.

"Would you like to come sailing again tomorrow Tuan," Doel asked? His words had the effect of the loud clanging of a cymbal in an orchestra at the wrong time and where the music script had clearly indicated pianissimo instead. It cut the silence to shreds. After a pause I nodded.

"I would like that very much," I said. We had sailed every day in his outrigger sailing canoe, with Lily hosing the boat dry at times. The sailor got up and wished me good night.

Long after he had left, I was still deep in thought. I stared over the open sea. The moon stood high and threw a silver sheen over the sleeping coconut palms, dreaming in the moonlight. My watch told me that it was well past midnight. Far away I heard the surf breaking over the coral reef. Apart from that nothing, you could hear the silence; you could almost feel it, touching you, enveloping you. I almost felt that I had to free myself before it choked me.

I got out of the hut and went for a walk. The dog, which had been sleeping peacefully, roused and stretched its legs before following behind me. I decided to walk along the beach, heading to where the fishermen had dragged their prahus over the shells on to the beach. The soft sand under my feet still felt warm from the heat of the sun during the day. Every bungalow of the Bungalow Park was in darkness, including the one Lily occupied. She must be asleep. But sleep was far from my mind. My brain was feverishly working overtime and was utterly disturbed.

The story the old sailor had told me came back in all its detail, slow and deliberate. He believed in the prophecy all right. The threatening eerie feeling produced by the story was still with me. Why had this prediction, if it was one, alarmed me? Did it stir awake a recognition of something in my memory that had happened to me in the long distance past, a former life perhaps? Or something more relevant: something about to happen in the future, not only to me, but also to others?

I interrupted him at the beginning of his story.

"Who is Djojo Bojo?" I asked.

"He was a holy man, a hadji. He lived in the south west of Java in the Kidoel Heights, a wise man," he added. "Djojo Bojo predicted long ago that there will not be peace in this beautiful land for much longer.

This land will be invaded by a warrior yellow race, which will come from across the sea. These invaders will occupy all these islands. But that won't last," he continued, speaking softly.

Was it the effort of remembering exactly how the prophecy went, that made him speak so softly and carefully?

His head was hidden in the darkness of the shadows cast by the flickering oil lamp. Once in a while a flicker of light from the lamp, intent on bypassing the shadow, jumped, caught his one eye blind from an old injury and reflected the light bright blood red in the dark.

"The yellow race will only stay for the duration of a maize harvest." He finished his sentence almost hesitantly.

"And then, and then?" I asked full of anticipation. The story began to fascinate me.

"The white buffalo will go back to its stable after that," he resumed.

"The white buffalo," I said. You talk in riddles, what or who is the white buffalo?"

"I am not certain," the sailor hesitated. "Maybe it is the white Tuan who rules these lands," he said. I thought it over.

"Carry on please." There was a long pause.

"The rest of the prophecy is not too clear Tuan. But one thing is certain, there will not be any peace even after the white buffalo has returned to its stable because the Solo river will be red from blood and puntjuk hats will flow down the Solo river."

"Whose hats are the puntjuk hats?" I wanted to know. The sailor shrugged his shoulders.

"Puntjuk hats are worn by Chinese coolies as the Tuan knows."

"It does not make sense," I said. "The maize harvest; the yellow race, the white buffalo and now the puntjuk hats. The Chinese already live in the islands and have lived here for centuries. Why should the Solo River be red from blood? Is it their blood, since you say there will be puntjuk hats flowing down the Solo River? The blood of Chinese, are you saying that?" I again pressed him.

"It is what Djojo Bojo predicted," the sailor repeated with finality in his voice. "There is nothing to understand. Puntjuk hats will flow down the Solo River and the river will be red from blood. It will come true. That is what the prediction says and it can not be changed." A shudder went through me at his words.

"But how do you know it will come true at this time?" I questioned him. "After all you yourself said that Djojo Bojo lived a long time ago and it has not happened so far. If it is going to happen why not a hundred years from now; two hundred years from now, when we are all dead."

"But the war is already there Tuan," the sailor reminded me. "The whole of Europe is in a turmoil. And did you not hear the dogs howling last week when there was the earth tremor from the Ringgit? There has not been an earth tremor from the Ringgit for centuries. The Tuan knows that the Ringgit is a sacred mountain because a holy man lies buried at the top. The Ringgit has spoken a message of doom.

Djojo Bojo meant this period no other." He said this with conviction in his voice. No, better still with resignation. It was the fatalistic acceptance of the East. To him there was no doubt in his mind; that is why what he said was so disturbing. No theory but reality, which was about to come true and impossible to alter.

The silvery moonlight and the walk gave me no peace of mind. The dog was at my heels and showed signs of restlessness too. Did my mood reflect in the way the dog felt also, I wondered? But then I remembered that I had seen a panther in the neighbourhood a few nights before. He might have got the smell of the big cat. I turned back on my heels and the dog gladly changed direction.

In the early morning of the next day I got up and shaved, the sun having just risen above the horizon. The sea was pink in hue, mixed with the blue of the sky. The blending of the colours was worthy of a painter's dream. Perfection!

Myriad droplets of seawater on the sand reflected the rays of the early sun in sparkling particles like jewels cascaded out of a giant's jewel box. The morning was as beautiful as all the mornings of Lily's and my holiday had been. The birds in the waroe trees above the roof of my bungalow had already left their nests. They were always early. But had they ever come back? They had left in a hurry after the earthquake I remembered now.

I had stayed two weeks in this paradise with Lily.

Another week and our holiday would be a past dream, but lovely to look back to. I decided to forget the Djojo story. On the veranda of the restaurant under the Waru tree I joined Blommesteyn, the owner of this idyllic bungalow complex, for breakfast.

"You were late last night," Blommesteyn remarked. "Did something keep you awake? What did Doel and you talk about?"

"Oh, it was nothing," I evaded the question, feeling edgy in my chair.

"He talked to me of Madura Island where he comes from and how to sail there." No use in making Blommesteyn worried about the Djojo Bojo story, a stupid tale besides, even though Doel believed it.

"Did he not tell you about Djojo Bojo?" Blommesteyn asked.

"He did," I now admitted.

"Do you believe the story?" I asked Blommesteyn.

"Difficult to say," he hesitated. "I never heard the story before. There is much detail in it. And it is not a story, which could be made up by an illiterate fisherman. I hope it has not caused you a sleepless night," he added. Blommesteyn was a retired planter and as solid as a rock. He was not inclined just to believe any story told to him, no matter how much it was believed by the person who told it.

"There was one detail I am puzzled about and I want to put it to you," I said. "Doel mentioned that the yellow race occupying these islands would only stay for the time of a maize harvest. I then asked him, more in order to show my interest rather than anything else; if this period was a fixed one? To my surprise he said that this period could be influenced: "but only by a very powerful person." I then asked him if a head of state such as the Queen of the Netherlands could be such a powerful person."

"And what did he say?"

"Well this is what is so strange: he thought about it for a long time, then broke a piece of straw and after thinking for a while, his eyes closed as though in a trance, he said: "I think that some other powerful person will do it. But that is the only variation possible in the prediction. Everything else will come out as I have told you." He was very certain when he said that. By this time a cold shiver passed through me and I did not dare question him any further."

"A pity," Blommesteyn said. "It seems to me then that Doel himself was not exactly certain about that period himself."

"On the contrary I would say: he was very certain and already seemed to know that the period is going to be altered by a very powerful person and that it is the only change in the original, but not envisaged in the early prediction. Perhaps in the original story of Djojo Bojo the person living at the present time and who is capable of influencing that period of the maize harvest; belongs to a country that did not exist at the time when Djojo Bojo lived. That could be a plausible explanation.

"Since it had to be a very powerful person, he must have referred to at least a head of state or something similar. That state or country could for instance be the USA. For the rest he did not waver about the authenticity of the prediction one bit. Oh and there is another thing: he also referred to the earth tremor of the Gunung Ringgit a week ago. He used this event to point out, that the prediction would come about at this time, not at any other."

"That was a strange happening, this earth tremor," Blommesteyn said pensively. "Incomprehensible. The Gunung Ringgit is an extinct volcano, as everybody knows. The dogs perceived the tremor before I did.

Another strange thing is that since that event some birds have abandoned their nests in the waroe trees yonder, for no good reason I can think of. You of course know that the natives consider the Ringgit a sacred mountain."

The shiver in my spine returned. We were both quiet for a while. Blommesteyn then resumed the conversation.

"Don't tell your fiancé about the prediction. It will only worry her."

"Lily," I said, "she is more skeptical than you are."

"Well," said Blommesteyn, "the yellow race is obviously a referral to the Japanese, but how would they ever be able to get here? There are the Philippines and there is Singapore also. They do a lot of sabre rattling, but that it seems, is as far as it goes."

"Quite," I said, my thoughts turning to more practical issues. "We would like to come back here on our honeymoon. We plan to get married in the next few months: on Lily's twenty-second birthday in fact. Would you keep a bungalow for us?"

"The best," Blommesteyn promised. "Where will you be posted for your next assignment?"

"Makasser," I said, "do you know it?"

"Very good; just what you would like. You will be able to sail with the Buginese, the best sailors in these islands."

"I know," I said, "I have already sailed with some of them. They seem to be true sailors; it is in their blood. Talking of Pasir Poetih; it is the most idyllic place of all the places I have seen. How did you find it?"

"I realized this very soon," Blommesteyn agreed. "When I was planting tobacco not so far from here and when my wife died, I decided that tobacco was not for me and I built this bungalow park for a living instead. I think that the tide kissing the sand comes straight from Bali. I have found flotsam: leaves and twigs, carvings of Balinese sculpture on the beach. The tide must have brought them straight from Bali. Their carving is unmistakable."

"I never knew that," I said.

"Well go to Bali one day and you will see it for yourself from the carvings on their temples. You need to know this for your work. Good gods, synonymous to good to men, always have beautiful slanting eyes; demons on the other hand, are always pictured with round protruding eyes and ugly faces; they are evil, ruining the wishes of man. Beware of them, they may influence your life too and spoil all your dreams.

"They; if you want to believe it, spoilt my life also; my wife died in childbirth. Fortunately my daughter survived." He paused for a long moment, memories of the past flooding back to him.

The eerie feeling of the night before crept into me again.

"Inside information for you governor," he finally said, returning from his dream.

"Well I am only an assistant governor; they call us civil servants."

"Low pay?" he asked.

"I can afford to marry and ask for the luxury bungalow for our honeymoon." Blommesteyn laughed.

"I will reduce the price for both of you," he said. "I know just the bungalow for you. Just drop me a line a week before and it will be ready for you both when you come down. Let us listen for the news from Batavia, the Netherlands Indies Radio Broadcasting System."

"I think I'll wake Lily," I said, pushing my chair back, while I put the slice of sandwich covered with anchovy paste into my mouth. As I emptied the last drop of my Java coffee from my cup, Blommesteyn turned on the radio. He punctually every morning, listened to the news at 7 o'clock. The war news from Europe was usually bad, and the Germans now dominated Europe after the fall of France Belgium and Holland.

The radio started off with the usual march like it did punctually every morning at seven. I stood at the veranda with my back against the wood of the railing. A small brown lizard scuttled at my feet and came to rest between my toes. His shining clever eyes looking up at me showed no fear, merely curiosity to know what I was thinking. He was perfectly happy with his lot in life and knew that I was too. A peacock in the jungle behind the bungalow across the road hooted for his mate. Nothing could be more peaceful than this earthly paradise, which seemed to have been made especially for Lily and I.

The voice of the radio commentator came over the air and ripped the peaceful setting to shreds. The Japanese Air force this morning of Sunday the 8th of December 1941 had bombed Pearl Harbor the American naval base in the Pacific, producing heavy damages and loss of lives. The news completely shattered us. President Roosevelt of America had made a speech about the treacherous attack and America had declared war to Japan. Our Governor General also spoke and reminded us, that Japan's attack on Pearl harbour meant also an attack on the Dutch East Indies; the war declaration had already been sent to Japan. The rest of the news was drowned by our excitement.

"I am going back today," I said. "Fortunately the USA is in this war too; this is going to be a short war. The Japanese made a big mistake to attack America, the strongest nation in the world."

"I would not count on that too much," Blommesteyn remarked soberly. "The Japanese have prepared for this war. America is totally unprepared and the US fleet was destroyed at Pearl Harbour. Did you not hear?"

"But the Philippines, what about the Philippines, and what about Singapore?" I protested. "The Japanese will never get anywhere."

"The British are totally committed in Europe," Blommesteyn said pensively. "But Singapore of course is heavily defended," he admitted. "The Japanese must have miscalculated Singapore badly."

I suddenly remembered what the old sailor had told me the previous night. The yellow warrior race was on the march. No longer was the war 8000 miles away. It had come a lot nearer to the Dutch East Indies. Still this was no proof at all! The prediction that the yellow race would invade and occupy all the islands of the Dutch East Indies was still utterly impossible. The Japanese had seas to cross before they even could reach the Dutch East Indies, let alone occupy them. And their stumbling block would be the Philippines and especially that British stronghold Singapore. The Japanese were fools. The war would not last long. And the detail in the prediction; as far as occupying the Dutch East Indies even if only for the short period of a maize harvest? Utter rubbish, I decided. But first I had preparations to make. The one and only bus for the day would leave at four p.m. for Probolingo.

From Probolingo I could catch the train to Batavia the capital of the Dutch East Indies where I would find my unit, the tenth battalion infantry. A formidable exhausting journey lay ahead for me. I would have to leave Lily behind. The travel would be too hectic for her.

She could travel by coach to Bandoeng, where her family lived and take two days over the journey.

First of all I had to tell Doel that I could not go sailing with him. I went down to the beach to look for him. Lily was there already, sitting in the sand, talking to Doel. Her slender hands playfully shifted the dry sand, to let it pass between her slender fingers. It reminded me of an hourglass, egg timer, where sand escaping through a narrow opening indicates minutes going by.

I told them about the war. Doel did not appear surprised. It was as though he already knew. He never referred with even one word to the prediction, which he had told me the night before.

"I won't be able to sail with you Doel; I'll have to join my unit because of the war."

"You will come back Tuan, one day you will. I'll miss you," he said sadly.

"So will I Doel, so will I. We had good times together. As soon as the war is over I'll come back again and we will sail again."

"I know that you will come back one day," he said again. He kissed my hand. It embarrassed me. He was truly a good friend and a good man.

"Good luck tuan and farewell."

"Not farewell Doel but only "au revoir." Doel didn't reply. That was strange. Only years later did I understand why.

Lily's first words were: "We still have to climb the Gunung Ringgit together, remember?"

"I do remember," I said forcing a smile and trying to forget about the war. "Yes we have to climb the Ringgit. It is our last chance."

The Gunung Ringgit lies behind Pasir Poetih. The mountain was a volcano once; the top split in half by a previous eruption in prehistoric times. Yet, so the local story goes, the Ringgit is far from dead. It is a living being with magic powers, able to influence the lives of mortals.

An old legend exists, which promises that he who climbs to the top of the Ringgit, and reaches the grave of a holy man, who lies buried there, without encountering a snake on his way up, shall be able to make a wish and the wish will come true. That was the guaranty given.

But only if no snake was met on the way up. That was the condition and which was not an easy one to meet. Nobody could remember why the holy man was buried up there, because the transport of a dead body up to the top of the Ringgit must have been an impossible climb. Nobody remembered, because it had happened generations ago.

I had climbed the Ringgit myself on previous occasions, but had never managed to reach the top, without encountering at least one snake on the way up, and of course because of the encounter, could not make my wish even though I had reached the top many times before.

I had told Lily the story and since then, she had been most insistent that we should climb the Ringgit together and make our wish. So far we had turned back every time we encountered a snake and never together made it to the top. But each time, the climb had been worth it, because of the beautiful views over the sea, from high up on the mountain.

One could see far over the water and sometimes see the mountains of the island of Bali, like in a mirage, shimmering in the distant light of the sun, if there were not too many clouds.

But only sometimes and only in the early morning, before the heat waves changed the sky and made the air thin, distorting the view, as broken glass does, when one looks into a fragmented mirror. This was early morning.

"Come on," I said to Lily. I took my 12-caliber bore gun with me. There were panthers in the woods and one had to be careful. The dog followed behind us. Lily danced and sung in front of me, climbing along the winding road.

The news of the war did not seem to matter to her although her father was a major in the forces and her brother a cadet officer in the navy. She must be convinced that the combined forces of America, Britain and the Netherlands would keep the enemy away so that no harm would come to her nearest and dearest and that was what I believed too.

At a turn of the path she looked back at me. Her beauty stunned me. Her dark blond hair was long and thick, wound into a knot for this occasion. Here was a young and lovely girl with dark green-brown eyes, barely twenty-one years old and answering my prayer to be loved by her.

"What do you want to wish?" I asked her.

"I'll tell you up there," she teased, "not before." I was overcome by her radiating personality and the vision has permanently, indelibly remained in my memory.

The first part of our journey led through heavy undergrowth and only the path was clear. All around us cicadas were singing away, but there was no singing of birds. That was very strange. Why were there no birds? They had also left their nests in the waroe trees above the roof of my bungalow. Why? Had they been scared away by the earthquake? I remembered the hooting of the peacock across the road just before the announcement of the war came through the radio. I had interpreted that as a calling for his mate, but perhaps it had been a warning signal! Who could tell? The forest of the Ringgit was normally a paradise for birds. But perhaps the explanation that we didn't hear any birds; was the cackle of a startled wood hen that we had heard earlier. She had betrayed our presence and the warning signal of the jungle, no matter which animal produces it; is understood by all the others and carries far.

It was humid and it had drizzled up here in the early hours of dawn. Now and then we stood still and watched the fresh hoof marks of wild deer, now turned into little pools by the drizzle at dawn. The deer had crossed the path from higher up on the mountain, probably coming down to the sea to lick the salt off the vegetation that grew in the marshes when the seawater had retreated. Much later we heard a band of black gibbons calling to each other and another troop replying to their call from across the valley.

The climb became difficult. Trees had fallen over the path in certain places and broken boulders were strewn about, crossing the trail also. In some places the rains had washed away the track, until we picked it up yards further along.

We progressed little. Tiny spotted butterflies, which seemed to have passed the cocoon-stage, only this morning, were kissing the little buttercups scattered about. We spoke little: reserving our breath for the effort of climbing only. The dog followed effortlessly but kept close behind us.

"He doesn't like the smell of panthers," Lily remarked. The slope became steeper, our feet loosening gravel that careered down the mountain slope only to be caught by the thick under growth. We came to an open stretch high up on the mountain slope. Higher than Lily and I had ever been together. I did not remember ever having been to this spot before.

"We must have taken a wrong turning," I said. "There must have been a bush fire here recently."

There was no sign of human interference with the jungle. Trees were not cut but some still standing, were dead and blackened by fire, leafless. We sank on a block of lava panting for breath. The blocks of lava reminded us that the Ringgit had been an active volcano once.

"Look," Lily pointed back. The panoramic view was overwhelming. Far out, shimmering in the distant light, lay the mysterious island of Bali; Island of the Gods, but also island of the Demons. A light blue haze covered the island. Just as if an inexperienced pupil artist had wanted to make a watercolour painting of it and then by lack of sufficient paint had decided to dilute all the blue colours in the painting. We looked mesmerized as though under a spell. The stretch of sea between us and the mirage of the island Bali, looked immaterial and I felt I had only to stretch out my hand to touch it. But then the spell would be broken, so I merely kept looking at it in a trance.

Little triangular white dots seem to be floating in the air. They were sails of fishermen on the sea, a sea, which had the same color as the sky, so that there was no dividing line between sea and sky. Doel had one of those sails. He was free, no spell on him. For a while we sat still; spellbound.

"What are you thinking of," Lily whispered softly so as not to disturb the dream.

"Of you," I said spontaneously. Lily's beautiful green brown eyes with long eyelashes fixed on mine. She drew close to me and threw her arms around my neck. As always when she did that, I felt quite embarrassed. But she did not seem to notice and put her head on my chest. The fragrance of her hair and body crept within me and I longed for her. Could she hear my thumping heart desiring her, I wondered.

We sat on the block of lava for a long, long time. We both knew we were in love; nothing else mattered. The world was far away. Only Lily and I existed and we existed only for each other as lovers do.

Slowly she raised her head again and kissed me: a long lingering kiss, which touched my soul.

"It was a beautiful holiday wasn't it," she whispered. I was touched by her tenderness, by the fragrance of her clean smelling hair mixed with the scent of jasmine the flower she always wore in her hair at night.

"We will have to part. You must go mustn't you?" she said. "Times will be uncertain for us. Will you come back to me?"

"Of course," I said, "of course I will. This war is not going to last forever, but we will not be able to keep our planned wedding day; I love you my dear Lily." She threw open the knot of her hair and draped her hair around my head.

"I will always wait for you," she whispered. We sat on the block of lava for a long time, forgotten was the war, forgotten any resemblance to reality, only thinking of our love for one another. At last I took her by the hand.

"Let us make our wish now Lily," I said getting up from the block of lava. "It will be granted this time, you'll see." I took her by the hand. "We are not even half way!"

I did not realize the symbolism with which I had spoken. This time I went up in front, my gun hanging from my shoulder. How often in the next years to come, have I carried a gun from my shoulder, as though a gun could have prevented the outcome of our fate and that of Indonesia.

How often in the next long years have I longed for that sublime moment, when I sat there with Lily by my side, on the slope of the Ringgit, looking at this dream island Bali. Would that sublime moment with Lily's hair draped around my head ever return?

If only the gods of the island of Bali would be merciful to us mortals today. If only we could make it to the grave of the holy man without meeting a snake on the way; we could then make our wish and it would come true, that was assured. Doel also would not doubt that for a minute.

My throat felt dry, not from the effort of climbing, but from my anxiety. If only it were possible to make that wish. We had to turn back so often in the past, please not this time, our last time, I prayed. We climbed the rest of the way fast and through the clearing between trees; I could already see the lonely grave and the large single cambodja tree, full with fragrant yellow flowers at the head of it.

I felt jubilant but nevertheless also prayed: "please don't let this climb be spoiled like the others."

Alas fate did not will it this way. This was the day of the demons, not of the Gods. Just as we were about to touch the wooden railing of the grave and make our wish, a green snake scuttled right in front of our approaching feet, from under the red broken slabs of stone, leading to the grave. It had been lying there peacefully, till we disturbed it from its slumber.

Dumbfounded and disappointed without speaking a word, we looked at each other. There was no point making a wish now. The prediction had been very clear. No snake was to be met on the way up for the guaranty of the wish to come true. The demons of Bali had denied us our wish. They had eternity to play with, but Lily and I mortals, only had today and our today was spent.

That afternoon I kissed Lily goodbye. There were tears in her eyes.

"Remember, we did make a wish even though before we reached the grave. I did. Long before I heard about the Ringgit I already knew that I loved you," she whispered. "Don't forget me."

"I never will; never," I said. But there was a strange foreboding in my heart when I spoke the words and in my head I heard the other words from Doel when he told me of Djojo Bojo and his predictions.

"The Gunung Ringgit has spoken a message of doom," he had finally said. What was to become of these islands that entwined the equator like a garland of emeralds and what was to become of Lily and I and of our promise to each other? Would I ever see her again and under what circumstances? Only time would tell and the demons of Bali already knew how the outcome of our lives would be.

As the bus turned the last corner of the bay, I looked back. There lay Pasir Poetih with its dazzling white sand beach. There also lay "Mon Mirroir"; Blommesteyn's Bungalow Park, of which he was so proud.

Would I ever come back here with Lily? The white patios of the neat bungalows were framed with frangi pangi trees and the purple dazzling bougainvillea flowers danced in the light of the bright afternoon sun. Far out on the turquoise sea, smooth like glass, but with here and there sometimes also a ripple, from a breeze seemingly arising from nowhere; little white triangular sails were visible. They were sails of fishermen. It felt as though they were trying to wave goodbye to me and beckoning me to come back soon.

The ripples on the sea appeared to me the frown of a wise, benign, supernatural spirit, which was surprised and questioning the wisdom of a mortal like me, leaving paradise and the girl Lily. Why did I expect that this miracle of our happiness would wait for my return?

It had been a free gift that came this way and at this time, only for Lily and me: "Serendipity" in essence. Did I not tempt fate by leaving and turning my back on this free gift? What choice did I have?

Can a mortal ever count on happiness coming his or her way and when it does come, is then able to hold on to this gift at will? I knew the answer already: There are always considerations, which make this a practical impossibility.

For Doel it was different. He did not have the same consideration for which I had to leave paradise. He was sailing away to his island Madura free as a bird. For him there was no Queen and country, nobody expected loyalty from him. There was no dishonour if he did not fight a war. He did not have to risk his life, barely twenty-four years old and there was no girl Lily waiting for him to come back to.

Chapter 3

Probolingo, where the bus came to a stop, was where the connecting station for the train to Surabaya, the capital of East Java, was located.

"No sleeper?"I queried the stationmaster, already expecting a negative answer. He was dressed in his impeccable white suit and red cap, the uniform of a stationmaster.

"This train does not carry sleepers and neither will you be able to get one in Surabaya; unfortunately not sir," he added taking off his red cap and rubbing his sweaty forehead. "All soldiers like you are making their way to their units. You don't have to change trains when you arrive in Surabaya if you have further to go, which is quite a help," he tried to soften the blow. He had guessed that Surabaja the capital of East Java was not my destination.

"Yours is a through train from then on," he added superfluously. "You are lucky. Alternatively you can go by bus. It will take you two days, but you can stop on the way to sleep and continue the next day. What about that possibility?"

"Not a chance," I said; "even if I have to sit all the way, the war will not wait that long. All soldiers have to report to their various units as soon as possible; mine is, as you have already guessed, in Batavia."

"Good luck soldier," he said. "You have a long and tiring journey ahead of you." With that he shrugged his shoulders and put his red cap on again. He was very meticulous that he was always wearing it, before he put his whistle to his mouth for the train to move. It was routine but it was an important detail. "I know my job" he proudly said to himself.

The shrill sound told the train to move. Slowly the stationmaster walked back to his office, after carefully noticing the effect his whistle had produced. It never failed to please him, to have this power to make a train move. Such a large locomotive only started on its way if he chose to blow his whistle. Not a moment before! Was this not something wonderful? He took off his red cap totally satisfied that he had become a stationmaster. That is what he had always wanted to be, as long as he could remember. He held such an important job! He was part of an organisation; saw to it that business was carried out properly; on time! The economy of the country depended on the railways and he was part of it. What could be more satisfying? His trains were now helping to win the war. And there was a bonus to being a stationmaster. He could look forward to the icy cold beer, always waiting for him in his office!

The train was already packed and I had to sit on a few crates, which were placed on the floor in the middle of the railway carriage. The stationmaster had already indicated that it would be getting worse in Surabaya. There was still one advantage however: I could stretch my legs

The train slowly started to move, accelerated little by little, till it reached its maximum speed. Like fate itself, the train moved undisturbed without feeling, along a determined track, to an already known destination which was Batavia the capital of the Dutch East Indies.

Again; exactly like fate, it was not interested who would die in this war. It felt no fear, no triumph, and no regret; a totally impartial and impassive juggernaut.

With every puff of smoke from the locomotive, it separated me from Lily and Pasir Poetih, the person I loved most and the place where I would like to be most.

I looked out from the window and heaved a big sigh. Life was exciting nevertheless. I never expected to be in a war and here I was.

Not that the war had not been talked about and even sometimes seriously discussed. Everybody knew about the photographer shops, the ice cream parlours, the different clothes shops, the fishing boats all over the coasts of Java and Sumatra. They all had one thing in common. They were all Japanese. Their owners all spies, openly making maps, gathering information and learning the language via a phonetic system called kata-kana. All this was carried out in preparation for a future invasion.

It was only a matter of time and their time had come.

And the different governments that should have known better, shut their eyes to the spying, and left the Japanese free to do what they wanted. The government had applied ridiculous standards.

The Dutch East Indies were ruled from overseas by a colonial power; 8000 miles away. Chinese and Indonesians were classified as Asians, but not so the Japanese. They were classified as white Orientals, at par with Europeans.

The Queen of the Netherlands had never visited and only a few of her top ministers, had ever visited this vast Empire, the largest area in longitude of all colonial powers in the world.

The present Governor-General, like many other government officials in the most important governing positions, had been sent out from the Netherlands. Only a few of these could speak Malay, the main language of the population, so that they were unable to speak to the indigenous people other than by an interpreter. The present Governor however, was trying hard to learn the language and made extensive journeys, to meet the local population and local rulers, who all had pledged allegiance to Her Majesty's representative.

From the window, I could see that the sun was already setting low, throwing long shadows of the telegraph poles that we passed. Soon the fishermen in Pasir Poetih would be dragging their boats out of the water. Many would not even know that there was a war on. And most of those who did know would not care one-way or the other.

They would accept their lot without complaint. Their way of life had not changed over the years and would not change whoever held rule over their islands. The air was free; equally so were the seas, the rivers and the mountains. There had always been an abundance of fruit trees, vegetables and fish. The odd times that they celebrated, such as their New Year, they slaughtered a goat, and enjoyed meat for a short period. Their life was peaceful, uncomplicated and had an enduring quality.

Their children often died of malaria or some other tropical disease, but then their own life was short too, an average of forty years perhaps. In any case, why would you want to live forever, when you could share the happy lives of your ancestors? And they could have plenty children to replace those that had died. It was a philosophy I could understand. It made for a happy outlook on life, in spite of the hardship and sadness that life also exacted at times.

The train slowed down for Surabaya, the capital of East Java. At last I could get something to eat and move my legs. They badly needed it. The platform was brightly lit. Quite a number of food vendors were exposing their cooked products on the platform. I chose two lempers (chicken meat rolled into glutenous rice like a sausage). One cent each. The vendor was pleased and showed me her worn red beetle nut teeth, exposed in a wide smile, when I gave her three cents. She also blessed me.

I looked round. There was a mood of excitement, which affected everyone. An already packed train was further packed to maximum. I would only be able to sit with my knees up drawn now. The prospect of that for the whole night and half a day; did not cheer me up. Fortunately I did not have to change compartments, as the stationmaster in Probolingo had already told me. The present carriages were simply shackled to two locomotives of much larger pulling capacity than the one we had before from Probolingo.

Conductors moved over the platform, trying to sound convincing saying: "There is another train due for Batavia in another hour."

Nobody seemed to believe them and the pushing into the train went on. Normally there was only one train each day from Surabaya to Batavia, colloquially called "the one per day train". Wives, mothers, sisters and sweet hearts, were saying goodbye to their men and crowded the platform to capacity. Most women cried and also some men kept a brave appearance, in spite of the fact that many a moist eye was secretly dabbed dry with a handkerchief.

I was glad when the train moved again, since the scene reminded me too much of my own farewell from Lily, a few hours earlier, when I had kissed her goodbye. The memory was still so fresh in my mind. She was now left alone in Pasir Poetih. However Blommesteyn had promised me that he would put her on the train in Probolingo himself.

I knew nobody in the train, but in Batavia, I would meet all my army friends again. The tenth battalion, of which I was a part, had its headquarters there.

It was just after mid-day the next day, when the train slowed down again, the first stop and destination after Surabaya, apart from the stations where the train had needed refuelling. No further passengers had been allowed to enter. It would have been totally impossible in any case.

I could already see the bridge over the Tjiliwoeng, the river, which approximately bisects Batavia. We had canoed the river when we were schoolboys, I myself and Mas, my best friend, and classmate, the Sultan's distant relative. The Sultan was the official ruler of Middle-Java, next to the Governor of that province. He owned a palace in Soerakarta the capital. He also ruled autonomously, had his own army and kept a harem of forty wives. Mas, my friend was the only son of his cousin, the Regent of West Java.

The Sultan was a benevolent ruler and I had been a guest at the Kraton, [the palace] once, in the company of his cousin's family.

Mas had three sisters, all from the same mother, a Dutch lady his father had married when he was still an oncoming young government official.

Mas had attended the same school as I did and was groomed to follow in the Sultan's footsteps, because the Sultan had specifically asked the Dutch government to implement this after his death.

The reason for this request was probably that thereby his many sons would not fight over the position. The result also was that Mas served in the Dutch army and not in the army of his uncle. He was a good sports-man. He and I had competed in sporting events regularly, like the one hundred meter crawl swimming, and also the high jump. He always had beaten me in the one hundred meter fast running.

We had already been in the army once in a unit, which was planned to make us reserve officers. Until the war was declared, we had been sent on long leave, very much to our relief, because the army had not appealed to us as a career. I looked very much forward to seeing him again.

The same panicky situation like the one in Surabaya, met us at Weltevreden the station of Batavia. A poster said: "spend the most wonderful time of your life in this idyllic cosmopolitan Capital." Cosmopolitan it certainly was but with a temperature of thirty degrees in the shade, it could hardly be called "idyllic".

Most people on the platform were in uniform and the ubiquitous sweethearts shedding tears, were clinging to their men, who had to move to their units elsewhere and who were leaving from, instead of going to Batavia.

A tall; conspicuously uniformed clad sergeant, spotted me and slapped my back. "Together again." I turned round. "Tjaden," I exclaimed, pleasantly surprised. I was very glad to see him again. He had been our sergeant in our last period in the army, only a few months ago. We shook hands warmly.

"I am here to meet whoever comes in from the crowd in Soemowono," he explained.

"Right, Tjaden, where are we off to?" I queried. "Back to Soemowono?" Soemowono, high up in the mountains above Semarang, had been where our camp of our last period in the army was situated.

"I am glad I found you Tjaden. It saves me a long walk to the tenth battalion."

"You did not find me," Tjaden said, "I found you. I saw you first and not so fast. There is another train due in just about an hour they tell me. I have to stay here, as I already told you, to see whoever of the soldiers from your unit, formerly from Soemowono, will arrive. I have been here all day."

He still had not told me where we were off to, but I hoped that it would be a place near Bandoeng where Lily lived, so that I perhaps could see her at weekends or whenever I had leave.

"I am hungry," I said, "nothing to eat?"

"Go outside the station, there are plenty food vendors. Here, have a drink on me" He pressed a guilder note in my hand. Tjaden was as generous as ever.

"Who will be our Captain?" I asked.

"You will find out," he replied.

"As long as it is not Captain Smyth again," I said. Tjaden did not say anything.

"Go outside and eat, you must be hungry," he said, pushing me into the direction of the exit.

Batavia was not a pretty city in general but this part of the town near the station although not pretty was designed spaciously. The whole of the station was separated from the main road by a long open grass field. Poincietta trees were planted at regular intervals and their bright red flowers were giving the intense white painted station a most festive appearance, more like a bank building issuing free X-mas bonuses.

Usually taxi's lined the approach road, but now there were no taxi's to be seen anywhere. They had all been hired by soldiers, who wanted to avoid the heat of the day and had made off to their different destinations. Betjaks as means of transport were in heavy demand too. I was only interested in food.

"Captain Smyth," I muttered, "I sincerely hope not." The lukewarm tjendol drink put me in a good mood, I also bought two more lempers , making a total of four. I felt quiet satisfied then. There were other soldiers on the grass lawn, making use of the shade from the poinsiettia trees and a small breeze was gratifying. The food and drink vendors were doing well.

A small native girl, hobbling on one leg with a stick under her right arm, came by to beg. I was pleased to notice that she got from every soldier. A hungry dog, his ribs nearly sticking out from his skin, was looking for scraps. His tail was wagging in a submissive attitude but we were afraid of him and only threw scraps at him from a distance. Rabies was rampant in stray dogs in Java at that time.

I suddenly remembered that a common friend of Mas and I myself was interned in Batavia as an unwanted alien. Schoppel, at the outbreak of the war with Germany, had been interned on a technicality. His father had been German and had never bothered to change his nationality. Schoppel, born and bred in the Dutch East Indies knew nothing of Germany and did not even know that he held German nationality. His father had died when Schoppel was only five years old. Because of red tape; Schoppel who was the gentlest of men, was locked up with other German men as an unwanted alien, whose supposed home country was at war with the Netherlands. How foolish can officialdom be? We, from his old school, regularly visited him and had written numerous petitions for his release, so far unsuccessful.

He was however allowed to continue his studies in medicine and had nearly completed the course. I vowed that I would look him up as soon as I could.

Tjaden arrived, as I was fully asleep, outstretched on the grass outside the station. During the past night in the train I had practically not slept. He shook me awake: "We're off."

"Mas," I shouted when my eyes adjusted to the light and focussed. Was I glad to see him! He also returned my enthusiasm and we embraced each other. Then I shook hands with the others; Werbata, Marcus and quite a few other friends, with whom I had served in the forces in Soemowono, some months before.

"Is it crowded where we are going Tjaden; where is it going to be?"

"I am not permitted to tell you," he said.

"Well we'll give you an idea; why don't we go where Captain Smyth is as far away from us as is possible," Marcus said.

"What," Werbata cried. "Did I hear the name of Captain Smyth? Surely we can't have bad luck twice! I hope we won't get him this time."

Tjaden did not say a word .We were very glad to see each other again and exchanged information about the events in the last five months that had elapsed.

Tjaden hailed the military trucks, which had been waiting in the shade. He lined us up.

"Sixteen per truck," Tjaden shouted. We were off to the headquarters of the 10th battalion.

I discussed Captain Smyth with Mas.

"Do you remember the punishment exercises in the burning sun at mid-day? Punishment given for petty offences. They were annoying. And the swine looking at us through binoculars from the shade in his staff car. And if you didn't do well enough, you had to march dressed in full military uniform and laden rucksack for hours till you nearly dropped. And he had the nerve later, to tell us that it made better soldiers out of us. He is a sadist Mas; he got pleasure from seeing our discomfort."

"I wonder what Tjaden thinks of him," Mas said. "He has neither said a word for, nor against him."

"No, but Tjaden would not. He is too much of a soldier to criticise his commanding officer, whether that officer is a bastard or not."

"We may get a completely different captain this time," Mas tried to pacify me. "This is wartime, real stuff soldiering this time. No time for petty punishment exercises now. We may even like to be soldiers; seeing that real issues are at stake now."

I was not convinced.

"We'll see Mas, but I am not prepared to take much more from anyone pushing us around. We will be officers soon ourselves anyway. Alternatively we can always ask for a transfer to a different unit. But we, you and I, should both do the same thing to stay together."

"Of course we will," Mas agreed.

"You know something Mas," I said: "I have an idea that Tjaden has shielded us against Captain Smyth on more than one occasion. He could not do that openly of course, but one day if you'll remember, he let us drink in that kampong in Bandoengan on the roadside pretending he was too tired to go on. We got back so late in the camp that day, that Captain Smyth had no time for his nonsense.

Tjaden took the blame for having "overworked" us that day. Can you imagine Tjaden being too tired? More tired than you or I? He is stronger than any of us."

"You are right," Mas said.

"When I come to think of it, it must be as you say. Tjaden did not want to get back that day because he very well knew what Captain Smyth had in store for us. Why worry in any case," he laughed. "We could take it then and we can take it again. Life is sweet."

"Indeed, why worry," I agreed.

"By the way Richard: what happens to you and Lily now? You were to get married, weren't you? You promised me that I would be your best man. Have you made further plans? It will have to be postponed won't it? I hope it won't be for long."

"Neither do I Mas. But the war won't last long. Imagine the Japanese taking on Britain and America at the same time! They must be out of their senses!"

In a good mood, full of hope, we entered the headquarters of the tenth battalion. It was already 4.p.m. The sentry at the gate stood to attention and presented arms, spotting Tjaden's rank. The salute was promptly returned. We were soldiers again.

Djojo Bojo would have a rotten time to make his silly prediction come true. Singapore and the Philippines stood firm like a rock and the Dutch East Indies equally so.

Chapter 4

Yamamoto hoped that he had sized up the hierarchy of Siam correctly. As far as he was concerned, there were only two kinds of people: wise ones and fools. The fools were the heroic ones. People generally pictured the heroic ones as tall, good looking and muscularly built, but especially alive and vibrant. This last assumption was where their thinking went wrong. Heroes are invariably dead he thought. If they were lucky they would not have been tortured or maimed before a bullet arrived in their head. They could have lived but were stupid enough to resist.

He thought, and fervently hoped; that the ministers of the country, and in particular of course the Prime Minister of Siam he was about to meet, would be wise men.

Siam also had a King but the King was too young to make decisions. He depended on the advice of his ministers. It was the Prime Minister; Yamamoto had to deal with.

Yamamoto had announced his visit from the embassy in Bangkok; but only minutes before his arrival. He did not want to give Pridi Panmyong time to think what he should do and possibly get advice from the other ministers. When he Yamamoto made the plans for the attack on Pearl Harbour he also had paid particular attention to this part of his carefully worked out schemes: namely the confrontation with this prime minister of Siam. About a successful outcome of this encounter however he was not at all certain. And it worried him! Occupation of Siam was indispensable for Yamamoto because he needed the air space for his planes. But not by force; certainly not!

Japan's excuse for the war, so Japan had claimed, was to free the oppressed colonials from their greedy masters. Thereby wanting the world to believe that theirs: Japan's war, was a just war.

But here exactly was where the difficulty lay. No foreign country had ever before occupied Siam, although it shared borders with two colonies, namely one of France and the other of Britain.

How therefore could Japan claim that occupation of Siam by Japanese military soldiers was justified?

Unless of course the hierarchy of Siam first, by signing a peace treaty with Japan, had in this way showed to agree that the country was to be occupied by Japanese soldiers. But how could he put this to the prime minister in such a way that this man would agree to the signing of the peace treaty?

Yamamoto did not waste time. He normally never did anyway. Without polite preliminaries such as asking for the prime minister's health, he shoved the peace treaty made up long before by him, towards Pridi Panmyong the prime minister.

"Will you please sign the peace treaty between your country and mine?" he spoke in perfect Siamese. He had practised the tone and the sequence of the words in front of a mirror. This was a request, which had to be presented with the necessary politeness, tact, but at the same time with a clear hint of demand also; of which the latter part, could not be misunderstood by anyone! He hoped that his demeanour was servile enough and that he could convince the prime minister that by signing the pact; all the advantages were on the side of Siam. A tall order indeed, because it wasn't altogether true.

"Will you sign the peace treaty?" he repeated in staccato guttural Siamese this time because he had become slightly nervous. While he spoke the words he leaned forward, his head as close to the minister as the available space would allow. He had learned that you should never lose eye contact with the person whom you wanted to ask a request from and also wanted to subdue at the same time. And subdue the minister he must, if he wanted him to sign the peace treaty with Japan.

His mouth whilst speaking had opened only ever so slightly. And the slit that substituted for his mouth, closed again, as though regretting that the luxury of it in the open position was made too hastily. Then the corners of the slit hardened in a downward direction coming to an abrupt halt.

To people who did not know Yamamoto this movement of his mouth could be interpreted as a smile if you were a kind person, a grin perhaps if you thought less of him. But persons, who knew him well, would know that it was a threat, and that it had nothing to do with a smile. Yamamoto had hoped to fool the Prime Minister so that the latter would interpret his mouth movement as a substitute for kindness.

Pridi Panmyong with his gut feeling and accustomed to thinking with an eastern mind, although not knowing Yamamoto, realised however that what some people would consider a grin or even a smile, with Yamamoto this was not the case. He was not fooled in the slightest and immediately and fully realised, that what he saw on the face of this Japanese was an unadulterated threat and he interpreted it correctly. He knew therefore that without being able to offer at least equal resistance to the force that opposed him, he was going to lose this contest to the man right in front of him, who regrettably held all the trump cards and whose ace in the pack was his army.

The minister nevertheless tried to win time. He was not going to be beaten that easily! He wished that it would be possible for him to show this officer, whom he considered ill mannered and now was trying to intimidate him, the door and to throw his ink blotter after him. Idle thought! The man in front of him would get away with what he wanted. He looked out from the palace gate. Where were his palace guards to remove the intruder? "Alas," he sighed; he remembered that he did not have them. Siam was a peace loving country, which never had needed an army. How he wished now that he had! All he saw were Japanese soldiers, with fixed bayonets glinting in the light of flickering fires as the evening was falling. The fires were lit by Yamamoto's forces on purpose, so as to demoralise the minister.

Yamamoto knew all about intimidation to get what he wanted. Again he had planned this confrontation to its finest detail, as much as possible like all his other plans had been. He was one step ahead of Pridi Panmyong. The latter of course was totally unprepared. Yamamoto knew that timing was the most important item; if you counted on success and success he had to have, come what may!

The attack on Pearl Harbour had been a case in point. He as a master planner equally carefully, already had an alternative in his mind, should the minister of Siam be so foolhardy as to offer objections. Some compromises he was willing to make in return, but Siam's air space was paramount. About the latter no compromise was possible.

"We cannot afford it that the minister refuses to sign," he had said to Suzuki, his aide-de-camp. "Finding a successor means delay," he had added.

The latter fervently hoped that the minister would sign forthwith. He was in a hurry. Singapore was waiting! The reunion with his concubine was all Suzuki had in his mind.

"Sign please," Yamamoto now spoke in Japanese. Yamamoto counted on the intelligence of the man in charge sitting in front of him. The minister would understand that a military confrontation would only mean one thing: the killing of many Siamese citizens especially the students who would take to arms, although poorly equipped and who were certainly no match for his superior army. A peace treaty on the other hand, although reluctantly agreed, would save lives. Pridi could convince the population that the King had agreed to the peace treaty and the Siamese loved their King and would obey.

Yamamoto put his head even closer to the minister: "Sign please," with hardening in his voice, he repeated in Japanese. The tension in the room had now risen to explosion point. Although the minister knew no Japanese, he perceived nevertheless very clearly the threat behind the plea. He needed no explanation to know what the next step of Yamamoto was going to be. He realised that the time for his life was running out. And not only for his life, but also for the lives of some of his people who would also die if a peace treaty were not signed. He saw no alternative but to give in. Yamamoto did not allow the minister to win more time. In his hand he held the golden pen with which he was now sure, this wise man opposite him, who had already capitulated, was going to sign. He waved the gold pen, between thumb and forefinger of his right hand in front of the minister's nose.

Pridi Panmyong for the last time looked out from the palace gates. He was not used to being dictated to! So far he had been the one to give orders. The amount of Japanese soldiers at the palace gate convinced Pridi that resistance was useless. Reluctantly he signed with the gold pen, which Yamamoto held in front of him.

This time Yamamoto allowed his mouth the luxury to widen as far as it would go, into what he himself would interpret as a smile. He was very pleased with the fact that he had won the contest against the minister. It confirmed his belief that the man was smart. Not all rulers were! It would save a lot of valuable time.

His wide mouth betrayed two gold molar teeth that reflected the light from the expensive candelabra hanging from the ornate ceiling of the palace. A worthy palace for himself, he thought. In due time it might even become his palace. The Emperor might reward him for past duties. King of Siam perhaps? Did he dare to dream that far? Why not? Had he not organised this whole campaign resulting in what had been accomplished so far?

The whole of the American fleet in tatters, possession of Indo-China, Hong Kong, the Siam Kingdom, plus the King maintained as King. Very soon he would have the Philippines and Singapore too.

At that moment his thoughts took a turning. The cold shiver returned. He knew the outcome well enough.

Sooner or later his luck would run out and all his achievements so far, would come to nothing. The Americans would be gunning for him. Sooner or later they would succeed in killing him. His Hara-kiri plan was getting nearer to fruition. And Japan would lose the war. He was certain of it.

"But Singapore first; then the Philippines. Let fate decide the issue; concentrate on the matter at hand," he thought. He had enough to think of!

The ink on the peace treaty had not run dry when Yamamoto walked down the palace steps, his Samurai sword clattering behind him. "Damn that sword," he thought. Why had the sword to be so long or alternatively; why was he built too short? He would have liked to be as tall as Suzuki, his aide-de-camp. This officer was wearing his sword correctly; off the ground.

He had not considered it worthwhile to shake the minister's hand when he left. He had simply put the signed peace treaty in the leather bag he had brought with him. It would be sent to the war minister Tukagoshi forthwith.

Intimidating the prime minister had worked! He had hoped that it would. The man fortunately was wise. It had saved time in needing to find a successor.

But Yamamoto had underrated Pridi Panmyong severely. Even before he signed, Pridi already in his mind had a resistance plan in his head. Not immediately but later when he could count on help from the Allies. He was one step ahead of Yamamoto and even cleverer than Yamamoto had imagined.

Expectantly Suzuki waited for Yamamoto at the bottom of the staircase.

"Singapore next," Yamamoto said, cold steel in his voice. Suzuki's eyes glittered. Yamamoto's words had opened paradise for him.

"Singapore next," he echoed, happy like a child unwrapping a Christmas present long overdue. To him this was the answer of his prayers to his Shinto God. Would she still be there? And his tailor shop from where he had been spying extensively? High-ranking society ladies had been coming to him to have their expensive clothes for their elaborate parties designed by him. It had been a pleasurable time. No thoughts of possibly losing the war could enter his head now. Indeed not. His thoughts were those of a conqueror. Life and love were too sweet.

These visits from his concubine, the wife of an English officer had been so lovely, they had made it all so worthwhile, this period out of the army. The army life he really enjoyed had to wait. There were more important things to do first. For the time being, he instead had to be satisfied being a tailor spying for Japan.

She regularly came to visit him in secret. How could anyone say that English women were cold? That was not his experience. No, not at all, he thought shivering with the pleasure of the memory of her and her body. He knew all her body measurements by heart and he had not come by those simply by being a tailor! In addition she had provided him with all the gossip and rumours in the military world. He had carefully noted down the important details and could draw maps of the military installations from the information she unwittingly had given him.

From the pocket of his tunic he extracted the fan she had presented him with and fanned his overheated brow, the result of thinking of the passion that had been between them. He would be able to help her now and she would be grateful to him. He came back as the victorious officer, no longer a tailor but a captain of the victorious Japanese army, no less, he reflected vainly; an army better equipped and with brave officers, not the spineless jellyfish, he considered her lieutenant husband to be. Suzuki was almost more in a hurry to leave the palace than Yamamoto.

Yamamoto walked as tall as he could, the tip of his sword only just missing the floor. What he had promised the Emperor at the war conference had nearly, almost totally, come true. Not entirely yet but he had no doubt that he would conquer Singapore, the so-called heavily defended fortress lying at the bottom of the Malaysian peninsula. He knew full well that the defence of that fortress was only directed at an enemy approach from the sea. His troops however, under the direction of General Yamashita were approaching Singapore from land, from the north. There was no defence there. No one in Singapore had given thought to the possibility of an enemy approach from the land but he Yamamoto had all his plans based on that simple fact, amazingly overlooked by the defenders. His plans for Singapore, the approach from land, would succeed.

The British foolhardy had tried to rectify the situation by sending the battleships the HMS Repulse and the HMS Prince of Wales to oppose a Japanese landing. Useless effort, too late! His troops had already landed without difficulty and both British ships hit by torpedoes fired from planes from the air were now lying at the bottom of the sea. His troops, thanks to superiority of airpower and their mobility by bicycles, now replaced by tanks; were already approaching the causeway joining Singapore with the mainland. It would only be a matter of weeks now he reckoned. His forces would then effectively cut off the enemy water supply. In his elaborate and carefully worked out plans, he had counted on this Achilles heel. Due to an unbelievable oversight by the British but incalculated by Yamamoto, the necessity for water, which could be cut off so easily, was overlooked by the defenders. This lack of water, even apart from anything else, would be the demoralising factor on which he had depended. The British would have to surrender.

"We have taken Siam in Your Highness name," his intelligence service radioed the Emperor.

"Singapore will follow shortly." What was important to Yamamoto was that he now had possession of the airbase near Bangkok.

Singapore now had become within striking distance of his warplanes. His grip on Singapore was tightening! He had maintained the King of Siam, for the time being at least. It suited his purpose. If guerrilla forces attacked his troops, he would have the King as hostage. His zero fighters would do the rest. They did not even wear parachutes, but preferred to die with their plane if they were shot down, rather than save their lives or be captured. That is the attitude that wins wars he reflected. He would show the world that Pearl Harbour was won by his warriors and this was not going to be an isolated victory: far from it he swore! It never occurred to him that this attitude to life could be interpreted as weakness. An attitude that preferred glorified brave death, rather than overcoming life's difficulties instead. How could he think differently? He was brought up to think this way.

Back in Japan at the Emperor's palace, the news reached the Emperor as he woke from his slumber. He was jubilant. In barely three weeks his forces had accomplished not only the downfall of the American fleet. There was much more! Siam was now virtually a puppet state at the mercy of Japan. He was now an Emperor who owned a King! The whole of Indo-China was his. Hong-Kong the prize possession of the British was now also Japanese territory. A new map was needed to include all the territories conquered by his forces. Or should he wait just a little bit longer with the instructions to make a new map? What about Australia? Perhaps? Better to wait just a bit longer! The Philippines and also the Dutch East Indies with its rich oil fields could then be included. Not to forget Singapore as well. He looked forward to see all the changes. It would be hanging on the wall of his bedroom of course, this map of his new Empire!

His reign had more than doubled in size and the campaign against Singapore was going to be successful: Yamamoto had assured him of this. He felt more of an Emperor than ever before. The white colonial rulers were no match for his brave forces. He believed it now. His ancestors had told him, that the Japanese are a superior race, and here was the evidence. All his misgivings about a successful outcome of the war now magically evaporated from his mind like a drop of water from a hot plate. His gut feeling about Yamamoto had been correct. He was the daring military genius Japan needed.

Tukagoshi, the war minister, was also informed. He felt overjoyed, as he had been once, when he was ten years old on a school picnic, and when the teacher treated the children with jam on their bread. This was not an occasion to drink sake he thought. No, instead it called for a white man's drink. From the drink cupboard he extracted the Scotch whiskey bottle he kept for happy occasions such as this one. He could hardly wait and poured the whiskey straight from the bottle into the first cup he could find. His wife could not stop him now. He downed the glass in one gulp. Then he sat down and belched. What good news! Had he not been right to recommend Yamamoto as supreme commander to the forces?

The Emperor would be pleased with his excellent judgement. He filled his glass for the third time. Where did whiskey come from again? His numbed brain already could not remember. In ten minutes he was asleep, his glass only half empty, dropped from his hand spilling the precious fluid on his expensive carpet showing, the rising sun, Japanese war emblem. He had bought the carpet only recently to commemorate the outbreak of the war. He was minister of war after all and owed it to himself to have such a distinctive carpet! Had he been awake, he would have had to admit that the kick from Scotch whiskey is at least equally as strong as that from sake.

When he came to, a few hours later, he noticed the whiskey stain on the rising sun decorating the carpet. It was an ominous sign but Tukagoshi was not superstitious. He just shrugged his shoulders. A pity about the spilt whiskey, but he had more. Another glass would settle things! It almost did but not quite. The hangman who was to hang him later, at that moment was drinking from a coca cola bottle in an American battleship that had survived Pearl Harbour! He preferred that taste to a good many others and he especially detested the taste of whiskey.

The news of Siam's co-operation with the Empire of Japan was broadcasted over the world news of the BBC. In the barracks of the tenth battalion infantry, a group of Dutch soldiers listened in silence to the radio broadcast. It didn't mean anything to them. Siam was on the other side of the world! They had no idea how serious this news was for them, since it brought Singapore within striking distance of Japan's bombers and all their hopes were pinned on Singapore. They believed implicitly in this impregnable fortress.

No force in the world could take it. The impregnable fortress would break Japan's neck. And with the help of the Americans the Japanese would be driven out of the Malaysian peninsula first, then out of Siam and then all the way back to Japan.

"Yes," I said to Mas. "Singapore will be a different story altogether. It won't be so easy like Siam was. The Japanese will find out what they have taken on. Let's make ourselves comfortable."

We searched for the canteen and had hot food served on a clean plate, by the glow of an oil lamp. It cost ten cents only. Our moral was high and our stomachs were full. The gramophone record in the corner of the canteen played the tune: "The very thought of you", sung by Billy Holiday. Life was wonderful!

***

The traffic on the fast side out of Batavia flowed like an artificial snake, purposeful and relentless. Bren carriers with all their lights ablaze were coming to us from the opposite direction. They crossed the bridge over the river one by one, like ducks following the narrow path of a paddy field. Our trucks were held up to let them pass. They reminded me of the dragon I had painted in class once. The art teacher, who had not approved of the dragon painted by me, had praised the dragon drawn by Wong instead. Wong had been my classmate and friend of Lily, Mas and I since our youth. What had happened to him?

Would he have joined the army as we had done? He did not have to. After all, he was considered an Asian, having no nationality. But he might well have done, because he hated the Japanese so much for what they had done to the Chinese in Nanking "Look what they do to women and children," he often said, showing us the atrocities of the Japanese troops in photographs.

"The western powers do nothing," he complained. He was right in a way, but China was so far removed so that compassion did not reach that far although we sympathised.

Our trucks only proceeded very slowly. Most of the traffic was heading in the same direction as we were going ourselves: Tanks, trucks, gun tractors and Bren carriers.

On the slow side of the highway with the tram rails in between, bullocks and horses were pulling fully laden carts, not much slower than we were going.

A flight of Brewster planes came over; we counted twenty-four of them. They were on their way to the new airport called Kemajoran, which was only built since Holland had been occupied by the Germans after a short war in which Rotterdam had been flattened by Hitler's bombers.

Marcus and Werbata were discussing Captain Smyth. At last this morning, Tjaden had told us that he was our commanding captain again and that our camp was going to be Tjipatat, a training camp to teach us how to fire with rifles again. Werbata was the oldest among us; he was twenty-seven; old as far as we were concerned. He was a planter on a sugar estate in east Java and married.

"The son of a bitch," was his first comment.

Slowly we succeeded to get away from the congested traffic. It had taken us more than half the day. The air was getting cool as we neared the end of our journey, passing through the Tjiater, a mountain pass connecting Batavia and Bandung. The pass was heavily defended. It could be freezing here at night. The views were stunning, overlooking the valleys from this high vantage point. I was pleased to be stationed in Tjipatat near Bandung, the second largest capital of west Java where Lily lived. I could perhaps visit her at weekends.

That evening the 13th of December I bunked above Mas in the fifth dormitory of shooting bivouac Tjipatat. It was exactly five days after the treacherous attack on Pearl Harbour. That night I dreamt of Lily embracing me and putting her arms around my neck. The demons of the isle of Bali watched us, watched us silently. At first I thought they were smiling; but no, as they approached, I could see that what I had first thought was a smile; was in fact a malicious cruel grin on their grotesque distorted faces with protruding round eyes, full of hate. They pointed at us with their ugly knotty fingers. My skin went cold with fear. I woke up and realised that my blanket had fallen down and that the cold came through the wide window of our dormitory.

***

Reveille was at six a.m. The air was cool we noticed when we went to the bathrooms to take a shower. The showers also were cold, causing goose pimples. Outside the barracks the sun was rising.

"Look at the twins," I shouted to Mas, pointing to the Pangrango and the Gedeh, the two volcanoes side by side nosing their tops curiously through banks of clouds. The sun would soon disperse the clouds and show the mountains in their true purple coloured majesty. Our hearts were full of anticipation. Who was going to be the lieutenant serving with Captain Smyth?

After breakfast the bugler called for assembly. Ninety men in three rows were lined up by Tjaden: thirty in each. A first lieutenant in full military uniform appeared. Tjaden made us stand to attention. The lieutenant climbed on a few crates in front of the kitchen. He was about twenty-five years old, certainly not older than Werbata we guessed. He was well dressed and close shaved, no moustache. He wore a leather strap round his chest, which held his sabre. He was the typical first lieutenant gentleman of the Dutch colonial army.

"Soldiers," he started to speak, "my name is Hes. I am new to you but I understand that most of you already are familiar with my superior officer. In name of Captain Smyth; I welcome you and trust that you had a comfortable night. The amenities are not at all bad; for instance there is also a swimming pool in the river and a canteen and I will see to it if they can be improved. As you already know Siam is in Japanese hands. The King of Siam has signed a so-called pact with Japan, obviously under duress.

"I mention this to you, to let you know that we are within striking range of enemy planes albeit at their furthest range. However always have your helmets ready as extra protection in case you need it. We are situated here for the protection of the town Bandoeng and also for the support of army unit called Left half of 21st brigade which is a regular infantry unit."

While he was speaking Captain Smyth appeared. He looked very pleased with himself. His gird had increased in size a little. Lieutenant Hes called us to attention and saluted. The salute was promptly returned.

Captain Smyth climbed on the platform next to Hes.

"Well, well, what have we here?" he started; "most of you I already know, so I don't have to tell you who I am." He droned on about what was required of us and said that in his opinion we deserved to be proud of having accomplished

46

what we had in our previous six months of army service. He then ended saying that he would leave no stone unturned to help us become reserve officers.

"In about six month time," he promised when he finished his sentence. "I have to recommend it of course, since you are an elite outfit," he added, waving with his hands at the "imaginary elite outfit."

"Would there be any questions? I would be happy to oblige."

Marcus waved with his hand mockingly, aping Captain Smyth's hand movement

"Yes soldier," Captain Smyth enquired kindly, adjusting his head to the listening position.

"How many of us will become officers, on average?" Marcus asked innocently.

"Oh I would say fifty percent," Captain Smyth replied encouragingly.

"In that case what would happen to the forty five officers who would qualify?"

"Forty five officers?" Captain Smyth frowned, taken aback by the staggering amount of possible qualifying officers.

"Yes Sir, fifty percent of ninety makes forty five, would you not say so?"

"Oh yes of course," Captain Smyth hastened to say. "Well, they will be distributed over other battalions of course."

"Sir, there aren't forty five battalions in the whole of the Dutch East Indies Army and unless these forty five volunteer to become administrative officers, they have no job." Captain Smyth felt decidedly uncomfortable. He now recognised in Marcus that same son of a gun soldier who had asked him impossible to answer questions on previous occasions. But he wasn't beaten so easily.

"Becoming reserve officers; indeed doesn't mean that all can be placed. That again depends of course on my recommendations. That also holds for the selection of those lucky ones to become officers of course. From the way he looked at Marcus, it wasn't likely that he ever would recommend Marcus.

"And you are right of course, places must be available first." He looked round to see if there were any more questions, pleased that he got off so lightly from that "son of a gun" he knew was studying to become a lawyer.

"Your duties will be conveyed to you by Lieutenant Hes." Then he left. So far so good we thought. His speech had been benign even when Marcus tackled him.

The first day was a holiday to settle in. In the afternoon Mas and I visited the native barracks. Their highest rank was held by a Sergeant Major who had a beautiful wife and four also beautiful children. His name was Soedirman.

"Why are you not an officer?" Mas asked him. The sergeant became quite embarrassed by the remark. I hastened to explain.

"What Mas means," I said, "is why you with your excellent qualities got stuck in the rank of Sergeant Major, instead of becoming an officer?"

"But sir, to become an officer, you need to finish high school first, then Military Academy. These studies cost a lot of money and I never attended high school."

"Then what education did you have?" Mas enquired

"Indonesian school which was free," the Sergeant replied.

"But you got nowhere with that, did you?" The sergeant did not reply.

"Yes it did," I said to Mas later. "His schooling got him the job he is in now."

"But do you not see the bias against the Indonesians? Even in the army it exists."

"Come off it Mas, you have been saying these thing to me as long as I can remember. You finished high school and you are elected to follow in the Sultan's footsteps. What more do you want? Here you are in a favoured position to become an officer, just like me, just like Werbata and Marcus. And talking of favoured positions: who is fighting for Indonesia? Certainly not the Indonesians apart from a handful like the Sergeant Major we have just visited. Had it not been for the Dutch, you would have had another colonial power ruling you. And what is wrong with the Dutch," I said, "Your mother is Dutch."

"She is fine," Mas said.

"Well then?" I said. "I am Dutch too and are we not the best of friends?" He pressed my hand warmly.

"Of course we are," he said.

"Look at the situation again Mas. This sergeant went into the army. He had free schooling. My father had to pay for my schooling and so did your father. Admittedly it will get us further or so we hope. The sergeant is a lot higher in rank than we are at the moment."

"I may never become an officer," Mas said. "Captain Smyth will discriminate against me. But I don't care; I didn't want the army as a career anyway."

"Neither do I," I said, "but why should Captain Smyth discriminate against you? There is no difference between you and me, our education is the same."

"Oh but I am Indonesian."

"So what," I said, "do you realise that a Dutch person cannot own land in Indonesia? But you can because you are Indonesian. A Dutch person can lease land but only up to seventy-five years and will never be able to possess it. This does not apply to you. Who is being discriminated against Mas?" I said.

"You will get your independence, probably sooner than later. And then you will be in trouble, because then you'll have to prove that you will treat your people better than the Dutch have done."

"Oh sure we will."

"I believe you have the best intention, I believe that, but before the Dutch colonisers arrived, Indonesia was ruled by a succession of Rajah's and Sultans, each not caring one fig about the welfare of the tani's. They were only interested in hunting and women and other pleasures like cock fighting. The tani's were badly oppressed. You learned your history like I did."

"I admit," he said. "Maybe we are not yet ready for Independence, but there is a lot of unrest. Indonesians want independence."

"And will get it; I have been taught officially at my education for governor, that the power for government should be handed over to people like you. Your father is a clear example. He already rules over a district autonomously."

"And is supervised," Mas reminded me.

"Only to the extent that the tani's are not suppressed as happened before the Dutch came," I replied. "The governor of West Java so far has never interfered with your fathers ruling and you are groomed to follow in your father's footsteps prior to taking up the position of Sultan when the present Sultan dies. You are in a very favoured position."

"But it is the army that wants to keep us slaves."

"Slaves", is a ridiculous word to use. Is the sergeant we just visited a slave? He has had eminent free schooling and has a good job. Which slave had that? And," I said: "the army is not the decisive factor. We, in the government, make the decisions, the government officers, not the army.

"Only in times of war such as now is the case, can it officially dictate to us and only in special circumstances. You'll get your independence and good luck to you then: you can't force a democracy. You must be mature to want it. And that means that your interest must succumb at times to the interest of the common denominator: the people! Human nature being what it is, it is a hard cookie; easy in concept but hard in execution."

"I know; you are right. Let us change the subject," Mas said. "What did you think of Captain Smyth so far?"

"He came out well didn't he," I said. "Even Marcus did not put him off, but if there is to be a selection who becomes an officer, Marcus is certainly going to be turned down."

"You can bet your life on that," Mas grinned.

"Marcus is quite a character; I wonder how his life will continue; he is a free spirit. No rule will hold him." I said.

"You are right,"Mas agreed.

Neither Mas nor I at that time had any idea how tragic Marcus' life would end. Such is the interfering of fate within human planning, even planning at its best. Was Djojo Bojo's prediction fate itself, which would come to pass no matter what; or did the wise man, Doel spoke about, have it wrong? The question was still unanswered.

Chapter 5

Captain Smyth sat behind his desk writing his day report. In it he omitted to mention the punishment exercises of the afternoon that day. That news was boring anyway. The report needed to be sent away with the messenger leaving on his motorbike in an hour. Captain Smyth was in a good mood. His brother in law, Colonel Arlen, senior in years, had told him that the rank he so fervently had been waiting for: namely that of Major; would soon be his.

Nothing could go wrong now, he was told. He had every reason to be pleased with himself.

The rap on the door was short but decisive.

"Come in," he shouted.

Lieutenant Hes appeared in the door opening, advanced and closed the door behind him, then stood to attention and saluted.

"At ease Hes," Captain Smyth said. "Take a chair." His voice was crisp. He had used a voice, which neither sounded pompous, nor condescending. He had acquired this military voice after years of practice and found it most effective when he had an argument with somebody. It seemed to him that this kind of voice was now perhaps required. Of course he sensed that the lieutenant had not come down to tell him that he considered him a good boy and that there would be a disagreement. Lieutenant Hes sat down.

"Anything bothering you Hes?"

"As a matter of fact there is Sir," Hes started. "It has been reported to me that the men are disgruntled."

Captain Smyth raised his eyebrows and leaned back in his chair. He decided to take some time out discussing the matter.

"What are they talking about?" he asked in a manner as though he cared.

"They did not like the punishment exercises this afternoon Sir."

"What a pity." Captain Smyth leaned forward. Was this all that Hes had come to see him for?

"That kind of thing makes good soldiers Hes. Did you not have those yourself? I did. Those exercises are good for discipline Hes."

"That is a matter of opinion Sir."

"An opinion you obviously don't share Hes. How long have you been in the army, two years, three years perhaps?"

"Two years Sir." "Oh yes and your first experience with militia soldiers, cadets to become officers. Well take it from me: these fellows need discipline. These boys have been mollycoddled, too much money. At their age I had none. They have led a life of luxury, servants, cars and that sort of thing. They have had their own way for far too long. Discipline is the keystone of an army, you know that yourself don't you Hes?"

"I agree," Hes resumed, "but discipline can be taught in other ways than by punishment."

"I am sorry we don't agree Hes, anything else?"

"Yes Sir, there is. The punishment exercises were given because the soldiers had a bad result target shooting this morning."

"Yes, yes," Captain Smyth' voice betraying impatience.

"All the rifles show a marked deviation," Hes continued; "I checked this, the punishment exercises were unfounded."

"Leave that decision to me Hes. Whether the rifles aim correctly or did not; the recruits should have taken the error into account."

"Not that great amount of error Sir. The rifles were tampered with."

Captain Smyth froze.

"What the devil do you mean Hes?"

"Somebody changed the visors deliberately to make the rifles overshoot the target."

"Impossible." Captain Smyth pushed his chair back and started to walk up and down the room, a frown on his forehead. His hands were clenched behind his back and the pressure on his fingers made the knuckles white.

"Who did that?" Captain Smyth' voice cut the silence like a guillotine blade.

Lieutenant Hes realised that he could never prove that Captain Smyth himself had tampered with the visors. He had to proceed very cautiously indeed. He tightened his jaw muscles.

"On your orders last night the rifles were placed in the guardhouse. You locked the door yourself and kept the key, the only key to it." As he said it he realised that he had made a cardinal mistake.

"The only key?" Captain Smyth said, using his steel voice for the occasion this time; and closing his eyes to tight slits. "What makes you so sure that there is no other key? Are you saying that I tampered with the rifles?"

Lieutenant Hes realised that he had gone too far.

"No Sir, I never said that."

"But that is what you insinuated didn't you?"

"I merely wanted to bring to your attention a sequence of events and the fact that the recruits are disgruntled."

"I can draw my own conclusion." Captain Smyth said abruptly.

"Lieutenant Hes; you find me the person who holds the other key and tampered with the rifles as you say. Dismissed!"

Lieutenant Hes rose from his chair, stood to attention and as he saluted, Captain Smyth had already returned to writing his report.

As far as he was concerned Lieutenant Hes had already become an unimportant part of the furniture in the room.

Back in his apartment Lieutenant Hes could kick himself. He had accomplished nothing and had antagonised Captain Smyth against himself and the men. How stupid he had been. He was on the defence now.

Captain Smyth would surely ask him about "the other person with the missing key to the guardroom," and of course that person did not exist. But didn't Captain Smyth appear most surprised when he was told about the visors being tampered with? Was he that good of an actor?

On the other hand he had not been concerned enough if he had been innocent. The possibility that somebody else, other than Captain Smyth had tampered with the rifles was a worrying thought to Lieutenant Hes. Their usefulness as a unit in times of war depended on rifles! The implication was so serious that he had to investigate whether he believed in Captain Smyth's innocence or not.

What was he to believe? He held his head in his hand. What a mess he was in! How different it all was from what he had imagined. Commanding a group of recruits most of them students, not much older than he himself of all things and all relatively green as soldiering went. In charge of them and himself, a Captain, the best that could be said about him was that he was odd. He felt downhearted. Studying in Breda at the military academy had been fun and the thought of a pleasant and rewarding career in the services of the Dutch Colonial Army, had filled him with elation. He was born and brought up in the Dutch East Indies and loved the country and its people. All through the years at Breda, he hankered to come back, although the military life in Breda suited him also.

But he missed the beautiful sunshine, the mountain streams with crystal clear water, the sail with the different crafts and then the majestic blue mountains in the distance, which he saw from the bedroom of the last house he had lived in, before he took up his military studies in Breda.

He could imagine the cool air blowing over his face, coming straight down from the Tankoeban Prahoe above Bandoeng. He remembered the hunting trips with his father, the large rivers they crossed; full of crocodiles on the mud banks at every turn the river made.

The Malays thought that they represented their forefathers and who was to say that they were not correct? The Malays were rowing him and his father to the different kampongs along the river, so that his father, a doctor appointed by the government, could carry out the inoculations necessary against smallpox, a disease that killed numerous people in a single outbreak if they were not inoculated.

No he did not want to become a doctor like his father. The military life was for him with the mingling of the numerous different races, all soldiering in the service of the Colonial army in the Dutch East Indies, with it's innumerable islands, keeping law and order.

He remembered the hospitality that was showered on them in the different kampongs along the river, treating him and his father like royalty.

And now there was this war. Germany had virtually occupied the whole of Europe, apart from Britain and the Japanese had started with their attempt to implement their Asia domination plan. "Asia for the Asian" their slogan had been.

This plan was long foreseen. Even before he went to military college, he remembered the Japanese shops, ice cream parlours, barbers, laundry man and especially [and this was most important] the many Japanese photographers all over the towns of the Dutch East Indies.

And not to forget the Japanese pearl fisherman along the coasts also. They freely roamed not supervised. They were all spies making maps, studying field situations and learning Malay right under the noses of so-called government security. What laughable security it had been. Where were those Japanese now? Most of them would be officers in the Japanese army with as much knowledge of the conditions and layouts of the different coastlines, as the Colonial Dutch army itself. Moreover Lieutenant Hes feared that their army would be better equipped than his own.

His uncle on his mother's side, General Berens had told him so himself. The General had requested the forces to be strengthened. But the government ignored his advice. It would cost too much money. General Berens perished in an air disaster. The plane crashed just after take off from the airport. In the initial version there had been a suggestion of sabotage but later in the official version of the crash, sabotage was ruled out.

In any case, whatever the truth, Berens had certainly been in the way of the Asia expansion plan of Japan.

"And here I am," Lieutenant Hes talked to himself. They were ill equipped as a unit: they were a student and Malay infantry and to top it, a crazy captain was in charge. What was he to do? Ask for a transfer? Back to his own unit the tank core where he belonged? This seemed the best idea. But then he thought although it being the best idea, it was also cowardly.

If he wanted to serve as an officer and really serve his Queen and country: not only under ideal conditions but also under conditions such as these; this was his chance of a lifetime.

He could make something of these recruits. Their opinion of the army so far couldn't be very high. He could see to it that they changed their opinion and make them realise that fair play did exist in the army. There would be clashes with Captain Smyth certainly. There would even be confrontation. His conduct record would be at stake if he clashed with Captain Smyth.

But he would be in a real situation, not a yes man. It would make or break him, and lieutenant Hes was determined that it was not going to break him.

Through the open window of his bedroom wafted the smell of tropical flowers. He recognised all of them. This one was the smell of the Cambodja, that one was unmistakably Jasmine, "Melati" in the Indonesian language.

Tonight the smell of the "Sedap Malam" would overpower the smell of all the others. The white flower and smell he remembered from the last house he had lived in before he took up his military studies. The flower grew right below his window.

He looked round his sitting room. The native craft oil paintings; depicted the beautiful sceneries of rice fields against majestic blue mountains, with hardly a cloud in the sky. This was indeed the life for him. He was not going to buckle under. This was a real army; an army you could be proud of and where fairness prevailed. He would see to it, in spite of Captain Smyth! You could meet someone like him in every walk of life and in the best of armies. Captain Smyth was certainly not a true representative of the Dutch Colonial Army. Not at all!

Two raps on the outside door of his room disturbed his thought process.

"Come in." He spoke the words roughly, a reflection of his mood. The sergeant at the other end of the door shook himself, gathered the necessary courage and entered the room like a dog that had just lost a bone in a fight. He stood to attention and saluted.

"What do you want?" Hes hurled the words at him. He was not in a mood to be pleasant. The sergeant swallowed first; then spoke:

"They are fighting Sir."

"Who are fighting?"

"One of the recruits and sergeant Geys, Sir."

"Well," Hes raised his eyebrows, "Sergeant Geys knows his job. He has the diploma of master of all combat arts. The recruit will be soundly beaten and that is that."

Hes strongly felt that he should not interfere. This was the type of discipline that he wanted. Not by punishment exercises like the ones Captain Smyth was in favour of.

Sergeant Geys would have to earn his reputation and would then be respected.

"That is not it Sir: the recruit has thrown sergeant Geys in the river. You got to save his reputation Sir."

"I cannot do that now, unless sergeant Geys gets out of that river himself and beats up the recruit."

"But sergeant Geys cannot swim Sir."

"What?" With one jump Hes leapt out of his bed and while he put on his trousers he shouted

" Geys is a damned fool, and you there," he said "What do you stand there for, get him out!"

"I cannot swim either Sir."

Lieutenant Hes had already pushed him out of the way in his haste to reach the river.

By the time he reached the river, sergeant Geys had already been dragged out and Hes observed that sergeant Geys was spluttering and regurgitating the water that he had swallowed. Then he sat upright and shook himself like a wet dog.

"What happened?" Lieutenant Hes asked, pushing some recruits away so that he could reach where Geys was sitting.

"It is time Sir you teach me how to swim." Lieutenant Hes could not contain himself: he burst out laughing. The spell was broken.

Everybody started giggling and then laughing. More and more joined in and the laughing reverberated from the boulders flanking the river. Master of all the fighting arts, eh? It was still no good unless you knew how to swim and if the fellow you were fighting would throw you in the water. He walked away: the recruit and sergeant Geys were shaking hands already. He shook his head.

The recruit was a big man. Hes was not all that convinced, that sergeant Geys would have won the fight in spite of his so called fighting abilities, even if he had been able to swim. Perhaps it was better that sergeant Geys' fighting skills had not been put to the test after all.

As he walked back to the officer's quarters, he noticed a glint of light coming from the window of rooms occupied by Captain Smyth. Captain Smyth had watched the scene at the pool through binoculars.

So what; lieutenant Hes thought. He shrugged his shoulders. Soldiers did fight among one another; no hard feelings were left afterwards.

He had hardly made himself comfortable in his room, than when the door of his sitting room burst open and Captain Smyth entered. His face predicted a coming thunderstorm. Lieutenant Hes got to his feet and stood to attention.

"You witnessed the fight and did nothing," Captain Smyth started accusingly.

"With respect Sir, the fight was already over when I arrived."

"I want the name of the recruit and I want him punished."

"Why?" Hes with genuine surprise asked.

"Why?" "Do you have to ask me that question?" "Hes, do I need to tell you that fighting among troops undermines moral?" Hes again showed genuine surprise.

"Surely that can't be so Sir; fighting among soldiers is very common, they fight over girls and over many other things, sometimes over very unimportant things. In this respect soldiers are no different from any other recruits any where in the world; did you not fight when you were in Breda Sir?"

Hes had touched a very tender nerve without realising it. Captain Smyth was a coward, he had avoided every confrontation. He had resented his cowardice, which he considered a blot on his manliness, whatever that meant. In spite of that, he could not behave differently. But his resentments towards his own incompetent feeling had produced a self-righteous attitude. Fighting was "ordinair". He, John Smyth, was above common things like that.

"We obviously don't see things the same way Hes. I want the recruit punished. Bring me his name and he is to stand guard duty, instead of going on leave this week-end."

He left the room, banging the door shut to show his displeasure. Hes shook his head: what nonsense, but he had to carry out what he had been ordered to do. He opened the door of his office and walked towards the pool. Many recruits were still at the discussing stage, which follows every fight. The recruit who had fought sergeant Geys was swimming. To him the incident was forgotten. Hes hated himself.

"Come this way," he shouted to the recruit, "I want to speak to you."

"Yes Sir," the recruit replied politely.

"Your name please, I have to report this incident, I am sorry."

"Sure," the recruit replied without resentment "My name is Frank Ahler."

"Ahler you said? Are you the son of General Ahler?"

"He is my father, yes." Hes knew enough. He walked up to Captain. Smyth rooms.

"You got his name?" Captain Smyth asked, icicles in his voice

"Yes Sir," the recruit's name is Ahler, he is the son of General Ahler." Captain Smyth went pale. His brother in law had told him that the rank of major he so desired was his. If General Ahler heard that his son was punished with guard duty and cancelling of leave, as punishment for a simple fight, he could forget promotion to the rank of major forever.

"Have you told him of the punishment yet?"

"No sir, I thought you would like to think it over first."

"Well done Hes; come to think of it; you may well be right, I will let it pass this time, it is not important. You thought so yourself."

"Yes I do sir," Hes saluted and went to his own quarters.

"Hypocrite," he murmured under his breath.

Chapter 6

Lily sat by the pool, drying her moist hair in the sunshine of the late afternoon. In her hand, she held the most recent letter from Richard. She had read it again and again till she knew it all by heart! Almost reluctantly she put it down at last. But where was he? He never wrote where he was posted. It must be a military secret, to tell where you were, she concluded. All letters were also censored these days. Sometimes a letter arrived with cut out pieces everywhere, so that the whole letter did not make any sense. Was this cloak and dagger stuff absolutely necessary? She had a vague idea that he was posted not too far away from Bandoeng, where she lived, because he mentioned in the letter that he could see the mountains that she could also see. Her father also did not know where he was. She wrote to Richard every day, the more letters she wrote she thought, the better the chance was that he would get at least a few of them. And it was fun to write to him. He had also written her that Mas was in the same unit as he himself. It pleased her to hear it. He was among friends. But there was no news from Wong. All Richard's letters were very neatly placed in her album. Once in a while she read them again before going to bed. She had carefully folded away her wedding dress. The war would not last long but in any case the dress was better kept in the hanging wardrobe so that it could not get spoiled.

She would love a cup of tea just now but her mother had taught her brother and herself, that she could only ask a servant to do a job for them, if they could not do it themselves or if they were too busy to do it. Her brother Peter in the Dutch Navy; was coming home this weekend. He would have plenty to tell and his fiancée would come too. How unfair compared to her, she thought. She could only hope that Richard would turn up, but she could never depend on it. And her marriage to Richard was to take place on her twenty second birthday, the fifth of April, now only a few months away.

She was sure it would not be on that day, but maybe in six months? That would be wonderful! Everybody said the war would not last that long. Nevertheless it had struck her how easy it had been for the Japanese to destroy most of the American fleet in Pearl Harbour and again, how easy had it been for them to sink two British warships. How could that be possible? Was their success purely based on luck, or had the Japanese been underrated badly?

As far as the Dutch East Indies went, there had been no enemy activity apart from one abortive attempt at bombing Bandoeng. Only little damage had been done. Toorop, the Dutch General had, broadcasting over the radio, spoken of the strength of the combined Allied forces. Yet it had again surprised her that he had not mentioned any aeroplanes with one word. But of course this was military secret. In spite of the optimistic reassuring words, which also appeared in the press, it was obvious to Lily that the war was getting nearer. The Japanese seemed to score success after success in the Malaysian peninsula. Surely their advance would be stopped at Singapore?

57

Her thoughts returned to her wedding. It was much more pleasant to think about that. They had already decided where the honeymoon was going to be. That was before Richard parted from her. This paradise on earth: Pasir Poetih of course. They would sail with Doel again. Then they would climb the Ringgit together and make a wish. By then however, she would have had her wish fulfilled already: She would have Richard! But there were still so many other things that she could wish.

When they climbed the Ringgit the last time, luck was not on their side. Nevertheless she did not believe in bad luck. Richard and she were going to be lucky, she knew it. She let her imagination run ahead of her.

"Tea Nonnie," the garden servant called to her, showing a beautiful row of healthy teeth. "It is half past four already." He was as lovely as ever, spoiling her.

"Yes please," she called out to him, glad that she didn't have to make the tea herself now. The big tray was put in front of her. The cook Sarinah had filled the tray with all sorts of cookies also wanting to spoil her. How lovely they all were. They were such gentle people, these Indonesian servants.

"Any news Slamet?"

"None Nonnie; your father has not come home yet. I'll let you know." Meanwhile he was pouring the tea for her.

"You are spoiling me Slamet."

"Don't get fat Nonnie, or you won't fit into your wedding dress. Will Mr Richard be coming this weekend Nonnie? He must be very busy not to come to see you. But look what Sarinah has put on the tray for you? You can feed three people on that."

"I will assure you Slamet that I won't eat it all."

After Slamet had left, she reminisced what good life they had led in the Dutch East Indies. How normal and peaceful everything was. Not only spoiled by the servants but by nature also, by their lives in general. She looked around her, at the majestic scenery surrounding her. This was paradise. Would it stay that way? Funny, she had lived in this paradise but never seen it as it really was. She always had accepted this beauty without a second thought: had never seen it as starkly as at this moment. She remembered some one saying: "that you don't realise that you have been in paradise till you are kicked out of it."

Fortunately she saw it in time and know that she had to be grateful for what she had and could still enjoy all the splendour of the people and nature surrounding her life.

In the distance she saw her mother doing the gardening and then she remembered the party to be given in Villa Isola in honour of a high ranking officer, an Englishman, who came to see how he could help protect the Dutch East Indies. Her father; mother and she were invited but since the party was only for officers and their wives, Richard was not. If he turned up at the weekend, she would not go but stay with Richard.

She was sure that the young handsome army lieutenant would miss her if she did not come. She had danced with him in Villa Isola a week ago when she was there too and was supposed to dance with the officers who were single and therefore had no partner. Entertaining the forces in this harmless way was almost a command. Lily only barely got his name but she could tell that he liked her.

She got up; her hair was dry now. She entered the house by the side door so that she did not have to talk to her mother. She would otherwise have to listen about the young lieutenant with whom she had danced at villa Isola. Her mother was so taken up with him she noticed. It was almost as though her mother did not know that she was engaged to Richard.

Running upstairs, she took two steps at a time. The coming of this British high ranking officer, would be good for moral, although Toorop, the army General in charge of the Dutch Forces had let it be known that they could hold off the Japanese by themselves and did not need any help from outside. So far there had only been this one abortive bombing raid by the enemy. Undoubtedly the British were responsible for holding the war away. Singapore was holding fast; what were the Japanese thinking of? And where was the young lieutenant stationed? Her thoughts strayed again. In spite of the fact that she had shown him her engagement ring he had asked her again and again for a dance. She had enjoyed dancing with him and he was extremely polite. But with a wink in his eye and in a whisper, he said that he could visit her at weekends. She had wagged her finger at him meaning: "nothing doing!"

All European women were told by the press and radio that they should provide hospitality to the military if at all possible. And what was the harm in that? It was time to do her wartime bit; arrange the flowers in villa Isola and prepare sandwiches for the guests.

After she had dressed and came down to the hall, she heard her father talking to a visitor. It was a man's voice but it was not her fiancée. As she entered she only saw the back of the visitor's head. When he stood up and faced her, she recognised him immediately: her dancing partner in Villa Isola. He looked very smart in his military uniform with the two stars at the collar of his green tunic, showing his rank. "You know each other then," her father remarked, surprised to see her reaction.

"I had the honour to dance with your daughter at the last ball in Villa Isola," Hes explained, giving her a wink that her father could not see.

"Are your whereabouts still a secret lieutenant?" she asked.

"Indeed miss Cane," Hes replied.

"You must never ask a soldier where he is stationed these days," her father said.

"Why this cloak and dagger stuff father?"

"Well, the enemy could draw conclusions from the position of troops, where our strength lies. Lieutenant Hes is with a unit training cadets to become officers; that is all we can tell you."

"But that is what Richard is training for; you could be in the same unit."

"Perhaps," Lieutenant Hes agreed. "What is his name?"

"Nevermind about that," her father cut into the conversation. "We are not here to discuss personal affairs. Be so good," turning to Lily," to get us some tea, or would you rather have something stronger?" He turned to the lieutenant.

"Tea is fine," Lieutenant Hes agreed. Lily went into the hall to ask Bai, the houseboy to prepare the tea. What did Lieutenant Hes and her father have to talk about? And why did her father stop him when he asked the name of her fiancée? Now that she thought about it, Richard had written about a young lieutenant in his training camp of whom he approved. He must be from the same unit and since Hes had teasingly said that he could visit her at weekends, Richard could be stationed not that far away. Richard did not like the captain of the outfit, and neither did any of his friends in his unit, he wrote.

She prepared to go back to her room when she met her mother in the hall.

"Have you seen Lieutenant Hes yet and isn't he handsome? I wonder why he is not married yet. Go and speak to him."

"But mother," Lily said, surprised at her mother's reaction, "I am engaged to be married to Richard. Have you forgotten?"

"Of course not dear. But Lieutenant Hes has such a brilliant future ahead of him. Richard is so young and you only know him from school. Your father rates Hes' chances of promotion very high." Lily shrugged her shoulders.

"Good for him, I am not interested. Moreover who says that Lieutenant Hes is interested in me anyway? I am going to marry Richard, I love him; what is wrong mother?"

"Nothing dear; but as you know your father is military and wants to maintain the status of the Dutch in Indonesia. Your fiancée has different ideas. That is all."

"But I hold the same ideas and you too mother."

"Oh no dear, I agree with your father in this. The Indonesians will get their independence but not just yet. The time is not ripe. There is plenty time. They still must learn a lot about democracy. Before the Dutch came rulers who exploited their own people, as you know, ruled the local population. If the Indonesians become independent now, they will return to the same savage situation all over again."

"You are biased mother. Indonesians are just as able as we are. They haven't been given the chance to govern themselves. There is hardly any Indonesian intellectual in the government. Not because they don't want to or because they are not able. No, it is because the Indonesians just have not been asked. And that is the truth mother; you know that just as well as I do."

"Nevermind dear, we won't talk politics you and I," her mother wisely ended the topic of that conversation. "Besides we have a lot to do. The sandwiches for tomorrow at villa Isola and have you got your dress with laces ready? I want you to look like a million dollars"

"To impress who mother: Lieutenant Hes?"

"Oh have it your way."

With that her mother walked away leaving Lily in a pensive mood. Did her parents not approve of the choice of her fiancé? She had always assumed that they liked Richard although he held different views on political issues. It was strange that they had never discussed her impending marriage to Richard with her. She knew also that her parents had not approved of her going on holiday with Richard. Did that mean that they did not approve of Richard altogether? In their outlook on Indonesian independence, it now became clear to her that they didn't think about it in the way that Richard and she did.

But was that important anyway? In the normal events of life the question never arose. Never in school neither on the tennis court was it ever discussed with her friends, except as a passing item; never seriously. It was never important enough. You don't talk politics in paradise! She had many Indonesian friends among whom there was Mas the son of the Regent of West Java, who, if she was to believe the rumours, was groomed to become the next Sultan of Middle Java and who was the bosom friend of her fiancee. Their association was in no way affected by this question of Indonesian independence. Nor was it affected in any way no matter what race they belonged to, whether Dutch, Indonesian, Chinese, Arab or whatever. With politics it was the same: it didn't matter in the slightest what your views were. Neither did it matter what religion you or the other practised. They didn't even know what religion their other friend confessed to. There were Jews, Mohammedans, Christians, Shintoists and many other religions. It did not matter. Their friendly relationships were totally unbiased!

Wong and Mas were her truly best friends and Mas invited Wong equally, like Richard and herself, to his father's holiday house high up in Tjipanas where they had had such good times in week ends, using the swimming pool and the tennis courts to amuse themselves even from the time when they were only children.

Wong was also interested in her, she realised. He adored her, she could tell from his looks. But he was such a good friend of Richard and would always respect her love for Richard. One day he would meet a nice girl and fall deeply in love with that girl, forgetting that he had ever admired her and had held an infatuation for her, she was sure. But at this time, she had to be extremely careful not to encourage him by even a word that could be interpreted wrongly.

She wondered where he could be. Perhaps he had also joined the forces. He had been so anti-Japanese, even long before the Japanese had bombed Pearl Harbour, pointing out the atrocities the Japanese had committed in China, against the civilian population. Neither Richard nor she herself knew anything of his whereabouts, since the outbreak of the war.

Back in her room upstairs she looked out from her window. Hes was just leaving and getting into his army jeep. He was handsome she admitted. He looked up and saw her standing in the window. Mockingly he bowed low and threw her a kiss. She waved back at him. Her father saw him do it. It left him in deep thoughts. What if Lily..?

Chapter 7

The meeting Colonel Arlen had arranged; was held in uttermost secrecy and strictly confidential. Only five other officers were present. The chairman, Colonel Arlen, had carefully selected them. They all had one thing in common. None of them wanted Indonesian independence in the foreseeable future.

The meeting was held in the prestigious boardroom of Hotel Homann's private wing. After Colonel Arlen arrived, he himself shut the doors to the west wing of the hotel. This action he considered highly necessary. He felt himself very important, at least as important as Clark Gable did in the film "Gone with the wind".

No other person could now enter and by chance overhear what was said in secret. If any of the officers present, had thought that this meeting was going to be an ordinary tea party, they were wrong! The behaviour of the chairman made it very obvious to the five officers already seated at the table in the boardroom, that the chairman had invited them to this meeting because he wanted to discuss an item with them, which in his opinion, needed high priority.

The chosen hotel, Hotel Homann, the most prestigious in Bandoeng at the time, was built very close to the Braga, the shopping centre of Bandoeng. Its location was perfect. Not only because it was situated near the main shopping centre but also because it was lying on the main road connecting the two main towns of the province of West Java. From the windows of this hotel's boardroom you could see the mountains Pangrango and the Gedeh, the twin volcanoes, like sentinels, which had protected a lake that was situated where now stood the town of Bandoeng.

A few millennia ago, an earthquake had punched a hole in the wall of the lake and all the water had streamed away, leaving a not too dry plateau with a radius of about ten kilometres. The town Bandoeng was built on this plateau. It was supposed to be a graveyard for children because of its damp climate.

After looking at the clock hanging on the wall, then consulting his wristwatch to make doubly sure that it was 5'clock PM exactly; Colonel Arlen cleared his throat extra loudly and dragged his chair nearer to the table. He then sat down with studied importance. After all he was a showman and what was to be discussed needed the utmost attention of those present. He hammered twice with his gavel on the table to indicate that the meeting had started and looked round at the assembled officers.

That the meeting was going to be a serious affair was now crystal clear to even the most non-intelligent of the five officers already seated at the table. Everyone therefore put on a sombre face for the occasion so as not to disappoint the chairman.

"Welcome," Colonel Arlen began. "First of all I must emphasise that this meeting is held in the utmost secrecy. Is that understood?" All the five other officers nodded in agreement.

Colonel Brink, one of the officers, shifted in his seat and even nearly raised his arm from emotion. He immediately was all ears. Subconsciously he was motivated by the fact that sharing confidential information, is human nature's easiest way of displaying ego. This was going to be fun: he liked secrets. Nothing he liked better than to share them with others. But only after a reasonable interval of time of course, in which you could hardly wait.

Colonel Arlen continued; "You may be wondering why I have selected you for this meeting. We all know," he looked round the table, "that there is a feeling among some Indonesians to want independence and that this is most unwise at the present time. There will be chaos if the Indonesians get their way. Their desire for what they call independence is premature. They certainly are not ready for it.

We also know that we cannot hold out against the Japanese forces if Singapore falls, and Singapore cannot last out much longer. It is only a question of time. The Japanese forces are already at the causeway connecting the stronghold with the mainland." His voice sounded grave.

"All of us have pinned our hopes on the strength of Singapore, a fatal mistake. Unless a miracle occurs Singapore will be lost within weeks, not months. Now I am coming to discuss what we are here for." He paused for a while so as to prepare the listeners for the dramatic effect of his coming words

"The Governor General wishes the son of the Regent of West Java to be evacuated to Australia. There is some urgency; the sooner the better, he reasons, while it is still possible, before we may also have to surrender. The son of the Regent is to be accompanied by his friend and confidant, the assistant controller of Buitenzorg. Both are at the moment in a shooting bivouac called Tjipatat, a training camp for soldiers to become officers under the command of captain Smyth present here." He nodded in the direction of Captain Smyth who acknowledged his nod.

"The Regent of West Java, his father, his mother and their three daughters are already in Australia; Canberra I believe. They all were evacuated at the request of the Governor-General.

"This plan of the Governor to evacuate the son of the Regent of West Java does not suit us and I'll tell you the reason."

"Why was the Soesoehoenan not evacuated instead?" Colonel Brink, (inferior in rank to Colonel Arlen but only in the duration of holding the rank) asked.

"He is totally ineffective," Colonel Arlen replied. "And that is why you and I would have preferred to have him evacuated rather than the Regent's son. We could have coped with him easily after the war. He has no following. His fat salary, which he receives from the Dutch government and his harem suits him perfectly. A change to an independent Indonesia would not suit him. He would have agreed with everything we propose to him in the future."

"But is he not the more powerful one?"

"In theory yes, but he does not have the backing of the Indonesian elite in contrast to the Regent or the Regent's son. "The main reason that the Governor wants the Regent's son in Australia; is that he is an influential spokesman for the Indonesians. He is well educated and cultured. He also has a Dutch mother. The most significant reason is that he is groomed to become the Sultan when his uncle, the present Sultan dies. This is the wish of his uncle, although why is not known as he has many sons himself. Perhaps he does not trust them. Each of his sons could kill him if they were in line of succession. Now they are not. Quite clever don't you think? In any case then, this Regent's son who is intelligent, is the one who acts against our aim. He wants independence at short notice, so our interests clash! We don't want our power handed over to the Indonesians just yet do we?"

"Certainly not," Captain Smyth spoke out, feeling good that Colonel Arlen could hear that he held the same opinion as his brother in law.

"This Regent's son," Colonel Arlen continued, "is what it is all about. He must not be groomed to become the next leader of the Indonesians, which is what the Governor-General wants. As far as we are concerned he has too much following as it is already. We certainly have no objection to the Regent, his father. He is pro-Dutch anyway and his wife is Dutch. Moreover he is already too old. No, it is his son we have to fear.

"This meeting I called for, is to have your opinion and agreement for a plan I have, and which we can carry out, to prevent him from getting away, so that it won't be possible for him to become groomed as the leader of the "pro freedom for Indonesia movement." In simple terms; we must prevent his evacuation to Australia."

"But this is contrary to the wishes of the Governor, contrary to law," Captain Draper remarked. "What will happen if the Governor finds out?"

"First of all," Colonel Arlen stated calmly: "we the army; in war time, at certain times can also be the law: secondly the Governor will never find out unless we tell him."

"I don't understand," Colonel Brink spoke. "What difference will it make whether the Regent's son is evacuated to Australia or not?"

"Just as I thought," Colonel Arlen spoke to himself. How could Colonel Brink be so dumb and yet have risen to the rank he held. There were always anomalies in any army he decided. He remembered someone saying to him once; speaking about the army in general, that he, Colonel Brink was so dumb that all the officers were surprised at his high rank. He knew that he had to explain to Brink slowly. Maybe even a few times for the benefit of Brink.

"There is every possibility that if Mas, the Regent's son is not evacuated, that he then will fall into Japanese hands. He is too well known not to have escaped their attention. Either they will kill him, which is also not what we want and is very unlikely, or they will use him for propaganda purposes, which is even better for us. If they let him live and will use him for their propaganda, he will have to broadcast everything he is not in agreement with and will hang himself. No intelligent Indonesian will agree with an Indonesia run by the Japanese or by someone who was a puppet of theirs during the war, which is what Mas will have become, irrespective whether he made his statements under duress or not. The Indonesians will be terribly disappointed with him and there will be nothing left of his popularity after the war. He will, even after the war, still be tainted, having been a puppet of the Japanese. Mas, that is his name; will have been disposed off neatly. Nobody will bother about him any longer. Are you all with me?"

He was relieved that he would not have to explain the plan to Colonel Brink for the second time, when everybody even Colonel Brink nodded.

"Thank God," he thought to himself. "Very good, we are all in agreement then, he continued. In that case we will send for the controller only, I'll explain to you later why only the controller, and we will tell him that he and Mas are to be evacuated soon."

Again Colonel Brink raised his finger. "He is still a schoolboy," Colonel Arlen thought.

"Yes?" he enquired kindly knowing full well the question that Colonel Brink wanted to ask. The man was so transparent.

"I still don't understand Colonel; first you say that they must not be evacuated and now you say that you are going to send for the controller and that you will tell the controller that they are.

"Colonel Arlen carefully chose his words. He explained slowly with patience, like a mother communicating with a child.

"What we say and what we do is not the same thing: of course not.

The controller must not know that he is not getting away to Australia, which is what the real plan is. On the contrary he must firmly believe by our action in this room, that is to say by what we tell him, when he is here, that we are fully for this plan of the Governor and that we intend to implement the request. After the war he must not be in a position to tell the Governor, that we didn't mean to carry out the order given by the highest in the land. He cannot deny now, that we have called him here and that we told him that he must escape with the Regent's son as soon as possible, as is the wish of the Governor. What we do thereafter is none of his business."

"Another point," he paused for a moment, to get the officer's attention: "Mas, the regent's son himself, will not be told by us that the Governor wants him evacuated. He must only hear it from the controller: second hand so to speak. This is done so that there is never a possibility that the two together can testify against us. If something unforeseen goes wrong we can always deny what the controller says. That is to say: it will only be his word against ours. Since Mas will never have heard of the plan for his evacuation from us ourselves directly, he might think that the controller has misunderstood what he was told. Preferably he may even believe that the controller is hoodwinking him. There has never been a better substitute for "divide and rule", if you know what I mean," he added, pleased with himself that he could slip in this wisdom.

Again this last remark escaped Colonel Brink totally.

"This is to safeguard us if something goes wrong," Colonel Arlen added superfluously for the benefit of Brink. "All blame for not succeeding in their plan of escape must never be traceable to us."

It was wasted effort. Colonel Brink was as much in the dark as he was before the explanation. It had the effect on him as though he had received the knock out blow in a boxing match and he slumped back in his leather chair into temporary oblivion: totally satisfied, warm and cosy. The manager of the hotel, to allow guests to take a nap if meetings would last too long or if they were boring, had put these kinds of chairs in the conference room.

Apart from the "divide and rule bit", Brink felt that he had understood the plan perfectly. Understanding something to him was almost as if he had thought it up entirely on his own. In secret he congratulated himself on being so clever.

"Does General Toorop know of our plan?" he asked innocently, when his mind came round again; his face full of honest anticipation.

"In heavens name," Colonel Arlen swore softly to himself. He again wondered: how could a fellow with the brains of a hen have risen to the rank he held himself. It occurred to him for the first time, that he should seriously question his own intelligence, seeing he held the same rank as Colonel Brink.

"Of course not," he grumbled.

To avoid further stupid questions coming from Colonel Brink, he quickly said:

"Are we all in agreement then?" Nobody spoke, but all raised their hands instead. Only Colonel Brink seemed to hesitate: he then also raised his. He was not sure whether he should raise his hand or not, but since the majority was in agreement it might show up his ignorance if he did not. To indicate that the meeting had come to an end, Colonel Arlen took the chairman's hammer and again knocked twice on the wooden table in front of him.

The officers left one by one. Colonel Brink was the last to leave the room: there was doubt in his mind. Had he really understood all that was talked about? If he had, it was a dirty trick they were playing.

Although he was not clever, he was scrupulously honest. He had risen to his rank because of his honesty, in contrast to Colonel Arlen, who had got there by manipulation. He was going to think about it and better still, make some notes. He always understood things better after he saw them written down and could then take his time to understand them.

Yes, he was going to write down the things discussed at the meeting. Especially the divide and rule bit he was puzzled about. What was it that Colonel Arlen had said again? He already could not remember because he had not understood the phrase in the first place. Of course he would keep his notes hidden even from his wife. After all he had promised to keep secret what was discussed. Later, after he had made his notes and after some time had gone by, he would talk about it, maybe only to his wife. She would enjoy the secret as much as he had.

A promise to keep something secret surely did not last a lifetime! After all there had to be an expiry period, otherwise there was no fun in knowing something and not being able to share that knowledge with any one. He never thought that Colonel Arlen was crooked. Maybe he had misunderstood the things that were said at the meeting. Must be that, he concluded. He closed the door of the boardroom very softly behind him because he felt that his next promotion depended on it. He need not have bothered; he was killed in the war. In spite of his lack of intelligence, or perhaps because of it, he died a war hero. Had Yamamoto known about him, it would not have surprised him: the latter had decided long ago that hero's invariably die an early death.

But Colonel Brink wrote the notes before he died! He was no wiser after having written them down but I was! His widow gave them to me after the war. They were dynamite! Two days after the original meeting, a second meeting was held in the same prestigious boardroom of hotel Homann. Colonel Arlen again chaired the meeting Present this time however were only four other officers, not five as before. I had been sent for and was told of the evacuation plan for myself and for Mas.

"For reasons of secrecy," the chairman told me, mysteriously, "Mas is not to be told of this plan until you reach Australia, do you understand?" Although I did not understand, I nodded.

"Did I have any question to ask?"

"Yes; would we get any assistance?"

"Of course," was the reply of the chairman; "every assistance possible." Not until much later, did I realise how deceitful his words had been and how twisted some people can be.

That Lily's father was involved in the plot I did not know then. He was one of the five officers initially present but he was not there when I was sent for. He did not want me to see him and know that he had agreed with the plan! But I did find out from Brink's notes much later that he had been present at the initial meeting when it was decided that neither Mas nor I should ever reach Australia. He had also raised his hand when Colonel Arlen asked if they were all in agreement. Had it not been for the explicit notes made by Colonel Brink and for the fact that his widow made me a present of them, I would never have known and certainly would never have been able to prove later, that this plan was made in the boardroom of Hotel Homann.

I was therefore, much later in court, even able to mention the names of the five officers who had taken part in the plot and even the dates at which the two meetings had been held!

This plan of the officers, contrary to the wishes of the Governor-General had unforeseen, and far reaching consequences, involving the future for many people, not least for Lily, myself and for the fifth person not present at the second meeting: Lily's father!

The guerrilla war in Indonesia, which followed shortly after the Japanese surrendered; to some extent, had its root in the wrong decision made and carried out, contrary to the wishes of the Governor. The honest spokesman for the Indonesians, my best friend Mas turned guerrilla fighter, which was just something the Governor had wanted to prevent.

Chapter 8

Kemajoran's airstrip at the outskirts of Batavia, the capital of the Dutch East Indies, still consisted of partly caked dry mud left alone to get hard and partly of asphalt mixed with concrete. Several Kampongs had been sacrificed for the construction of this strip and its adjoining hangars. The inhabitants of the kampongs and their herd of cattle and other livestock; were housed on the free land on either side of the airfield complex. It was the second largest airfield of Batavia and had only hurriedly been built, since the importance of Batavia, the capital of the Dutch East Indies, had increased in the years 1940- '41, now that Holland and the Hague as seat of government, had been occupied by the Germans. The Queen of Holland and her close advisers including her adjutant (and son in law) Prince Bernhard had fled to London, where they enjoyed British hospitality.

Today: February 19th, 1942, Kemajoran expected an important visitor; General Wensel, commander in chief of the British forces in the Pacific.

Toorop, holding the rank of General in charge of the Dutch Indonesian army, and his staff, waited in the open sun, where the airstrip ended and the complex of hangars began. They were sweating like pigs in a basket, dressed in top uniform and even the uppermost button of their tunic was closed and that in the heat of Batavia, in the monsoon at 30 degrees in the shade!

"Why on earth did Wensel have to arrive at mid day," Toorop swore softly to himself. The heat undermined his strength and the DC 16 was late in arriving. He had been standing in the unrelenting sun for half an hour already. When Wensel's plane finally appeared it started to circle the airfield first. Perhaps the pilot wanted to give Wensel a view of the capital of the Dutch East Indies from the air before landing.

"Why this Goddamn delay?" Toorop sighed, feeling the temperature in his tunic rise to boiling point. Being an airline pilot himself, he concluded there being no wind to speak of, the pilot could have landed from any direction earlier. The sweat from his body, so far collecting around his navel only; now made its way downward, steadily but with determination. He had only this morning arrived from his cool headquarters Villa Isola, high above Bandoeng in the mountains, with the active vulcano Tankuban Prahoe (upturned boat) in the background.

"Villa Isola", as it was called had been declared the Headquarters of the army since the outbreak of the war. The villa was still the private home of the millionaire Alberti, who was pleased to help in the war effort and had gracefully loaned the villa to the forces for the duration of the war. Villa Isola's setting in a tropical garden full of orchids; was stunning. Alberti and his wife were living elsewhere in any case at the outbreak of the war.

His wife had loved Villa Isola, this idyllic Garden of Eden especially built for her.

Toorop was more than happy to have the Villa as his headquarters and so was his fair-haired secretary, lascivious in every way, the divorced wife of General Aitkin.

"I am in love with you," Toorop had once told her, "I want to marry you." She had wisely desisted after the experience of having been a wife once. The role of concubine suited her much better she thought and she was right. After a while Toorop agreed. She was always right of course; she was indispensable.

The D.C. at last to the relief of Toorop and his staff, lowered its wheels under the fuselage, poised for touch down.

In a cloud of dust, Wensel descended the steps of the plane. The dust filled his nostrils and lungs. At the same time, the cacophony of the local, improvised military band, reached his ears. It played "God save the King" or some sort of version of it. It was only just recognizable as the British national anthem. General Wensel had to stop his descent from the plane, to stand to attention. This was far from easy in the position he found himself, standing on the third step from the top of the airoplane's ladder. It was quite uncomfortable. He could still topple down, five feet if he lost his balance. To Toorop, the music did not at all sound bad. He was tone deaf and he felt that at least an effort was being made to honor his visitor. He joined the melody with his base voice softly, as far as the Anthem was discernable so as to take the attention away from his discomfort, produced by the heat.

He made a mental note to congratulate the Malay bandleader later for his efforts.

Wensel reflected that his senses were severely tested by the heat; the dust, and now this awful music. When the band stopped he resumed his descent from the airplane, carrying his wooden baton with the silver knob at one end under his arm. Silly habit Toorop thought. Again a snobbish Englishman his thinking concluded. He, Toorop, would never carry a baton like that; but if Wensel liked it…., "O.K," he said aloud.

"What was that General?" his adjutant Colonel Bresle standing by his side said nervously; startled by the remark.

"Never mind," Toorop added. "I was just talking to myself." He stepped forward leaving Colonel Brestle wondering if the heat had been too much for Toorop, upsetting the brain functions of his superior.

With a warm smile Toorop extended his sweaty hand.

"Welcome to the Dutch East Indies General," he said. "My staff car will pull up later; would you like to inspect the guard of honor first?"

General Wensel, to whom the heat of the airport had felt as though he had entered a crematorium by the back door, sighed. He felt trapped. He had looked forward to a cool bar, a fan blowing clean cold air to his overheated head and in his hand a glass of ice cold gin and lime, with an extra generous measure of ice lumps in it.

"Another wretched inspection of troops," he sighed. Resignedly he nodded. He could have expected this pomp. Toorop would have seen to it that everything was done as it ought to be done. After all, it was done to honor him. The gin and lime with the extra ice blocks in it; would have to wait.

So this was Toorop, Berens's successor. He had liked Berens whom he had met in Singapore before the war. But Berens was killed in a plane disaster a few months before the war. Undoubtedly sabotage he had decided, although the official statement did not say that. The war had started shortly afterwards. Did the Japanese want Berens out of the way? It was difficult to say.

Toorop was altogether different. His uniform fitted him badly and the sweat had penetrated his tunic at the lowest point of his body and under the arm pits. He looked like a peasant and Wensel did not like peasants. Toorop had quickly sized Wensel up correctly; Wensel was a snob.

"Glad to be here," he lied, dabbing his forehead where the sweat started to accumulate.

Wensel's objective was to find out how long the Dutch East Indies forces could resist the Japanese, although he did not have much hope on this score. The Dutch East Indies forces consisted of an army and a navy. He was aware that the Japanese did not rate these forces highly: they certainly did not pose a threat to their expansion desires. He knew also that the army was more like a police force, aimed at keeping law and order and only was meant to deal with local uprisings when necessary. Certainly not strong enough to resist anything like the Japanese army, well equipped with modern airoplanes. About the Navy part he knew nothing to his regret.

However he knew that the Dutch had helped in the European war, by sending aeroplanes to Britain even before the Japanese entered into the war. They were used with success in the battle of Britain. The Dutch surely must have many more planes for the defence of the Dutch East Indies than only those that were sent to the European war scene. And planes would make up for what he knew was a small army.

It was natural for him to expect that, since Toorop being a pilot himself, would naturally have favoured equipping the air force especially. General Wensel was to find out that apart from a miserable squadron of old fashioned Brewster planes remaining; the planes that had been sent to Britain; were practically all the planes that the Dutch East Indies forces possessed. The information shocked him.

"Are you absolutely sure," he even asked Toorop between two sips of his cherished gin and lime.

"Absolutely," Toorop assured him, drinking his pait (genever) straight and knocking his fifth drink back in less than a second flat. "Some more ice General?" Toorop offered with a smile.

Wensel sank back in his leather chair deep in thought, deflated.

"Good God," he thought. Here was a police force devoid of air power and their government had just declared war on a country whose air power had only recently inflicted a loss of 18 battle ships and 2000 lives in Pearl Harbour.

The electric fan above his head kept supplying him with cool air that he needed to think straight. No aeroplanes! What was the world coming to! In this respect though, they were no worse off than his own forces in Malay and Singapore. They did not possess air power either. But then he had already decided that the Malayan campaign was lost and that Singapore could not be held. He now realised that what applied to Singapore equally applied to the Dutch East Indies. Another lost case. How unfortunate! He considered air power as absolutely indispensable in modern warfare. Politely he listened when Toorop pointed out that aeroplanes were not of much use anyway in a jungle war, which in itself did not sound so bad. In this he found Toorop naive. To hear that from a man who was a pilot himself. How could he say such glorious nonsense! Obviously the man was ignorant that he, Wensel had written a book on modern warfare. In the book he had insisted that aeroplanes were essential in a modern war. "Typically a peasant brought up on potatoes, gravy and cauliflower, posing as a war strategist," Wensel thought to himself. What would he know of modern warfare? Berens would have seen his argument in a second flat.

In a conversation between him and Berens in Singapore, a few months before, they had discussed the danger the Japanese presented. What if the Japanese bombed Batavia and Bandoeng, two towns full of people with intensity, and that intensity was undoubtedly to come after Singapore had surrendered. About this he was sure. What if this bombing resulted in the killing of large amounts of women and children? Would Toorop not be forced to agree to an unconditional surrender once that happened? That time had not arrived, but it would make the Dutch East Indies indefensible without a large air force to resist the enemy.

"Another drink General?" Toorop cheerfully offered, as though he was presiding at a birthday party, blissfully unaware what Wensel was thinking of.

"Yes, a stiff double whiskey," Wensel ordered unhesitatingly to steady his nerves. But Wensel had underrated Toorop. This officer had only put up a brave face to support morale.

Long before, Toorop was aware of the impossible situation he would be in if the Americans surrendered but especially if the British stronghold Singapore was to fall.

Wensel was still sober when they arrived at Villa Isola high up in the mountains above Bandoeng. Villa Isola took his breath away. He had never expected such luxury. His room had been tastefully furnished and lavishly decorated by a millionaire with cultured taste, Wensel coolly deduced

The view from his window looked out over the expanse of the town Bandoeng several miles below him, with lush wooded vegetation in between. The very few houses below Villa Isola were built with flat roofs. Alberti had paid every house owner, who was building a house below Isola, to construct a flat roof on his or her house instead of a tiled one. In this way it assured him of an unimpeded view from Villa Isola at the town of Bandoeng far below. He had succeeded well. Wensel was impressed.

The coolness of the falling of the night, felt pleasant on his skin; quite a difference of temperature compared to that of his arrival in the heat of Kemajoran's airport. On the other side of Bandoeng, Wensel observed the active twin volcanoes the Pangerango and the Gedeh, the latter spewing out a cloud of smoke at the top. He could also see the twinkling of the lights of Bandoeng, now that the night was falling. From the other window of his room, he could see the mountain called "Tankoeban Prahu" very nearby. It looked exactly like an upturned boat hence the name. The explosion, to shape the mountain the way it looked, must have been colossal! Wensel had seen many a beautiful view in his life, but this was special.

He lay on his bed and wondered who had slept in this bed before? Alberti and his wife perhaps; had they made love in this room? It was the most ideal honeymoon setting; but what would be left of this beautiful place once the heavy boot of the Japanese destroyed its happiness?

Wearily he got up from the bed and took a shower before dinner. He found the water surprisingly cool and refreshing.

On his first evening he was introduced at dinner to Toorop's secretary. She was charming and he could understand that Toorop was fond of her. He concluded that she possessed everything in the way of beauty that a woman could wish.

"Gin and lime General?" Toorop asked. Later at dinner to the left of him, was seated Toorop's adjutant whose name he had already forgotten, having been introduced to so many new people. The talk inevitably led to the progress of the war.

"Where will you go back to General; Australia perhaps? Or will it be Ceylon?"

"What do you mean?" Wensel asked, amazed that the Colonel mentioned Australia and also Ceylon.

"I beg your pardon," the officer said. "Surely you are not going back to Singapore to stay? It cannot be held." Wensel felt trapped. Could this fellow have read his thoughts?

"Is that your opinion?" Wensel asked sarcastically, knowing full well it was his own opinion also. The Colonel was not embarrassed.

"I did not want to offend you sir, but I read your book on warfare. You believe in air power as absolutely indispensable in order to win a battle. Seeing we have no air power and neither do you: the conclusion in your mind must be obvious. Neither Singapore nor the Dutch East Indies will be able to stop the Japanese." Wensel felt flattered. The fellow had read his book and could discuss it, giving his opinion too.

"What was your name again?" he turned to his neighbour.

"Bresle Sir, Michael Bresle."

"Yes," Wensel thought with satisfaction. The upper strata in any army were no fools. He had always held that view. This officer was no exception and confirmed his belief. Of course: after all he Wensel belonged in the upper strata of the British army himself.

Villa Isola, Mrs Aitken, the food and drink and now this officer who had read his book, made good the miserable "God save the King" at the airport and the information on the lack of airpower, the airpower he had so much counted on and he knew to be indispensable. One could almost forget the war in this environment. The excellent "rijsttafel" was by far the best food he had ever tasted.

The free flowing gin blotted out his natural defences and the heavy perfume escaping from between Mrs. Aitkens well formed breasts soothed his numbing brain. This was living in the tropics, as it ought to be.

"Damn the Japanese who attempted to destroy this heavenly peace," he thought.

"What do you drink?" he turned to Bresle. He could see that Mrs. Aitken was already heavily involved with Toorop on the other side of her. No use spoiling Toorop's fun now. Leave him be. He would soon have more problems than he could cope with.

He heard Bresle reply:

"Lemon juice please, sir." It sounded to Wensel that Bresle's voice came from a far distance, although the man was sitting next to him. Also Bresle's face was seen as though it was in a haze. The man of course had drunk too much; could it be? Bresle had asked for lemon juice. Surely there must be some mistake? Had he heard correctly?

Bresle nodded when the question was put to him for the second time, to make sure what Bresle was drinking. Wensel could not be more surprised when Bresle confirmed that it was indeed plain lemòn juice he had asked for. This man mysteriously could get drunk on lemon juice! The drink arrived, served with ice as well.

The degree of euphoria from alcohol took over from Wensel's previously sombre mood. He ordered his fifth gin and lime, or was it his sixth? The world seemed to be a better place than when he arrived and were aeroplanes that important after all?

In his state of mind at the moment, he wondered if he should not have a reprint of his book, questioning soberly the wisdom of the need for aeroplanes after all. At this stage he would even have consented to bows and arrows as a means of defence.

After the splendid dinner and pleasant company, as he walked on the thick carpeted covered floor back to his room, a large lizard creeping on the roof above his head, called the melancholy call tokèh's [lizards] make, through the empty hallway. It was an eerie sound, Wensel thought. Subconsciously he started to count the wailing cries till the lizard stopped its calls.

"Seven times." He had counted distinctly. No doubt about that. His brain was now clear again! Had Wensel grown up in the Dutch East Indies, he would quickly have made a wish, because he would have known that when a tokèh cries seven times, a mortal can make a wish and the wish would come true. A sky full of aeroplanes is what he would have wished, his planes, and plenty modern ones. They would soon drive the enemy away. Unfortunately he did not know that he could make that wish. Because of it, he let an invaluable chance go by. Sadly he realised that without planes the Dutch East Indies could not be held and he did not have any to give away.

Another officer whose room opened unto the same hallway had also heard the calls of the lizard. His wish had been a modest one and when Wensel passed the doorway to the officer's bedroom the next morning, Mrs Aitkens' perfume coming from that bedroom met his nostrils. The officer had had his wish fulfilled. He had capitalised on the chance the seven cries of the tokeh had given him and had received even more than he could have imagined!

Wensel only stayed another two days. He was sad to leave. All defence had to be concentrated on Australia now. He explained this and Toorop saw his point of view and reluctantly agreed. The Dutch forces had to do the best they could do under the circumstances delaying the advance of the Japanese army, an army well equipped with a superior air force. The only hope for the Dutch lay in their navy and in their determination to hold on and fight as long as they could.

Wensel left from the same airport and in the same aeroplane that had brought him; one of the few planes the Dutch still possessed. He had to admit that Toorop had been a generous host. Toorop saw him off.

In their short time together they had come to like and respect each other. He no longer saw Toorop as a peasant. He realised that Toorop was in an impossible position. The Dutch armed forces small as they were, were up against a numerically superior army well equipped with modern planes. He really felt sorry for Toorop. What could this man do other than show a brave face although he knew very well himself that he was losing the war?

In turn Toorop appreciated that Wensel was genuinely interested in the fate of the Dutch East Indies and Toorop never again referred to "that snobbish Englishman," when talking about Wensel in future. He realised that in Wensel he had met a true gentleman.

The fate of the Dutch East Indies was sealed. Their hope pinned on the fortress Singapore and the presence of the Americans in the Philippines, would be proven to be misplaced. The Dutch navy lost the battle of the Java Sea and its army was continually bombed from the air. They were about to lose the war.

Djojo Bojo's prediction, as far as the occupation of the Dutch East Indies by a yellow warrior race was concerned, seemed about to become true. Radio Preanger's closing song "Sag beim Abschied leise Servus" meaning "goodbye" would sadly soon be heard for the last time when Radio Preanger would cease to exist altogether.

And Mas and I were still waiting for our "urgent evacuation," promised to me by Colonel Arlen.

Chapter 9

The Sergeant major of the platoon coming down the hill in his jeep looked worn out. His face was blotched. Deep cringes of coagulated sweat had accumulated around his mouth. His clothes were torn and his right arm was held in a sling. He was obviously wounded. He had not slept for forty-eight hours.

The platoon had started from the North Coast of Java fighting a retreating battle through the Tjiater mountain pass, which connects Soebang with the city of Bandoeng, which lies in a plateau, surrounded by a group of mountains. Twelve Bren Carrier trucks bore bullet holes from machine gun fire and were also covered with mud and dust.

"The Tjiater pass has been abandoned," he said in a hoarse voice: "the Japanese have taken the airport in Soebang."

That was demoralising news.

"Where is your captain?" he asked me in the same monotonous tone.

"I don't know," I said, "but Lieutenant Hes, our lieutenant is here. Just follow this gravel road down." The Sergeant major frowned.

"Your captain is not here? I have been given instructions to report to him. You are from shooting bivouac Tjipatat?" he verified

"Yes," I assured him.

The twelve Bren Carriers followed him down the gravel track to the camp. It was a pitiable sight. I heard later that his platoon had lost five trucks already due to bombardment from the air, while he was on the retreat.

I resumed watching the road. So far I had not seen any sign of life. The Kampong people had either left or kept themselves in their houses out of fear. Indeed, why was Captain Smyth not here? That is what we all wanted to know! Surely he had not run away?

After about half an hour Tjaden and Mas came to relieve me.

"Noticed anything?" Tjaden asked.

"Nothing," I replied, "no sign of life, not even from the kampong."

I shouldered my gun as Tjaden looked at his watch

"One thirty," he said. Then he turned to Mas.

"Anything suspicious that you see is immediately worth reporting, you understand?" Mas nodded and repeated the order given.

Tjaden and I marched back.

"You saw the Bren Carriers and the retreating platoon?" I turned to Tjaden: "what do you make of it?"

"The Japanese are winning this war," Tjaden said solemnly; "and there is nothing we can do about it; we haven't got the means to hold them. You heard of the defeat of Singapore of course?"

"Yes," I replied. "How is that possible? What disaster! We have all counted on the stronghold of Singapore and it turned out to be a total failure. And where are the Americans? The strongest nation on earth made to look ridiculous by the

Japanese. The Japanese are supposed to be incompetent; wearing poorly fitting eye glasses because they are short sighted and are also bow-legged.

In reality they have crippled the American fleet, sunk the " Prince of Wales" and the "Repulse". They now have taken Singapore! In fact they also have superiority in the air and all we can do is shelter from their bombing.

And they are fanatics; they like to die for their Emperor. That makes them doubly dangerous and the results are there to see. Now we are next on their list with outmoded aeroplanes, of which in any case there are only a few. Their Zero's have passed low overhead a few times and they don't even machine-gun us, saving their bullets, knowing that we can't do anything and that they don't consider us a threat. We are useless." Tjaden just nodded but didn't say anything. He had always been a man of few words.

Back in the Camp I went to report to Lieutenant Hes. He was sitting at his desk, his body bent over a local map spread out in front of him. He held a magnifying glass in his right hand. I saluted and stood to attention.

"Yes," he said without turning round.

"Nothing to report Sir," I said. "You know of the platoon of retreating soldiers no doubt?" Lieutenant Hes nodded.

"No sign of Captain Smyth?" he asked

"Not yet sir."

"All right you can go."

From the tone of his voice I knew he was worried. He had reason to be. The retreating soldiers were sheltering and had horror stories to tell of their journey. The sergeant major had lost his captain in the skirmish of their retreat. He might have been killed, wounded or captured by the enemy. If he had been captured, he would most probably have been killed, perhaps tortured first. It did nothing to raise our morale.

Lieutenant Hes had no one to turn to and yet had to make important decisions, involving the lives of these recruits and a small contingent Indonesian infantry. Those were his fighting forces, equipped with only outdated rifles. A small, already beaten force on the retreat had now joined them. The latter force would be no use at all in holding the Japanese back. With a few exceptions such as Richard Searle and a few others who had been brought up with guns for hunting; his recruits hardly knew how to shoot. Too little time had been spent on it.

Richard Searle was the only outstanding one when it came to handling a gun.

Hes recalled the shooting incident. Captain Smyth had blamed him for the shooting and had wanted him to charge the controller, Richard Searl, with criminal intent, incompetent to be in the Army. Not so in Hes opinion and he had voiced this opinion to Captain Smyth.

Everybody knew that controller Searl was the sharpshooter of the platoon. The controller had fired his gun, yes, because the password had not been given. His own words were that he had not fired at his troops but in the air. He had done this on purpose to point out the grave mistake the relieving guard had made. Had he really fired on the relieving guard, he would not have missed. Searl referred to his marksmanship being the best in the platoon.

He had done the right thing in Hes' opinion. Eventually Captain Smyth also agreed and Lieutenant Hes had impressed on his soldiers that giving the correct password was of the utmost importance in wartime and especially when the enemy could already be expected at any time.

Now Hes alone was in command. Was he also to retreat to Bandoeng, the stronghold of the forces, or was he to battle to the very end with the approaching Japanese and the odds very much against him? Suicide would be the proper word for it. He would probably be killed and would never see her again, the girl who he was in love with. She was engaged, she had shown him her ring, yet he had hoped that may be one day, he might see her again.

Who was her fiancé; where was he stationed? He was also in the forces; somewhere near Bandoeng but where exactly? And he envied her fiancé. He had never got to know his name. He turned to the letter of farewell which he had written to her and which was still lying on the table.

He decided to keep the letter after all. If he were killed there would be no point that she would ever see it. And if not, he might send her another letter at a later date. In this war, there was no certainty who might be killed. It was all up to the Gods.

And there was this other letter written to him by Captain Smyth. What was he to make of it? Whatever the reason the letter was written for, it was an important piece of evidence perhaps later on.

"Dear Hes," it started: "I have secret orders not to be divulged to anyone, to leave the command of Tjipatat open. There may be a replacement for me. On the other hand there may not be. I wish you good luck and let bygones be bygones, signed Smyth, Captain."

Hes did not understand what it was all about. Now he had a decision to make and he did not have enough evidence in order to make that decision. "Bloody hell," he swore and meant it.

The field telephone suddenly came on the air, just as he had straightened his back. He didn't remember which came first. He looked at his watch to verify the time before picking up the phone: 2 p.m. or just after. At last some news of Captain Smyth and his whereabouts. Perhaps of his successor, as was mentioned in his letter?

Hopefully he picked up the phone.

"Yes; Lieutenant Hes speaking."

"Hello, hello," the impatient voice at the other end was shouting, obviously not having heard Hes, so Hes repeated who he was.

"Ah there you are, Colonel Xant at this end speaking; headquarters," he clarified; "I wish to speak to captain Smyth."

"Not here Sir," Lieutenant Hes replied.

"That is most irregular at this time," Colonel Xant remarked. "Where is he?"

"He has gone to Bandoeng."

"To do what and on whose authority?" Colonel Xant insisted.

"I don't know Sir," Lieutenant Hes said, feeling the tension rise: "perhaps for instructions," he tried hesitatingly.

"Instructions?" What kind of instructions?" the impatient voice on the other end persisted: then continued: "well never mind. Lieutenant Hes is that your name? I have instructions for you too but let me finish this first.

"You got two soldiers under your command, one is a Regent's son by the name Mas; the other his best friend we understand, private Searle, controller in private life. They immediately have to be transported to Bandoeng's airport Andir, to be evacuated. This is urgent, you understand?"

"Yes sir, understood." He repeated the message to the satisfaction of Colonel Xant.

"Oh sir," Lieutenant Hes paused for a moment, "we have just received a contingent of the fifth Batallion, engineering division. They say that they had to evacuate their original position on the Tjiater pass, by orders from Colonel Arlen. They were sent to the north coast, to stop Japanese landings. But now they are here in diminished numbers."

"Yes I know all that," Colonel Xant resumed; "the captain in charge of that outfit made his way to Bandoeng on foot all the way. He was nearly captured. I don't understand the order for them to proceed to the north coast. They should have stayed at the Tjiater pass. Now it is too late. The pass is in Japanese hands.

"What I want to know is when you expect your superior back?"

Lieutenant Hes didn't know what to say. The letter lying on his desk was clear enough; Captain Smyth had no intention of coming back. But could he say this to Colonel Xant? Colonel Xant sensed his indecision; something was wrong.

"What is it lieutenant, you better tell me, this is war time. No use beating around the bush."

"To tell you the truth sir, I don't think that Captain Smyth is coming back."

"All right; in that case Colonel Arlen will send a replacement for him no doubt. Perhaps the replacement will be the officer who originally was in command of the unit now sheltering with you. Major Cane is the name.

"In any case you yourself must also leave Tjipatat and join the fighting unit south of the Tjiater pass, but that will not be for a day or two. In the meantime you remain in command of this unit in Tjipatat. But you must not remain in Tjipatat to wait until a replacement for you arrives, once you receive your order to leave. I repeat: you do not remain where you are at present, waiting for a replacement to arrive, should you receive your orders to join the tank unit to which you in fact belong.

"Instead you must go and join that unit immediately even if no replacement for you will have arrived as yet. Your tank unit is to recover the pass. This is high priority, is that understood? All orders need to be implemented immediately, you understand?"

"I do sir."

"About the two soldiers we spoke about: in case Andir is closed they are to proceed by car immediately to Kemajoran airport, a lot further to travel, but they have this priority, you got that?"

"Yes sir," Lieutenant Hes replied.

"That is all then lieutenant; give me your name again; I want to verify that I spoke to the correct person."

Lieutenant Hes repeated his name.

"Yes correct, you're the one I wanted to speak to. You belong to the tank unit I spoke about. Nice talking to you," Colonel Xant added and before Lieutenant Hes could say anyting further, the phone went dead.

Lieutenant Hes was puzzled. He was perhaps going to be replaced by Major Cane, Lily's father. Lily the girl he was in love with. He already felt sorry for Major Cane. There was no doubt that Tjipatat was in the fighting line, now that the Tjiater pass was abandoned. Unless Tjipatat was reinforced, it would be a hard job to retain it. The already beaten contingent was not going to be of help. Their morale was low and this could be infectious for this group of greenhorn soldiers barely trained to handle rifles, let alone fit for ground combat.

From the very beginning he had hated the position of the camp. It was lying in a low position surrounded by hills. Instead of having a command strategic position, it could be shot at by an enemy lying in those hills. Madness or incompetence of the people who had built the camp where it stood he thought. He opened the door of his office. The sentry posted in front of the door clicked his heels, stood to attention and saluted smartly.

"Make a jeep available and tell private Mas and private Searle to report to me pronto you hear," Hes barked at the sentry.

"Yes sir," the sentry already running to obey the order, shouted over his shoulder. Lieutenant Hes stepped into the corridor.

"Geys," he shouted. The sergeant in the office opposite appeared in the doorway, a face full of wrinkles and questions but with calm steady eyes met his gaze.

"Yes?"

"I want you to escort two of our men by jeep to Andir. And listen well. If Andir is not available you have to get them to Kemajoran by country roads, haphazardous no doubt, but these are the orders I got from H.Q." Seeing Geys' questioning frown he added,

"I know what you are thinking, but don't ask me more than I know."

"Yes Sir."

Geys saluted and sped away to the motor pool. Many questions arose in his mind but he knew that this was not the time to ask them.

The sentry returned bringing private Mas and private Searl with him. They stood to attention.

"At ease," Lieutenant Hes said. "You two," pointing to Mas and the controller, "in company of Sergeant Geys are to leave immediately by jeep to Andir airport. Let us hope that Andir is still available. Otherwise you have to proceed to Kemajoran which is much more difficult and fraught with danger.

You are requested by head quarters to be evacuated. Where to I don't know and you don't have to know it. These are the orders that came by phone a few minutes ago. Now off you go and join sergeant Geys at the motor pool, he is waiting for you."

At last Mas and I were evacuated, just as Colonel Arlen had told me. I realised that Lieutenant Hes did not know the reason for us to be sent to Andir and I had promised that I would tell no one of my interview with the officers in Hotel Homann one week ago. Neither had I told Mas the reason for our evacuation. In due time I could tell him this but not yet, not till we reached Australia Colonel Arlen had insisted.

When Lieutenant Hes returned to his room he muttered under his breath: "Lucky devils." He sat down heavily and studied the map in front of him again. The rottan chair under him squeaked in loud protest.

They were dead ducks in this position but on the map he had found an escape route in the pass back to Bandoeng. The headman of the village had also mentioned this path to him on another occasion but at that time the information had not sounded important enough to him. But now it was a very important piece of knowledge should the time come that he was to evacuate the unit.

But of course he needed to be ordered to evacuate Tjipatat first and that order had not been given. And Captain Smyth who could make that decision independently was not here.

"Damn it, " he said and scratched his head.

***

Andir airport was famous. Emilia Erhard had landed there and had taken off from here on her fatal last flight over the Timor Sea to Australia. She never arrived and nobody ever knew what had happened to her and her co- pilot. There was even a suggestion that she crashed and was captured by Japanese fishermen who wanted to have information about the plane. However that was quite unlikely. It had happened at least some years before the war started. But that was an unimportant event now.

As soon as we arrived Mas and I got out of the jeep and Sergeant Geys reported us to the control tower. We could see that it had been badly damaged by machine gun bullets. The officer in charge inspected us and sent us through. A Boeing plane was just landing, but it had to circle low over the airport twice, before landing in order to avoid the crater holes produced by Japanese bombing, twice in the last week. The damage to the hangars however was minimal and the Brewsters were still operational.

There was a lot of activity loading and unloading artillery. The officer who had received us, Lieutenant Tims was his name, led us through a doorway into the waiting room.

"Wait here," he said. Two officers were seated in the corner, drinking and talking to each other. They were in full uniform; one was a captain, the other a Major. We immediately recognised the captain as being Captain Smyth. What was he doing here? We stood to attention while lieutenant Tims pointed to us.

"These two are not coming," Captain Smyth said. "Is that is what you're asking?"

"They are on the list as first priority sir."

"Lieutenant," Captain Smyth said, "I make out the list and nobody told me that these two soldiers are having first priority."

"With respect, that cannot be correct Sir," the lieutenant stood his ground.

"Your priority list is second to the priority list I have of these two soldiers."

"Impossible lieutenant, you are mistaken, I have a list made out today by Major Cane. I pricked up my ears. Did I hear correctly? Major Cane had not been at Hotel Homann when I was briefed. But Colonel Arlen and the other officers including Captain Smyth at the meeting in Hotel Homann had told me that Mas and I should get away as first priority. Although therefore perhaps Major Cane, because he had not been there, was not informed; Captain Smyth certainly knew of the priority. And here he pretended to know nothing of the urgency. Of course at that time I was completely unaware of Major Cane's complicity.

Perhaps something drastic had happened needing a change of plans?

"Whose orders are you acting upon?" Captain Smyth wished to know.

"Colonel Xant's orders sir," the lieutenant replied.

"Well there must be some misunderstanding; my list which is today's list, is signed by Major Cane by order of Colonel Arlen, not by Colonel Xant. Can you show me your list? It has to have today's date on it lieutenant. If not, please get out of my way and take these two soldiers with you." It was an order and the lieutenant could do no more. He took us out of the waiting room but we could see that he was fuming. Suddenly Captain Smyth's voice sounded behind us.

"I remember now, they are to be evacuated by ship from Tjilatjap. There are plenty ships leaving for Australia; that is where they should go, our evacuation plans had to be changed."

"That is at least a day's journey. That can hardly be called a priority evacuation," Lieutenant Tims remarked angrily.

"Take it or leave it lieutenant."

We had no choice. Mas and especially I, were as surprised as the lieutenant was furious.

"Your sergeant plus jeep have already left: we have to find alternative transport to get you to the station, but you must get away. I am sure that the captain is mistaken. There is something I don't understand."

Then lieutenant Tims left to find transport for us.

"What is going on?" I asked. "Why is Captain Smyth not in Tjipatat?" Mas shrugged his shoulders.

"Beats me too," he said.

Shortly afterwards Lieutenant Tims returned.

"What are the odds?" I asked him. The officer's face betrayed hidden frustrations.

"I can only find an ambulance for you but you must get away at all costs. You were top priority; about that I am sure. That is what Colonel Xant intended and it must be executed. I cannot overrule Captain Smyth's decision and what is more I cannot reach Colonel Xant to ask questions. Colonel Xant made out the initial list, which I have in my possession. Where does Colonel Arlen come into it?" he said puzzled.

He suddenly felt he had said too much about a superior officer and was about to explain, when the air siren went and broke off any conversation. A squadron of six Brewsters immediately took to the air as fast as they could.

High above, about twenty silvery white aeroplanes appeared, Zero's they were called, faster than any Brewster. These were the Japanese planes that had bombed Pearl harbour and sunk many a battleship. And now they were here! Puffs of smoke from anti aircraft guns appeared. None of the planes got hit. The explosions from the anti aircraft guns although occurring high in the air seemed to happen too low to produce any damage.

No sign of the Brewsters, which were supposed to attack them so far. We raced to the nearest air shelter and noticed that captain Smyth was in the same shelter already. His face was white and his hands trembled. His knuckles were clamped over the stengun he was holding.

An American pilot who's plane was already hit and on fire, jumped in next to us, emptying his Colt revolver indiscriminately at the enemy planes with the red ball painted on the underside of their wings; the emblem of the Japanese. They came down in a low dive now, aiming directly at the airfield. We saw the bombs dropping above us and could also see the faces of the pilots and rear gunner clearly. The bombs dropped on the airfield and hangar and exploded like eggs hitting a concrete floor. The murderous explosions shook the earth around and below us violently, bursting drainpipes open and showering our pillar-box with their content of dirt and mud. The hangars were already hit and ablaze.

The bombardment lasted ten minutes, but they were ten minutes of hell. The Japanese plan obviously, was to immobilise the airfield but their mission had only half succeeded. They were retreating now.

One of the bombers in the rear collided with a Brewster plane that had dived straight into it. The explosion of the two colliding planes was even louder than the sound of the bombing. We felt an awful pang of pain for the fate of the two fliers in the Brewster. They had sacrificed their lives by attacking the bomber.

Captain Smyth crawled out of the air raid shelter. His pompous attitude had totally vanished and he was trembling like a dog in a vet's surgery. Then he saw us watching him. He knew that we knew that he was afraid. Without saying a word he disappeared into one of the hangar buildings, which were still standing. The Boeing which had just landed shortly before the bombardment, was on fire and although the fire service was extremely busy trying to douse the fire, it was obvious that the plane would not be fit to be flown at least till the damage was repaired: if the damage could be repaired at all!

Ambulance men were quite active evacuating the dead and dying and palls of smoke rose in the still mountain air, blanketing the surrounding mountain range around the city of Bandoeng. The sudden silence, contrasting to the bombing enveloped us like a blanket. It took a while before Lieutenant Tims appeared.

"I got through to Major Cane," he said. "Colonel Xant is not available. But Major Cane also wants you to proceed to Tjilatjap. He says that these latest orders came from Colonel Arlen. These orders are in complete contrast to the ones I received from Colonel Xant. I guess I will sort this out some day," he added.

"We will undoubtedly have more air raids soon, the quicker you leave the better." The wrinkles in his face had become deeper and his voice crisp and precise before, now had a knife sharp edge to it.

"Tjilatjap has got to be your next destination. I know the journey is difficult but it is the only way."

"Does Major Cane know our names?" I asked him. Of course I did not know at the time, that Major Cane was merely carrying out the plan concocted by Colonel Arlen and which had the approval of him also. Because I did not know this, I wondered if Major Cane was aware what took place in the meeting with Colonel Arlen, the one I attended and in which I was told that Mas and I would get first priority and all possible help to get to Australia but which now did not seem to be the case!

I reasoned that even if Major Cane knew nothing of our priority; Colonel Arlen would have put that straight when he passed on the instructions to Major Cane. Apparently he hadn't. That was very strange. Something was wrong; things did not fit.

"Yes", Lieutenant Tims said. He even repeated your name especially."

"I don't understand," I said.

"Nevermind, get into that ambulance," the lieutenant urged; "it will drop you at the station. I can't get a taxi, they all seem occupied or non-willing Perhaps they are frightened of a repeat bombing. There is a Mitchell bomber plane at Tjilatjap tomorrow at noon. Your names are on the list, Major Cane said so." Captain Smyth was nowhere to be seen. Not that we missed him.

The lieutenant guessed what we were thinking.

"I'll explain it to him" he said, "but only after you are away," he added. The ambulance drove off avoiding many bomb craters.

Bandoeng's station was packed full. One could hardly reach the train. But we had to get away and pushed ourself through the crowd. A stationmaster appeared from nowhere.

"Have you just come from Andir?" he asked. "No soldiers are to leave Bandoeng; this applies to you both." From one of the carriages a sergeant appeared.

"What are you doing here?" he asked sternly. "Are you deserting your post?"

"Not at all," we assured him, we have orders to proceed to Tjilatjap. He was not convinced but it did not interest us.

"Has the train for Tjilatjap left," I asked him.

"As far as I know, this is the one," he said. Without explaining further, we plonked ourselves down on the floor of the carriage and the sergeant realising that he could not remove us forcibly, disappeared, maybe even to get help. The stationmaster looked on but did nothing.

We were beyond caring: one way or the other. But why had the stationmaster told us that we were not allowed to go to Tjilatjap? And he knew that we had come from Andir. Had he been told to prevent us from getting away? Everything was puzzling to me now and suspicion had taken over. Was our escape to Australia thwarted on purpose?

At last the train got into motion. Although the locomotive was extra ordinary large, it started very slowly due to the extra amount of carriages it had to pull. I consoled myself that at least we were on our way to Australia now. The first stop gave us a chance to eat from the platform. Mas was quiet; he was brooding about something.

And where was Lily? Her father surely would inform her that I was sent to Australia. There had been no time to say good-bye to her. The only time I had seen her again since Pasir Poetih was on a short leave of a few hours to Bandoeng. We reiterated our pledge to each other then and as we said good-bye, I wondered again if the demons of Bali had other plans for us. Her father, Major Cane, might be able to evacuate her and her mother to Australia and we would perhaps meet. Who could tell what your fate was in these uncertain times? How true as it turned out!

The next morning at Tjilatjap Mas and I saw a large number of soldiers wearing diverse uniforms: British, Dutch, American and Australian. They had one thing in common: they were all dishevelled and looking tired. Nobody seemed to know what there was to be done here. Mas and I quickly tried to find out where the airport was.

We found a sergeant with a band round his arm on which was written airport. He surprised us:

"There is no airport but there is an airstrip where even large aeroplanes are able to land. Yes we are expecting a Mitchell bomber at noon, what are your names?" Before we told him he already said: "but you don't have a hope, there are so many people who want to be evacuated."

"Oh but we have good hopes," I said. "We are on the priority list."

"I don't have the list," he said. "There is an officer on the air strip; he will know."

We left him in the best of spirits, full of hope. It was still half an hour to walk. We arrived and settled ourselves in a Chinese restaurant with a cup of coffee. The officer the sergeant had referred to was nowhere to be seen.

The dog of the owner lying by my side suddenly pricked up its ears. True enough; the Mitchell bomber arrived bang on time and the dog had heard the engines long before we had. A throng of people moved forward but the platoon of soldiers who had arrived with a lieutenant barred the way. One by one the officer checked his list. Only a handful of people were selected to board the plane before our turn came. We were confident and then our hope was shattered. The officer shook his head.

"I am sorry he said, you were on the list but I was instructed to refuse you passage, I don't know anything more. "Next," he shouted.

Mas and I looked at each other. What were we to do now?

"But we have special priority," I managed to say lamely.

"You had," the lieutenant agreed.

"Who changed that," I asked?

"I am not permitted to say," the officer replied.

Mas was speechless, he then took me aside.

"This has all been planned; we are not to get away, don't you understand it?"

"It doesn't matter," I said," we are going by ship or boat or whatever we can find. We owe it to ourselves; we have come this far."

I was puzzled too. The Governor-General wanted to get us evacuated but I had promised the officers in Hotel Homann not to tell that to Mas for the time being, "not till we had got away," Colonel Arlen had said. I had not understood why that was and still didn't! The lieutenant at Andir airport also knew that the Governor-General wanted us to get first priority.

The list he had held in his hand was made out by Colonel Xant and not by Colonel Arlen. Neither had it been made out by Major Cane. The list that Captain Smyth held however was; and the two lists were conflicting. What were we to believe? Of course I was on the wrong track from the very start, but did not know it.

Suddenly Mas said: "I am going no further."

"What!" I exclaimed. "You and I are both going to Australia. You are the representative of your people. I can now tell you what took place at Hotel Homann, the day that I was absent from Tjipatat. "I was sent for by officers, who included Captain Smith. They told me that the Governor-General wanted you to be evacuated to Australia. About that I am very sure. The Governor gave specific instructions. Somehow someone or some group of people are trying to prevent this. You notice that everywhere we appear, a previous order was cancelled. The previous order is obviously the correct genuine one."

I now related to Mas what took place at my meeting with the officers in Hotel Homann. He listened carefully.

"Why have you not told me this before," he asked?

"I promised that I would not," I said.

"But why this secrecy?" he demanded?

"I don't know Mas," I said. "I also wondered about that myself at the time."

"The Governor-General is afraid that if you stay, you will fall in Japanese hands. The Japanese will realise, perhaps even already know, that you are a spokesman for the Indonesians. You will be used for their propaganda and you will be killed if you don't agree. Let us find a boat. Your father and family are already in Australia, I was given that assurance."

"The assurance given by the same clique of officers that put us on the priority list," Mas sneered. "What guarantee do we have that they are not going to kill us if we try?"

It was the first time that I considered this myself. Had the clique of officers in Homann deceived me? They had assured me "every possible help" to get away. Why then was there a list from Major Cane acting on orders from Colonel Arlen denying us departure from Andir. Instead we had been sent to Tjilatjap. It didn't make sense. Was it all a trick? But of course it could not be. Lily's father had sent us to Tjilatjap. Did he not want us to succeed in getting away? I corrected my thinking quickly. How could I think such a thing of him? My future father in law would certainly not do such a thing!

"Mas, your father and mother are waiting for you in Australia; the orders to evacuate you were genuine. There is a plan for you and me, you must listen."

"But have you not seen the attitude of Captain Smyth at Andir airport? He is an army officer too and he doesn't want us to get away."

"But he is small fry; the Governor wants you to be evacuated." None of my pleading had any effect. Suddenly Mas said:

"Have you not noticed that we are being shadowed by the officer who refused us entry into the plane? He wants to know what we are doing next it seems. You must go," he urged me.

"Go alone, your chances of staying alive when the Japanese capture you are much worse than mine. I am a native; I can disappear among the people. I can even get a guerrilla force together and keep fighting. Your knowledge of the country will help my father in Australia. We will meet again in better circumstances after the war. Japan will lose eventually, perhaps earlier than we think." I thought of Djojo Bojo. Six months was the duration of a maize harvest.

"I will look after Lily," Mas continued, "don't worry about her." He embraced me like a brother. Then he was gone in the crowd and I was by myself to think what to do. It was only half past twelve.

The priority to escape to Australia was for the two of us. Now that I was alone did the urgency remain? Should I not to return to my unit in Tjipatat instead? Would I not be considered a deserter as the sergeant at the station in Bandoeng had wondered?

Walking aimlessly I reached the harbour. Everything was disorganised; a general exodus was taking place. Everybody was trying to leave the sinking ship Java. Nobody believed any longer in the ability of the military to hold Java.

Although it was afternoon it was still cool. I looked across the small strip of sea between the mainland and the island Noesa Kembangan, covered with thick jungle.

The harbour was a mess. Large oil slicks covered the water. Crabs covered with shining oil on their backs wandered aimlessly among the rocks reminding me of my own situation. Buginese sailing boats were much in evidence, sailing in, or were anchored in between K.P.M. steamers, small coasters, which in normal times had been plying between the different islands of the Dutch East Indies. In normal times they also delivered mail among other business errands.

Every so often a ship left: sloshing the oily muck back and forth between the ships lying at anchor. The ships did not leave with the usual happy hooting, the way they used to do in former peace times.

The chance of getting passage on a ship was nil. But how about a Buginese sailing craft? The Buginese were excellent sailors, and would be able to sail to Australia without any trouble.

My thoughts were interrupted by machine gun fire, which was soon joined by every firing power available. High up in the air a silvery plane was visible. It did not seem bothered by any of the shooting aimed at it.

"It is a reconnaissance plane": a sergeant walking up as aimlessly as I was, said. The nearest airstrip to Tjilatjap was Solo, The headquarters of the Sultan. The Japanese were there already. There was no time to lose.

I joined a group of four soldiers in discussion with a Buginese captain. They turned to me;

"Would you come along?" they asked me. The invitation was genuine and so was my acceptance. This was my chance to get away.

"Where are we going?" I asked the captain.

"New Guinea first, then Australia," he replied.

"How many crew?" I asked.

"Two," he replied, pointing to two sailors with frizzy hair; Timorese, I decided, totally reliable.

The Buginese captain wasted no time.

"The wind is favourable," he said. "I have plenty water for drinking and food for ten people for 2 weeks. That should be sufficient to get ourselves to Van Diemensland. But you must change your clothes; no military uniforms and you must hide under the tarpaulin canvas for cover, in case we are inspected from the air." The tarpaulin cover was stretched over the copra on deck; stacks of it.

The Buginese plied between Tjilatjap and Van Diemensland, buying and selling copra, a business that brought in enough money for himself and his crew to live on. We lifted anchor, passing lots of oil spills, which were clinging to the different boats we were passing. A tugboat was pulling a K.P.M. ship into deeper water. It had got stuck in the mud as the tide went out.

We motored past sunken ships, their metal twisted and rusted, metal giants of a bygone age. At one time they were proud possessions of some wealthy owner or company, now forgotten. We were in a cheerful mood.

The Captain however in contrast, seemed to be preoccupied with something. Perhaps he was thinking of the spy plane earlier in the day and realising that fact might mean that Japanese planes might appear at any time; the anxiety showed up on his face. A lonely otter was busy cracking shells on the banks, totally happy in contrast to the captain.

After about an hour we were in deep water. Nusa Kembangan was left to starboard and the Indian Ocean opened up in front of us. It was just past 2 pm. Our uniforms were stacked below and we were wearing native clothes the captain had handed to us. Our guns and ammunition, what little there was, was put in the captain's hut under the deck.

The roar of the Mitchell bomber taking off filled the air. For a split second we saw the plane levelling off, then an enormous explosion. The plane disappeared, another explosion, then a pall of smoke where the plane went down rose in the air.

"Good God," said one of us. We looked in horror at each other. We were totally shocked by what we had seen. Another sabotage? It seemed very likely. All the passengers must have been killed. And Mas and I might have been on that plane! Little did I know then that my name was still on the passenger list in spite of the fact that I was refused to board the plane and that unfortunately Lily was told: (and later saw for herself) that my name was on the list. There were no survivors.

Chapter 10

In my mind I saw the Goenoeng Ringgit again. I smelled Lily's fragrant hair mixed with the fresh Jasmine flower smell, the flower she used to wear in her hair at night. She whispered to me. I tried to catch the words.

Why did she not speak louder? I tried hard to make out what she said. The effort of listening was too much. Just before I could understand what she was saying to me, I heard another sound mixed through her whisper. What was it? At last I heard what she was saying and now I also understood why she was speaking so softly.

"Will you come back to me?" She had asked me that before; on the slope of the Ringgit, also in a whisper. I had made a pledge to her then that I would. But something was not quite right. What was this chugging sound in my ears? At times it became louder, and then faded again as though the wind carried the sound away.

There it was again, becoming louder as I gained consciousness. What could it be, and why was my head so heavy? I also felt nauseated and my left arm hurt. It was easier to keep my eyes closed; the light was too bright. But was it the light that was so bright, or was it just the thought of it, which made me wince with pain? Then the light was gone again. Had someone switched off a torch? The noise of the buzzing became too intense. Flurries of memory returned.

The smell now was that of the sea and I distinctly felt the swell of waves. Was I in a vessel; a Buginese sailing vessel perhaps? But the chugging I could not explain. That did not fit. Now I recognised the sound; a diesel engine, trying to dominate the sound of the waves! I felt the wind blowing over my face. A ship!

The surprise that it was possible for me to recognise that it was a ship's engine I was hearing; made me try to open my eyes again. I could not but I tried again. Undoubtedly a ship! It must be; my ears did not deceive me. A diesel engine makes a distinct sound. Unmistakable. The simple act of trying to open my eyes drained my remaining energy and I felt the darkness trying to engulf me again.

Lily's face which had just taken shape, receded and the contours of her face blotted out like water on an aquarelle painting. Desperately I clung to her memory, I mustn't pass out, I mustn't, but I did. When I woke again, I knew that it was dark. The engine of the ship was very distinct now and I could also hear the waves clearly. Also voices! In my head I felt a sharp pain and when I passed my hand over my head to the spot where I felt the pain, my fingers passed over a bandage which was wet and my fingers became sticky: blood!

I heard someone shouting: "nurse." I opened my eyes. In the darkness I noticed that I was lying on the floor in a room and that there were others in the room also lying on the floor. Who were they? There was a door facing me and when the door opened for a moment, I could see a sky full of stars.

A woman entered, she wore a white hospital uniform. In spite of the darkness I could see that clearly. There was nothing wrong with my eyes. She walked straight up to me.

"How do you feel? Here let me adjust your bandage. Would you like something to drink? You were unconscious for a few hours and you got a gash in your head but it will heal. You must also have dislocated your left shoulder but it corrected itself when we lifted you on board. We have no doctor on the ship."

"On board," I said, "where am I?"

"You are on the "S.S. Jansen," on our way to Australia. You were half submerged on an abandoned raft in the sea. You were extremely lucky that we found you. We thought at first that you were dead and wanted to leave you, seeing that we have so many refugees on board. The ship is brimful of people. I'll bring you some tea with sugar and you should try to sleep again, it is only just passed midnight. Is your pillow comfortable?" I assured her that it was. Then she left me.

On the "S.S Jansen," she had said, on the way to Australia. They found me at a raft at sea.

I remembered now; the Buginese sailing boat. Yes, of course; now I remembered. I had boarded the 60 feet vessel with four other soldiers at the stinking oily harbour Tjilatjap. The Buginese Captain had promised to take us to Van Diemansland near Australia and after fuelling even perhaps further on. Further to Australia itself: to freedom. He had thrown sheets over the tarpaulin cover for us to hide under and also to protect us against the sun, because we would be exposed to the sun for days. That was after the Mitchell bomber had exploded on take off and dived into the sea. But what had happened after that?

What had become of the sailing boat, the Captain, the crew of two and the four others on the boat? The effort of trying to remember exhausted me. The nurse returned.

"I have a bowl of soup and a slice of bread, can you eat?" Only now did I realise how hungry I was.

"Tell me," I said, "what about the others on the raft?"

"Others?" "There were no others."

"What about the sailing vessel, a Buginese prahu?" I insisted.

"You were the only one on the raft. There was no boat, only splintered wreckage. We came upon you by pure chance. But let that rest now. Tomorrow you can ask the Captain about the details. For now just try to sleep, you suffer from brain concussion and you must try to rest."

"What about my friends?" I sank back, "no others?" What had happened? Unhappily my mind was blank and I had to be content with having to wait till daylight for the answer: if there was an answer. My mind drifted off again in a sea of nothingness but now the dream became reality, no longer a dream. I was with Lily again, climbing the Ringgit not far from the top.

"We make it, we make it," I said jubilantly. Then I remembered, the reality had been different and that dreams are only dreams, even though they can seem real even to the finest detail. But was it a dream? While I pondered the question I fell asleep. When I woke the next morning it was bright daylight. The horizon was endless and the long swell was that of an ocean, the mighty Indian Ocean, which stretches from the south of Java uninterruptedly till the South Pole. Nothing that Captain Blomme told me that morning made me remember more of what had actually happened. I could not fill in on the scant knowledge I already had. He had found me stretched out on a bamboo raft half submerged with netting attached to it. Splintered painted wood was floating around me. The painted wood must have come from a native vessel such as indeed from a Buginese sailing prahu.

"I think that you must have been bombed," he suggested. "A bomb," he repeated; that must be it." About the Mitchell bomber he was short. "Sabotage, undoubtedly. It is not likely that there were any survivors," he concluded.

"We picked you up about twenty miles south of Nusa Kembangan. We spotted you by pure chance. You should count your lucky stars that our look out has such sharp eyes. If we had passed you by even for two miles either west or east of your position, we would not have spotted you! How is your head?" I assured him that I was in good care by his nurse on board.

"We won't have a doctor until we get to Australia. You should have an X-ray of your head then. The Dutch- East-Indies is in Japanese hands. You got away in the nick of time. The army has ceased to exist, according to the last communication by General Toorop. But of course his radio broadcast was under duress.

He and the Governor are prisoners." That was bad news indeed. What had happened to major Cane; his wife, Lily and her brother? What had happened to the Buginese boat the Captain and his crew and all the other people who were on board apart from me?

"We are now out of reach of enemy planes," the Captain resumed his explanation, "but as I do not have any idea where the Japanese fleet is, we could still run into enemy shipping with unhappy consequences to say the least.

Yesterday we were lucky; maybe it was the same Zero that bombed you. He also strafed us. But we shot him down; he came too low thinking we had no anti- aircraft gun. But we had: he found out," he said with satisfaction pointing to a machine gun mounted on the foredeck were two soldiers were posted. "You may have had your revenge."

I knew that my revenge would never make up for the lives that were lost; my comrades in arms on the Buginese sailing ship and the sailors: the Captain and his crew.

"Hopefully the pilot of the Zero plane has not radioed our position to enemy vessels before he went down," the Captain added. In a sombre mood I went on deck.

The whole deck was occupied with people of all ages, military and civilian;

also quite a number of children. They were making themselves as comfortable as they possibly could. Fortunately the weather was good. Everybody was happy in the belief of being safe and having escaped a callous enemy. The journey was uneventful and the happy atmosphere persisted till we reached Perth, the nearest free harbour to Tjilatjap. Nobody was happier than the Captain himself. He had had the most memorable sea journey of his life but at the same time the most responsible as far as lives were concerned. Most people shook his hand and thanked him and his crew. I also personally thanked the nurse who had looked after me.

"I don't think I will have that X-ray after all," I said to her; "my head wound has healed. A doctor could not have done a better job." She wagged her finger at me.

"Look after yourself," she shouted as I descended the gangplank.

***

The journey eastwards from Perth took days and I quickly realized that Australia is a continent. I was pleased that I had no further problems with my head. The journey was uneventful but I was lonely and my thoughts regularly drifted off to Pasir poetih and Lily. Had she managed to escape from Java perhaps with her mother? The chances were of course very small.

Three days later I arrived. The Regent himself welcomed me from the train. With outstretched hands he pressed mine.

"I am glad you have been detailed to help me out," were his first words. "I need a good aid who speaks English, Bahasa and Dutch," he said. He was older since I had seen him last and he looked worried. "Come, I'll show you to the family first." The chauffeur in an old rickety Chrysler car took us to the house that the Regent and his family had been allocated to. It lay in the outskirts of Canberra and the house was large, colonial style; the lane from the road flanked by casuarina trees. Parakeets nestling in the larger branches were making a din of a noise. So far he hadn't mentioned Mas, his son with one word, but I realized, that he wanted to wait with that till his wife was also present.

"You will have this car at your disposal too," he informed me. The barracks where you are billeted are about a mile north of here and I expect you here every morning to help me out with various correspondences, especially English, at which I am not good."

The car came to a stop. The Indonesian driver got out and opened the door for us.

"Come controller;" the Regent invited me in. His Dutch wife and his three daughters, who were standing on the veranda, welcomed me heartily.

"Tea?" his wife asked.

"I could do with a cup," I said. I felt it was time to open up why Mas wasn't here.

"Mas and I didn't agree," I started. "It seemed that Mas wanted to do something different. He perhaps knew something, which I didn't. He wanted me to get away at all cost. He said that if we stayed together that we never would have a chance to get away and that if he left me, I would stand a better chance. He perhaps was right, I don't know."

"Why was that, I mean why did he say that?" the Regent's wife asked.

"Well," I hesitated, "when Mas and I got the order to be ready to be taken to the airport Andir and to fly out to Australia, the order seemed genuine. However arriving at the airport, the lieutenant who had us on the list of passengers, as a first priority, was overruled by a captain who said that we couldn't go on that plane although I am sure we had first priority as the lieutenant had claimed. We then were ordered to go to Tjilatjap but no taxi was available so eventually an ambulance took us to the station. When we finally appeared at the station, the stationmaster told us that we were not allowed to enter the train for Tjilatjap, the town where we were to leave from to Australia, as an alternative. We both had become suspicious by then. It seemed as though our plan of escape was thwarted on purpose every time.

When we finally got to Tjilatjap after a hectic journey without food or drink we were again told by the officer in charge of the allocation of priority seats; that we were not on the list any longer. He said that we had been on the list, but that on orders he was not permitted to disclose, we were not allowed on the plane. Nevertheless our names were there.

"There were so many people trying to get away. I have never seen such a panicky situation. Then Mas suddenly decided that he didn't want to go any further. He said that if he stayed with me that we would never get away."

"Why did he say that?" the Regent asked, with worry in his voice.

"I suppose he rightly or wrongly had come to the conclusion that we should separate. He said that he hoped that I would make it and send you his best; that is all I know."

"Strange," his father said pensively. "I was personally informed by the Governor that he and you were especially chosen to come out to Australia. I had asked the Governor for you to accompany Mas. If Mas now left you of his own free will and you made it to Australia, then he will be considered a deserter and that is the last thing I want my son to be."

"Well," I said, "there is something in the theory that our so-called privileged air evacuation was thwarted on purpose, because the officer in charge seemed to be bound by higher orders to refuse us passage. It seemed he was particularly interested that we shouldn't get away from Tjilatjap either, because he kept following us and I think that is the reason that your son disappeared. The officer in question must have known that we had first priority; moreover we told him so. He even admitted as I mentioned before, that we had been on his list. That I got away is pure luck. Shortly after Mas left, I got together with a group of four soldiers; We agreed with a Buginese Captain that he would take us to Australia for a sum of money we had agreed upon and we were on our way when an explosion must have happened; we may have been bombed from the air; at least I think that is what must have happened; I cannot remember the details as I was concussed. I only remember that we boarded the Buginese vessel. There were eight of us: Five soldiers; myself included; then the Captain and a crew of two Timorese. The boat was full of copra. The Captain sailed between Tjilatjap and van Diemens land regularly. The boat must have been wrecked and must have sunk, since I was the only survivor.

"At the time the Captain of the "S.S. Jansen", from the ship that rescued me, said that we were about twenty miles south from Nusa Kembangan. There was only wreckage of a boat when I was picked up. My friends and the Captain plus his two-man crew must have been killed by the bomb, maybe drowned. As I said, I was concussed and only vaguely remember the explosion; I can't be sure of the details.

"When I was picked up from the sea, I was found on a bamboo raft. I appeared dead and they nearly left me because they thought I was dead. There was hardly any space on board. The "Jansen" just happened to pass by. I was the only one on the raft. It has kept me wondering ever since what exactly happened."

"Sabotage," the Regent said. "You perhaps knew too much?"

"But what do I know?" I said. "Nothing other but that I think that the officer in charge in Tjilatjap was acting on higher orders and that is only a guess. On second thought, and I thought about it a lot as you can imagine, it must have been an aeroplane that dropped a bomb on us. The other possibility is a submerged mine, but that is highly unlikely."

The Regent was deep in thought.

"Did Mas say where he was going?" he asked.

"No; he only said, "find me after the war and I'll do likewise. He seemed to have a plan."

"If Mas falls into Japanese hands they will use him for propaganda or will kill him," the Regent remarked somberly. "That is exactly the reason why the Governor wanted him to be evacuated to Australia; the Governor told me so personally. There is nothing more we can do for him. Japan has occupied most of the Indies by now." I noticed that he didn't use the word Indonesia.

"I hope the Sultan won't be killed," he resumed, "maybe the Japanese will retain him as a puppet, he is the official ruler; I wonder why he was not evacuated instead of myself and my family." I of course knew why but I could not tell him.

"The Governor is in enemy hands," the Regent continued; "it is terrible he is such a courageous man. The war has been lost, Australia may be next and America does not seem to have the power, which we expected. I am very grateful that the Governor evacuated me and my family"

"The war won't be long," I said. "The fall of Singapore was indeed unexpected and once our fleet was annihilated, it was only a minority army that stood in the way of the Japanese."

"That is true," the Regent said. "But it is also true to say that there was no cohesion between the different forces; Indonesian, Dutch, English, Australian, and American, were all independently taking part.

The Dutch military commander, General Toorop, gets all the blame for losing the war and the unconditional surrender. He always pretended that the Dutch forces did not need any help from outside; but of course he had to say that for the morale of the troops. He himself knew very well that he did not have a chance. It is unfair to blame him. Without planes and no cohesion between the forces, what could he do? And what happened at the armistice conference was, that the Governor was initially instructed to undertake the negotiations and that at the last moment whilst in conference with the Japanese army General about these armistice negotiations, the buck was suddenly passed to General Toorop.

The Japanese immediately grasped the contradiction in thinking between the two top men and capitalized on the situation. It should have been clear from the outset which person was to undertake these negotiations: either the Governor or preferably the top of the military, General Toorop of course."

"Is that the way it happened," I said. I was most interested. "No wonder there was an unconditional surrender then," I said. "But I don't think it would have made much difference; as you said, the Royal Dutch Indonesian Army, had no air support and was bombed and shelled from the air almost continually."

"Toorop," the Regent said "counted on a possible guerilla war in the jungle but nothing had been planned that could make such a war a possible alternative. What is sad is that this war was long foreseen and nobody did anything," he sighed.

"What will happen now is that freedom for Indonesia from their oppressors as the Japanese will call the Dutch, will be preached by the Japanese, only to hide their own intention and that is to make Indonesia a part of their great Asia expansion scheme under the heel of the Japanese. Yet the man in the street will fall for it and not only he; but there are also numerous power seekers who will turn and will condemn the Dutch for everything that went wrong.

"That is not fair. Although it must also be said, that several good Indonesians with the best intent, have tried to obtain independence in the past without a hearing from the Dutch. Now we will only get the traitors raising their ugly heads, sympathizing with the Japanese."

During his talk he had been walking up and down with his hands behind his back, his head bent forward. He must be thinking about his son I thought.

"What about your family?" he said. You must be worried about them also."

"My family fortunately is in the Netherlands. Perhaps it is not too bad for them."

My thoughts turned to Lily again. The situation for her; her father, mother and brother would be serious. Her brother was probably dead already. The navy was destroyed. Every Dutch family in the Dutch East Indies would have something to fear now. And also those that had sympathies with the Dutch; the numerous Chinese "well to do", who had helped in the war effort or had openly, fought on the Dutch side.

Maybe Wong was one of those also. Many Indonesian families also would now feel abandoned and fearing for their lives. The Japanese atrocities were well known from the war in China.

And what about Australia? I wondered. The date was March the twenty sixth. Would the Japanese push through to Australia also or had their plan to conquer stopped? To extend their territory further would make their occupation thin on the ground; they could not have so many troops to occupy all this gained territory. Was that the reason that they hadn't invaded Australia already?

My stay as aid to the Regent was a happy one. Every morning I was picked up by car by the Indonesian chauffeur, who wished me a long life and a good morning in that order. Once in a while he said:

"I hope you will have a wife soon."

"Ahmed," I said one day "What about you? Do you not have a wife?"

"Oh yes tuan," he said, "and I have four children with her. But what is the good of that; she had to stay behind. She and the children are now in occupied territory. Still we have family; she will be taken care of. And the war will not last long. Do you not see that more and more Americans are coming? What is more, they bring their planes with them. Planes is what we should have had tuan."

I more then anyone knew that.

The Regent's family settled in well into a mixed community. Of course the daughters went to school and were already fluent in English. Life in that part of Australia was almost normal. My rank now was first lieutenant and I was delegated to liaise between the Regent and the army.

The Royal Dutch Indonesian Army, or K.N.I.L. in Dutch; here only consisted of the men who by hook or by crook had managed to escape, some by dug out canoe from Arnhem's land in New Guinea. But some had arrived by Catalina plane from East Java. I often looked at the names of arrivals, but Mas' name was never among them.

I was sure that he could escape if he wanted to. Why then didn't he? As a native it would not be difficult even though it needed several stops on the way and maybe would take weeks. But getting to Australia was not a big problem for a determined native person. I therefore concluded that for reasons only known to him he did not want to. Weeks passed by, followed by months.

Then one day I understood. The newspaper was directly from Djakarta Indonesia. There was a large photograph of Mas belonging to the "Freedom Party of Indonesia." I could not believe my eyes. There must be a mistake. I kept the paper hidden from his family; they would be upset. But the news bore

Japanese characters also. Mas would not be able to say what he wanted. I was certain that he was only allowed to say what the Japanese wanted him to say.

There was a knock on the door of my office interrupting my thoughts. The sergeant messenger who had come by motorbike; handed me the letter on which was written: "Personal" and a request for me to sign that I had received the letter.

In the letter Major Van Dam of intelligence asked me to visit him the next morning at 9.A.M. What was it about?

I got in touch with the Regent to ask him for permission to attend, since he, and not Major Van Dam was my direct superior. He already knew.

"You must go," he said."Major van Dam has asked me to release you for the time being. I don't know how long for. Come back as soon as you can."

Did van Dam make it seem as though I would be away for a long time I wondered?

The next morning I walked to the barracks. I was very curious. Why was I sent for? It was not far to go. The building, which Van Dam occupied, was flanked by a bougainvillea array of flowers in three different layers: purple, crimson and gold yellow.

I told the secretary my name; she asked me to wait. The office was decorated with different pictures from Indonesia tacked to the walls. There was even a picture of "Villa Isola". I had lived very close to it. Looking at the picture, made me feel quite homesick and I longed for Lily. I wondered how she was. Maybe she was already dead I thought somberly.

After ten minutes a female receptionist appeared and asked me to follow her to a door on the outside of which was printed: "do not disturb." She knocked and the voice from inside called "enter." The receptionist opened the door and I faced Major van Dam.

"Come in," he said getting up from behind the bureau. He looked too young to have the rank he held. We shook hands.

"You are controller Searle?" he asked: "at least in civilian life you were a controller. Now you are aide-de-camp to the Regent of West Java is that not so?" I affirmed what he said.

"This is going to be an "informal chat", he said. "Nevertheless it is strictly confidential." I pricked up my ears at the words confidential.

"Smoke?" he asked pointing to the cigarette stand on his desk. I declined. He lit a pipe and inhaled the smoke deeply.

"How did you get to Australia?" he asked.

"Well sir," I said, "that is an extremely long story but the gist is that I was picked up from a raft in the Indian Ocean by a ship called the "Jansen." You must have heard that this ship made it from Tjilatjap with quite a number of refugees." The Major nodded.

"It must have been a rough trip with so many people on board."

"It wasn't too bad, everybody helped to make the trip as enjoyable as possible."

"Tell me," he said: "I have been informed that the Regent's son was under your care," he inhaled deeply again," and that you lost him."

"No sir, that is not correct," I said. "I was only to accompany him. He was supposed to be evacuated by orders of the Governor. We both were meant to be seconded to his father the Regent of West Java, who in normal circumstances would also be my superior."

"But where is Mas?" Major van Dam asked shaking the ashes from his pipe.

"Good question," I said, "he left me in Tjilatjap. He said that he perhaps was going to lead a guerrilla war. That is what he saw as the only thing left to do."

"The only thing left to do? I don't follow." Major van Dam was leaning forward.

"Yes," I said, "we were supposed to be evacuated from Andir's airport and later from Tjilatjap. Twice we were told that we were on an emergency list. Yet both times we were told that our emergency rating was cancelled, no reason given. The second time the plane on which we were booked exploded. Had we been in that plane we would have been dead."

"Quite," the major carefully remarked. He pushed his chair back.

"But you," turning his gaze to the ceiling: "why did you not go back to Tjipatat where your unit was, when you found yourself not to be on the priority list any longer and after Mas left you? Why did you continue with your plan to escape? Were you not afraid that your action might be interpreted as cowardice and desertion?"

"I hardly think so," I said. "I was told to proceed with Mas to Australia; not at any time was that order repealed. Reaching Tjilatjap was the normal sequence of events of an order to accompany Mas to Australia. True I was in a predicament since Mas on his free will did not want to go further, but I had been interviewed by a group of officers who intimated to me the wishes of the Governor himself. Those wishes were that the two of us were to proceed to Australia and that the army would help us in the execution of that plan. I thought that to proceed was better than turning back."

The major pondered about what I had told him. Then he said:

"Would you be willing to volunteer for a mission into enemy occupied territory? It is important that we find your friend Mas. We not only want to find him but we still want him to be evacuated to Australia even at this late hour. The mission has to be conducted in the utmost secrecy and carefully planned. It mustn't fail. You are aware of the consequences if you are caught? We have already lost quite a number of good men. I am sure they were caught and executed. They all must have been betrayed."

He lent back in his chair and with a tone becoming serious he continued: "in fact none of the missions we have had thus far; were successful."

I thought over what he had said.

"The trouble is," he continued, "that we no longer know where Mas' allegiance lies. He has appeared, as you well know, in newspapers, which you have seen and we know that you have been very careful to hide the content from the Regent and his family. But eventually the Regent will find out about his son of course. In these papers he is full of propaganda; "Asia for the Asians," is the slogan in Indonesia now. He seems to be a puppet of the Japanese."

"Yes I know," I said; "however I know Mas. He is certainly in favor of freedom for the Indonesians but he is not a traitor. He is saying what he says solely under duress."

"That is exactly what we think also. However since he is such an important person to the Indonesians, his broadcasts and statements in the papers are very damaging to our cause. He must not be seen to be in favour of the "Asia for Asians," plan which is exactly what he is saying."

"And that is where I come in?" I said.

"Yes indeed, we think that if you found him, he would listen to you and would be persuaded to come to Australia with you. You would be about the only one he would listen to."

"About that I would not at all be sure," I said. "He left me in Tjilatjap remember, not the other way round."

"Be that as it may," the major said. "It is his only chance."

"What do you mean by that?" I asked.

"I will tell you later," he said mysteriously. "You would of course get any assistance available."

"And that is?" I asked.

"We envisage a landing on the South coast of Java by submarine. You will be rowed ashore on a to be arranged beach, so as to meet with Mas. We could get a message to him to meet you there at that beach."

"Suppose that meeting can be arranged," I said, "though that will be difficult enough: then what are we to do, if he does not want to come or if he for some reason or other cannot come?"

"That will depend on the circumstances. In any case we can pass the message to him. We have Buginese Sea Captains who still sail beween van Diemensland and Java, for instance to Surabaja. When you meet Mas you must implore him to come with you. To us, the army that is, it is immaterial whether he is in politics under duress or not. He must be stopped."

"In other words he will be abducted if he does not come voluntarily, that is what you have in mind; don't you?"

"Correct!" Major van Dam said tugging at his pipe.

"That will not be so easy," I said.

"Of course not, but there is only one other alternative if Mas doesn't come either willingly or unwillingly."

"And that is?"

"He will be eliminated."

"What?" You must be joking.

"I am far from joking," van Dam said. "Mas in the present form, is a danger to us. As a result of his condemnation of us; many European women and children will be killed by the natives, once the Japanese lose the war and that will happen. Mas will have stirred up their feelings. It makes no difference to us whether what he says is to save his own skin or not. Unless you succeed in bringing him to Australia, we will eliminate him. We have the means. We will obtain the services of a hired killer."

"That will be cold blooded murder," I heard myself say.

"Not so, we don't want to harm him if we possibly can. Let us hope it won't come to that. But should it be necessary, we have paid assassins. It is up to you."

I suddenly felt a chill creeping up my spine. How could I persuade Mas to come with me, even if he was willing to speak to me? And in order to speak to him I would be running into quite some danger by entering into enemy occupied territory. The major had already indicated that none of previous undertakings into enemy occupied territory had been successful. All the unfortunate agents had been caught and killed. But if I did not go along with Major van Dam's plan, Mas would sooner or later be assassinated.

I wanted some time to think about it and told Major van Dam my decision.

"Don't think too long about it," he warned me. "And another thing; we have already cancelled your return to the Regent. You cannot act normally now and will betray yourself by your behaviour: you see that don't you?"

Although I could understand that he was correct, I still resented that I had had no say in this particular part of the deal, if there was to be a deal with him. But I agreed that I could not possibly act normal to Mas' father, his mother or family under the present circumstances.

"Damn," I thought; Mas had brought this situation unto himself. Why had he not listened to me? The Governor-General had wanted to protect him from the Japanese. True, it seemed that there had been an attempt, on the part of who or what that I did not know; wanting to prevent us from reaching Australia.

Nevertheless he should have listened to me and have tried with me to get to Australia.

But then I thought how I had reached Australia against all odds. I easily could never have made it and that I did, in spite of all the obstructions along the way, was sheer luck. The whoever, that had wanted to block our escape and why; had nearly achieved that goal. And I still did not know what I was up to and who or what the enemy was. My life was going to be in danger again if I agreed with Major van Dam's plan. If I did not agree, Mas' would be eliminated van Dam had warned me.

It boiled down to this simple fact: Mas's life against possibly mine. What about my family, what about Lily? All considerations I could think of again and again always came down to the same thing: It was his life against possibly mine.

I did not need long to think. The odds were decidedly in my favour, or so I thought.

"Yes I will go," I told Van Dam.

Chapter 11

The night was still and only a faint moon accompanied us. It was a waning moon. The timing of it was carefully chosen so that it would not be totally dark when we would row ashore at Pang Pang bay.

The lights to the entrance of the harbour of Perth slowly faded in the distance behind us. An hour later they could not be seen any longer. The K12 submarine behaved like a young dog off the leash looking for new adventures!

I breathed the freshness of the air deep into my lungs and realized how much I had missed it. Two long months had passed since my meeting with van Dam. Every day since, I queried the wisdom of van Dam and my decision to agree to this dangerous plan of his. The overriding factor each time was that Mas would be assassinated if I did not agree with van Dam's plan. The reason for the long wait, apart from the state of the moon, was that we also had to wait until we received a message from the Buginese Captain that Mas would meet me at "Pang Pang" bay.

Thoughts like: "Would we be able meet at the specified place and was there a trap?" kept returning regularly in my head. The date and the hour of rendez-vous had finally been specified. All the time we were painfully aware that of all the secret missions into Japanese territory, none of the agents had ever returned. They must all have been betrayed.

Inevitably we had to make the Buginese captain a confidant of our plan. He therefore knew the meeting place, the date and the hour. But could we trust him? It would be easy enough for him to betray us if he wanted to. The Japanese would pay him well for doing so.

And what about Mas? He might be blackmailed tortured or even killed if the Japanese discovered that he had agreed to the meeting. And by torturing him he could perhaps not avoid betraying us against his will by giving away our meeting place. Nothing was certain, except that our lives were going to pay the price if we failed for one reason or the other. None of us felt too happy, with our lives at stake!

But it was the only way. Either we accepted the risk with all the consequences involved or Mas would be assassinated. I had already fully come to terms with the risks and so must the others be although I hardly knew my companions.

The submarine was old. Everything about this navy was old, except the captain and her crew. They had managed to send a Japanese destroyer to the bottom when the submarine was lying in the mud off Tamarkan's oil field in Borneo, waiting for the Japanese to appear.

Immediately afterwards they managed to escape still undetected and were able to make their way to Australia.

The large rollers of the Indian Ocean behaved gently like a wrestler having his tea break. By day we submerged at periscope level. We did not encounter native craft till we were about 100 miles from our destination. Apart from these vessels, mostly large fishing vessels, we had not spotted any shipping.

At night we surfaced and admired the myriad of stars and the phosphorescence of the sea. We then enjoyed the salty fresh air, quite a change from the stale air mixed with the oil smell down below.

The sea always appeared like a virgin, staying the way she had appeared millions of years ago. Only we humans, plants and animals grow old.

On the twenty ninth of November '42 late in the afternoon the Captain through his periscope saw the surf pounding the rocks on either side of "Pang Pang" bay. He had calculated the moment of arrival precisely. He kept the submarine at periscope level and kept scanning the deserted coastline.

"No sign of life," he said. But that meant nothing. The Japanese could be lying in hiding. After a while he grunted with satisfaction.

"I just saw a pack of wild dogs," he said. "This means that there are no humans such as Japanese nearby."

The meeting with Mas was scheduled to take place at midnight. Five and a half hours to wait.

If the Japanese knew that we would come by submarine, they could still be hiding elsewhere and wait there till it was dark before coming to the beach to hide here.

But we had plenty to do to keep our minds occupied with other things. There was no turning back now. We checked the rubber boat and our rubber suits. Then we checked our guns with rounds of ammunition.

I looked at the two sergeants who handled their guns in a business like manner. Major van Dam had carefully selected them. They were strong men in their middle thirties, both very well acquainted with Indonesian territory and its people. They were to row and accompany me to the shore.

Night came and it went quite dark. At last it was time, thirty-five minutes to midnight. Only then did the captain surface the submarine. We lowered the rubber boat into the water. The last of the waning moon, only a faint crescent, was hidden in a bank of clouds. The darkness was just as we had planned it. Yet the surf on the beach was still clearly visible.

Although the darkness was meant to conceal the floating submarine, an observer from the beach might nevertheless spot us against the faint horizon line.

My heart was pounding loudly in my chest, every beat an accompaniment to the oars that dipped in the water. This could well be the last night of our lives. I sat in front of the rubber boat, my gun at the ready; the two rowers dipping their oars in the water as quietly as possible were sitting directly behind me.

My eyes accustomed to the dark now, scanned the beach. I would never be able to detect people hidden in the foliage flanking the beach! Once in a while I held my breath as though that action would make me see better in the dim light, which of course was not possible. The last surf catapulted us ashore.

We scrambled up onto the beach dripping with water The salty taste made me reminisce the many times I had scrambled ashore in happier times at Pasir Poetih's beach, sailing with Doel and Lily. Apart from the surf on the shore, there was only silence and near darkness surrounding us.

We looked at our luminescent watches. One quarter of an hour to go. We dragged the boat up the shore for a short distance only. We should be able to make our get away in a hurry when necessary. If the Japanese were there already we would not get that chance.

We then could only fight till we died there. We certainly did not want to be taken prisoner. Prisoners were first tortured for information and then beheaded. Anxiously we peered into the darkness imagining that we saw Japanese everywhere, our automatic guns clicked at the ready.

After what seemed an eternity but in fact was only a quarter of an hour, a lone figure appeared out of the bushes, which flanked the beach. My heart was even beating faster than it already was; could this be Mas or was it a Japanese?

He was neither, but the Indonesian told us to wait and whistled. We became even more suspicious, our guns ready to fire.

The first one to be killed if this was a trap, would be this Indonesian for betraying us. My throat felt dry. Another figure loomed out of the dark. Unmistakably Mas this time. We embraced each other.

"You are running into great danger," he said. "I chose this spot not expecting that there would be an Islam festival here this time of the year. There is a kampong just over that hill. He pointed to a hill covered by dense foliage and only just visible in the darkness around us. "I am lodging there; so called taking part in this Islam festival. I can't stay more than about half an hour. Then they will miss me and they will go looking for me."

"Mas," I said." We have come to fetch you. We want you to come to Australia with us. This is your only chance to get away. We cannot come back again."

"I cannot come with you now; the Japanese hold me here by blackmail. I should have come with you when I had the chance in Tjilatjap. They have threatened to kill Lily if I escape."

"Lily?" I said. "How is she Mas?" Mas went quiet.

"She is well Richard, but she thinks that you are dead. So did I. After I left you, I heard that a Japanese plane had bombed a Buginese prahu and I was certain that it was the same vessel in which you and others had planned to escape. And Lily saw the list of passengers of the crashed airoplane and searched for your name. It was still on that list. We both; independently of each other, thought that you were dead. How did you manage to escape?"

"Never mind Mas: it is too long a story." The whole situation had suddenly changed. The well-being of Lily depended on his presence! He could not escape without jeopardising her life.

A light in the distance appeared; it was still far off.

"You must go immediately." Mas pushed me away.

Suddenly there was an enormous retort from a shot on my right. To my horror the retort came from Sergeant Boon's gun. Instinctively I had deflected his aim and the bullet went wide. His aim had been at Mas! I was stunned.

Sergeant Boon again aimed at Mas. It was only a short distance between Mas and the muzzle of the gun. The gun never fired! Reflex, instinct action and the handling of guns all my life, had prevented that. I had thrown myself bodily on Sergeant Boon and fought with him. His gun was now in my hands.

The other sergeant was still fumbling with the trigger. I hit his hand hard with the butt of the rifle I now held in my hands and he dropped his gun with a scream of pain. All this happened by reflex action and in a time span of seconds! Mas ran off into the bushes as fast as he could.

Major Van Dam had deceived me. I had been unaware of the real plan he had worked out behind my back. The two sergeants had been instructed to kill Mas if he didn't want to come with us, but van Dam had not told me anything about this.

Two hired assassins had come with me and I had led them straight to Mas innocently. There was no time now, no matter how I felt. We had to get away from the beach as fast as we could.

We reached the submarine in record time panting hard. We had not spoken one word to each other. Other lights had appeared on the beach. Within three minutes the submarine dived at periscope level.

"Don't ever come near me," I hissed at the sergeants. "I'll have both of you court marshalled acting without my orders."

"I only acted according to my instructions from Major van Dam," sergeant Boon miserably defended himself. The other said nothing. His hand was quite swollen where I had hit it.

Is it not amazing that hired killers look no different from ordinary people? On the street they would not pass up a collection box for the Salvation Army without a donation and would rescue a dog about to drown, which had fallen through broken ice in a lake, at great danger to their own life. The sergeants exactly fitted this description.

Our mission had been a failure. Mas would never again trust us, nor would I ever trust van Dam again. I only hoped that Mas had noticed that I had saved his life and that I had had nothing to do with this treacherous plot that had ended catastrophically. I now also feared for Mas' life. If the Japanese found out that he had allowed himself to have a rendez vous with the enemy, he might well be killed. Others must have heard the noise of the shot on the beach. There was nothing I could do about that.

The Captain of the submarine was equally furious. He also had been kept in the dark and he would never have agreed to the assassination part of the undertaking. Major Van Dam would not hear the last of it. What were we to think of him? I had liked him before, but he now had betrayed my trust

"Damn you Van Dam," I spoke out loudly; "I swear that I will take my revenge out on you and take you before a military court." During the passage home I never spoke one word to the two sergeants again. They had carried out their instructions, but I wanted nothing more to do with them and they wisely kept out of my way. It was Van Dam I needed to speak to and I would tell him what I thought of him. Who did he think he was; to scheme up this treacherous plot and making me an accomplice to murder without telling me?

In his office Major Van Dam felt distinctly uneasy. The taste of whiskey in his mouth relaxed him a little. The Captain of the submarine had sent a wireless report straight to van Dam's office. The ending of the wireless was not flattering. Van Dam took another mouthful straight from the bottle, got up from his chair and looked in the mirror on the wall. The face that met his gaze was grooved in all the anatomical places where a person who is expecting the worst shows his fear. He adjusted his tie with trembling fingers. The plan he had worked out had not succeeded the way he had hoped. And he alone was responsible. His superiors had made it plain to him that they wanted nothing to do with the plan and would certainly never have agreed with the assassination part of it. They had never given him "carte blanche" as far as that was concerned.

Eventually he had made his decision. It meant deceiving Richard Searle of course. The latter had to believe that the army through van Dam could and would assassinate Mas in Japanese occupied territory, which of course was only a remote possibility. Only because Richard Searl had believed that Mas otherwise would be assasinated, had he agreed to the meeting with Mas at Pang Pang bay. Had the plan come off and had Mas come along voluntarily, it would have been a great success for van Dam. Now however, the controller would be fuming with anger, not having been told about the alternative that he had planned if Mas would not agree to come along.

Had Mas been killed, the controller could say what he liked. The two sergeants would tell that they had acted in self-defence by killing Mas. Proof would be lacking and even the Governor-General would never believe that the army would have killed Mas. But now Mas was alive. The controller also had the Captain of the submarine as witness.

And now the controller was on his way back with rage like that of a betrayed tiger. There was only one good thing: he could pull rank. He held the rank of major and Richard Searle was only a lieutenant. But he discarded the idea quickly. He was sure that in this case, the anger from Lieutenant Searle was not going to be intimidated by van Dam's superiority in rank. He was equally sure that the controller would relate what had happened to the Regent, Mas father. In this latter assumption he was wrong. I kept the assassination attempt well out of the story. I told the Regent and his family only that I had been sent on a reconnoitre expedition. They had no reason not to believe me and were glad to see me back alive and well.

"Were you successful?" the Regent queried. I nodded. How could anyone tell a father that an assassination attempt on his son had just failed?

I agreed with the Captain of the submarine that I would make out the report of what happened in Pang Pang bay and he would sign it also.

I looked forward to meeting Major Van Dam the next day after our return to tell him what I thought of him.

As I walked into his office his secretary met me. "Your appointment with Major Van Dam has been cancelled. He has been transferred: "destination secret."

I had to postpone my meeting with him but vowed that he and I would meet again one day; preferably in a military court. It took me three and a half years, before I found out that I would never see him again. I visited his grave. He died at the hands of the Japanese when he led an underground mission in Java when he also was betrayed. My mind was not at ease. Why did he go on that mission? Did he go because he felt responsible for the failure at "Pang Pang" bay or was there another reason? Perhaps somebody or perhaps more than one person wanted to prevent him from being able to tell the truth about what really happened? I never found out.

Later, much later I met his parents. They were very pleased that I had known their son, their only son. I have always kept the assassination attempt to myself.

Chapter 12

After the Japanese surrender, General Mac.Arthur had delegated the liberation of the Dutch East Indies to the British and the Dutch. The U.S.A. did not want to become involved in the freedom fight of Indonesia.

The Japanese occupation of Asia had shown the colonial indigenous populations that their so called masters of the past, far from being superior, were in fact weak, not only in a militarily sense, but were also divided politically.

This latter fact had not escaped the Indonesians either. The majority parties in the Netherlands favoured independence for the Indonesians but not all political parties agreed. In any case, all parties had one thing in common: law and order should be restored first, before entering into any discussions.

The Indonesians in the meantime had unilaterally declared themselves independent. They had entered into a guerrilla war, killing European and Chinese, not only men, but also women and children. The British were also plagued with demands for freedom in their own colonies namely India, Malaysia and also Singapore.

It was perhaps for this reason that their forces seemed unable or did not have the will to keep law and order, since many of their soldiers came from the British colonies that wanted independence themselves and therefore sympathised with the Indonesian freedom fighters. And there were not enough Dutch troops around to fight the fanatical Indonesian fighters.

I found this chaotic situation when I came back to my homeland after an absence of four years!

In all that time I had not seen nor heard anything about Lily apart from the one abortive encounter on the beach of Pang pang bay where Mas told me that she was alive. She would be twenty-five years old now. Was she still alive and how would I go about finding her again?

Whole families were missing and large areas of Indonesia were held by Indonesian freedom fighters, some of who were cold-blooded killers, to whom the so-called freedom fight was only an excuse to indulge in killing. Their past Japanese masters had taught them to hate every white person. It was quite possible that Lily had been killed and that I would never see her again.

One day early in February 1946 I was ordered to appear for a talk with the Governor. It was a meeting I had very much looked forward to. Maybe just maybe he would give me the instructions I required:

A pardon for Mas and an invitation to talk with him about the matter of Indonesian independence, which had arrived at an impasse! An Indonesian soldier clad in official uniform, to indicate that he belonged to the entourage of the Governor General, handed the message to me.

"Please report to me." the wording simply stated, signed St Cyr. The letter bore the Governor's official stamp. The chauffeur opened the car door for me and an hour later I was beckoned to enter the room, which I knew to be the office of the Governor-General. The building was located in the beautiful

111

botanic gardens in Bogor, originally founded by Junghuns and later enlarged by Sir Charles Stamford Raffles.

The Governor was alone and rose from behind his desk when I walked in. He had aged. The time as a hostage under the Japanese had produced grooves in his face and his hair black before had turned grey around the temples. He wore the usual white tunic, which was worn by Government officials before the war. The worry about his wife and daughters in Japanese captivity must have been simply awful to him because he was known to be a close family man and he never had any communication with them in all the three and a half years that he was held prisoner. We shook hands warmly.

"How have you been?" he greeted me.

"Reasonably well," I replied. I related my experience and time with the Regent in Australia but also and especially, told him of our failure trying to get ourselves; Mas and I myself; out of Indonesia and to Australia. I ended by telling him about the abortive assassination attempt on Mas' life at Pang Pang bay.

He listened intently and did not ask any questions while I was telling my story. When I had finished my tale he shifted his seat back. He looked even more tired, rubbed his hand over his forehead and sighed.

"It is important that we locate Mas and speak to him. How can we now establish contact with him after the attempt on his life? What can he think of us? We know that he is very much alive and a freedom fighter; enforcing by his example, resistance to the Dutch return as rulers. He holds many clandestine radio broadcasts. He is even known by different names condemning the Dutch for wanting to create a police state oppressing the natives.

He knows full well that is not so and never has been. We also want independence for Indonesia but it has to happen by peaceful means. Is there no possibility by which you can contact him?"

I had not seen Mas since "Pang Pang" bay's attempt to persuade him to come with me to Australia and which had ended in total failure.

"That may not be so easy now," I heard myself say. "He must be suspicious; there was this assassination attempt on his life, remember?"

"What stupidity," St Cyr sighed. "The situation which faces us now is the result of it.

Instead of an intellectual rapport with the Indonesians we can trust, which situation we could have had; we have nothing less than another war on our hands, this time a guerrilla war, which may be lasting for years. And it is so unnecessary.

"The Queen also wishes freedom for Indonesia. Here is where your friendship with Mas is invaluable. You can approach him and talk with him. He surely will not believe that you meant him any harm although you were present at the assassination attempt; after all you deflected the bullet."

"Hopefully he noticed," I said. But there was no time to find out whether he did or did not. Moreover he may believe that I wanted to abduct him, which is also not true. And from the evidence of his subsequent broadcasts, he may well feel very badly about what happened in Pang Pang bay. He seems particularly anti-Dutch now; he was never like that before."

"I have a request to make," St Cyr came to the point, "but this is entirely up to you, no pressure whatsoever is exerted upon you, since there is considerable danger attached to what I will ask of you."

"You want me to find Mas and speak to him," I said, making it easy for St Cyr to say it.

"Correct," he nodded obviously pleased that I had taken the words out of his mouth. "You were his best friend. If anyone can establish contact, you can. The difficulty is finding him. There are reports of him being everywhere, just like the Scarlet Pimpernel."

"Not like that exactly," I said. "I have a good idea where he might be. He is in the non-military occupied area in Semarang and calls himself a freedom fighter much to the regret of his Indonesian father and his Dutch mother. I am still in contact with his family and can locate him at any time through his father and mother.

"They know where he is. He is also accused by the military that he has, or rather that his troops have committed several murders on Dutch, other European and also Chinese women and children, and he knows that there is a price on his head."

"I do not believe that Mas had anything to do with those murders," I heard St Cyr give his opinion.

"I don't believe that either; I know Mas."

"Nevertheless," the Governor continued, "his orations sweep up hatred against us and there is an anti-Dutch feeling already that does not need fuelling. And the anti-Dutch propaganda is also present in Australia, which is supposed to be an ally. The dock workers in Australia refuse to load and unload Dutch ships have you not heard?"

"I have," I said; "this is something recent because when I was in Australia the Australians were more than kind. It is all the more incomprehensible that this is so, because the Australians suffered very badly during the war.

The Governor looked at the ceiling as though to get inspiration for what he was going to say. He must felt awkward to ask me what he wanted me to do. Almost apologetically he said:

"The only solution is you finding him and speaking to him."

"This time I will go alone," I said. "My intention must not be known by the army, especially not the military."

"How can you conceal that, since you will have to pass army controlled posts before you can enter Indonesian occupied territory?"

"That is true," I said, "but I'll tell you how: I will enter Semarang's most southern military post.

Could you use your influence to tell the commanding officer there to let me have a jeep? I will proceed from there. Once I have the O.K, I'll proceed at once so that nobody else but only that particular outpost knows of my intent. On that I must insist; I don't want another Pang Pang bay incident."

"You can count on that," the Governor assured me. "I'll find out who is in command there and I will request that you be given that jeep. What about weapons," he asked.

"Indeed," I said, I need to be seen armed to the teeth; not that I have any illusion that the guerrilla fighters will not disarm me quickly, but I will automatically gain respect, because the Indonesian guerrilla's like a man carrying weapons."

"So be it," the Governor sighed relieved. "I'll be in touch and you don't know how grateful I am. I can only wish you good luck." We shook hands and I was alone with my thoughts, contemplating how to arrange a meeting between Mas and the Governor-General: the official government in power. Of course Mas could be suspicious if and when I offered him the opportunity to talk with the Governor but I was convinced that he would not harm me.

However before I could reach him I would encounter hostile Indonesians. They might kill me then and there, before I could explain what it was that I wanted and which was only to see their leader.

Somehow I thought that with my knowledge of the Indonesian language and knowledge of their ways; that would not happen. I had yet another equally important reason for finding Mas. He undoubtedly knew where Lily was.

The day was fine when I visited Kedi, the last outpost of the Dutch military occupation. It represented the borderline just before the area, which was held by what the Dutch called "Indonesian extremists". The military post was heavily defended and had repulsed several Indonesian attacks on it, causing heavy casualties on the attacker.

One of the captured officers was Commander Hat. He had lost the forefoot of his left leg due to an explosion by a strategically placed mine by the people he considered his "enemies", but he was otherwise recovering well. I decided to interview this officer in the army hospital where he was held prisoner. I perceived some resistance from the Dutch commanding captain but could well understand his behaviour. He had lost a few of his men and possibly dear friends also; such is the foolishness of war. I shook hands with Hat, the captured Indonesian officer, conveying my regrets about his injury.

"It is tragic," I said "that we are at opposing ends, while we are in fact friends." He nodded.

"Yes," he said. "All we want is to be free and you people are trying to prevent it." I again could see his argument and at the same time could also see the other point of view, namely that independence should not be achieved by means of force. And if I could convince Mas of this and bring him to the conference table, the mutual understanding between him and the Governor might just bring about this peaceful solution.

"That may appear to be so to you," I said to commander Hat, "but you are wrong. The Governor has to carry out the instructions of the government of the Netherlands to grant Indonesia its freedom and that view prevails in the Netherlands today. But you must realise that you are trying to get it at the end of the muzzle of a gun. Those tactics nobody can agree with.

"The demand is law and order first; then we can discuss freedom for Indonesia in a context with the Netherlands which satisfies all parties. The Netherlands government has responsibility not only for the Indonesians, but also for every citizen; Chinese, Indonesian, and Dutch etc. who live in Indonesia, so that the transfer of sovereignty occurs in an orderly manner, not by force.

"In any case I have not come to speak to you about those issues, important though they may be. I intend to speak to Mas. He and I were bosom friends before the war and as far as I am concerned we still are. I want to know where he is."

"That information I cannot give you. That would be betrayal."

"But I only want to speak to him," I said.

"Who guarantees that?" he asked me. "Mas is safe where he is; you will not find him."

"I suggest," I said to Hat; "that I will go into your occupied territory by jeep and when I am halted by your men; that I then will ask them to take me to Mas."

"You are risking your life, I won't guarantee your safety," he said ominously. "The Indonesians you meet may be trigger-happy; however I can give you an idea how to get through if your intentions are really peaceful.

"Produce a Merah Putih flag and have it signed by me, then put it on your vehicle in a place where it is easily seen in front of your engine on the bonnet. When you are stopped deliver this letter in which I ask for you to be taken to Mas. This is your chance of getting to him alive."

I realised that this was sound advice given to me by an "enemy" and I thanked him.

When I set out in the early morning the sun had just risen over the Merapi, the mountain guarding the town of Semarang, but the top of it was still hidden from view as though too shy to face the world.

The morning was cool and it occurred to me that this might be the last morning I would experience in my life. I had the red and white flag flowing on the right and a large white flag on the left of the jeep. The flags could be easily seen from a mile away, since they were in front of the car.

I covered about twenty kilometres. Every time I expected the retort of a rifle and a bullet in my neck. I now also considered myself a fool to run such risks.

The Governor had given me the option to refuse. Why had I not done that? Maybe Mas had changed; maybe he was to all intents and purposes responsible for the attacks on women and children murdered by the Indonesians. Maybe he did not deserve a hearing, if this turned out to be the case. Also maybe he would kill me but I immediately discarded this possibility.

My reverie came to an end when I suddenly saw the roadblock. A large tree was pulled over the road, making any progress impossible. By instinct I wanted to go for my gun but I checked myself. Had I done so I would have been killed instantly.

Almost at once Indonesian freedom fighters appeared out of the foliage bordering the road. There were about twenty of them. They all wore a black band around their upper arm with a white skull painted on it and were armed with automatic rifles aimed at me. They also carried hand grenades in their belts.

Again I wondered what on earth had persuaded me to be here, now that their menacing faces confronted me from every direction as they approached me closely. Before they could say anything, I addressed them very loudly in Indonesian:

"I want to speak to Mas your leader."

There was no response and as they approached, their guns were all the time aimed at me. I prayed that they had had enough training how to handle guns so that I would not be shot accidentally. They stopped at five paces from me. Then one of them stepped forward.

"I am Ahmed," he said. He was obviously the headman; probably a ruthless killer.

"Get out of the car," he ordered. I got out of the jeep, hoping to appear unconcerned although my heart was pounding loudly in my chest.

"Your guns if you please."

I handed him the gun first and then the revolver with the barrel turned towards me very slowly so that my meaning could not be wrongly interpreted. This was not an occasion to be misunderstood or show bravery but required steel nerves instead. Two others now proceeded to search me bodily and removed my hunting knife from my belt also. I felt reassured.

At least they had not shot me yet. Satisfied that I was now unarmed; Ahmed beckoned me to follow him.

"The flag," I said to him, "Captain Hat' s name is on it, he has given it to me to hand it to anyone of you who would arrest me. I also have a letter written by him in which he explains that I came here of my own free will."

Ahmed opened the letter and read it but said nothing, he then removed the red and white flag from the car with Hat's writing clearly on it. His poker face showed no emotion. He obviously wanted to intimidate me. Again I wondered if I would see the next day alive.

We went along a small footpath with Ahmed in front and two others behind me. The remaining soldiers stayed behind, no doubt guarding the roadblock. No word was spoken since we left the jeep. I did not consider that a good omen.

After about half an hour we reached a village. Dogs and children played together but it had struck me that we had zigzagged into the kampong and that all the dogs were on a leash. Many more freedom fighters appeared; hatred on their faces when they looked at me and the children stopped their playing.

The men wore the same black bands with the white skull painted on it on their upper arms and they wore their hair long. I knew why. They had vowed not to cut their hair till the Dutch were driven out from Indonesia.

Ahmed ordered a chair for me to sit on and he and about five others sat themselves down on a baleh- baleh in front of me.

Ahmed started to speak: "You are a spy: you know what we do with spies?" He drew the forefinger of his right hand across his throat, the meaning of which was unmistakable. Before he could go on I had already decided to call his bluff.

"A spy you call me?" You must be joking; I came here alone in a jeep along a road, which I knew would lead me into territory occupied by your forces. Any intelligent person would deduce that I wanted to contact you."

I could see that I could needle Ahmed easily but I had to be careful doing so.

"And what about the flags I carried and the letter from your officer Hat?" I continued.

"The letter could have been written under duress," Ahmed retorted: "you keep him prisoner. You ran into us too obviously, why did you let yourself be captured?"

"Captured?" I said, "I didn't know I was a prisoner. I came to see Mas, to speak to him."

"Why?"

"Because he is my friend, we grew up together."

"You are lying, you want to kill him."

"Without a gun?"

"Of course you haven't got a gun now; we took it away from you."

"So you did and Mas won't be pleased about it when he finds out that you did not trust me in spite of my coming here on my free will and carrying the Merah Putih flag plus the letter from your commander Hat. If you keep me prisoner as you say you do, Mas will undoubtedly hear about it and he won't be pleased that you did that to his best friend."

Ahmed shifted uncomfortably on the baleh baleh. My bluff had the necessary effect, I noticed to my satisfaction. Not knowing anything about me, my story could be true and he had no way of knowing otherwise.

I decided to press the point.

"You must stop these childish accusations you know very well not to be true," I said.

"Well," he hesitated, "Mas is not here."

117

"Then I'll wait for him," I said. "Alternatively you can take me to him."
Ahmed turned to the others. After a long discussion, which they knew I could
follow, he said sullenly:

"All right, we'll send a message to Mas and tell him you are here. If he
denounces you, and says that he is not your friend you have signed your own
death warrant. Perhaps he will be here by tomorrow."

"That will please me," I said

"We give you this house on stilts to stay in," Ahmed continued; "don't try to
escape, don't even walk around, you will be free but the kampong is surrounded
with hidden mines and we won't tell you where they are."

"That is fine with me," I said.

Now I understood why the dogs were on the leash; so that they could not
step on the mines by mistake. The children had been warned not to go outside
the safe area.

So far my mission was going as I had planned it, and I was still alive. How
long for? But I banned those negative thoughts from my mind. It was only a
matter of time before Mas would appear. I had food and drink served regularly.

For toilet facilities I shouted to a sentry who then accompanied me to a little
stream. Even on the first occasion I had decided that by crossing this stream I
could then disappear in the jungle behind it and so escape. Of course I needed
to do away with the sentry first; and I sincerely hoped that it would never come
to that.

In the meantime I explored the hut I was in. It was only one large open
space; there was no partition between the kitchen in the corner and the sleeping
quarters; the total screened off from the outside by billik matting. Through the
matting I could observe what was going on in the village. The floor of the hut
made of split bamboo was about eight feet from the ground.

Through the slits in the bamboo floor I saw chickens roaming underneath
me, scratching the earth looking for scraps of food dropped through the
bamboo matting of the floor.

It occurred to me suddenly. I was stretching myself on the mattress put on
the bamboo floor, when I paid attention to the red stained beetle nut patches on
the mattress I was lying on. But were they red from beetle nut stains? I inspected
them closely, no; ....they were patches of caked blood! Someone had bled on this
mattress, and was probably tortured or murdered on it.

Who? The bristles on the back of my neck stood up, I could be murdered
here and no one would know. And I was given the same hut as the person who
bled on this mattress. What was I doing here? No one would be grateful. I did
not even exist. The Governor had made it plain that I was on my own. I did not
need to have come.

Damn Mas, his credibility and his so-called freedom fight! He was, even if
only indirectly, still responsible for the murders of Dutch women and children.

So why should I, or the Governor be concerned about him? The military were probably right. Fight it out with the guerrilla fighters.

Quite a number of them were undoubtedly bloodthirsty killers and enjoyed murdering for murdering sake. It had nothing any more to do with freedom as they claimed. I did not want to admit that Mas was like that and neither did the Governor. That was why St Cyr; who knew Mas's father well, had sent me to find him. We could not be so wrong about him.

It was then that another thought suddenly occurred to me. What if Mas were killed? He was my only key to safety. Ahmed would only be too happy to kill me, once he knew that Mas was out of the way.

I suddenly felt a shiver of fear running up my spine. I had no weapon left. Not that a weapon would do me any good now even if I had one.

I contemplated escape again and I would possibly succeed. But then my whole purpose of coming so far would be lost. I was surprised at myself for not having thought of the all too obvious possibility that Mas might be killed. After all he was fighting the Dutch in a real war.

Anxiously I looked out from the billik matting. My nerves were strained. There was no suggestion that I was being watched though I knew that I was. If only I could talk with Ahmed. But he must have decided that he didn't want to speak to me. Enquiring after him, that I wanted to speak to him had no effect.

The next day passed without a sign of Mas. Also again there was no sign of Ahmed. He was apparently unconcerned about what was happening to me for the time being. The cat was playing with the mouse and I was the mouse! The second night I slept soundly in spite of my sombre thoughts.

At about noon the following day there was excitement in the village, I could feel it from the restlessness of the inhabitants and of the children and even notice it from the tense behaviour of the dogs. Mas' impending arrival was many times talked about. It was obvious to me that the whole Kampong considered him an important person. It was time he appeared. My safety depended on it!

Chapter 13

I recognised him immediately. At last he had arrived with a detachment of twenty well-armed soldiers. Their army uniforms were caked with mud and sweat and they looked haggard. Some blood was also apparent on the clothing of some of the men who appeared wounded and were limping in, supported by their comrades.

Although uniforms varied, most of them wore American battle dress, invariably stolen from ammunition arms depots that the Dutch had taken over from the Americans. Also many of these uniforms had ended up on the black market.

Many of the soldiers were wearing the black band with the white painted skull on it around their upper arm, but Mas' black band was different. It had a red elephant painted on it.

The red elephant like the one painted on Mas'armband indicates an emblem of strength in Indonesia. Mas' clothing also differed from the others in that he didn't wear his hair long like the others did. I was pleased to see that. Did that mean that he did not hate the Dutch and did not want to drive them out of Indonesia? I knew that his mother was Dutch. Was that the only reason that he didn't?

I had not seen Mas since the abortive attempt to speak to him in Pang Pang bay. At that time I had never had the opportunity to vent my dissatisfaction to Major van Dam personally.

Mas welcomed me with outstretched hands. We embraced each other.

"I am so glad to see you," were his first words. "It has been too long. Thank God you survived the war." We embraced each other again and he slapped my back.

Ahmed who was standing behind Mas looked at me like a cat whose prey had just flown away and spit on the ground to show his disapproval at what was happening.

"Too long indeed Mas," I said. "I have come to talk to you and to bring you a message from St.Cyr."

"Have my men treated you well?" he asked me.

"Yes they have," I said, ignoring Ahmed's unfriendly gesture.

"Come," Mas invited me, you have met Ahmed, he was a sergeant in the Dutch East Indies army; did he not tell you?"

"No he did not," I said. "In that case he swore allegiance to the Queen of the Netherlands. Can you now trust a man like that?" Ahmed stared hard at me. There was no doubt in my mind that he would kill me if he had half the chance.

"Well," Mas said: "times have changed. He now sees that his allegiance is with Indonesia and the Indonesian uprising."

"A point of view I don't share," I said, "do you?" Mas did not reply. He was brooding about something..., I could tell because I knew him so well. He changed the subject.

"What is the message from St Cyr and how did you bring it and why you?"

"Steady," I said to him. "Do you remember Pang Pang bay?" I asked.

"I surely do; if you had not saved me I would have been dead."

"I was not aware of the plot Mas; you must believe me."

"Do not worry about that; I had that worked out a long time ago since you deflected the bullet that was meant for me. I have also since heard the true story from my father although you tried to keep the truth to yourself."

"But why Mas did you never come to Australia? It would have been easy enough for you."

"I told you why in Pang pang bay, do you not remember? I couldn't, I wanted to explain the whole story to you then, but I never got the chance. I was being blackmailed; although I never wanted to explain it to her, and only sporadically saw her in all these years. The Japanese threatened to kill Lily if I did not work for them."

"Lily?" I said. "Where is she?"

"She is safe but she is still in occupied territory with Wong her husband."

"Her husband you said, Lily?" I exclaimed. "You said husband?"

"Yes, Richard. I had hoped that I would be the one to tell you first. She thought that you were dead because she saw your name on the list of the passengers which were in the plane that blew up in Tjilatjap At one time I myself also thought that you were dead although not in that plane disaster since we both were refused entry in the plane. You were going to Australia last I heard. But I also heard later that a Buginese vessel was bombed and sank about twenty miles south of Tjilatjap.

I was sure that was the boat you were on. As far as Lily and I were concerned you had died."

"And she married Wong?"

"Yes, she was very heartbroken about you. But times were made impossible for her. She thought you were dead. Try to understand Richard! Wong was very good to her and with Wong as an Asian husband; she was at least protected against the Japanese and had a chance of survival.

Try Richard, it is hard for you I know, but try to understand it, she thought you were dead. So did I, so did Wong."

I could not have been more shocked. Lily married! It was as though a mortar bomb had hit me. All my dreams of finding her back again and marrying her, evaporated into nothingness. What had happened to the goenoeng Ringgit and the promise we had made to one another? I needed to sit down.

"Yes Richard, I was blackmailed. The Japanese had found out about the friendship I felt for Lily. I also asked Wong to marry her to protect her. I even contemplated to marry her myself to protect her, but even believing in your death I still could not do that to you. Wong tried to protect her that is all; you must believe me. The circumstances were altogether impossible."

I nodded but still felt dazed. Lily married to Wong. What irony! Lily, Wong, Mas and I had been the closest of friends but the cards had been shuffled totally the wrong way. Nothing had turned out as expected. It seemed that fate wanted to handle the outcome of things her own way, not caring in the slightest about the feelings of the people who were involved.

Mas continued: "The Japanese threatened me by saying that they would accuse Lily of an imaginary plot if I did not co-operate with them. I knew what that meant. After a short trial, imaginary accusations corroborated by a few false witnesses would have been levied against her.

She would have been found guilty of collaboration with the enemy and she would have been beheaded. "Fortunately, Lily does not know anything about this. I did not want to see her lest I would betray myself and tell her why I behaved the way I did. And after finding out at "Pang Pang" bay that you against all odds were still alive; she was already married and I could not bring myself to disturb her already difficult position further, by saying that you were alive.

That would have been cruel. Sooner or later of course she will have to be told. That is why I never escaped to Australia, but you and my parents of course could not understand why. Now you know why I could not come."

"Nevertheless you are a freedom fighter now Mas and your radio broadcasts are very well known to be nationalistic. They do a lot of damage and make it impossible to go into discussions with you."

"They may well be nationalistic as you say but they are not necessarily anti-Dutch, now that I am no longer blackmailed by the Japanese and can speak my mind."

"We; meaning by that the Governor and others, myself included, don't agree with that, but we won't argue about little details. I came because the Governor has asked me if I can persuade you to speak to him. The Governor still considers you the spokesman for the Indonesian cause and would like to hold frank discussions with you and your party of freedom fighters. As soon as possible; in order to avoid further unnecessary bloodshed."

"The climate is no longer suitable for discussion, Mas said."

"On the contrary," I said. "The prevailing mood in the Netherlands today is to grant Indonesia independence as I already told you. To talk with the Governor can only be helpful. He wants a temporary treaty to discuss an eventual freedom for Indonesia, though on a yet to be agreed short term basis and through a democratically elected government."

Mas weighted my words.

"That I fear is not acceptable by me and I speak with a certain authority for my people. I know the mood; we prefer to be free now. If not peacefully then by force, we will fight to get it."

It was not at all what I had hoped to hear.

"Mas," I said; "you have the option to be free by peaceful means, why do you choose war? You are the leading figure for your people."

"Richard, unfortunately that is no longer so. Perhaps before the war what you say applied. Other people have taken over from me. I am now only in command when it comes to military matters. Unfortunately so, he sighed. In the months to come even if I am not killed, the sons of the Sultan, my cousins, will want to be in charge. And apart from my cousins there are other power seekers. As ever in history there is this craving of power and I am not immune to it. I recognise it in myself.

"Militarily speaking, I have observed the increasing military strength of the Dutch army. We have a chance to become free now. If we wait longer your forces will become stronger. I see it happening already. I lose more and more of my men. The chances of freedom for Indonesia, which is almost certain within our grasp, may recede again if we delay. Have you forgotten that in the last three hundred and fifty years when we were dominated by the Dutch; that we have had no freedom of choice for our own affairs?"

"But things are different now Mas. Indonesia will be given a much larger freedom of government and the Dutch rule will soon be replaced by your own altogether."

"Too late," Mas said. "That kind of agreement would have been perfectly acceptable, had it come before the war. The mood now is to fight for freedom. I speak for the mood of the people."

I noticed that he had used the word Indonesia as though Indonesia was a free country already.

"Nevertheless, consider the options, you have death and destruction on the one hand and freedom, democratic freedom that is; all be it on a to be arranged basis on the other."

"Richard, can you in all honesty speak for all the government officials and for all the military?" Mas interrupted. "They would not understand your language. They did not understand that language before. They still want to rule, they want to turn the clock back, as it was before the war. That won't do any longer. I have to be practical and move with the tide."

"In any case, let there be a conference," I said; "you have nothing to lose by what the Governor has to say."

"That is true," he said. Mas was thinking very hard.

"When and where?" he said at last.

"At the Governor's place: Tjisarua."

"And who guarantees that I won't be captured? You know what happened to Diponegoro don't you?"

"The blackest page in the Dutch-Indonesian history" I said. "That won't happen again."

"How much guarantee can you offer me?"

"The Governor is in charge again Mas" I said. "You know that he is an honest man."

"But you wear a military uniform", Mas said. "I only have your word that I will return free. Every army rank higher than you can arrest me by overruling you and you cannot change that."

"No; not true; I had a letter from the Governor with me. Ahmed took it away from me. Ask him for it. It guarantees your immunity from prosecution if you attend the meeting; if you consent to meeting the Governor on a selected date and place." Mas was quiet, deep in thought and I left him to ponder on the offer of the governor.

"What about the Romusha's Mas?" I said suddenly. "Have you ever felt sorry about what happened to them?" He looked up surprised.

"What about the Romusha's?" he asked.

"They died in their hundreds," I said and you sent them to Siam."

"Yes I know, terrible, they died in slave labour being used by the Japanese at the Siamese death railway, so did hundreds of P.O.W's. But what does that have to do with me? The Japanese offered them work for payment."

"Only because of your propaganda talks did they accept this kind of work, but did it not occur to you that the Siamese themselves never accepted these jobs? Why not? Because they very well knew of the very dangerous working conditions they would be exposed to: cholera, dysentery, malaria and other tropical diseases."

"You can hardly blame me for that, I did not know about all these conditions. That is not fair Richard. As far as I could see they would have work and food for their families. Don't forget that the Dutch abandoned them in the first place. Many of us and of those that were sent to Siam had no work; the conditions of war had changed all that."

"You can't blame the Dutch for that either; they lost the war and we; you and I, have lost many a friend Mas, good friends they were. Mas went quiet.

"And the many Dutch women and children who were killed by your murderers, your so-called freedom fighters, are you innocent of that too?"

"I have never killed any women and children, Dutch or otherwise. Do you believe I did?"

"No Mas", I did not really think so."

"But Richard, now that you have brought up our freedom fighters behaving like murderers, I like to ask you: what did you do to our leaders in the past? They were jailed for expressing their opinion and sent to impossible places to get them out of the way. Is that democracy, the democracy you are advocating?"

"I agree with all that Mas; we have made many mistakes but we are willing to make amends, this is precisely what the offer of the Governor is all about. The situation is so out of hand that even your father and mother, back in Bantam, are being threatened by your own people. Why? The only reason is that they don't agree with the way the freedom fighters have behaved, and your father dared to voice his opinion. You are responsible if something happens to him; to all your family; have you ever thought about that?"

"If they happen to be killed for the cause of freedom for Indonesia, so be it." Mas said.

"What?" I said. I was horrified. "You can't be serious about that Mas, you never used to be like that."

"I am sorry but I now have to believe in the cause for Indonesia first and if I don't think like this, we will never get our freedom. The Japanese occupation has shown us, that far from being superior, the Dutch forces are in fact very weak. The Indonesian freedom fighters are in a guerrilla war, also badly equipped but we can disappear in the masses without being detected, and moreover the Dutch troops cannot patrol such a large area as Indonesia. We hold the trump cards this time."

I realised that I was speaking to a different Mas than the one I had known before the war.

How confused things had become. The Indonesians did not trust the Dutch; the Dutch did not trust the Indonesians and the British who were given the task of keeping law and order by consent with General Mac. Arthur, seemed to be incapable of preventing bloodshed and murder: not only of European women and children, but also and perhaps especially, Chinese citizens.

The Djojo Bojo prediction had mentioned the Solo river red from blood and puntjuk hats floating down the river. This was now happening already if the Chinese who were indeed wearing puntjuk hats, were the ones meant in the prediction.

"I have to get you out of here," Mas said after a pause. "I understand that you came by jeep. I'll take you to no man's land. You must go straight back along the road you came, carrying all your weapons. Don't look back: I will control my men. And don't drive off the road; some mines are placed there, where exactly I don't even know myself. I will be at the place and time set by the governor. You can send the message via my spy. He lives in Kemajoran kampong. His name is Haroen Janoedi. Ask for him, I will let him know that you will contact him. Richard; I will be taking a great risk by coming to this meeting with the Governor. Please make sure that I won't be betrayed like Diponegoro was."

I again reassured Mas that the Governor had already guaranteed his safe return.

He walked me to the jeep, which was left by the roadside. I still felt the hatred in my back from the looks the villagers gave me as I left the kampong; Ahmed was one of them, spitting on the ground for me to see, but my feelings towards him were not that friendly either. I gave him the military salute nevertheless. He returned mine. He could hardly have done less in Mas' presence.

We left by the same zigzagging path, which we, Ahmed and I, had used on our approach to the kampong before; obviously to avoid concealed mines I now knew.

"I am so sorry about you and Lily," Mas said when we parted; his eyes were moist when he spoke. At least she is alive and you are alive. All of us could have been dead Richard; think about that. It is some small consolation.

"Maybe you could still mean something to each other in the future; you still could be good friends and think well of one another. She has had a hard time. So did Wong. He was tortured by the Japanese and is in bad health. Wong and Lily both are still in occupied territory. I will let you know when she will be released. I have been trying to make it soon; probably in two weeks or so. It also means that I need cooperation from the Dutch military for the transfer evacuation. In this respect we fully cooperate with each other. Plans are already on their way. I wish we could be like that in other matters too." I heard regret in his voice and it gave me hope. We embraced as we parted.

When I got to the first Dutch military post where I had borrowed the jeep, I received a message that the captain in charge, Captain Hensen, wanted to see me. He was seated on a camp bed in his tent and asked me to sit down.

"You have just returned from kampong Tjilan?" he began.

"Yes," I said.

"Did you return the jeep we loaned you?"

"Yes, thank you for the loan of it," I replied.

"Good! I aim to attack the kampong tomorrow at dawn. First I want you to tell me the layout of the kampong, the number of men, amount and kind of weapons they carry, minefield situation if there is any and how many women and children there are? Also any other thing you can think of which may be important."

He leaned forward pen in hand with a blank white sheet of paper in front of him.

"Well?" he asked expectantly.

"I'm sorry captain," I said. "You will not get that information from me. If you attack that kampong tomorrow you will be acting against the orders of the Governor. I have just had a meeting with Mas. He trusts the Governor and me. I protest in the strongest terms possible and refuse to give you any information of the kind you asked me."

"Will you remember that I can have you court-martialled for withholding the information I asked you? You are still in the army and I am senior in rank to you."

"Don't be silly captain; you know full well that the Governor has given you an order to assist me. You may not like it but there it is. And are you also not aware that that order was endorsed by your highest in command? Threatening me are you? "You must be joking. Your action will be reported by me personally to your highest in command, if you insist in your demand.

As for attacking this kampong, you will lose many men and I for one, will not keep my mouth shut that I did not warn you of the consequences if you do. I am warning you captain: we have the trust of Mas now. I will not be able to persuade him to talk to the Governor ever again if you attack that kampong; Mas will never trust me again. He will think that I betrayed him."

"And are you afraid of that? He is a murderer and needs to be executed like a mad dog."

"We obviously have different opinions captain. I remain with my refusal and on your head be it, if you attack that village. Moreover, I repeat, you will lose many men if you do. The place is booby trapped and extensively so, from my observation of the kampong these few days. That much I will let you know. And now," I said, "I want to be taken to Tjisarua, where the Governor will be waiting for me and my report." I started to get up.

"Sit down again please," the captain said, changing his unfriendly stand.

"I can see that you do not see things as I do, but just think of the women and children who are at this moment in danger because you want to protect your friend. You knew him before the war and were his best friend, I heard. He has changed you know, take my word for it. He would even sacrifice his friends; he is obsessed with freedom for Indonesia and would condone murder to accomplish that."

I thought of the words, which Mas had just spoken to me, when he referred to his father and mother: "If they are killed for the cause of Indonesia, so be it." His words had shocked me. Could he be serious? Was this Mas my best friend in whom I had always believed and still did even now?

If he could sacrifice his parents for the cause of Indonesia, he had indeed become a fanatic.

Was the captain wrong? He obviously saw Mas in a totally different light than I did but was I not biased? I knew the Mas from my youth. But what about this new Mas? Did I know him? I needed to think hard.

"One more question please lieutenant. Did he wear his hair long?"

"I know why you asked me the question captain. No, he didn't. It may be relevant that Mas has a Dutch mother."

"I did not know that. Nevertheless, that doesn't change much. I can see that you don't believe me and for your sake, I hope I am wrong; good day to you lieutenant."

I left the tent, my head in turmoil. The captain was still sitting where he was, the blank sheet of paper still in his hands.

Less than two months later a civilian post not far from Tjilan where women and children had been kept prisoner against their will by the freedom fighters, was freed by the Dutch military forces of Captain Hensen.

Among the items left by their jailers was a torn armband. It was a black one without the white skull painted on it. I identified it. Mas had worn it when I talked with him in kampong Tjilan two months before. Unmistakably a red elephant was painted on the black band. Five Dutch women and three Chinese children were found murdered, hacked to death, before the Dutch forces could rescue them. The description of the freedom fighter's leader fitted Mas exactly. Could I have been so wrong about him?

Chapter 14

Major Cane inspected his troops with a weary heart. His soldiers were not in the best physical condition, which was plain to see. Even their clothes lacked uniformity. They looked like a bunch of amateurs.

The majority of his troops had only recently been liberated from a protracted period of oppression, torture, brutal beatings and famine; in other words they had been prisoners of war of the Japanese.

Now again they were supposed to fight, another war this time. An unnecessary war; full of frustrations! If only politicians had not interfered! If only the politicians e.g. the Governor and his kind, like Richard Searle, had kept their noses out of it, law and order would have been established long ago. The military forces weak as they were; but given a free hand, would soon have established that.

At the moment however his forces were fighting a war with their hands tied behind their back! Every time they had gained territory the army was ordered to stop fighting for yet another conference taking place between politicians from the Netherlands and Indonesians bombarded to be representatives for Indonesia.

Who were these latter men? There had never been a democratic election, so how could these people represent the majority of the Indonesian people and know what they: the majority, wanted?

They were in the foreground, certainly, but only because they had pushed themselves there or had taken up arms for what they called fighting for the freedom of Indonesia. Once they would be in power, their so-called freedom fight would amount only to one thing: dictatorship and corruption! The majority of peaceful and honest Indonesians would never be heard. And the Dutch politicians were not dealing with these peaceful representatives but only with the loud troublemakers.

What nonsense! When the so-called political meetings broke down, which they always did, the army was then called in again, having to gain lost territory first, which could have been avoided if the Dutch politicians had only stuck to their demands.

It was frustrating and the army in the eyes of pro-Dutch Indonesians and pro-Dutch Chinese was losing credibility. They saw the so-called freedom fighters winning; law and order seemed to be missing and many pro-Dutch Indonesian citizens and pro-Dutch Chinese citizens were murdered and tortured, only through the incompetence of the government.

He held his own opinion of how the situation should be handled: First law and order. Then an honest negotiation with the really peaceful Indonesians of whom he knew there were many.

But certainly not with the type of freedom fighters who were murdering women and children, and pretended to fight for the freedom of Indonesia. Could Mas, the Sultan's nephew be one of those?

129

The war with Japan had not passed major Cane by lightly. His wife had become an invalid, suffering from frequent headaches and nightmares from having been beaten severely. His daughter's whereabouts were still vague. He had already lost his son in the battle of the Java Sea, a naval battle against a numerically far superior enemy. In this encounter when the odds were very much against them, the Dutch had lost practically every ship they possessed, apart from some submarines. In this battle again there was no cohesion between the different nationalities taking part, resulting in this disastrous consequence.

Richard Searl had visited him that evening, and had told him that his daughter was safe, protected by Mas. It was the news that he had hoped to hear. Thank God she was alive then. But could he believe a person like Mas these days? Had he not turned into a renegade? At least that was the name he was now known by.

Major Cane however could never believe that Mas deserved this bad name.

"I do not believe all the bad things they say about him," he said to his wife.

We know Mas, don't we? He has frequently visited us before the war. You and I have always liked him. Richard, Wong and Mas have always been good friends of Lily. Of course a man can change but I doubt that Mas ever would."

As far as his daughter was concerned however, he wondered what she had ever seen in Richard. Richard had always stood for freedom for Indonesia, where was his loyalty? He was also a friend of Mas and Mas was now a genuine freedom fighter, fighting him and his men. That was unfortunate, but he was certainly not a murderer. That he could never believe. The accusation that Mas murdered, tortured, mutilated and killed not only European but also Chinese women and children was certainly false in his opinion.

Richard had also informed him that Lily had married Wong. It was the first time he had heard it.

He knew Wong as a youngster and knew that Wong had always been keen on his daughter. But Lily had never given Wong an indication that she was interested; not even by a word that could be interpreted wrongly. She had always been careful to show that she held his friendship dear, but that was all. How did it come about that she married him? Why had she not waited for Lieutenant Hes? He was the kind of son in law he would have wished. He had seen Hes blowing a kiss to his daughter. He had held high hopes then that Richard would be replaced. How would Lily feel about Richard, once she knew that he was alive? Did she know that he had survived the war? Richard had not said anything about that.

And Richard had not visited him to tell him about Lily only. He had outright told him what he thought of him and it was not flattering what he had said.

"You are a coward," Richard had started accusingly. Fine; hard as it was to admit it; Major Cane knew it.

"You left us to ourselves in Tjipatat. And Lieutenant Hes was not there either."

"That is right, I had Lieutenant Hes transferred to the tank brigade to which he originally belonged. He was completely out of place in Tjipatat. He should never have been placed there. Nobody should have, it was a waste of men.

The place was a lost case. It could not be defended. The tank unit was where Hes belonged. That was where he was most useful. I finally gave him the order to leave Tjipatat and that was not only my own decision. Colonel Xant also wanted that."

"But you were to replace Hes. That is what Colonel Arlen ordered you to do. And you never turned up. That meant that Tjipatat was completely abandoned by officers. You deserted!"

"Yes; hard as it is for you to accept, your unit was expendable, yet was not evacuated in time as in my opinion it should have been. Again, I did not make that decision. I was; wrongly in my opinion, taken away from my own unit which was to defend the Tjiater pass."

"Does it not bother you to see the graves of the soldiers who were my friends, now lying on the lonely graveyard in Tjipatat because you did not follow orders?"

"Richard, this was war. I didn't want it this way. Do you think I did? My presence would have made no difference; you must believe me. No difference whatever. Tjipatat should have been evacuated in time. That would have been the correct decision. But as I told you, it was not up to me to make the decision as I saw it.

"I became a prisoner of war of the Japanese. It was there where I was confronted with naked reality. Have you never seen the graveyards along the river Kwai in Siam? These men were all expendable as far as the Japanese were concerned. It was the same story with Tjipatat. Everybody abandoned us. First Singapore fell then the Philippines. Do you know how it feels to be completely at the mercy of your enemies? We all, when we become expendable are left to die. It is the law of nature. It is the law of the jungle. It takes one to be prisoner of the Japanese to realise this truth.

"You all were equally expendable in Tjipatat. But not only you! We all lost the war. Look for yourself at the graves along the railroad in Siam, the ones I talk about. One grave for every sleeper; but of course you haven't. You fortunately were safe in Australia"

"That is right; that is where you were supposed to have sent us; I myself and Mas. That is where the Governor wanted Mas and me to go. But your clique of officers did not want that. No you put every obstacle in the way, so that we could not get there. Not thanks to your help did I eventually make it. I could easily never have made it and nearly drowned in the Indian Ocean. I have since heard that you also were part of a clique of officers that put yourselves above the law. And I am sure that my information is correct. You all decided that you knew better than the Governor. You did not even know that the Governor long before, foresaw what chaos would arise by not evacuating Mas.

"With a peaceful spokesman, the like of which Mas could have been now; would through his influence have brought the Dutch and the Indonesians together at this stage. You forever ruined that chance. I am sure judging from putting two and two together that you were part of a group of officers who misled Mas and myself, from trying to get away. But you were such a coward that you didn't want to be seen by me that you also belonged to that group. That is why you were not present in hotel Homann when I received my briefing, which was to accompany Mas to Australia. But I have discovered since, that you nevertheless were also present at the initial meeting in Hotel Homann. I will collect more and more evidence till I have definite proof that you raised your hand also: indicating that you were in agreement with the plan of Colonel Arlen thereby acting against the wishes of the Governor.

At first I would never have believed that you would do a thing like that to me, but I think that there is definite evidence of your betrayal of me.

"Because of you and your clique of officers in hotel Homann, are we now saddled with this impossible guerrilla war. You seem still to be so naive as to think that you can suppress this freedom feeling of the Indonesians by force? There will never be peace from now on, if the Indonesians don't get their independence. Do you really believe that we can turn the clock back to what it was like before the war, which is what you want? This guerrilla war is extremely destructive.

"I am not blaming you for the viewpoint you hold as far as the freedom of Indonesia is concerned. You are entitled to hold a different view than the one I hold. But your clique deceived us; Mas and me. You are equally guilty; have you no shame?

The army intends taking you to court, a military court, for what they consider misdeeds. Apparently more than one I have been told. One of which is that you are also accused of not helping an escaped prisoner. As it so happens he was a friend of mine, a comrade in arms. Do you know what that means? The doctor in camp Tamarkan in which you were the allied camp commander, tried to save his life. Again you were a coward on that occasion. You did not help Marcus that is his name; which is what you should have done in your capacity as Major in the forces. You did not dare to take any chances.

As a result of your cowardice Marcus was beheaded. Where is your conscience?

"I have been approached by the military court to be the prosecutor in your trial. And I have accepted. You deceived me but that is not the reason that I have accepted. Mainly I agreed to do this because I owe all my dead army friends; Marcus my beheaded friend lying in this lonely graveyard in Tamarkan included."

Richard's voice had raised a few decibels.

"What will Lily think about all this, you prosecuting me in a military trial?" Major Cane had touched a tender nerve and knew that he had scored. Lily would be broken-hearted, her father accused of being a coward.

But what about Marcus who had been so happy with his life, beheaded? What about all the others lying dead under their marble slabs which were already overgrown with moss on the grave yard in Tjipatat? Did I not owe my allegiance to them, my army friends in the first place?

I ignored his remark about what Lily would think.

"There is more; you are also accused of slapping your men in the face, even using your fist at times. Thereby you stooped as low as the Japanese; accepting their standards of behaviour, abhorrent to Dutch military practice" I continued accusingly. "I am sorry to prosecute you but only because you are Lily's father. I only came here to tell you that Lily is alive thank God. Mas will free her. He has promised. I had no other reason for coming to see you. Goodbye."

Richard had left him then before he could defend himself. Major Cane felt awful. Long ago he knew he was a coward. He remembered Breda and his humiliation at military college when he had refused to defend his honour when he was challenged to a dual. He had been scared!

And Richard had every reason to be angry and feel let down by him. It had been a dirty trick played on him. And Richard would never believe him that he was sorry later and that he finally had sent him to Tjilatjap in the hope that he would get away, knowing that Richard had always sailed yachts and was a good sailor.

As far as the case in Tamarkan was concerned however, what could he have done differently? He was still convinced that he had done the right thing not to agree with what the doctor had urged he should do. He also had persuaded Colonel Xant to transfer Lieutenant Hes. Not only because the lieutenant himself had asked for transfer to the tank unit to which he originally belonged, but secondly because he was a valiant officer. Hes had only been temporary delegated to training cadet officers with Captain Smyth. It would be such a pity if he were to be sacrificed at Tjipatat. What for? For no good reason at all. He didn't belong there in the first place. And secretly he liked Lieutenant Hes.

Secretly he would have liked to be like him, tall, good-looking and especially brave. Could he, Major Cane, only have been as brave! He would then have forced himself to proceed to Tjipatat like it or not and he would have fought to the last men. He would have died on the battlefield of course. Suddenly the terror of fear with which he was born, when he imagined himself dying on the battlefield, took possession of him again and he broke out in cold sweat.

Richard must have found out that he was involved in the officers' clique so that Mas could not reach Australia contrary to the wishes of the Governor. How did Richard find out? Somebody must have talked! And soon the Governor would know. Perhaps he already did. His military career would be in tatters.

Richard was going to bring this forward; even in court. That would expose all those officers who had not carried out the wishes of the Governor.

His conduct with regard to the beheading of this friend of Richard was going to be questioned. Here he felt that he could not have behaved differently although the doctor of the camp would probably condemn him too. The doctor would be in court asked by Richard to testify against him in his prosecution. What would his opinion be? The doctor had offered to help Marcus. That was brave but not wise and he was certain that in this case, he had taken the correct decision not to let the doctor have his way.

Slapping his soldiers the Japanese way was also one of the accusations made against him. Indeed; but this had been the only way to maintain at least some form of discipline. Abnormal situations required a different set of rules. How else could he have maintained even only that little remnant of discipline by other means? And Richard knew nothing of the circumstances! He had been sitting pretty in Australia safe from all the clatter of weapons, famine, fear as he had never experienced before, diseases such as cholera, dysentery, tropical ulcers, regular beatings by the Japanese for imaginary and petty offences, starvation etc. and this man was going to judge him in court. The world was unjust!

His thoughts returned to his daughter. Could it be true that she was alive? She would be his only child now that his son had died. She had been engaged to Richard. Was one of the reasons that he had Lieutenant Hes recalled, because he knew that Lieutenant Hes liked his daughter and that he had also noticed that she had danced with him at the Villa Isola parties and liked him too? How much better would it have been if she had waited for Lieutenant Hes instead of marrying this Chinese Wong, whom he knew was also in favour of Indonesian independence, being a friend of Richard?

Why a Chinese would be in favour of Indonesian independence, was very difficult to understand. The Chinese would be discriminated against, if Indonesia ever became independent. Why did Wong not understand that?

His thoughts returned to the question of what had happened to his daughter and her whereabouts. Although he had heard about her at last and that she was safe, it still kept his thoughts occupied. How could Mas rescue her? He himself had looked for her without even knowing where to look. Richard had spoken to Mas and Mas had said that he would free her. But still Lily was not free even now. The war was finished more than six months ago!

Ten days later he got the letter handed to him late at night.

"It was delivered by an Indonesian katjong," his batmen said. He tore open the letter; "your daughter will arrive at Weltevreden station on the morning train." signed Mas.

"Where is the katjong," he asked the batman.

"He went away, he seemed frightened being here, but he told me, that the man who gave him the letter had given him five guilders for delivering it. He also said that the man who gave him the letter was heavily armed and wore a black band around his upper arm with something red on it."

A freedom fighter! Could the man have been Mas himself perhaps? The letter was signed by him yes; but the man who brought the letter could also only have been his messenger.

Major Cane felt grateful, she was still alive then and he would see her tomorrow. He had not seen Lily for four years. From Batavia she would take the connecting train to Bandoeng from where he could meet her at the station. Would she look like her mother? Richard was in Batavia; would Mas have informed him of Lily's arrival also? Did Lily know that Richard was alive? Would Mas have told him?

Major Cane recalled that he himself had never been able to tell his daughter that Richard was not killed in the plane disaster in Tjilatjap. Richard, thanks to the deceitful plan of which he, major Cane, was partly guilty, had been refused entry into the plane. He had wanted; even planned to tell Lily that, but it was the last thing he heard that himself before he was interned as a POW. Since then all contact between him and his family: in particular Lily, had been lost. Maybe that was the reason that she had married Wong. Of course, she must have thought that Richard was dead. How unfortunate.

Suddenly it occurred to him that he could have been killed by the freedom fighter that brought the letter, if the man had wanted to do so. Where was security? The compound he lived in was a military camp with a gate and a sentry post! How did the nightly visitor manage to enter so easily? The freedom fighter that had brought the letter certainly did not mean to harm him. He already could have done so had he wanted to. The only conclusion he could come to, was that the silent night visitor had indeed been Mas himself and that Lily owed her freedom to him.

"Mas, I am not disappointed in you," he whispered.

Chapter 15

Sooner or later, I would meet Lily again. How would I behave towards her? I knew now that she was married to Wong, thinking that I was dead. She was four years older; more than four years had passed since we had seen each other the last time and everything was different. We could not possibly carry on where we had left off. My head told me that I should forget about her, but my instincts did not want to.

Lily had been part of my life. I had longed for her and dreamt about her all these four years of our forced separation! Could I give her up so easily? "She is married," I told myself time and again when I thought of her, but she kept returning in my thoughts and in my dreams. And we had planned to marry on her twenty-second birthday. She was twenty-six years old now and we had not only lost four years of our lives, but we had lost each other. Yet she could not feel so different about me. I knew that she had been deeply in love with me once.

All the same she was unattainable to me now. To make matters worse I had accepted the task to collect evidence against her father's conduct during the war. The committee that commissioned me had only mentioned his name to me in passing. Yet it was obvious that by sending me to Japan to find and interview the Japanese camp commander of the camp Tamarkan in Siam that the army wanted to hear evidence from me in favour of, but as I later understood, rather against Major Cane preferably.

Lily's father had lost his son, Lily's brother when the latter perished in the battleship "De Ruyter" sunk in the combined allied fleet sea battle of the Java Sea against the Japanese. The Japanese had been more than victorious in this encounter, perhaps because there had been no cohesion among the allies. There were too many nationalities involved and too many different opinions on how it should have been fought.

Lily's mother had suffered hardship humiliation and famine. She had been kept in a women's concentration camp, ruled by a particularly brutal and callous Japanese camp commander called Sonei who was executed after the war for beastly crimes against the women. She was suffering from severe headaches and often woke up during the night screaming, plagued with nightmares. I felt deeply sorry for her, but I could not find pity in my heart for Major Cane.

Since I had accepted my commission, which mainly was to find out what exactly happened at Tamarkan camp in Thailand during the war; I had also heard that out of cowardice he had never appeared in Tjipatat, where he had been sent in order to relieve Lieutenant Hes. That meant that I held yet another grievance against him: namely abandoning my friends in Tjipatat resulting indirectly in their deaths!

Lieutenant Hes had been called away to his tank unit, which was trying desperately to regain the stronghold, the Tjiater pass, and the airport Soebang in order to stop the upward march of the Japanese to Bandoeng. In the process

Lieutenant Hes had become wounded, a bullet had passed through his thigh but the wound was now healed and I knew he was in active duty again although he still walked with a limp as a result of the injury. I met him briefly and we talked about the sad event in Tjipatat four years ago. He also felt deeply sorry about the unnecessary loss of life of his former recruits some of whom had become good friends to him.

I informed him that he would be called to testify in the pending court case against major Cane.

"Why is major Cane on trial?" he wanted to know.

"It has something to do with his war record," I said, but he had to be satisfied when I told him that the case was still in it's early stages and that I therefore could not tell him more. He had become a Captain and he held a medal for bravery, awarded for carrying his dying captain to the first field hospital post, in spite of the fact that the bullet through his thigh had broken a bone and he was bleeding heavily. Up to that time I did not even know that he knew Lily and that he was in love with her. We had never mentioned her name because there was no occasion to do so.

The week after my meeting with Mas near Tjilan I received the message from him, which I had been waiting for, namely that Lily would be arriving at Weltevreden, the station of Batavia. It was already near June 1946. How could it be possible that I had not seen her all these years? Although four and a half years is a long time, the years seemed to have flown by.

For Lily, Batavia would only be a short stop on her way to Bandoeng where she would join her father and mother whom she had not seen since the occupation of Indonesia by the Japanese, now more than four years ago. Lily had been free during the Japanese occupation on account of her marriage to Wong. Yet Wong had not escaped the war unscathed. Mas had already told me that.

And where was Wong? The message from Mas had not mentioned him. I decided that I would go to meet Lily at the station. I had to confront myself with the reality that Lily was lost for me but I still had to see her again; I just had to. We could not part just like that! Mas must have felt the same: otherwise he would not have let me know that she was arriving.

Had Mas told her that I was alive? She believed all through the war that I was dead.

The night before, I hardly slept but tossed and turned repeatedly. What would she look like? Would I recognise her; would she recognise me? Did she think of me sometimes? The train coming in was a relief train, bringing women and children from occupied territory, territory occupied by freedom fighters as they called themselves. I had been at the station hours before, getting more and more nervous pacing the platform up and down. Would there be a hitch? Maybe Mas had it wrong. After all he was not in complete control himself. The Dutch military also were involved in the evacuation and could have made a mistake. The more I thought about it, the more nervous I became.

My fears were unfounded.

"Lily," I shouted when I saw her stepping down on the platform. She turned and stood nailed to the ground, as though she did not comprehend who I was.

"It is I, Richard." I ran towards her, embraced and kissed her. She looked bewildered.

"You are alive! It can't be," she sobbed. "Oh what can I say? Richard you look different but you look even more handsome!"

"Did Mas not tell you that I am alive?" I asked her. She held my face and sobbed and sobbed.

"You don't understand Richard. I thought you were dead."

"I know Lily," I said, "the plane in which I was supposed to be a passenger, crashed and caught fire. Luckily I was not on board."

"But your name was on the list."

"Yes officially, but I was refused passage."

"You are alive, thank God." She embraced me again. "It is so good to see you. How are you, what has happened to you?"

"I know you are married Lily, I only came here to see you again. I needed to see you again, I just had to."

"Richard, I was so heartbroken when I heard you were dead. And when Wong wanted to marry me it did not matter to me. Nothing mattered to me any more. Wong was so good to me. He knew that I married him to forget you. He never made demands on me but I know that he needs me now. I can't undo things."

"And I Lily: what about me?" She looked more mature; she had also suffered which was noticeable from her face. No longer just the glamorous girl I had fallen in love with and who had once appealed to my physical, instinctive senses mainly. No: what this Lily did to me now, was worse, much worse. She was part of my heart I realised once more. I would always miss her terribly and my life would be empty with that awful feeling of always longing for her. I pressed her close to me and for a tender magic moment while I held her, I could feel her resolve wavering. Could she not hear my heart that was laid bare before her? Then she slowly freed herself from my embrace. Her beautiful green eyes with specks of brown looked up at me.

"It is too late for you and I, Richard. Time has passed us by. It came our way on the Ringgit but we could not grab it then. It was beyond our means. Everything has changed now. The circumstances, oh it is impossible but you are alive, thank God. If only I had known that you were alive. What can I say Richard? You don't know what it was like. I owe Wong my life."

She kissed me, "I am married to Wong. I don't love him as I should; he knows it but he needs me. He needs me very badly. You will understand when you see him. He has been good to me Richard. You don't know how he was tortured. Being married to me put him under suspicion by the Japanese. He protected me as much as he could. I can't abandon him. He is not well Richard; the Japanese torture left him an invalid. His lungs are bad and he won't recover. The doctor told him that he is lucky to be alive. Don't make it more difficult for me than it is already. Goodbye Richard, you will always be part of my life; a good positive influence, but our lives went different ways, we have to part. I will always think of you as we were on the Ringgit.

"And to think that we were to be married!" She shook her head wanting in a physical way to rid herself of the mental agony she was enduring.

"Please keep in touch with me Richard; please keep in touch with me and Wong. He will be so pleased to hear that you are alive. He was very sad when he thought you had died. We all were." Her eyes were full of tears again.

She boarded the train. The shrill whistle blew and with it the train set in motion. With it disappeared my dreams and a part of me. I was totally desolate. Why had I survived this war and the political upheaval when so many of my friends had died? Yet I was alive. I owed my dead friends that they would get a hearing and a hearing they were to get even if it would hurt Lily. I had an obligation to my dead friends. That I could never forget. It was like a quirk of fate that I would be the one left to do it. Yes it would hurt Lily and perhaps bring to an end the relationship, whatever there was left of it, for good. I had no choice. The military court wanted to investigate Major Cane's behaviour just before and during the war. I was given the opportunity to do it and I wanted to expose whoever was responsible for the death of my friends in Tjipatat. That I was used by Colonel Arlen for his own ends to cover up his incompetence by focussing the attention on major Cane, I was not yet aware of. Lily's father was going to be the scapegoat and I was given the ammunition to shoot the goat, thinking in all honesty that I did the right thing by my friends.

Chapter 16

It was not until two months later that I met up with the Governor again. He had been unavoidably detained on a visit to the Netherlands. This fact as it turned out later, proved to have unwanted consequences, which never could have been foreseen at the time.

"There is something fishy here, the total does not add up to his character," the Governor addressed me. "We know him don't we? The whole purpose of you getting in touch with Mas at great peril to yourself; seems to have been wasted effort now. What a pity!" He got up from his chair, deep frowns appearing on his brow.

Our talk had lasted no more than five minutes. He walked to the window of his mountain retreat. From there he had a beautiful view of the scenery of the Preanger. He probably needed a pleasant panorama to clear his mind and to think that some of the things that he had done after the war still mattered. In the lull that ensued, I thought for a while about what he Governor had said. Almost reluctantly I spoke:

"It probably does add up to his character now; the way he acts recently," I said. "He has changed it seems to me; I did find something wrong with him when we spoke with each other the last time. He mentioned that even if his parents were killed and if that was a good thing for the Indonesian freedom cause, that he then would condone it.

"Did he say that?"

"He did, and he was perfectly serious." The Governor paced up and down looking at the floor:

"Then I must reluctantly conclude that there is no point talking to him any longer. I regret that very much. He appears to have become a fanatic. The elite Indonesians have also dropped him. They have let me know, that they no longer consider Mas a spokesman for them. They do not agree with his stand and his tactics any longer. He is thought to have blood on his hands, although I personally still don't believe that this is so.

"The moderate Indonesians also want independence of course; but by peaceful means. I also heard that it is not the only objection they have. They also say that he was a puppet of the Japanese in wartime.

"We cannot negotiate with Mas any longer if indeed it is proven that he is guilty of murder.

What about the recent accusation that he was involved in the massacre in camp Tjilan? Do you believe that he was involved in the killing of women and children in that camp?"

"I would hate to admit it to myself, if the answer to your question might be yes! It cannot be. That I will never believe. I have known Mas from my youth. I know who is responsible for this news. His name is Captain Hensen. I met him when I borrowed a jeep from him the day I was looking for Mas. He is an honest man and he must firmly believe it himself. One of these days I hope that he will find out that he was wrong and he will then apologise to Mas personally I am sure. He is that kind of man.

"Still I have difficulty with an armband that has been found in the liberated camp. I have identified it because the military asked me to do it. Of course I also wanted to be sure myself. It was indeed the armband Mas wore when I met him, now approximately two months ago before this latest incident. I wish I could be wrong. I must be wrong! There must be another satisfactory explanation.

"I would now like to tell you something. But this has nothing to do with why Mas behaves the way he does recently. I had a long time to think about it, in fact the whole war. I eventually came to the conclusion that Mas and myself were hampered on purpose in our attempt to escape to Australia contrary to your wishes."

"The last time you spoke to me about your escape to Australia you did mention that you encountered one difficulty after another. Is that what you are referring to?"

"Yes, but at that time I only had suspicions and nothing more. There was no point telling you what I thought. However I now not only think but I am sure that we were hampered in our escape on purpose."

"Hampered by whom?"

"Rather hampered by many people you should say. At Andir, which was the most logical place to leave from by plane, and in fact where we had been ordered to go to, in order to be evacuated; we were told that there was no place for us in the plane and that we needed to go to Tjilatjap. The officer who had our names on the list was a lieutenant and the officer who refused us passage and told us to proceed to Tjilatjap instead, was a captain. Hence by superiority of rank the lieutenant had no option but to give way.

"Suppose this captain belonged to a clique of officers which wanted to prevent our escape, so that we, but especially of course, Mas, because he was the one you wanted to evacuate mainly, should never reach Australia and instead counted on the fact that the Japanese would use him for propaganda purposes because he was such a conspicuous figure."

"Unfortunately that is exactly what has happened," the Governor interrupted.

"That is the point I wanted to make," I said.

"Most unfortunate for him," the Governor shook his head. "Of course from then on he had to broadcast whatever the Japanese wished him to say. And by doing that, he lost the support of the intelligentsia of the Indonesians who now consider that he was a puppet of the Japanese regime and no longer wish to see him as a member of the "Freedom for Indonesia" movement which is the party Mas fervently wanted to belong to. That party has now been robbed of an important spokesman."

"That is the way I see it it also." I said. Most unfortunate."

"But you could also argue that Mas perhaps could have escaped by himself to Australia even in war time so as not having to make the broadcasts the Japanese wanted him to make. For a native this I believe would have been very possible. Why did he not at least try that? He did not, which is surprising. Some Indonesians have accused him exactly of that and maybe they have a point here."

"I can tell you exactly why he didn't. He could not. The Japanese blackmailed him. Had he done so my fiancee, who was also a friend of his since his youth would have been killed. The Japanese had found out that she was very important to him and threatened him that she would be beheaded if he tried."

"What awful predicament he was in."

"And even now he doesn't want to clear his name by explaining to his accusers the reason why he never absconded to Australia. I am the only one who knows the true story."

"Did you find your fiancee?" the Governor changed the subject. The last time we spoke you mentioned that you were engaged before the war and that you had heard nothing of her whereabouts. Any progress there?"

"Yes I found her. Unfortunately too late! She got married in the meantime."

"I am awfuly sorry," the Governor said.

"She has only recently been released from enemy occupied territory," I continued. "She thought that I was dead; that I was killed in a plane crash. Somehow the news leaked out, false as it was that I was on the plane that crashed in Tjilatjap. My name happened to be on the list and there were no survivors. She saw the list and concluded that I had perished."

"What rotten luck! How unfortunate that she drew the wrong conclusion.

"I want to come back to what you said before Richard," the Governor resumed. "Do you mean to say that there could be some high ranking officers in the army who were opposed to freedom for Indonesia in the near future?"

"I am no longer only thinking that. I am nearly convinced about it. I perhaps later, will be in possession of proof of what I am saying. At one time; as I said, it was pure speculation. Not any longer however. This latest information came my way by pure chance.

Mrs. Brink, the widow of Colonel Brink promised me that she will supply me with notes that she found in her late husbands belongings. And because my name was mentioned in them she has offered me these notes, which were made by him and refer to a meeting held in the boardroom in hotel Homann where this matter was discussed. I don't think the feeling is universal among army officers, no certainly not, but there is this clique of officers that felt that way and maybe still do."

"That is a lot of accusation so far not backed by evidence, at least not yet, for what you say. I am not saying that you could not be correct: in fact I rather believe that you are correct. However I would like to see some concrete evidence first that could back up your theory because the implication could well be serious."

"As I have already told you it is no longer only theory but I haven't yet got the notes in my possession to prove what I am saying."

"Then that being so does not get us any further," he said still walking up and down in deep thought with his hands behind his back as he always did when he was thinking hard.

"If Mas has come to the same conclusion as you yourself that there was an attempt to stop you both from reaching Australia, would that explain his present behaviour? Is he resentful? Is that why you said you can explain his behaviour?"

"No sir; that is not what I meant when I said I know why he behaves the way he does. He is not looking for revenge. It is different with me: I do! I nearly drowned. No, with Mas it is a different thing. Mas; as far as I am aware, doesn't hold anything against the army as such. He may not even agree with my view about this clique of officers who opposed your intention wanting to send Mas and myself to Australia. I have not spoken to him about that.

"No, I think there is an altogether different problem here. Mas is fighting himself. He must realise that he has lost the support he at one time held among the intelligentsia of the Indonesians as you already have stated. Through no fault of his own, he was made a puppet of the Japanese. He is still tainted by having been made a spokesman for the Japanese albeit under pressure. He will never be clean of that again. Yet he still wants to be important. He is ambitious. The only way he can be that now is by force: taking up arms, which he did. To be a freedom fighter is still acceptable in my view and possibly in his thinking too.

"Remember we, the Dutch, fought the Spaniards for independence in the "eighty year war" and that was very acceptable in our history. Then why not the freedoms fight of the Indonesians? But that still does not condone the method he uses to achieve his goal, if he is found guilty of murder and which I will never believe." We were quiet for a while. Then the Governor took up the conversation again.

"How was your fiancée freed and how is her health?"

"For her freedom and well being I have to thank Mas again. He promised me when I saw him last, that he would do all he could to free her, which he has done. It may not sound strange to you that I have implicit faith in Mas because I have noticed that you have the same faith in him. In this respect I am sure that he has done his utmost that my former fiancee came to no harm.

"He has protected her all through the war. In her case there was one extra danger because she happens to be the daughter of Major Cane and if the Indonesian freedom fighters had found out, that she is the daughter of a high-ranking military officer, she could well have been killed or held for ransom. It may well be that they did find out and that but for Mas' intervention she would not be alive. And I couldn't have done anything to help her. Thank God; nothing like that has happened."

143

"Coming back to Mas again the Governor resumed, "in a way I also blame myself for having been absent on business the last two months in the Netherlands. We should have negotiated with Mas immediately after you had spoken with him. I should have postponed my business in the Netherlands even if only to meet Mas again before I went. His father would have liked me to do that. The problem is that I can now no longer honestly negotiate with him in the belief that he almost certainly murdered women and children.

"For having missed that chance to speak to him I am deeply sorry." I nodded. I understood his reasoning perfectly. His honesty indeed forbade him to negotiate with a possible murderer. Also because he was the highest official spokesman in the land he could not do that.

"Still that same reasoning does not apply to you Richard. Why don't you get in touch with the "go in between?" That doesn't expose you to danger, should it?"

"That is indeed what I really regret; this difficulty to get in touch with him," I said.

"If I only could get in touch with him more easily, we could then communicate much more frequently and more often on a personal level. He gave me the name of the contact you referred to. I could perhaps try to get in touch with him as you suggest. I, for my own satisfaction, want to ask him how it is that his armband was found in the camp which was liberated by the military and why five women and three children were found killed and mutilated. The question haunts me. I want to ask Mas outright if he is guilty."

"Then you are still not certain about Mas, are you?" the Governor said.

"I also find it difficult to know what the truth is since you found his armband at the scene of the crime. You must follow your own conscience and instinct. But don't take unnecessary risks; you have done enough, having risked your life on more than one occasion."

I thought of Lily again. Was it not ridiculous that I could have done nothing to help her? She was lost for me in any case although I had found her. But even if only for my own satisfaction, did I need to see her again. Lily and Wong together. Were they happy? I also had to speak to Mas again. Ask him outright if he was responsible for the killings and if he was not, to explain to me why his armband was found at the scene of the crime?

More than ever did I need to speak to him. In any case, I also had to tell him that the Governor no longer wished to speak to him; no longer considered him a spokesman for the Indonesian freedom negotiations with the Governor as long as he was under the suspicion of guilt about what happened at Tjilan. That would be very difficult for me to say to him. It would be quite a blow to him. And I was sorry deeply sorry. Not only for Mas alone, but also for all the innocents who were going to die in this unnecessary guerrilla war. And I still had not progressed any further with my feelings toward Lily if ever I would. As far as that was concerned my feelings were in a complete turmoil. The case was further complicated by the fact that I was the prosecutor for the army, in the trial against her father!

Chapter 17

Wong was lying on his bed. He didn't look well to me. We were happy to see each other again. It had been years ago and a lot had happened in those years.

When we shook hands, I immediately felt that his hands were scarred. Although I tried to appear as though I was not surprised he had noticed my embarrassment.

"A remnant of Japanese "hospitality"! he joked, as he extended his hands and showed them to me.

"They put the leg of a chair on your open hand and then sat on the chair for hours, interrogating you. The tendons of my hands are partially cut; they did not survive."

I kept holding his hand in mine. His grip at one time immensely strong, I remembered, was weak now.

"How are you Wong; it has been ages."

"Four years Richard. I am no longer what I used to be. But you," he said, "you look good. We all; Mas, Lily and I thought you were dead and here you are well and you have become a captain I see. When will you be demobilised?"

"That won't be for quite a while Wong, if ever. The army still needs me. I'll probably make it my career now. Indonesia will become independent and there will be no more work for me in civil service as a controller. I am the last of the breed you can say. What are you doing these days?"

"Would you believe it, I also work for the army; intelligence they call it. They are very good to me. When I am ill they allow me sick leave and sometimes Lily takes over. She knows more about the job than I do, but then she has always been the clever one. I am a burden to every one now."

"Don't say that Wong. The doctors can perform miracles these days and there are a lot of new wonder drugs also. You will get better you'll see." Lily walked into the room with a tray of coffee cups, a jug of coffee and pressed citrus juice. She sat down on the bed.

"Is your chest any better this morning Wong?" She patted his hands gently.

"I was also drowned Richard," he continued. The Japanese wanted information from me about weapons. Some gangs of Indonesians around where we lived, had taken up arms against the Japanese you understand.

Chinese, including myself, were immediately suspected. I knew nothing and that was fortunate.

"At first they accused Lily pretending to find out if she knew something. Of course it was all an act. Lily was completely innocent and they knew that from the beginning. But they wanted a guilty person and afterwards they focussed on me. You don't know what their secret police is like. First they beat me. They broke my front teeth and sat on my hands via the leg of a chair as I said. I had nothing to confess. Out of frustration they eventually put me in a round glass bowl, a large one; then closed the lid.

There was only one small opening in the lid for the air to escape. The glass bowl stood in the middle of a room full of mirrors on the walls and on the ceiling. Then they opened a water tap inside the bowl. The water was rising and I could not close the tap. I fought like mad to get out, but the glass of the bowl was strong. I could see myself drowning in all the mirrors on the walls surrounding me. At the last moment when I was already unconscious they got me out."

"May I interrupt; would you like some coffee?" Lily turned to me. I nodded to her. Wong's story was horrible. How could the Japanese, anybody, do that to another human being?

"After they had revived me," Wong continued, "they asked me to sign a document declaring that I held no ill feelings against Japan for the way they had treated me because they now believed that I was after all innocent. So they said. Thinking that that would be the end of the matter, I was very eager to sign of course. No sooner had I done so, or they put me back in the bowl. They said that because I was so eager to sign, I must be guilty. When I was back in the glass bowl the tap was turned on again and then they said that this time they would let me drown if I did not confess.

I can tell you that I would have confessed to anything I knew, had I known something they wanted to know. Fortunately I did not know anything. I would almost certainly have betrayed no matter who it might be, out of sheer panic. You don't know what it is like, to see yourself drown in all the mirrors of that room. They took me out of the bowl again when I was already unconscious and then they let me go for good this time.

They now realised that there was nothing I could tell them. I am still surprised that they did not kill me anyway. I was of no use to them any longer. Since then my chest is not all that good. I am very breathless."

I drank my coffee in silence. No wonder he was ill. I strongly felt that I should not have come. I had no business here. Something made me do it, I did not know what. I had told myself that I wanted to see Wong. He was my friend and he was ill.

Lily had told me that at the station in Batavia, when I met her there. But Wong was not the only reason. I wanted to know more. Were Lily and Wong happy? Was Lily happy? She had told me that she did not love Wong but that she felt gratitude towards him. I wondered how much gratitude is needed to replace absent love, the genuine love that she once felt for me. And what right did Wong have over me? She had been my fiancée and we had pledged to marry each other. Circumstances had brought Lily and Wong together; not love, at least not Lily's love.

But I should not think like that any longer. Lily and I were things of the past; only memories to look back to. No longer desires to be kept alive. The demons on the isle of Bali had denied us our love. "You can't turn the clock back," I kept reminding myself. What was it again that Lily said to me at one time?

"Beautiful events are only loaned to us. The only true possessions we have, and which linger, are the happy memories of those events."

Lily and I were memories. I felt that my presence only caused awkwardness. To change the mood I asked for Mas.

"I see him regularly," Lily said. I was utterly surprised.

"Where?" I asked her.

"I can't tell you that; the military would like to know; wouldn't you Richard?"

"Mas has nothing to fear from me Lily," I said.

"I know that, but you may inadvertently mention it. You are still his friend, aren't you Richard? I sincerely hope you are."

"I certainly was," I said hesitatingly.

"You said was?" Lily asked surprised. "Not any longer? You and Mas were always inseparable."

"You forget," Wong interrupted, "that Mas has become a freedom fighter. He thereby has officially become an enemy of Richard."

"Yes but what nonsense; surely only in name; he would never hurt Richard nor Richard him. He only wants freedom for Indonesia; what is wrong with that?" Lily retorted.

"Nothing as long as it is not accomplished by force and murder," I said.

"Are you accusing him of murder Richard?"

"Aren't you Lily? Do you see this torn armband here," I continued, producing the torn black armband with the red elephant painted on it from my coat pocket.

"This armband was found in camp Tjilan. It used to belong to Mas. The camp was freed by the military but they could not prevent the murder of five European women and three Chinese children who were hacked to death before the military could reach them. The children were three, five and six years old. If you see him so often, ask him where he was on Tuesday July the third when these women and children were murdered in camp Tjilan?"

"Why that is easy; I paid him a visit on that day."

"No you did not," Wong corrected her. "You celebrated your mother's birth day; do you not remember? We had just been evacuated from occupied territory six weeks before that."

Lily blushed; I could see that she had been caught out lying.

"Oh of course," she said, "it slipped my mind. I don't believe you; anyone could have worn an armband like that. You are implying that Mas murdered the women and children?"

"No, I don't believe that he personally did that, but he must be held responsible yes."

"How horrible," Wong said."How can anybody kill a child? Could Mas have done that? No; I can't believe that either, you must be mistaken Richard."

"I sincerely hope I am," I said.

"You want to prosecute my father through the military I heard; is that true Richard?"

"Unfortunately that is so Lily, I am deeply sorry for you."

"Why do you do this to him Richard, no matter what he did or did not do, please don't prosecute him. He is a broken man, he lost his beloved son, my brother in the battle of the Java Sea and my mother is no longer a companion to him; she is too ill to care. Please Richard, please don't." Her face was full of tears.

"I have to Lily, my dead friends deserve a hearing too. I walked out the door and felt awful. I had not expected that she already knew about the pending court case, since I had agreed with the Judge of the military court that he would wait until I returned from Japan with evidence against her father. Again I felt that I should not have come to see Lily and Wong. I did not belong with them any more. There was no happiness in seeing Wong a cripple compared to his former self. Lily followed me to the gate.

"Do you prosecute my father because I married Wong, Richard? Do you hate me because I did not wait for you? I thought you were dead; can't you understand? I wanted to marry you. The war upset all that. Richard don't be hateful, I can't bear it. I wanted to wait for you."

Her voice was thick with emotion. I realised that no matter what I would be saying now, was going to be of any help. I would not be sincere about how I felt. I was confused in my own mind. I started the car and drove off without replying to her. In the rear mirror I looked at Lily, a small figure at the gate. I was not proud of myself.

***

When I arrived at my quarters I wondered why Lily had lied. Had she really been to see Mas or had she gone to her mother's birthday celebration when Wong corrected her first statement? She obviously had wanted to protect Mas by giving him this alibi. I very much wanted to know the truth because it could exonerate Mas if she had really been with him. But why was she there anyway? She also had said that she saw Mas often. Did Mas visit her and Wong together or did Lily go to see him, perhaps on her own? I could not be certain and a nagging doubt remained in my mind. I also had to see Mas again. He expected me to inform him of the date when he would meet with the Governor and that meeting was not going to take place now.

One week later I went into the village Kemajoran. Although it officially was considered a safe area: meaning that it was not infiltrated with freedom fighters, I took no chances but carried my Smith and Wesson under my blouse in a holster. It could not be seen that I was carrying a gun, yet I could get at it very quickly in case I needed it.

I left my jeep at the outskirts of the kampong and went into the kampong itself by foot. The kepala kampong (headman of the village) knew Haroen Janoedi.

"What do you want with him; has he done something wrong?" seeing my military uniform.

"No not at all," I said. "I just want him to deliver a message for me."

"I will send for him. Would you like to wait in my house tuan?" I thanked him but refused. In any case I was safer in the open. I could not be ambushed there. He called a little boy.

"Do you know where Haroen Janoedi lives? Ask him to come here; this gentleman wants to speak to him, hurry," he told the boy who ran off to deliver the message. It didn't take long. He was about forty years old, and wore an Indonesian headdress worn by nobility. His whole appearance spoke of a confident man of distinction.

"You wish to speak to me?" he asked bowing his head.

"Mas gave me your name, I am a friend of his; my name is Richard Searle."

"Ah," he said; "Mas told me that you would come with a message for him."

"Yes, but unfortunately I have bad news for Mas; the meeting with the Governor-General has been called off." Haroen Janoedi showed his surprise by raising his eyebrows.

"Mas indeed told me that there was going to be a meeting with the Governor. Do you know why this meeting has been cancelled?" Of course Haroen didn't know and I could not tell him why.

"I know that Mas is accused of the murders in camp Tjilan. Is that the reason why the meeting with the Governor has been cancelled? I can tell you that Mas was never at camp Tjilan" he volunteered. I was flabbergasted. How did he know about camp Tjilan and know that Mas had not been there? He saw my surprise.

"On that day Lily was with him at his house above Bandoeng, I am not allowed to tell you where. I was there also. Mas could not possibly have been at camp Tjilan." This came as a complete surprise to me.

"Lily was with him?"

"Yes she meets often with him but her husband doesn't know. She is his concubine." I could have been knocked down with a feather.

"What you say is true?" I asked him.

"Of course," he said. "You seem surprised; did you not know?"

I was dazed. None of this had I ever suspected. Was Janoudi also lying wanting to give Mas an alibi or was he speaking the truth? I turned to him:

"I would like to meet Mas. If he can prove his innocence to me as far as camp Tjilan is concerned and it seems that he can; we can still have a deal with the Governor."

Lily apparently had spoken the truth. She had not told Wong that she had gone to visit Mas that day. Instead she had told him that she went to her mother's birthday. But what was really the truth? It was important for me to know. She had given Mas an alibi if she indeed had been with Mas that day. But then she had lied to Wong. Did Wong know that she was Mas' concubine?

Wong had suggested that my friendship with Mas probably was not the same any longer since Mas had become a freedom fighter. But he had not given his own opinion about Mas. Mas had protected him and Lily throughout the war. As such he was bound to be grateful. And we; Wong, Mas, Lily and I myself had been the closest of friends. But did he condone Mas' behaviour lately?

I wanted to meet Mas more than ever now. I arranged that Haroen would stipulate a place of meeting in territory not occupied with freedom fighters,

In that way I did not have to fear for my safety. At the same time the date and hour would only be known to me when Haroen would come to fetch me and would stay with me and not let me out of sight, so that it would not be possible for me to telephone someone or contact someone, had I wanted Mas to be apprehended. His safety would thereby be guaranteed like mine was in turn. I went back to my quarters with my head in turmoil

Five days later Haroen called. This time he wore a European dress, no headdress to show that he was of noble birth. We travelled in my car to the centre of Bandoeng. I knew the district. The restaurant where the car came to a stop, had changed little. The meeting place was chosen by Mas. Lily and I had been here sometimes before the war, when we were still deeply in love and wanted to be by ourselves. How long ago that seemed now.

Haroen and I made our way upstairs, we could talk more easily there. Mas was already seated at a table, his back turned to the entrance. It was immediately apparent to me that he felt completely at ease here, otherwise he would have been alert and would have watched the people walking in.

"Hello Mas," I said, "we meet again." We shook hands warmly. In no way did he show any trace of embarrassment.

"You got my armband haven't you?" were his first words. "Is that why it took you so long to contact me?"

"Not only that; the governor was called to the Netherlands. He was away for six weeks. He only recently returned. As far as your armband is concerned however, I have to say that; yes Mas, the Governor believes that you were in camp Tjilan and that you may be responsible for the murdered women and children."

"First let me say that I was shocked to hear it. I very much regret it happened. But I was never there Richard."

"Then how did your armband got there? It is yours isn't it?"

"It is, except that I did not wear it. I suspect that one of my men stole it and left it there to incriminate me. Don't you believe me Richard?"

"There is nothing I want to believe more Mas; I want to believe in your innocence but my instinct does not believe in you. You have changed Mas."

"Yes; a lot has changed Richard. Once we were the best of friends. This freedom for Indonesia keeps us apart. Basically of course we are still and always will be good friends. Only our interests separate us. You are also one of us you know; why don't you join our movement? We need you: you were born and brought up in this country. Why is your loyalty not with us? Lily's loyalty is."

"What has Lily got to do with all this?"

"She works for us."

"In what way does she work for you Mas?"

"Forget it Richard; forget that I ever mentioned it to you."

"I want to know Mas, I want to know where I stand."

"I said forget it Richard, it would not make you happy to know. I should not have spoken. Let us turn to business; can we have that meeting with the Governor-General? I am anxious to stop this useless fighting. It only causes death and destruction."

"I am so glad to hear you say that Mas; I am sure the Governor will be delighted too. I have to tell him that we met and that you were not responsible for the death of women and children in camp Tjilan. It will most likely be in Tjisarua again: the meeting I mean. I'll pass the message to you via Haroen; is that agreed?"

When I got to my quarters the nagging doubt returned. How did Mas know that I had his armband? The only persons I had shown the band to were Wong and Lily. He must have got this information from Lily. I wanted to believe that Mas was innocent of the murder of the women and children at camp Tjilan. Lily was anxious for me to believe that she was with him on the day; thereby wanting to exonerate him. Yet Lily had told Wong that she had gone to celebrate her mother's birthday. What was the truth? Did she go to Mas and did Haroen really see her there that day, giving Mas an alibi or were they both lying? Did she not meet Mas that day and was she instead at her mother's birthday? I was convinced that Lily knew more than she had wanted me to know.

Haroen also wanted to convince me that Mas was innocent. And Mas himself?

"I was never there Richard," he had said to me. For the first time in my life did I not believe him! Too many people, including Mas, had tried too hard to make me believe that he was innocent. It had exactly the opposite effect. Mas was guilty! I needed good evidence to the contrary first that he was not; before I could believe him. Could my suspicion about what exactly happened in camp Tjilan be wrong?

Chapter 18

The morning mist jealously guarded the mountain scenery of the Preanger and in particular the Tjiater pass through which I was travelling in my jeep. In a few hours the sun would wrestle through, when the mist would resentfully be forced to give up its secrets and the majestic scenery would be exposed like the face of a bride, when her veil is withdrawn at the end of the wedding ceremony.

How ironic; barely four years ago, Japanese forces had marched through this pass on their way to Bandoeng, in their lightning conquest of Asia! Japan was at the peak of its victory in the war then, having accomplished the destruction of eighteen battle ships of the American Navy in one swoop, the sinking of the "Prince of Wales" and the "Repulse" and the surrender of the supposedly impenetrable fortress Singapore. Thereafter the combined American and Philippine forces, after fierce fighting together against an overwhelming, numerically superior enemy, had surrendered.

The Japanese had also conquered the rich oil fields of the Dutch East Indies after the battle of the Java Sea in which the Dutch Navy lost most of its fleet. At the time Japan appeared unconquerable. Now they had lost the war.

Not unlike the conquests of Alexander the great and Djenghis Khan, Japan had lost all the territory it once had conquered. How could all that have happened in four years? And the Americans could have won the war in a much shorter time, had they not been fighting the war in Europe also. It was only because Germany had declared war on America that the country became involved in the European war scene.

Tukagoshi, the Japanese minister of war, was hanged as war criminal; perhaps unjustly so. He had accepted blame for war crimes committed by others, of which he certainly was not guilty. There was no evidence that he had committed any other offence than declaring war on America. He had tried Hara-kiri to atone for this failure, but had not succeeded in killing himself. Most of the war criminals had escaped the hangman, including the Japanese camp commander of camp Tamarkan in Siam who had executed my friend and comrade in arm Marcus. He was one of those whose crimes had been overlooked like those of many others who had been given a reprieve, in spite of the fact that their crimes were all too well known!

The law and justice were not one and the same.

He was the one I wanted to find and speak to, in order to find out exactly where Major Cane stood as far as the beheading of Marcus was concerned.

Yamamoto would undoubtedly have been executed, probably hanged also, as the ultimate humiliation, had he survived the war. He knew that the Americans would kill him for masterminding what they called; the treacherous attack on Pearl Harbour although the declaration of war came minutes before the attack. Yet the deception by moving the Japanese fleet within striking distance of Pearl Harbour just before declaring war, no matter how you looked at it, was a treacherous act, as Yamamoto well knew! Two thousand Americans were killed in the attack on Pearl Harbour as a consequence. That "criminal" behaviour the Americans had never forgiven and neither forgotten. His plane was shot down by three American warplanes over Rabaul in New Guinea even already early in the war. The Americans had managed to break the code and knew that he was flying to Rabaul in New Guinea. Yamamoto knew that his life would not end on the gallows by hanging. He would die a warrior. He wanted a hero's death, not led to the scaffold and blindfolded like a criminal. Only he did not know exactly how it would end. That it would end violently he had no doubt and justice would be done. The Americans would kill him, but in a fight!

Yamamoto also knew the outcome of the war. Japan never had a chance of winning it. Only he could not confide his fears to anyone. Nobody would have wanted to listen to him. The warlords were arrogant. He knew their thinking and that he could not change their minds His fate was sealed but equally so was Japan's. Japan would only seem to be winning initially. It would not last long.

Japan's so-called "victories", had only been possible because America was unprepared. Ultimately the might of America would crush Japan and him too. What about the British? Would they ever be able to overcome the humiliation of Singapore's loss to an enemy, which they had so seriously underrated?

But Japan was not alone in losing the war. We the Royal Dutch Indian Army had also lost the war. The consequences of having lost to the Japanese meant that the Indonesians now believed that the time for their independence had come. They saw the weak position of the Dutch government. Either the Dutch gave in, or the Indonesians would fight for it.

The Dutch suddenly, against expectations, now had a guerrilla war on their hands for which they were unprepared, and was very much against their will. Friends were fighting friends. And my best friend and classmate from before the war, was fighting in the guerrilla forces against my forces. How crazy things had become. Marcus, Werbata, and the others from the camp Tjipatat were dead. Amazing changes had taken place in these four years! Wong my surviving friend married to Lily was quite ill, as a result of Japanese torture. And Lily found herself shackled duty bound to him. Maybe that was a high form of love on her part! Sacrificing her wishes because Wong needed her. But had she not come to love Wong also? I had observed that she did everything for him and she was a lovable person.

Djojo Bojo had been correct so far, with his prediction, that a yellow warrior race would occupy all the islands of the Dutch East Indies and then would leave again. There was one exception to the otherwise exact outcome of the prediction: the time of occupation by the "yellow warriors" had been wrong. Yet even that part of the prediction could still be correct, since an influential important person might have changed the period of occupation as Doel had also said. And the person in question could even be unaware of having done so.

I wondered about the second part of the prediction. Doel had mentioned the white buffalo. But who or what was the white buffalo? If the Dutch were meant by the white buffalo in the prophecy; then the Dutch would leave and Indonesia would become independent. But how long would the guerilla war last, before the white buffalo would leave and what would the cost of lives be in the "in between" period? When Doel told me the prediction of Djojo Bojo, I had known instinctively deep down that it would influence my life dramatically also.

I had lost more than only the war. I had lost Lily also! What further calamities lay in store for me?

When I received St.Cyr's invitation to attend a meeting with himself; Colonel Xant, plus three delegates from the Netherlands, I was pleased. I could now also tell the Governor-General of my last encounter with Mas and tell him that although his armband was found at Tjilan, Mas had nothing to do with the murders in Tjilan.

I had to believe that. What I thought deep down didn't matter; I could not prove it and I didn't want to know the truth.

The three civilians of the Dutch delegation were dressed in white clothes; the upper button closed. Here in Tjisarua the air was cold but they would soon find out that their tunics were not suitable for the tropics. They had been wrongly advised about tropical clothing. What other wrong advice were they sent out to Indonesia with?

I was the last one who arrived for the meeting; the chairman shook my hand and introduced me to the others. His name was Thyssen. He was in his middle fifties, bald and his head without protection would quickly be sun burnt.

They had never been in the Indies, which was nothing new to me but worse: they had no clue of the military situation without which an understanding of a civilian solution to the problem of Indonesian independence was impossible. Nevertheless their ideas were stubbornly aired as though we knew nothing. "No concessions" the spokesman pompously stated.

Colonel Xant spoke:

"Are you not aware that the largest part of Java is in the hands of freedom fighters and that they hold quite a large number of Dutch and Chinese women and children as hostages?"

"Why can't they be set free?"

"Do you know how large the area of Java is? For your information it is three times the size of the Netherlands, not even speaking of the size of the other islands; Sumatra and Borneo each are bigger still, and New Guinea is the biggest. The total area is perhaps twenty five times the size of the Netherlands. Does that give you any idea?"

"You have enough troops."

"We never had, otherwise we would not have lost the war. Moreover," Colonel Xant continued, "the majority of the troops we have now, are former POW's and have as yet to recover from that ordeal."

"You will soon have volunteers from the Netherlands. They will form a special division that should help you. I expect that they will be sent out very soon. They will of course have their own officers."

His news was received with a frown from Colonel Xant. I guessed that it was the last part of the remark: "they will of course have their own officers," which had made him frown. The delegate seemed to bypass subtleties like a charging rhinoceros.

Thyssen, with the bald head, now turned to me:

"You are a friend of the murderer Mas who calls himself a freedom fighter. He wants independence by force, is that correct?"

"You assume three things," I replied; first that I am a friend of his, second that he is a murderer and third, that he wants independence by force. Yes I am an old friend of his and have only recently spoken to him. He expressed a desire to have a meeting with the Governor-General in order to come to a peaceful understanding."

"An understanding with a freedom fighter, who has as we know, just been declared guilty of murdering women and children."

"That we don't know for sure," Colonel Xant interrupted. "There are so many units operating in the same area that it is impossible to know who is responsible for what."

The bald headed man Max Thysen again turned to me.

"Do you have any evidence to suggest that Mas is not guilty of these murders?"

"Should I have?" I said innocently, "I thought you had an open and shut case. At least that is what it sounded to me."

The Governor-General gave me a disapproving look and I decided to be more co-operative, although the attitude of this bald man started to irritate me.

"I have Mas' statement that he was never in camp Tjilan, the camp you are referring to and where the murders took place." I said. "Then there is the statement from his messenger through whom Mas and I liase. The messenger claims that Mas was with someone I also know. She is the third person, the daughter of major Cane who claims that she indeed was with Mas at his secret hideout the day that the Tjilan camp was freed and when the murders were taking place. Consequently he could not have committed the murders he is accused of."

"We can exclude Mas himself and his messenger also, from telling the truth surely; but who is the third person you mentioned? Where does she fit into the picture?"

"Lily Cane," I said. "She, Mas and I were schoolmates and close friends many years ago. She also was my fiancée."

"Was?"

"Yes, she married some one else."

"I am sorry," Thysen said.

I kept quiet letting my thoughts wander. They were not pleasant thoughts. The Governor-General now spoke:

"Is it not time that we speak to Mas, what is your opinion Colonel Xant?"

"I think that any communication with the opposition is useful and welcome" was Colonel Xant's opinion.

"Hold it, we are very much against the idea," Thysen said. "We have specific instruction that there can be no deal with the freedom fighters until they lay down their arms."

"In that case there will never be a useful discussion. I don't think you have heard what I said before," Colonel Xant reminded him. "It is the Indonesian fighters who hold the trump cards at the moment, and if we can have some understanding between us, it will be more to our advantage than the other way round. Until we are better equipped and at least have another division of healthy soldiers; instead of these former POW's, only just out of Japanese concentration camps, we should in the meantime try to negotiate. There is nothing wrong with that. Moreover who is talking about a deal? We don't know what Mas is going to offer."

"I am surprised," Thysen said, "that you don't show any muscle. If that is your attitude, then it is no surprise to us that you lost the war against the Japanese. It was of course lost exactly because of this weak attitude of yours."

"I don't think so," Colonel Xant said calmly; "the war was lost because too little money was spent on equipping the forces. The successive governments here relied on being defended by the British in Singapore and by the Americans in the Philippines. Both as it turned out, were utterly overrated by the Dutch.

In contrast the Japanese were very much under rated. If you are not in agreement with my point of view, namely one relying on the other for protection: explain to me then, why you didn't do any better against the Germans in Holland? Again the government there relied on the strength of the British and the French. Also perhaps because the Netherlands had not been attacked by the Germans in the Great War of 1914-1918. False hopes as it turned out. No one except Churchill liked to see the reality and face it squarely.

"It is typical that Churchill was fired immediately the danger of the war passed. Nobody wanted to see the next danger lurking behind the iron curtain: Russia!

And you tend to put the blame on the army? What nonsense; put the blame where it belongs and leave the army out of it. The successive governments are to blame. Not only the Dutch government; but also the British, the French and the American governments refused to look the impending danger; then Japan, in the face. Each counted on the other to do the job they should have done themselves."

I could see that none of what Colonel Xant said made any difference to the delegates. They had already made up their minds beforehand, or had received instructions how to behave before they came. The "colonials", which they considered us to be; could only see the problems in a short sighted way and which was not their way of seeing things.

The Governor-General so far had not said much. It was difficult for him to suggest anything to a group of people, who had already made up their mind and already proved to be inflexible. We first had to find out if the delegates had an alternative to offer. If not, it was useless to proceed. He put the question to them.

"Well it seems that without the army here willing to fight it out, we can't do anything," the head of the delegates said. "Which then means that we have to have discussions between the new contingent of soldiers arriving from the Netherlands and yourselves," he turned to Colonel Xant.

"I have never said that we were not willing to fight," Colonel Xant defended himself. "The question surely is: are we wise to do that and are we not better with a compromise? Mas is willing to talk. It binds us to nothing. On the contrary, he has to declare his hand. The attitude he will take for instance; will show us his strength. Although here we must also read between the lines. He will be bluffing and appear over confident. But even that will tell us something. I think the controller should convene a meeting with us all here and invite Mas."

"Why can't you apprehend him when he turns up?"

"Before he comes he will want immunity so that he is guaranteed a safe return to wherever he came from. We don't get him to agree to come otherwise. You would have wanted the same conditions were you in his place."

"You would not be obliged to keep your word to a murderer."

"The idea is tempting but no. There would never be any further negotiations between us and even the most moderate Indonesians, if it ever leaked out that we did this. And leak out it will! You perhaps don't recall that our government has exactly done that in the past. The name of the Indonesian who trusted us was Diponegoro. He was betrayed and the story is very well known in Indonesian circles.

Thysen knew what Colonel Xant was referring to. He thought for a long time. It seemed we had arrived at a decision and I was already satisfied that I could inform Mas of the agreement to meet with the Governor-General. My hopes were dashed.

"We don't agree, the delegate leader said. We are bound by instructions to a great extent."

I could see that the Governor General was taken aback

"In fact," the delegate continued, "and please don't take it too hard; I have been empowered by the Dutch government to stop further negotiations with the government presently in power in the Indies. That means that you Sir," he bowed to St.Cyr, "will be replaced. Your successor is already under consideration but it was left to my judgement, whether to implement this appointment or not. We are not pleased with this attitude of pacifism and this half-baked attitude from the army, which we have encountered here today. A new commander for the army is also being considered."

I was stunned! Did the delegates have this power to dismiss even St.Cyr?

Dejectedly I drove back with thousands of questions racing round in my head waiting to be answered. This was something I had never expected. St.Cyr replaced! He was the best. I had seen how he could handle really difficult situations through tact and forbearance. The handling of the independence of Indonesia would go through an even more difficult time without him. It was now up to me to inform Mas of the new situation.

When I got to the officers quarters in Bandoeng where I was billeted, there was a message from Lily waiting for me. The message was simple: "Meet me tonight at restaurant Braga", it said. It was the same restaurant where Mas and I had met recently and where Lily and I in the past had sometimes booked a table if we didn't want to be disturbed.

Our encounter would open bleeding wounds again: mine!

I arrived early and I was anxious. There would be tears again. I had nothing new to offer. The court case against her father was already filed officially. I still needed to go to Japan hoping to find out more about the execution of Marcus, but I did not expect too much that would make any material difference to the case. Major Cane, her father was accused of cowardice by the army and even putting that aside I had a personal score to even with him. My going to Japan was the idea of the army. It suited my own original intention to go to Japan myself exactly, but primarily the idea was theirs. I was merely the executioner to a plan, which had been concocted by Colonel Arlen.

However, I also wanted to find out about my own feelings first and foremost. Why was Marcus killed? Was Lily's father really guilty for not trying to save him? Was my eagerness to find out the truth, coloured by the fact that Lily had married Wong instead of me? I paced the floor up and down beleaguered by my own questions to which I had never received an answer.

Lily arrived exactly on time. She wore high heels and a lot of make-up. Her face was nevertheless still pale. The rouge and mascara had failed in the attempt to cover up where nature had decided to miss out. I felt suddenly such a great pity for her. At the same time I also felt cold. Her pleas would fall on deaf ears. I had a job to do. Lily was no longer my responsibility. My dead friends were. It was to them I owed my loyalty. Not to Lily any longer. Lily and I were past tense, finished and at the same time unfinished business. It would always remain unfinished business in my mind.

As I kissed her when she arrived, I could see that she was close to tears.

"Would you like to go somewhere else," I offered. She shook her head.

"We buried mother today Richard: she was ill you knew that didn't you?" I took her hand in mine.

"I am so very sorry Lily, I knew she was ill but I did not know the extent of her illness. When did she die?"

"Yesterday afternoon, she must have had a brain haemorrhage. She fell and was comatose. She never came to again."

"Oh Lily, I am so sorry for you." We sat there for a long time. I realised how different things had become between us.

"How is your father taking it?"

"He is devastated; mother and he were always very close as you know." I nodded.

"Is there anything else Lily, anything I can do?"

"No there isn't if you have nothing more to say."

"Lily I am so sorry.

I can't say anything to you now. I can't tell you how sorry I feel for you. We have always been able to talk to each other. Now the words fail me. It has been so long since we talked confidentially and so much has happened to keep us apart."

"It doesn't have to be like that Richard. You will always be in my heart."

In spite of the fact that I had hardened myself against her I could almost have wept.

"Lily we will even be driven further apart and you will hate me for it. You will hate me for trying your father in court."

"Has he not had enough Richard? Must you also take his honour away by taking him to a military court?"

How could I tell Lily about the fifty war graves in Tjipatat. How could I tell her of the moss already growing through the cracks in the marble slabs covering their graves? How could I tell her of Marcus, crazy Marcus with his ready smile? He had been so happy with his life. I was quiet. Lily could never realise that I was torn apart in my feelings toward her and on the other side by the loyalty I felt towards my dead friends.

"How is Wong?"

"Play chess once in a while with him Richard. He would like that. He often talks of you and why I don't go back to you."

"I'll take you home Lily; there is nothing more to say." She nodded.

At her front door I held her hand for a long time. "Oh Lily, dear Lily when did we ever part like this?

I wish things were different between us and I am very sorry about your mother." She bit her lips not to cry. I felt awful. We parted almost like strangers. I looked back at Lily in the rear mirror when I drove away. I only saw the blurred image of her. I didn't have anything with me to dry my eyes.

Chapter 19

Major Cane felt no remorse for not having proceeded to Tjipatat where he had been ordered to go. As far as he was concerned the camp was doomed. It could not be held. Strategically it was a mistake, to have built it where it was, lying low in a valley as it did, instead of it being situated on top of a hill.

You could attack the camp from three sides and only if approached from the riverside by the enemy, would it stand a chance of offering resistance and possible (still doubtful) successful defence. But which enemy would be foolish enough to approach it from that direction if there were three other more successful alternatives? In any case it was never meant to be a bastion of strength. Only a fool of the upper hierarchy had wanted it held. And that decision only at the last minute when it was already too late.

In his opinion the camp should have been evacuated long ago.

In contrast an important stronghold; the Tjiater pass, which could have been defended well by him and his soldiers, was for no good reason left to be defended by troops unfamiliar with it's lay out.

His soldiers who knew all about the pass and its structure, since they had built the tunnels and bunkers; had been wrongly sent to the north coast of Java to oppose a Japanese landing under the command of a captain they did not even know. In the process he, Major Cane, was separated from his troops. After his soldiers had unsuccessfully tried to stem the Japanese landing on the north coast of Java and were exhausted from the battle, they were sent to this useless outpost Tjipatat to shelter there. Why of all things? It was unbelievable!

He and his soldiers; should have been left at the Tjiater pass

And in the hurried decision the soldiers replacing him and his platoon, knowing nothing of the lay-out of the pass; were only given a road map of the area to familiarise themselves with the defence of the region! All the expensively built bunker and tunnel system was unknown to them and was therefore wasted! The pass if properly defended, would have been a problem for the Japanese

He knew who the blundering idiot was, who had been responsible for this. Sending him to relieve Lieutenant Hes who was called away from Tjipatat to recapture the airport Soebang and which had fallen into Japanese hands was equally foolish!

He would be called a deserter if it ever came out that he never followed up this latest order, but he never felt a deserter. The truth was that his post had been taken away from him. That was the reality. And only at the last moment did he receive orders to proceed to Tjipatat where he did not belong in the first place. Most of the soldiers at that post were already beaten anyway. Their commanding officer, Captain Smyth had been called away, or had deserted, he did not know the exact reason for Captain Smyth' absence from Tjipatat.

The upper echelon might call him in front of a military court and urge for his dismissal on the grounds of desertion. If that happened and if it became clear that he would be fired dishonourably, he would point out the obvious mistake of the Tjiater pass and its consequent disaster. His superiors also had something to hide! They also should have known that Tjipatat could not be defended; the outcome showed it. His presence would have made no difference. But maybe nobody would ever raise the question. Maybe it would never come to light that he did not follow orders.

He had never been happy to be in charge in a situation where he needed to be brave. He knew of himself that he was not. And now he was in charge of and confronted with this new problem where he needed good judgement and courage: namely the question of the escaped soldier who had come back after the Japanese had noticed his absence for three days! It was of course impossible to hide him for long. There were always informers. The news that the escaped prisoner had come back would inevitably leak out.

Had the Japanese not found the secret radio constructed from spare parts by two British lieutenants and had he not been made to watch them being beaten to death? He tried to interfere then. Yes, he had exonerated himself from being a coward that time. The Japanese had beaten him mercilessly till he became unconscious for trying to interfere and help the two unfortunate officers. He thought they would kill him too.

The interpreter was also beaten up and kicked and he and the interpreter, after they regained consciousness, were put in front of the Japanese guardhouse, standing right in front of a machine gun not knowing whether they would be shot any minute. Thirty six hours later, standing in front of this machine gun without food or drink, they both passed out, one after the other. When they came to, they were in the hospital tent under the care of Dr. Stam. Eventually the Japanese had released them.

He had known nothing about the radio but that did not make any difference to the Japanese. He was held responsible. And how else but through informers did the Japanese find out the secret that there was a radio?

And they would also find out about Marcus who had escaped and had come back, the fool!

Major Cane had warned his men not to escape. Practically all prisoners who had escaped had been betrayed by Siamese boat people for money and had been beheaded! He could do nothing for Marcus but first he wanted to speak to Dr. Stam, even if only to have somebody to speak to.

Dr. Stam opened the flap of the cholera tent when he heard his name called.

"He has returned and I am stuck with him," Major Cane blurted out.

"Who and what do you mean?" Dr. Stam replied.

"Three days ago Marcus escaped as you know. He did not make it. But what is worse is that he has come back." Nervously he wiped the sweat from his clammy forehead, shifting his weight from the left foot to the right. "I believe that you to some extent only; yet nevertheless also, encouraged him to escape." he added.

"We can hide him in a tent under the barrack beds for a few days but very soon the numbers will be detected at roll call as having been increased with one number since Marcus' escape. Pressure will be exerted on us to reveal the person who escaped and came back. You know how that is being done. The Japanese will take one prisoner and shoot him and will take the next one, till we reveal the identity of the person who escaped."

"We all know about these beastly procedures, I don't have to tell you the gory details. We cannot protect him." He sighed heavily.

"He should not have come back and has to try to escape again. There is nothing else for it, we cannot take the risk."

"There is an alternative," Dr. Stam interrupted calmly.

"How?" Major Cane wiped the excess sweat, dripping into his eyes from his brow. The question was full of hope but deep lines on his forehead had appeared and now joined the anxious expression on his face.

"Well," doctor Stam continued: "I will hide him in the cholera tent till we have a death. The Japanese never look there. They are scared of contracting cholera themselves. The death won't be reported. Instead we will bury the deceased under the earthen floor of the tent and Marcus will take on the identity of the deceased. The total number of men will be correct again and the Japanese will be none the wiser. The dead man buried under the floor of the tent won't be detected and will have a proper burial after the war. Marcus will not be noticed as having come back since he will now be considered a recovered patient having recovered from cholera"

Major Cane considered what Dr. Stam had suggested. It sounded a marvellous idea! The escaped soldier could be saved that way. He thought about it for a while: eventually he sighed. He discarded the idea.

"Impossible, there are always informers. The danger is too great. The Japanese may already have discovered that he is back. They may be waiting for us just to do such a thing as what you have in mind. Not only will Marcus be executed but you will also suffer the same fate. I cannot accept that risk. And I myself will be executed also," he added as an afterthought.

"Marcus either escapes again or presents himself to the Japanese, there is no other way." The anxious expression on his face if anything; had increased in intensity. "I have no choice."

"But Major Cane," Dr. Stam began: "if he presents himself to the Japanese, you know full well that he will be executed. This has happened to all escaped prisoners who were caught; you know this just as well as I do. The plan to hide Marcus in the cholera tent till we have one death; and we may well have one soon," he added,"is the best I can think of. Again as I said the Japanese are only interested in numbers, they don't recognise faces. Marcus will take the identity and number of the dead man and the Japanese will be none the wiser. Believe me Major, this is a way out. It is your duty to protect your men; I am willing to take the risk and so should you."

Major Cane went pale. "That is an enormous danger to you, to me and to all the men in the camp. Marcus knew the consequences of escaping and not succeeding. Turning back was the worst thing he could have done. He should have thought of it. I already got beaten when the Japanese discovered that there had been an escape. You see this blue bump on my forehead and my face is still black and blue. I still don't understand why they have not already executed a few men as a consequence of Marcus' escape. But if the Japanese find out about this plan of yours and we follow it up, we are done for.

"Marcus has to escape again and must not come back this time. He still has a chance. I will not accept the risk that you, Dr Stam may be executed as a result of Marcus' escape. He should not have tried."

"But Major Cane; have you forgotten that it is the duty of every soldier who has been made a prisoner of war to escape if at all possible. Look at it in that way."

"No," Major Cane interrupted, "that may be so in a civilised society. The Germans would not execute an escaped prisoner, let alone execute remaining prisoners of war if one of theirs escaped, which is what these captors of us do as a deterrent. "This is completely different. We are dealing with cruel barbarians passing themselves off as civilised. For one prisoner escaped from Konkwita's camp a week ago, the Japanese have shot four of his innocent friends. It is impossible and highly selfish to want to escape under conditions such as these. I must insist that he either escapes again or gives himself up. The consequences are his and his alone." Dr. Stam didn't reply, he was in deep thought. After a while which seemed like a century to Major Cane, he spoke slowly.

"Perhaps you are right Major. I make the same offer nevertheless."

Major Cane walked away. He felt beaten and especially lonely. How lonely could life be in situations such as these, when there is no one else but you yourself and God to make a decision of the utmost importance: namely the life of another person!

It was all good and well for Dr. Stam to speak the way he did. He did not have the ultimate responsibility. He Major Cane, on the other hand had. He was responsible for the life and safety of the doctor too. Some patients without him would undoubtedly die.

"Damn," he swore. Why was it up to him to tell Marcus to go? But what else was he to do?

Back in his tent he threw himself on the baleh- baleh where he slept. Marcus had to accept the consequences of his escape. But his men would not be pleased about that. They would accuse him of cowardice. The doctor had shown him a way out. Dr. Stam was courageous and willing to take the risk of being found out by the Japanese and being killed for it as a consequence. But he Major Cane had the ultimate responsibility. He had accepted long ago that he was a coward. During his military training he was once challenged to a dual with swords. He had refused the challenge. Out of fear he had accepted impossible humiliation

It was then for the first time that he came face to face with himself and admitted to himself that he was a coward. On that occasion he wondered if he was fit to live the life of a soldier. But to give up the life he had been so looking forward to all his young days was impossible for him. And when would his courage ever be tested anyway? But now, totally unforeseen, it was, and it had been challenged in Tjipatat and he had failed there too.

His excuse there was that the post Tjipatat had only been a shooting bivouac. It was meant to teach soldiers how to use a rifle. He was convinced that Tjipatat could not be defended against a determined attack by the Japanese. It would mean suicide to go there. His presence would not have mattered. The defenders were militia greenhorns plus an already beaten contingent of his soldiers whose morale was bound to be low. What was the point of his going there? Only to be killed also. The outcome would be the same: annihilation of the post. The camp should never have been used in wartime. The soldiers should have been located elsewhere.

But were these arguments not just excuses? Excuses he was bringing forward because he did not want to face up to the truth, namely the fact that out of fear he had not followed up his orders to go where he was sent? Now again he was presented with another predicament that required courage. Why was this so easy to accept for the doctor but not for him? True the doctor did not have the ultimate responsibility, but there was more to it. The doctor had courage and courage you probably had to be born with. You probably either possessed it or you didn't.

He heaved a deep sigh. God, what was he to tell Marcus? He had no choice. The doctor was needed; there was a cholera epidemic. And in any case, the life of other people including his own could also be at stake if the Japanese suspected and found out that they were cheated. The consequences could be staggering. To escape from the Japanese was impossible. If it had been possible, he would have had a try himself. They were surrounded by impenetrable jungle. It would mean trekking through jungle for a thousand miles at least, if you were lucky at the end of it, to arrive at an allied military post. The chances that you would run into Japanese or be detected by Siamese, who could get a good price for you if you were caught, were much greater. There was also the danger of tigers, panthers and poisonous snakes. But even that was not the worst. There also was malaria and starvation but that also was not the worst.

No, the worst was that innocent friends were made to suffer for you if you escaped. That was unacceptable. This should have weighted uppermost in Marcus's mind before planning to escape. And to some extent he held the doctor responsible. Had he not openly said once, that in his opinion prisoners of war were supposed not to collaborate with the enemy and that escape should be tried if at all possible. This was the result of such irresponsible talk!

But it was also true that Dr. Stam had corrected his opinion later and had advised the men to escape only if they could be sure that they were not jeopardising the lives of their friends. Marcus still had a chance: escape again! As far as the Japanese were concerned, he had already done so anyway. His friends surprisingly had not been made to pay with their lives; the possible reprisals, this time. At least not yet! Why, Major Cane did not know. Only he had received a beating.

Slowly and reluctantly he rose from his baleh-baleh. This was awful. It would be the most heartless thing he was going to say.

"Marcus" he called softly. From under the top bed of the common bamboo beds, a figure crawled, blinking against the bright light of the sun.

"Did you talk to Dr. Stam?" he enquired anxiously.

"It is no good," Major Cane forced himself to say. "You have to go; try to escape again, you still have a chance. We can give you enough dry rice for a week. You have got a boiling container. You can also have this knife. I am giving it to you; I managed to keep it hidden all this time but I am more than pleased for you to have it. Within a week you could be contacting an allied outpost. Have courage, don't give up."

"No," he heard Marcus say, "I will go to the Japanese camp commander and give myself up. I trusted a Siamese boat family; they betrayed me to the Japanese and I was chased. The jungle is an awful place when you are out there alone and hunted. I don't want to go through the same experience again. If they kill me so be it. I cannot face the jungle again."

He then left without saying another word. Mayor Cane was alone with his own thoughts and prayers.

***

The execution was planned at midday. Every POW.was forcibly ordered to attend and watch. Marcus was led from the bamboo jail in which he had spent the night. Major Cane stepped forward with the interpreter. Immediately three Japanese soldiers attacked both men and threatened to bayonet them then and there. They were hit with rifle butts. Major Cane fell first. The soldiers kicked him to the head and abdomen. The interpreter tried to protect himself and Major Cane, by saying something loud in Japanese. A rain of rifle butts landed on his head and he also went down.

The machine gun in front of the prisoners was clicked to readiness. Not one of the prisoners moved. Orders in Japanese were shouted. All the rifles of the Japanese guards facing the odd one hundred prisoners of war in front of them were ready to be fired into them. The situation was electric.

Marcus was dragged over the mud into the central square. He was bleeding from the head and nose. He had obviously been beaten. His clothes were hanging loose from his body. It was an impossible situation. Nobody could do anything to help Marcus.

His head was cleanly severed from his body by one stroke from the executioner's sword. Three prisoners were ordered to bury Marcus. They tried to put him in the rough, wooden coffin. He was too tall even with his head cut off. It was no problem for the executioner. He merely cut off the legs, threw Marcus and his legs and severed head into the coffin and ordered the three men to burn him.

From an improvised raised platform, the Japanese camp commander Yakumi was looking on. This was what he had been ordered to do. Produce dissatisfaction between the prisoners and their leading officers. The men would be dissatisfied with Major Cane's conduct for not having protected Marcus' life. This was exactly as he had planned it. Divide and rule. Produce dissatisfaction and terror at the same time. This was the way to guard prisoners of war with only a handful of men, so that the majority of Japanese soldiers could be used for the war effort and were not burdened with guard duty. Years later I was to find out this truth.

Dr. Stam wrote to Marcus' mother after the war.

"Your son, he wrote, died as a brave soldier trying to escape as was his duty."

She never found out until much later at the court case, that her son would have had a chance to live, if Major Cane had been brave enough to face the risks that the doctor was willing to take. I heard the story from doctor Stam.

Marcus had been my friend and comrade in arms and I knew that I would not be satisfied until I knew exactly what had taken place. That Major Cane happened to be the father of the girl I once had been in love with and who had married someone else made no difference. Or did it?

I decided to investigate; not least my own motives!

I needed to find the Japanese camp commander of the camp in which the execution had taken place. What exactly had happened? Did I have the right to judge Major Cane, Lily's father, without knowing the exact circumstances?

By what I at first thought was just a stroke of luck; I was asked to investigate the circumstances surrounding more than one crime committed by the Japanese at Tamarkan camp. I could not have been more pleased. The name of Major Cane was only mentioned in passing, with respect to the beheading of my friend Marcus, but I understood later that this was the main reason why I was sent. The request came from headquarters. It seemed altogether straightforward and innocent to me.

The military; I read between the lines, needed a detailed report about Major Cane but I was not told that in so many words. I was merely sent to probe into the murder of Marcus and perhaps other misdeeds that I would uncover, and which had happened during the war in the Siamese POW-camp Tamarkan on the river Kwai. That is the way I saw it.

Colonel Arlen was the one who presided at the official briefing. He pretended not to know me. I in turn did not care to remind him that he had promised Mas and me every help to get us to Australia which had turned out not to be the case. As far as that was concerned I was promised possession of the notes made by Colonel Brink and I was biding my time. Sooner or later I would take my revenge out on Colonel Arlen. What was he up to this time sending me to Japan? That dawned on me clearly only later.

"You are to go to Japan and come back with information from the Japanese camp commander of Tamarkan camp in Siam. We don't have his name nor do we know his present whereabouts exactly but we know that he was released by the general pardon of President Truman, although he is considered a war criminal. The last information we have is that he was released in Fukuoka on the Japanese island named Kyushu. He was a Kempetai officer. That means that he held the rank of Colonel in the Japanese army. That is all the information we have. We want to know about the conduct of certain officers in relation to all POW soldiers executions."

Again Major Cane's name was not mentioned. It was as though he was not involved in the execution case of Marcus whereas I knew that the purpose of sending me was to investigate Major Cane's role and conduct in the case.

"The name of the person who was beheaded is Marcus, Colonel Arlen continued. We are informed that you have a special interest in this case since you are the victim's friend, and it should therefore be helpful to you, to be in this position to investigate. You were stationed in war time in Tjipatat weren't you?"

I pricked up my ears and suddenly became suspicious. Why did he bring up Tjipatat? I of course knew already that Major Cane had never arrived in Tjipatat although he had been ordered to go there by Colonel Arlen.

My experience of Colonel Arlen made me think twice! Did major Cane's refusal to go to Tjipatat have a bearing on sending me to Japan? What were Colonel Arlen's real motives in this case? Maybe nothing other than those he had mentioned but I was not certain that that was all it was. I had learned that Colonel Arlen did nothing without a purpose beneficial to himself in the first place!

I decided to let my suspicions rest. I could not be happier. I could now test my own feelings and motivation. Did I want to prosecute Major Cane for the love of my friends and for refusing to help Marcus, resulting in his death, or was my motive revenge because Lily had married Wong and had not waited for me? I hoped to find the answer for my feelings in Japan.

***

The Dutch consul in Fukuoka occupied the smallest offices that I have ever visited. But he still had a secretary in his service and who showed polite interest. She had just had a hairdo Japanese style. I didn't like it. She had blond hair. There are no blond Japanese females. Their hair style only suits women with dark hair.

After introducing myself to her, she said:

"The consul is expecting you." It was a superfluous remark since I had phoned him from Tokyo of my impending visit and we had agreed on the date and hour. I was made to sit and wait in an even smaller anteroom in which I barely could stretch my legs. After a few minutes the consul breezed in, bringing with him the pungent pleasant smell of after-shave lotion. He was in his early fifties, wore a tweed suit and treated me to a warm smile, which showed a regular set of false teeth. I wondered where he had lost his own.

We entered his office and he invited me to sit down. After the usual pleasantries we came down to business.

"What can I do for you?" he eventually asked, with the kind of interest a tiger looks at his prey.

"I am here to establish whether a high ranking Dutch officer is guilty of misbehaviour and should be prosecuted." The consul indicated with a move of his hand that he was interested.

"I heard of such cases," he said.

"I want to find the Japanese camp commander of a camp in Siam, now called Thailand. Atrocities of a certain nature have occurred there," I continued. "The camp was on the river Kwai called Tamarkan and the event occurred in December 1943."

The consul pushed his chair back.

"That will be difficult," he said pensively.

"No I don't think so," I said. You have the power to ask for the list of released Japanese who were pardoned by resident Truman but who were nevertheless suspected of having committed war crimes. There were too many of them and they could not all be tried. This man I am looking for was recently released from a jail in Thailand."

"That will only give us a list of names but that does not bring us any further," the consul remarked.

"It does," I said. "This Japanese I am looking for should at least have the rank of Colonel, since he was also a Kempetai officer. We happen to have this information and all Kempetai officers held this rank. The position is comparable to the S.S. officers in the Nazi corps in Germany. It would be most unlikely that there should be two Colonels of the same rank who were in Tamarkan at the same time."

"You better consult the customs or the police; they have such a list."

"But you can help me to get in touch with the police. I am officially investigating this case."

"On whose authority?" the consul asked turning up his eyebrows so that they met in the middle. He must have studied this pose in the mirror.

"The authority of the Dutch Colonial Forces." I said. "You are supposed to assist me in any way that you can," I added.

He mused this over in his mind while moving the ink blotter from one end of the table to the other. To show that he was further interested he lent forward as though he had something confidential to tell me which he hadn't.

"And your motive?" he asked slyly; "your role in this holds nothing personal?"

"My role in this is indeed more than impersonal.

"How is that?" he wanted to know.

"I don't want to enlarge on this," I cut him short. " It is sufficient to say that a soldier was beheaded by the Japanese and that this soldier was a friend of mine."

"I am very sorry," the consul said with understanding. "I will introduce you to the local police but that will only be the beginning of your problem. You don't speak Japanese or do you?"

"Yes I do a little," I said. He was about to pick up the phone when I stopped him.

"There is more," I said, deciding to tell him the rest because he otherwise would not sleep well, by reason of his curiosity not having been satisfied.

"Oh," he said, waiting with an innocence becoming a newly born baby.

"The officer whose conduct I am investigating happens to be the father of my former fiancée." The consul got up from his chair and started whistling through his false teeth. He said nothing, just looked satisfied that he had been taken into confidence and picked up the phone. He dialled the number and got through immediately. He spoke in Japanese haltingly, leaning against one wall of his office, which was easy to do because all four of the walls were in close proximity.

"All right," he said when he put the phone down; "a taxi will take you." I thanked him and left. The taxi took me to the correct address and I was received by a Japanese police officer in American uniform, who escorted me to a door on which in Japanese writing was written: "Chief of Police". He knocked on the door twice and a voice from inside shouted, "Come in."

The police chief was about forty years of age and sported a moustache. When he got up, I saw the bulk of his body. He could easily pass for a Sumo wrestler. No tailor, unless he belonged to a magicians club, would ever be able to provide him with a suit that would fit all the contours of his body. He wore the same American clothes like those of the sergeant who had brought me, except that everything hung loose about his body in this man. The sleeves of his shirt were too short. The same held for his trouser legs. The tailor apparently had given up in despair short of committing Hara-kiri.

The chief's name was Soto he told me and after offering me a sweaty handshake he continued:

"You want to find the name and whereabouts of the Japanese prisoner of war commander of a camp called Tamarkan, on the river Kwai in Siam. Have I got that correctly?" he stated letting me know that he already knew what it was I had come for.

"Correct." I said.

"Do you know that the person you are looking for lives in this part of Japan?"

"I do," I said. "That is why I am here. We know of only one Colonel of the Kempetai and he was shipped back to Fukuoka."

The chief's face lit up.

"Yakumi." he said. "He is your man, he returned about six months ago. He lived here before the outbreak of the war; he also was police chief then. This man is dangerous; have nothing to do with him. You want revenge, is that your motive?"

"No," I said. "I only want to know exactly what took place in that camp, at the time when this Kempetai officer was in charge of it."

At least I had his name now, I was thinking to myself.

"I want to find out if there were mitigating circumstances for the Dutch major to act the way he did."

"How is that?"

"Well it may be that he had no choice but to hand over this prisoner we are talking about to your butchers as it appears. The prisoner had escaped but had to turn back. The Dutch camp commander then handed the prisoner of war over to this man Yakumi."

"And Yakumi killed him?"

"Yes, the Dutch major's role is investigated because of this. The Dutch doctor of the camp tried in vain to change the major's mind in order to save the prisoner's life."

"How could that have been done?" he asked.

I told him the whole story.

"Very clever," Sato was impressed. "All the same, I am surprised that my people did that. Kill an escaped prisoner of war I mean. I think that the Emperor did not know this."

"That may be, but is quite unbelievable; after all he was the one in supreme charge. Some people think that he must have known and also consider him responsible."

"You better rest the case, it happened so long ago and in order to find out, you will upset quite a number of people, moreover you are running into considerable danger," Soto was thinking aloud.

For a few moments I considered what Soto had said.

Although I had told him that there was no motive of revenge; my motive could be revenge of a completely different order than Sato was thinking of. How could I be so sure that my motive was all that clean? Did I feel hurt that Lily had not waited for my return? Did I not want to take it out on her in return? But I quickly dismissed the thought. Lily had never abandoned me. The circumstances were to blame. There were other considerations! I had to be clear in my mind about this.

What about Marcus? He had also been a friend of mine. We had been in the same outfit together and he had been ruthlessly killed! It might as well have been Major Cane who had beheaded him.

"I am hoping that I find an excuse so that Major Cane will not be prosecuted," I said. Did I really believe what I was saying?

"Suppose you do not find an excuse what then?"

"In that case the military court will consider all the circumstances and pass judgement."

"And your role in all this?"

"I will be the prosecutor."

Sato was deep in thought.

"This man Yakumi is dangerous, I have already told you so already and we have no control over the area where he lives. I cannot guarantee your safety; there is a chance that you will not come back alive, you may be murdered in that district."

"That is absurd," I said, "I don't pose a threat to Yakumi so why would he be a danger to me? All I want from him is information. Why can't you ask Yakumi to come here? I can offer him money for the information."

"He won't come; he doesn't want anything to do with us. He knows that we know that he is a war criminal and he is suspicious. When he hears that a foreigner like you is interested in him he will not come. He has not only killed once but many times. He will undoubtedly think that it has something to do with his war record and it is true, only in a different way than he thinks. It will be dangerous for you to press the point.

"We have on more than one occasion asked him for help to solve a crime for us in this area. Not once has he helped us in this respect. He knows the district well and knows everything that goes on. He is feared but above all respected. He is "one of them," if you know what I mean. His life is guaranteed so long as he keeps the information of this district to himself."

"I only want information from him," I said. "I am not interested in the crimes which were committed neither in this district nor in any other district for that matter. All I want to know is what happened in Tamarkan camp in December 1943."

"You forget that war criminals were tried and executed. Yakumi will think that you have a score to even just because he got off scot-free. He won't give you a chance to deny or explain. Go back while you can, there is nothing here for you. The war is over; forget the whole thing. You still carry the burden of guilt or whatever it is, that you have survived and your friends have not. A lot of survivors of this war feel this way."

"I can't go back," I said. The dead soldier was a companion of mine, a companion soldier of mine. You cannot forget that sort of thing; there is an obligation. He must have a hearing and if Major Cane is guilty of misconduct; incidentally there are other accusations against this officer; then he must take the consequences."

"Punishment you mean; loss of rank? You appear to be extra concerned that justice is done. Make sure that you don't get hurt."

Had Sato perceived more than I had been prepared to tell him I wondered? But that could not be, I was imagining things.

"I told you that the honour of my friend is involved. You Japanese know all about preserving honour: your whole cult is based on that."

Sato rubbed over his eyes with his hands. His sigh would have lifted a helicopter. A thought suddenly struck me.

"Why don't you give me an escort, a female escort? That will show that my intentions are harmless."

Sato was thinking hard: he shoved his chair back, swallowed a few times.

"I could perhaps let you have an officer, a female officer," he said at last. I never thought of it. O.K. he said rubbing his eyes again. On your head it will be! You are a fool, your consul already said that, but I do understand your motive. I lost a few friends myself in this useless war. No woman is worth the trouble you are inflicting upon yourself."

"Damn," I thought, had Sato perceived that I was involved in finding out the truth for more than just one reason?

***

She was quite tall by Japanese standards, five feet seven and her name was Kuri San. An attractive face with a slim and well built body, clear skin, laughing creases around her eyes and when she smiled, which was often, she showed a row of healthy pearly white teeth. When we were introduced she bowed low. But she did not wear a kimono as I had expected.

Instead she wore a tweed jacket obviously made by a local tailor and the large pockets of that jacket were brimful of items I could not place.

"Firecrackers," she explained seeing the query in my eyes.

"Firecrackers?" I asked surprised.

"Yes to keep the dogs away," she smiled, "very effective," she added.

"Do you know the district?" I asked her.

"Yes I know it well; I have an uncle who lives there."

"What about Yakumi?"

"I don't know him, but I am sure my uncle does. We have to stay with my uncle for a few nights."

"A few nights;" I exclaimed. "Is it so difficult to find Yakumi?"

"If we stay a few nights with my uncle and news gets around, it may be that Yakumi hears about it and becomes curious. He knows what goes on and will want to know about you. As long as we stay with my uncle we will be safe.

Yakumi will respect the guest of elders, my uncle being one of them. We must hope that his curiosity is great enough so that he will come; there is nothing else we can do.

"The best policy is that he comes to the house. That way there is no danger."

"What if he does not come?"

"Then we can send a message through my uncle that you want to speak to him. We don't want to do that initially so as not to make him suspicious. If you and I stay at my uncle we must pretend to be married."

"Married, you and I?" She giggled.

"Well, even my uncle must not know that we are not. We must also sleep in the same bed."

"In the same bed?" I exclaimed.

"Am I that unattractive to you?" she queried.

"No not in the least," I hastened to say. "Only it is so unexpected."

"Be that as it may," Sato butted into our conversation, "this is the best policy and we are lucky that Kuri San has consented to help you."

"I am more than grateful," I said. "What may I call you?"

"You don't call me by my name; you say "shin a naru" which is something like "darling" in Japanese. Not exactly that but it will do. I also call you by that name. My uncle won't suspect anything wrong if we call each other by that name. You have to wear these clothes," she pointed to a duffel bag. You leave your own clothes behind."

The bag was already carefully packed.

"I packed it with clothes that are worn by the biggest size Japanese men," Kuri San giggled, "but you have to try the size in any case also; here put the trousers on," she said, handing me a pair of trousers.

"Here?" I said, looking for a changing room.

"Well you two are married aren't you," Sato remarked with a smile. Reluctantly I undressed till my under wear. The giggling of Kuri San did nothing to improve my embarrassment. The trousers fitted perfectly and in no time at all I was dressed in Japanese civilian clothes. The chief of police inspected me:

"Perfect," he said looking at me approvingly. "This way you don't look conspicuous," he said satisfied. Have you had something to eat?" he asked.

"I have," I said, still recovering from my embarrassment.

"Well then; I think you should be off, the taxi is already at the door. It will take you half way; taxis don't like to go into that district, you have to walk the rest."

"Shin a naru," Kuri San bowed, "you go first. Here in Japan the husband goes first; he is the boss."

I had to get used to this. We went on our way. The outskirts of Fukuoka were drab and filthy looking, full of soot, smog and mist. This was an active mining district. There were no children playing in the small parks adjoining the squalid buildings, no dogs either, in spite of the fact that Kuri San's pockets were full of firecrackers as a protection against dogs.

The car came to a stop.

"We walk the rest," Kuri San said. "And don't help me out of the car. Japanese men don't do that and you must not be conspicuous. The chief police officer warned you about that."

After I paid the driver and gave him a tip the man disappeared in a cloud of smoke anxiously looking back over his shoulder. He was glad to leave this infamous district.

"Since you follow me shin a naru, which way do I go?" I had already got used to calling her that. She pointed with her finger to a lane leading from the small square where the taxi driver had left us.

Our steps sounded hollow. The lane was bordered with two story wooden houses on either side. There was also a central hedgerow, which was supposed to be green. Instead there was so much coal dust on the leaves that they appeared grey. The chimneys emitted a sooty smoke, which also penetrated our nostrils.

After half an hours walk, I saw a wooden bench. Kuri San directed me to it.

"Go and sit down there. My uncle already knows we are coming, he lives in the next block; he will pick us up here." We waited on the wooden bench for another half hour. Then a small figure appeared out of the mist like a ghost.

"My uncle," Kuri San said. They bowed to each other. Next I was introduced as her husband. We bowed to each other also. I studied him.

He was small, only just over half my height. His eyes furtive but intelligent studied my face and tried to probe my secrets. He seemed to approve of me, which I, surprised about myself, rather liked. He indicated that we should go.

He went first. It wasn't too far to walk and after ten minutes we stopped in front of one of a row of small wooden houses. He slid the door open. It hadn't been locked! Was this district such a dangerous district after all? Inside it was cosy. A meal had been prepared and I was hungry. I learned that the uncle was not married.

In spite of the fact that I spoke some Japanese, the conversation was halting with Kury San interpreting. Talk was about the person I was and that we were only just married. It seemed to please her uncle, but I wondered suddenly to what extent I had let myself become involved in, to find out about what exactly had happened in Tamarkan camp so many years ago.

And how would Kuri San ever be able to explain to the old man our true relationship after I had left? A lot of questions needed to be answered and I did not have the answers.

The name Yakumi suddenly fell from the girl's lips. I saw the surprised look on her uncle's face but could not follow what had been said. After an hour's chatting the old man suggested that we should go to bed. Kuri San agreed and beckoned me into one of the two sleeping rooms. The uncle took the other one.

We were to sleep on the matted floor with a quilt under us, the Japanese way of a bed and a blanket on top. Kuri San helped me out of my tunic, but I insisted in sleeping in my underwear. She stripped naked, then put on a kimono and covered me with a blanket. After wishing me good night she nestled against me under another blanket and went out like a light.

I was alone with my thoughts. How long could I keep up this pretence I wondered.

When would I give up and come to my senses and leave? Leave this whole project; admit to myself that it was revenge I wanted. The police inspector had queried my motives. If Lily had not married Wong before I came back from the war, would I try to convict her father as I did now?

But no, "I had to be clear about this," I spoke to myself; "perhaps it wasn't personal revenge I was seeking."

I had visited the lonely graveyard in Tjipatat when I came back to Java after the end of the war. Every name on the crosses conjured up a face of a friend. The oldest age on the cross of the militia soldiers buried there was twenty-seven years; Werbata. They all died for nothing. The Cambodia trees planted between the graves were already higher than I myself was and through the cracks of the marble slabs, plants already had started growing. No one was looking after these graves. The low sun of the late afternoon threw long shadows of the crosses on the sand.

The scene dispirited me. The Indonesian bedoek from the Kampong in the distance reminded me that I must go.

Japan had got nowhere with their extended Asia plan and had lost the war. Yet their formerly occupied territories were either already independent or were in the process of getting it.

I was alive and I was able to find out why these friends of mine had been abandoned at a time that they needed help. Perhaps they should have been evacuated in time. In any case there had not been an officer who could have told them what to do for their defence. And the officer who was ordered to go to Tjipatat had never turned up and his name was Major Cane, Lily's father!

That was the real reason for which I was here, not revenge against Lily. Yet I was not altogether convinced. I fell asleep pondering the question

When I woke up the next morning, Kuri San was already talking to her uncle in the next room. I got up slowly and found my clothes neatly pressed by my side. I had to admit that she was looking after me well. After breakfast she suggested that we should go for a stroll.

"Tell me," she said: "what are you going to do when you have accomplished your mission. Are you going back to your wife?"

"I have no wife." "Before the war I had a fiancée. We would have married but the war changed all that."

"And I would not have lost my husband," Kuri San sadly remarked. "Had you been married a long time?" I asked her.

176

"No, a few months only. My husband volunteered to become a Kami Kaze pilot. He committed suicide for his country."

"What a waste," I said; he could have been here with you." She was quiet for a while.

"But giving your life for your country is a great honour," she said.

I looked at her out of the corner of my eye, so that she could not observe me. I could not believe that anyone would have preferred love for his country rather than the love from this marvellous girl sitting next to me. But then I had never been able to understand this exaggerated Bushido chivalry; preferring glorious death above life.

If dying gloriously was so fantastic in the Japanese mind, then I was far removed from being Japanese although I was dressed in a Japanese outfit and out for a stroll with my so-called Japanese wife.

The situation was so artificial that I again queried my motives for being here. Colonel Arlen had given me the task to find out what happened about attrocities committed in the POW camp Tamarkan in Siam. Not once had he mentioned Major Cane by name. Neither had he referred to the absence of Major Cane in Tjipatat although he must have known that I knew that Major Cane never arrived in Tjipatat where he was sent!

What were Colonel Arlen's motives for sending me to Japan? It had of course already occurred to me that he might have a personal motive too and that he was not acting only for the army. I might be a stool pigeon for some reason I was not informed about. Not for the first time the thought nagged in my mind that Colonel Arlen was up to something. What?

Dr. Stam had admonished me. Yes he would give evidence against Major Cane but he thought that mitigating factors should be explored also. What these mitigating factors could be, I was here to investigate.

Lily had begged me not to proceed. Her father had suffered enough. He had lost his wife and his son. And I was jeopardising his career now as well.

"Do you do it out of spite against me because I married Wong?" she had asked me.

I had never given Lily a reply to that question; simply because I did not know. Was I here in Japan trying to find mitigating circumstances or just the opposite? Was I hoping that the case against Major Cane would hold?

Once more I realised that I had to be absolutely clear about this. What about those graves I had visited in Tjipatat? I could all see them again in my mind and my feelings toward Major Cane became ice-cold.

What about Marcus? Did he not deserve a hearing? He tried to escape which was the proper thing to do as far as he could see it. Of course he should not have turned back. All right, his efforts only resulted in his death, but should Major Cane not have tried harder to protect him? Doctor Stam had wanted to.

Kuri San turned to me:

"You are far away with your thoughts "shin a naru," they upset you. Why do you do this? You only make yourself suffer." Her concern for me was genuine and I loved her for it. But I hardened myself against her too. I was here for a purpose and I could not afford to let my feelings interfere with my job at hand. How did she spot my unhappiness? Was it so obvious that I hated myself for wanting to persecute Lily's father or was it just a loose remark?

"What can I expect Kuri San," I said to her. "Is there any point waiting longer?" She put the index finger of her right hand to her lips as though wanting to soothe an impetuous child.

"Have patience," she replied. "My uncle promised me that he would make contact with Yakumi."

The weather did not improve. It rains in June in Japan and the Fukuoka district was no exception; the drizzle lasted and my mood degenerated. Kuri San's presence only made matters worse.

I felt guilty that I was such rotten company for her. She certainly did not deserve this. Then on the third day there was some activity. Kuri San shook me awake.

"Good news," she said. He is coming in the afternoon." I didn't need to be reminded who "he" was. I got up. Again my clothes were neatly pressed by my side. I owed the girl but I could not feel grateful. She was Japanese and as such she belonged to the same race that had murdered my friends. I could not afford to feel friendship toward her. My loyalty stood in the way, and I did not feel happy about that because she deserved better from me. Hours ticked by and time and again I wished that I had never come: that I would never have started this mission although I felt that the end of it was now in sight.

At last in the late morning I heard the sliding door to the street move. A voice, a gruff voice was calling from the open door. A man came in. He was not at all what I had been expecting. He was small wore a mining suit and looked altogether down and out. Could this be Yakumi?

No, he was not Yakumi but Yakumi had sent him.

"What was it that I wanted?" he would pass on the message, and Yakumi would try to reply. This was not at all what I wanted; what I wanted was to speak to Yakumi myself.

"Kuri San," I turned to her "I must speak to Yakumi myself. Will you please convey this to the messenger?" I realised full well that this could be the end of the whole mission and that I would have to return as ill informed as I was when I arrived. Kuri San spoke to the messenger.

"Impossible;" he shook his head. Kuri San translated:

"He does not want to speak to you." I had already gathered that. What was I to do now?

Suddenly I had a brainwave.

"Kuri San," I said to her, "would you be willing to go in my place? What I want to know is if Yakumi can remember the execution of a prisoner of war in

Tamarkan camp where he was in command. If so he will remember the circumstances no doubt and may be, just may be; he will change his mind about speaking to me. If he sees you he might not think there is any danger for him to come here."

"I think," replied Kuri San, "that he already knows that he has nothing to fear from you. His spies have already informed him about that."

"In that case, offer him a bribe." I said and I put 5000 yen down on the table as I spoke. "This is for half an hour interview; he cannot lose." She nodded.

"I will do that and pass on your message." Then she left with the messenger and the waiting game started anew. An hour went by then another one.

Just as I had given up all hope, suddenly Kuri San appeared, wet, carrying an umbrella but nevertheless soaked to the skin. A large broad shouldered man totally wet from the rain also, accompanied her. He wore the same type of clothes I was wearing, the typical average Japanese men's clothes. Instinct warned me that he was ruthless.

This was the Yakumi as I had pictured him all right.

"I am Yakumi and since when do you send a woman to do your errands?" he said in a reproaching voice. I decided to ignore his remarks. There would be nothing about the man that I would like; I had made up my mind about that long ago. He was a war criminal who had escaped the hangman's noose undeservedly.

At that moment I wished that I could be the hangman. He had killed Marcus.

"What do you want to know?" Yakumi resumed. I started hesitatingly:

"Do you remember the execution of a prisoner of war in Tamarkan?"

"The one that we had planned should escape? Of course I do. The whole incident was planned so that Major Cane would get a bad name among his soldiers. Divide and rule. Marcus was the victim of this plot. We wanted him to escape, made it easy for him initially to do so, but later put so many obstacles in his way that he had to come back.

"One of my men pretended to be friendly and put the idea of escape into his head; made it seem easy. We knew when he was back; we also knew of the plan of the doctor whose name I have forgotten and who had wanted to shield him in the cholera hospital by letting him take the identity of a deceased patient when one died. Spies had already informed us of this plan. Had Major Cane gone ahead with this plan we would have prevented it. We purposely wanted Major Cane to have a bad name among his soldiers for not protecting the escaped prisoner. He had to have a bad name. It suited our purpose. How do you think we otherwise could control so many prisoners of war with so few men?

"What did you come here for? Is Major Cane on trial and if so what for? Are you not aware that Major Cane was helpless and did not get any support from his men? He also did not try to please us: as some officers did, to win some favour from us. His men also disliked him because he had adopted our method of instilling discipline; slapping the faces of his men if they committed an offence. Here again; ask yourself. How else was he able to keep up some discipline under those circumstances?

Of course you know nothing of those circumstances. Major Cane was as much a victim of circumstances as we all were. I needed to execute the escaped prisoner. I needed the drama so that no one dared to escape afterwards. At the same time I wanted Major Cane to appear in a bad light, so that his men would be disgruntled with him. They already were because he had adopted our method of punishment as I already said. In the circumstances he was right. He did it because it was the only way. He reluctantly had come to the conclusion that to have some sort of discipline, he had to adopt our method of punishment. His thinking was correct. So was mine. I had a railroad to finish so that our troops could be used in Burma. The sea transport of troops had become too dangerous. What did it matter that one person, your friend was killed? We were all expendable."

"What did you do in the war, hide in some safe corner? Major Cane did not; he was a POW because his government did not equip your army sufficiently. We also treated our prisoners the way we had been told. Our methods were brutal, expressly so, in order that we could rule with only a handful of men. When you get back greet Major Cane from me. He was not a coward, not in my eyes. He stepped forward trying to stop the execution. I had given specific instructions that he was not to be killed. I needed him to be hated, not killed. It suited my purpose to have him alive. In any case we sometimes, and I repeat only sometimes, held back. He is alive isn't he and you want to prosecute him? That is absurd; you do not know what you are talking about. The circumstances were altogether abnormal."

"Go home; Major Cane did what he had to do as we all had to. Does this satisfy your coming here?" Before I could reply he got up, bowed to Kuri San, ignored me and was out of the door. The 5000 yen was still lying on the table untouched. I have never seen him again.

Late that afternoon waiting for a taxi I said good-bye to Kuri San. She had helped me enormously. Without her help I would have accomplished nothing and I realised that I owed her a great deal of gratitude; yet I could not bring myself to feel it. Her people had caused an enormous amount of harm and bloodshed. She undoubtedly felt my reticence.

"Shin a naru," I started: "you helped me so much."........ But before I could thank her, she had kissed me on my lips and was gone. I had no further business here; yet I felt a pang in my heart.

"Your taxi Sir," Sato the police officer said, holding the door open for me and handing me my bag. I knew I had to go. Via the Dutch embassy in Tokyo I obtained an airline ticket and my flight from Tokyo to Batavia left the next day at 3pm. precisely. I was on board, but the niggling feelings in my head persisted. Yakumi's story had put my thinking upside down. And how would Kuri San's life develop? Kuri San whose husband had been killed in the war and who had helped me, expecting nothing in return. These were new disturbing questions forming in my mind and I knew I would never get any answers to these. There was no way I could ever be certain now, realising the turmoil in my head, and being more confused than ever about my own feelings. It was especially about the latter that I had been seeking and trying in vain, in Japan to find an answer!

Chapter 20

Here was the start of the preliminary hearings in the military court case against Major Cane, Lily's father and in which court I was appointed the military prosecutor. I had plenty time to think about the arguments I was going to present. They had bothered me time and again, thinking about what they were exactly, since I now held a different point of view than the one I held before I went to Japan. My head was in turmoil.

It wasn't long before Major Cane entered the courtroom. Once he had been an imposing figure; before the war; when he was impeccably dressed in full military uniform. Now only a sick man appeared. Even his clothes seemed far too big for him. The sunlight's probing fingers falling from the upper windows of the courtroom, betrayed the dust in the air, showing up tiny floating particles reflecting the light. They also showed up well deserved numerous gleaming medals on Major Cane's chest. In spite of the fact that he seemed very ill he managed to walk in tall and straight.

Was this ill man the man I really wanted to prosecute even though every fibre in me at this time could find a hundred reasons for exonerating him? But I was not my own master here. My dead comrades in arms were. They needed a hearing. They had died. I was alive. I had to be acting on their behalf only. My arguments should only be their arguments. How I felt did not matter.

Who was the guilty person who had abandoned my comrades? I felt more than uncertain. How could I sound convincing when I was not at ease about the accusations I was going to present against major Cane?

I looked round the courtroom. My gaze stopped when I saw Lily sitting on the upper wooden benches. Her face was pale and contrasted starkly with her dark blond hair, combed back and held by a black ribbon. She looked straight ahead of her and did not seem to notice anybody.

My emotions nearly got the better of me and I had great difficulty refraining myself from wanting to comfort her. Not that she would have accepted that, I sadly reflected. It showed me how far against our will we had separated from one another. She had begged me not to proceed with the prosecution of her father but I had ignored her pleas. She knew only vaguely how I felt deep down about prosecuting her father. I had tried to explain this to her but probably only in summary terms. I was not sure myself what to think. I certainly did not want to upset her too much since of course her father was dear to her.

But equally so were my friends to me; and until not so long ago did I hold her father responsible for their deaths.

Recently however, I was not as certain about the facts as I was before. Was I mellowing or had I seen reason?

I had not yet asked Captain Hes to be in the courtroom, since I did not need him at this time. But he knew that I wanted him to possibly be a witness in this case later. After all he had been the last officer in Tjipatat before the men were left to themselves. He agreed to testify although he was not sure what was expected of him.

A thin small figure, clad in the dress of a native Indonesian woman, sat in the far corner of the room. The dress was beautifully ironed but in spite of the meticulous care, which had been lavished on it, it was obvious that it had seen better days. She held a white handkerchief in her tiny hand, while she uncomfortably fidgeted in her chair.

This was what it was about: This was Marcus' mother! She would hear about her son's premature death and the army's point of view, after having investigated Major Cane's involvement in her son's execution by the Japanese camp commander Yakumi.

I felt helpless; she had lost the son she loved in a war with which he had nothing to do. It had killed thousands of people, most of whom had not wanted anything else but to be left alone and get on with their lives. The unfortunate death of her son; was the result of cowardice on the part of Major Cane. So the military would make it appear and probably genuinely even believed. But was it cowardice? I had done the investigation by going to Japan and heard the story first hand from Yakumi himself.

What accusations remained against major Cane as far as the death of her son was concerned? After hearing Yakumi's story, I had come to totally different ideas than those I had held, before I went.

Major Cane could not be blamed for this death I had concluded. And I would bring this up in his defence; the truth as I saw it, the truth even in spite of the fact that I was officially the prosecutor in the case. What was truth, apart from merely being a point of view anyway?

The clerk of the court got up. He expected the Judge to walk in any moment now, but he had to get up because his pen had run dry. Without a proper workable pen, he could not make any notes. Of course he should have made sure in time; that his pen was in good working order. He accepted the blame in his mind. This was going to be an interesting case, he thought. It would be different from the usual boring cases. The Judge would be in his element. He would see to it; make sure that it was all recorded, as it should be.

It was not long afterwards when Judge Penn walked in, wearing his black gown with a swagger, which would have made a Roman Senator feel jealous. He was twenty minutes late as becomes an officer of the law.

Facing the Judge on the wall opposite the room as he entered, was hanging the photograph of a serious looking man, pointing an accusing finger at him. Underneath the photograph was written: "Don't talk about secret information." The photograph was a remnant from the time when the war had started and was left hanging in the room. Even the Japanese in the three and a half year occupation, had not bothered to remove it.

No matter at which angle you approached the photograph, the accusing finger was always directed straight at you. Judge Penn felt decidedly uncomfortable. He had many secrets in the course of his working life he could not talk about. The remark underneath the photograph was eminently applicable to him. He scratched his neck. He had not worn his black gown for quite a while and the laundry servant had put too much starch on his collar. In spite of his confident appearance, he felt a little nervous. Everybody had got up, and then sat down again after the Judge was seated.

The clerk of the court returned. His face for this particular occasion was set in the: "didn't I tell you that he would come in just as I was away" position. As though this was not enough, he pointed to the clock hanging on the wall, seemingly wanting to remind himself and others, what time it was and accepting the blame for being late.

In the silence of the room a small lizard on the wall climbed ever so carefully to a mosquito, resting still on the white wall at times, so as not to scare away his meal ticket for today. To him the court case was totally unimportant. What did it matter what the court decided? His life depended on this mosquito. Secretly I agreed. Did we need all this pomposity?

The case against major Cane appeared straightforward, but only when viewed from a purely military point of view. However that was not my opinion any longer. Major Cane was supposed to be a coward because he had not wanted to help by shielding Marcus. That he had not helped Marcus was fact. Seeing it from his point of view and taking account of the circumstances however, it was also a fact that the doctor was running the risk that he would be killed also if Major Cane had let the doctor have his way. Major Cane had not wanted to agree to that risk. The doctor had been brave, yes, because he had accepted the awful possibility that he could be killed by the Japanese also, not only Marcus, if the ploy he intended to carry out, would have been detected by the Japanese. Nevertheless he clearly had accepted this risk, wanting to help. That was courageous.

Yet the doctor had been far too optimistic, thinking that the Japanese had not noticed Marcus' return. Personally I had heard from Yakumi that the return of Marcus had been noticed. The Japanese even knew of the plan of the doctor. They would have prevented it. Major Cane's concern could not be directed only to saving Marcus' life but also had to be for the doctor and for the other POW's too! What if the doctor would also have been executed? A doctor was sorely needed. Too many POW's already died as it was: through hardship, disease and lack of medicines and food. Without some medical care, the situation would be many times worse! Had major Cane not been correct to refuse the risk the doctor was willing to take?

With regards to the second point the army held against Major Cane: using Japanese tactics in order to maintain discipline, slapping the faces of his soldiers. Was that wrong? It was a very debatable point. How else could he have kept even a token of discipline under these abnormal circumstances? Abnormal circumstances sometimes required abnormal behaviour to cope with those circumstances. Did Major Cane have any other choice?

What remained of the accusation of cowardice that had been made? If major Cane was indeed a coward, then he should never have been placed in a position where he had to be brave. He certainly then should never have been promoted to be in command. My arguments for the defence of Major Cane, in spite of the fact that I, at the same time, was accusing him; were due to my belief that nobody can choose whether one is born a coward or not. If major Cane indeed was born a coward, then because he could not help being that; this factor should be taken into account in his defence for the way he had behaved.

He simply could not be different from what he was; that is to say "suddenly" become brave, when he found himself in a position where this new quality was now required of him. I intended to air this viewpoint in court.

Nevertheless I already knew that I would never be able to convince any military court to see it my way. No military court throughout history ever had.

The fact that I could reason in my mind that Major Cane had not proceeded to Tjipatat out of fear; weakened my case considerably. Did that imply then also, that I could not hold him responsible for the death of my friends any longer? My visit to the graveyard in Tjipatat had shown me the names on their graves. For each name I saw on a cross, I felt a pang in my heart. I had known them so well! This was the real issue for which I personally had held him responsible. I had sworn then on that lonely graveyard that I would take Major Cane to court. And here I was, unsure of myself. By army standards this was considered desertion, but that was not the way I saw it. My argument was that he had abandoned my friends. That was what I had intended to bring forward. That was the real issue for me and was the only reason why I strongly felt that my dead friends deserved a court hearing. And I was now stuck with my own argument, namely that if major Cane was born a coward, he simply could not bring himself to go to Tjipatat when he realised that he would die by going there. Could I still argue my debatable point of view, namely that he was guilty because he had abandoned my friends? What in the end can anyone accuse a person of? What therefore remained of the strong case, which I thought I had when I started my investigations?

There was another debatable issue here in major Cane's favour. You could argue that the charge of desertion held no foundation at all. Major Cane had reasoned that by going to Tjipatat he only would put his own life in danger as well. The outcome would have been the same: annihilation of the camp. The proper question should be: why was Tjipatat not evacuated in time? That was the real issue. Not why Major Cane did not follow up an impossible order given by an incompetent superior. You could argue that he had not left his post; the Tjiater pass. No; instead Colonel Arlen had taken his post away from him.

Although these points were so clear to me now; they had not been like that before I went to Japan. Yakumi in a way had opened my eyes. He had said to me that everybody in the war had become expendable. He had murdered Marcus because he reasoned that a railroad from Siam to Burma for his soldiers, needed to be finished as quickly as possible. What was the life of one enemy soldier who had surrendered, worth; compared to the lives, which were going to be saved of so many Japanese soldiers, his soldiers, by this vital railroad? No POW would dare to escape from now on, and therefore his railroad had the highest number of prisoners working on it and the highest priority to get it ready for troop movements in the shortest possible time. Winning the war for Japan was, and had to be, uppermost in Yakumi's mind. There was even a bonus point, which equally suited him. Major Cane would be hated even more by his men. He already was, because of his Japanese manners in maintaining discipline.

The argument of his men; that Major Cane should have done more to help Marcus, would be brought forward. But how could he, considering all the other facts?

Seeing it from Yakumi's point of view; it made perfect sense, brutal though his reasoning had been. The more disenchantment there was between the soldiers and their officers the better it was for him, guarding the POW's with only a handful of men.

Major Cane could have done nothing to help Marcus. The only really remaining grievance which I held against major Cane, was my personal one: he was one of the officers who had stopped Mas and I from reaching Australia, thereby secretly thwarting the wishes of the Governor. He was certainly guilty of that. In a personal way he had betrayed me at the time that I had still been Lily's fiancée and when I had trusted him! His reasoning was that he did not want a free Indonesia as yet. In this he was entitled to his opinion, but not at my expense and certainly not against the wishes of the Governor-General, the highest official body in the land at that time.

Colonel Arlen, it was plain to me, wanted major Cane out of the way. He was a liability to him and to the army generally. After all Major Cane was truly a deserter in the military sense of the word: he had refused to follow up an order to take up the post where he was ordered to go. The army wanted him punished. In wartime he might even have been shot. Everything was correct in that respect, looking at it from a military point of view. His defence that he had not abandoned his initial post, the Tjiater pass, would probably not help him

If I could not hold Major Cane any longer responsible for the death of my friends, was it then "one of those things" that happens in a war situation when no one can really be blamed? But no! Someone was to blame. My dead comrades still deserved a hearing. I still needed to bring their case forward as best as I could.

Colonel Arlen had an important reason for himself; apart from the desertion issue, for wanting to get rid of Major Cane. Major Cane knew of the unforgivable blunder, which Colonel Arlen had made by sending the soldiers who had built the bunkers of the Tjiater pass, to the north coast of Java. They were sent there, wrongly as could have been foreseen, to oppose a Japanese landing. And wanting to replace that unit when he realised his mistake, Colonel Arlen at the last moment had moved a contingent of the tenth battalion to the now deserted pass instead. They knew nothing of its lay out! To make matters worse in the hurried decision they were only given a road map of the area! The pass with its expensive elaborate bunker system would have been a problem for the Japanese, had the unit commanded by Major Cane who built the bunkers, been left there to defend it.

Moreover the soldiers who had built the expensive bunkers of the Tjiater pass were sent away under the command of a captain, who was a total stranger to them. Not under the command of their own officer: Major Cane. The result was that with a commanding officer unfamiliar to them; they retreated by lack of morale, already disenchanted by having had to move from their initial position. Eventually beaten, scattered and demoralised, when they had lost their captain in their retreat, they were then ordered to move to Tjipatat thereby only aggravating the already untenable position of this camp further. The outcome of that one mistake was a disaster with far reaching consequences. Major Cane, who had been their true commanding officer, was only at the last moment, ordered to go to Tjipatat because Colonel Arlen didn't know any more what to do with him. He did not belong anywhere by then. Major Cane disenchanted with the whole affair now refused to carry out the order, which he considered stupid!

Colonel Arlen was now faced with a dilemma. He wanted rid of Major Cane, but he also knew that Major Cane would expose his mistake if he were pushed. It wouldn't do his future career any good if the truth came to light. He therefore had to cover up the mistake, for which only he, was to blame. He had to find a way round the problem.

The solution Colonel Arlen came up with was that I could do the dirty job for him. "Give Richard Searle all the ammunition required," he reasoned. The controller clearly had a score to even. Colonel Arlen had probed carefully into the reasons for the disenchanted feeling the controller held against major Cane. And he had found the reasons!

The controller held Major Cane directly responsible for his friend's death, executed by the Japanese in Siam.

And there was more: he also found out that Richard Searle had discovered that Major Cane had not followed orders and therefore must have concluded that since his friends had been abandoned by Major Cane; they were killed unnecessarily. And Richard Searle had moreover discovered that Major Cane not only did not go to Tjipatat as he should have done but that he also had called Lieutenant Hes away: leaving Tjipatat without an officer!

Colonel Arlen reasoned that the gory details of the beheading in Tamarkan camp by itself; and brought up in court by Richard Searle, full of discontent after he came back from Japan; apart from anything else, would already be sufficient to show up Major Cane's wrongdoings to the extent that he Colonel Arlen could pretend in court be on Major Cane's side; thereby avoiding the wrath of Major Cane. That would cover up his mistake nicely.

Major Cane never felt that he was a deserter. Instead he correctly reasoned that the blame of the Tjiater pass lay with his superior Colonel Arlen, who had separated him from his men and taking them away from the Tjiater pass, which they had built. He was the one who should be on trial for incompetence. Not he, Major Cane for desertion, which is what he was blamed for.

Major Cane had given Colonel Arlen an ultimatum and counted on the fact that Colonel Arlen would keep his mouth shut about his desertion.

"You keep your mouth shut and I'll do likewise," he warned Colonel Arlen. It was now up to Colonel Arlen to solve the problem: how to get rid of Major Cane in such a way that he, Colonel Arlen, at the same time came out of the entanglement unscathed.

Now the controller was back from Japan with the information that would nail Major Cane, so Colonel Arlen believed. He looked forward to that. Purposely he avoided every contact with the controller. To see him and talk to him before the proceedings started was suspicious. Let Richard Searle speak out in court. Give him leeway! It would be enough to get rid of Major Cane. He, Colonel Arlen, would be there to handle the court case. It had to be done in such a way that there could not be any suspicion by Major Cane that he, Colonel Arlen, was the culprit behind condemning him.

Major Cane would be dishonourably fired from the army and Colonel Arlen's blunder would never come to light. He would commiserate; he would even appear to be seen on major Cane's side in court, to get Major Cane's goodwill. That would be easy enough.

In order to appear to be on major Cane's side, he would first discredit the controller from the start of the proceedings. The controller could also be accused of desertion and firing on his own relieving guard. Whether these events were true or not didn't matter. He would bring it up. The innuendo would be enough. Maybe Captain Hes was going to support him there.

Unbeknown to Colonel Arlen, Hes wanted to protect Major Cane, not condemn him. Lieutenant Hes had also discovered the true events with regard to the situation in Tjipatat and also knew that Major Cane had evacuated him from Tjipatat to save his life. He owed Major Cane a service in return. Apart from that he was also in love with his daughter.

When Colonel Arlen took his usual morning shower before getting dressed to go to the courtroom he was in a splendid mood. He could dispose of the controller and Major Cane at one and the same time. He even whistled when he was shaving in front of the mirror. Colonel Arlen was a master in duplicity. He should have been a lawyer! But he should have been more cautious. Even the best thought out plans, he had to admit later, have a habit of going wrong.

Because Colonel Arlen had made one further cardinal mistake than just the Tjiater pass affair! He had relied on utter secrecy at the meeting between him and the five officers who were present in hotel Homann, which turned out not to be as watertight as he had expected. Unbeknown to him I now possessed the notes of Colonel Brink, which were given to me by his widow and which were dealing with the official proceedings in hotel Homann before the war. I knew for some time already exactly the dirty dealings Colonel Arlen had been involved in, but I could now in court prove what I would accuse him of and show what he was capable of.

Initially I did not know and had wondered what the real reason for sending me to Japan had been for. Now I was perfectly aware what he had planned, expecting me to come back with ammunition against Major Cane and where he then could afford to appear on Major Cane's side, thereby avoiding the wrath of Major Cane.

That I had come back with new ideas, thinking altogether differently about Major Cane's involvement in the Marcus affair was something contrary to his plans and something he could never have anticipated. I had become wise to him. This time I was one step ahead! He would find out that he could not twist me around his little finger any longer! The new ammunition I now had in my possession was not directed against Major Cane in the first place, but rather against Colonel Arlen! And I was ready to use that ammunition.

Chapter 21

Colonel Arlen strutted across the courtroom like a Roman gladiator. He was determined; his whole composure showed that. But his determination was not directed towards defending Major Cane, his client, as he was supposed to do, but instead towards condemning him! I was probably the only one in the courtroom to know this.

I had to supply the ammunition; do the dirty job for him and he would give the appearance that he Colonel Arlen really did not want to find Major Cane guilty.

He had planned on sending me to Japan, so that I would come back with damning evidence against Major Cane. That damning evidence I would be coming back with, so Colonel Arlen reasoned, would be sufficient to get rid of Major Cane neatly. But he would get a nasty surprise! That I had returned with a totally different point of view than the one I had held before I went to Japan was unfortunate for Colonel Arlen.

Also unfortunate for him, was the fact that he did not know that I was going to take out my revenge on him personally for deceiving Mas and myself in the past. I had waited a long time for this! The subject of my revenge had shifted altogether and the revenge was going to be sweet! Of course I still had not totally forgotten that I held Major Cane responsible for the death of my friends. That however would come up later and was my main reason for being here.

"This man is a nut!" Colonel Arlen declared, opening his assault referring to me. I expected this. His ploy would be to discredit me from the start so as to get the goodwill of Major Cane and fool him as to his real intent. Still referring to me he went on:

"Searle accuses a clique of officers of a plot to interfere with the wishes of the Governor-General. Where did he get such nonsense? It is a grave accusation and I will get back to this point later.

For the time being I wish to show what he is capable of in his fantasies. You will then be able to decide what value to attach to the so-called evidence he is going to present in this court.

I am referring to a book he has written. In his introduction to the story he states that he probably won't be believed anyhow, but that he has written the book for a particular person who will believe his story although he does not want to name the person. He goes on to say that the reader will know eventually who the person is by reading the book. This he states mysteriously at the very beginning and on the face of it; this seems harmless enough.

"Perhaps it is a children's story you may think. When you start reading it however, you realise that he tried to write an account of a prediction, told to him on the eve of the attack on Pearl harbour. At least this is what he wants you to believe.

It is only then when reading the book that you realise that the book is full of serious inaccuracies; for instance in his book he claims to be able to see the island of Bali from the Goenoeng Ringgit in Pasir Poetih, a distance of at least two hundred miles! And then this story of Djojo Bojo, the prediction he refers to: pure fabrication in my opinion.

"In the book he claims that he was told that a yellow, war like race, would come and occupy the islands of the Dutch East Indies for the period of a maize harvest, which is approximately six months. All of us however know now, that this period has lasted three and a half years instead! I wonder what Richard Searle has to say to this; another one of his many inaccuracies?"

I got up.

"Your Honour," I addressed the Judge: "Some accusations are brought up against me by Colonel Arlen. Let us examine a few. Let me just refer to the last statement he made. If he had read my book accurately, he would have noticed, that I referred to a prediction made hundreds of years ago and that this prediction was not made by me. That prediction was made by a holy man, a Hadji and was told to me by a Madurese fisherman.

"The true authenticity of the story cannot therefore be confirmed; for that you would have to go back a few hundred years. Let me make that clear first. And my notes about the event when I was told the story; unfortunately can no longer be traced. They got lost during the war.

"The prediction was told to me on the evening before the day of the attack on Pearl harbour, as I have stated in the book. The person who told me the story was very convincing about what he said. The last time I saw him was the day following the day Pearl Harbour was bombed. I was saying goodbye to him then.

"What was interesting of course was the fact that he had told me the story the night before the attack. In his mind there was no doubt that the prediction would come true and would start happening soon. The fact that Pearl Harbour was attacked the day after he told me the story was relevant to me. That is strictly personal. It might not have been convincing enough to another person. However my story in the book, which is really his story, also refers to a possibility that the period of occupation by the Japanese might last longer than a maize harvest. I asked the fisherman who told me the prediction about this possibility specifically. I asked him this question, because it seemed to me that the period of occupation that he mentioned was very short. And in light of the fact that this period lasted three and a half years as Colonel Arlen rightly states, indeed therefore seems as though at least the time of occupation of the Dutch East Indies in the prediction was wrong. It could also mean therefore that the whole prediction is in jeopardy as far as time is concerned.

"The fisherman's reply was very clear however. He stated that this period could be influenced: but only by a very powerful person. I then asked him, would the Queen of the Netherlands be able to influence this period?

"After thinking for a while he said that another person would do it. He implied thereby that it would not be the Queen of the Netherlands who would be able to change that part of the prediction. He seemed to know already that the period would be altered and even by whom, although he didn't want to say it. Whether he really knew or didn't is not for me to say. I was brought up in the East Indies and there are many bizarre phenomena for which there are no explanations.

"The story by itself, as far as predicting that a yellow race would come from overseas to occupy the Dutch East Indies, is so exceptional; even if some inaccuracies would have crept in, which they haven't, I hasten to add; that he could never have made it up himself.

"Moreover, and of course this is the striking bit, he told me this prediction one night before the attack. Personally I believe in what the fisherman told me. I was there myself on that night and at the time that he told me the story, there was an altogether eerie quality about that night. I have never been able to explain it. I didn't get the story second hand.

"A few other remarkable things had occurred before that night, such as an earthquake a few days before. Totally unexpected! The mountain at the foot of which Pasir poetih is located is well known to be an extinct volcano.

"I want to refer again to the part of the prediction mentioned earlier, namely the one where he said that the yellow race would occupy the Dutch East Indies only for the duration of a maize harvest. At the time I did not know what to make of it. Now I know that president Roosevelt could be the person who changed that period unaware of having done that. He gave precedence to the war in Europe, which is very well documented. This decision was his personal one. It was not agreed; by for instance Admiral King, who wanted to finish the war in the Pacific first. Had it not been for that fact, the war in the Pacific might not have lasted three and a half years, which it did.

"Another alternative explanation for the discrepancy, as far as the time of occupation by the Japanese is concerned, is that the prediction was made at a time when America did not yet exist. This to my mind is a valid argument and the correction factor in the original prediction of Djojo Bojo was thereby taken into account by the fisherman."

There was total silence for minutes hanging heavily in the courtroom

"A very remarkable story," the Judge said. "Were you told that a yellow race would occupy the Dutch East Indies islands even before the attack on Pearl harbour?"

"That is correct," I said, "whether Colonel Arlen believes it or not."

Colonel Arlen got up.

"Amazing," he sneered waving his arm towards the audience in the courtroom. "We now have heard the fabrication of a story from what sounds like coming from a mentally disturbed. Anybody else who can testify that this story is not your own fabrication of events but really the story of a fisherman in Pasir Poetih?" he turned to me.

"I don't know," I replied; "the only other person I know whom the fisherman told the story of Djojo Bojo to, is a certain Mr. Blommesteyn who was the owner of the bungalows where I stayed and where the fisherman Doel, that is his name, told me the story. He may remember; if he is still alive."

"How convenient," Colonel Arlen remarked sarcastically. "We only have the word of Richard Searl himself, that this "tale", as I rather wish to call it, was told to him by a Madurese fisherman; no evidence whatever that he did not make this whole nonsense up himself. All the persons he referred to in his book, who could be questioned about the authenticity of the story are not available, perhaps even dead he now says.

"But let us continue," he said turning to the Judge. "This soldier is a friend of a freedom fighter of dubious reputation. He recently visited this friend, who I hasten to add, is not a friend of ours and who has committed murder of women and children. Nevertheless Richard Searle refused to give information, which could have been helpful in apprehending this so called "freedom" fighter.

"Recently he went to Japan, sent by the army to collect evidence against an officer whom he has accused of cowardice and desertion and returned with a detailed rapport in which all sorts of accusations and inaccuracies were introduced." He looked in my direction hoping that I would now explain that what he liked to hear and was counting on.

I kept quiet. My chance would come later. I would let him ramble on first. Let him think that he was succeeding in getting rid of Major Cane which of course I knew was his real intent, while at the same time making it seem, and was in fact, putting a slur on my record in the army. I could see that he was already slightly taken aback because I was not doing, which he had relied upon; namely give incriminating evidence against Major Cane, at this stage. Since I did not oblige, he had no option but to carry on.

"We have it," he continued slightly losing confidence and with uncertainty in his voice, "that Richard Seale went as far as to sleep with a Japanese female, in order to get this information he wanted."

I realised that Colonel Arlen's accusation although incorrect, was obtained from the consul in Fukuoka. The whole gimmick of course was to discredit me by putting a slur on my military career. Indeed I was not mistaken.

"With regard to his military conduct," Colonel Arlen continued, "it is also known that this soldier has fired on his own troops on one occasion. Fortunately since he was such a bad marksman he missed. His explanation is that the incident occurred because the password by the relieving guard was not given. This of course is again his interpretation of events, but I would call it another "inaccuracy". We will have Captain Hes in the courtroom later, to tell us exactly what happened.

"But there is more and this is serious. When he failed in his attempt to get away with the Regents' son from Tjilatjap by air, which is what his orders were, he should have returned to his unit in Tjipatat. He had orders to proceed to

Australia with the Regent's son. There is no reason whatever, that he needed to proceed to Australia on his own, after he had lost the Regent's son. He is lucky that he got away with not being called a deserter; instead of making accusations of desertion against Major Cane."

I realised that he had subtly managed to introduce desertion in connection with Major Cane. He continued:

"Mas, the son of the Regent of West Java and Searl, were both soldiers in the Royal Colonial Army and both absconded in wartime. Draw your own conclusions! There is more to say about his escape to Australia. He claims to have got away with four other soldiers in a Buginese sailing vessel with a crew of three. All the soldiers of course were deserters if you ask me. Richard Searle claims that they were bombed and that the boat sank. Afterwards the S.S. Jansen rescued him from the sea. This latter event is the only one we could corroborate. Searle says that he can't remember what happened exactly, because, so he claims, he was knocked unconscious. Therefore nobody knows the true story.

"On the face of it, it seems that he was the only survivor on the Buginese vessel. The boat with four soldiers plus three-crew personel disappeared. That is if you believe his story and that he again has not made it up. His friendship with Indonesians, who want independence by force and are opposed to law and order, is well known. Even his former fiancée has given him up to marry someone else. In short he is lucky that he is not court marshalled for desertion himself, instead of bringing up these false accusations against an officer of the forces."

For the second time Colonel Arlen had referred to desertion, although in a very subtle way, by instead accusing me of it, rather than Major Cane. I had to admit that he was clever! After a short pause he went on. Still referring to me he continued:

"A psychiater, who has examined his book at our request recently, has diagnosed him a pathological case of impersonation. He is pathologically in love with the characters in his novel, full of fantasies.

He believes that his stories are true and identifies himself with the characters in the book to the extent that the world is no longer real to him. He believes only in his own interpretation of reality. His "fantasies", as I rather call the book, are inconsistent, with reality, as we understand it, yet perfectly consistent with that of a schizophrenic person. No wonder that he needs a foreword, already stating that he won't be believed. At least it shows that he has some insight into his nonsense."

I got up again. I decided that I now had had enough of him. I turned to the Judge.

"Is it my wrong interpretation of reality your Honour, that I counted more than fifty war graves in Tjipatat; mostly friends of mine who were abandoned because there was no officer present who could tell them what to do?"

"Abandoned you say," Colonel Arlen spoke out of turn, "this was wartime, every unit had to fight the best they could. There were at least two sergeants in Tjipatat who were competent to instruct the soldiers what to do. These soldiers had been trained to fight; what were they there for otherwise?"

"Exactly that is what I would like to know. In my opinion they were sacrificed and they should have been evacuated."

"How much military training have you acquired to be able to give an opinion when it comes to military strategy Richard Searle? Were you not trained to become a civil servant?"

"Although I was not trained to become a military strategist as you imply, I can nevertheless reason that a military unit should be commanded by an officer; otherwise what are you there for, if a sergeant could do your job?" This was a question I knew he could not answer.

"But," I continued, "I was under the impression that this court was convened to investigate the conduct of Major Cane or am I mistaken? Because if I am mistaken and the court wants to investigate my conduct during the war; then in my defence, I am perfectly willing to tell my story of events." I turned to the Judge.

"Which is it to be your Honour?"

Colonel Arlen got up again before the Judge could reply.

"Your Honour," he said; "the defence is surely allowed to probe into the motives and rule conduct of the prosecution. In this particular case the person acting for the prosecution is the controller Richard Searle. Surely you will allow the defence this freedom and opportunity?"

The Judge nodded.

"However," he said,"we have not even heard what the army, through the controller, is accusing Major Cane of. I am now quite confused. It indeed seems to me now, that you meant the trial to be conducted against the controller, instead of what we are here for; namely for the trial of Major Cane, in which I wish to remind you, that you are acting for his defence."

This statement from the Judge unwittingly made, would be exactly what Colonel Arlen wanted to hear. He had managed to appear to be on Major Cane's side in court. Even the Judge was fooled! Again he wanted to get up but the Judge beckoned him to sit down.

"You will get your chance I promise, but I want to hear from the controller first."

"Thank you your Honour," I said getting up. "For the record, there were three accusations I wanted to make against Major Cane. Thereafter, I intended also to introduce mitigating circumstances contrary to usual procedure your Honour. Normally these mitigating circumstances are brought up by the defence; therefore they should belong to the realm of Colonel Arlen.

"That is where I beg your indulgence, because although appointed prosecutor in this court, I also wish to deal with these mitigating factors myself.

The reason that I wish to bring these mitigating factors forward myself, is because I know that the defence will not do so; will not bring them forward in the way I will and can."

The Judge stopped me short:

"Are you not presumptuous, thinking that you can do better than the defence? This is most irregular."

"Here is where I want to apologise," I said. "Indeed it sounds very pompous of me to state that I know better than the defence. Yet I believe that this is so, purely because I heard what happened in Tamarkan camp in Siam first hand.

I want to make it plain at the outset, that I have only had a cursory amount of training in law. In no way am I pretending to be a lawyer. What I bring forward at this moment will be in laymen's language and again I apologize for it.

"However before coming to the real issue, namely the three accusations against Major Cane, and at the same time also the mitigating circumstances in favour of Major Cane, to which I referred earlier; there are other accusations I wish to make first. In case these accusations don't seem to be relevant to you at first, I beg your indulgence your Honour:

"They may be relevant as I think you will agree, once you have heard me out. You can then of course decide whether you want the evidence retained as relevant, or otherwise decide."

"You may proceed," the Judge nodded in my direction. I thanked him, and resumed.

"This time my accusations are directed not against Major Cane only, but especially against a clique of officers that has been acting on its own: contrary to the wishes of the Governor-General. Major Cane happens to be only one member of this clique of officers. He is undoubtedly guilty but perhaps only in a minor way. The major culprit is Colonel Arlen present here."

There was a deadly silence. The defence being accused in court! It was unheard of.

Colonel Arlen got up like a jojo again.

"You hear that? The controller goes off into a tangent again. He brings up all sorts of incorrect accusations and imaginary happenings; none of which can be corroborated; let him specify what he means."

The Judge turned to me:

"The defence is perfectly entitled to an explanation. You have accused the defence of a grave misdeed. You better substantiate your accusation. Otherwise the defence is entitled to an apology, which if not accepted can lead to a court case proceeding directed against you."

"I certainly will substantiate my claim," I said calmly and extracted notes from my leather case.

"Your Honour; I happen to have in my hand notes made by a certain Colonel Brink, now diseased, who was present in the boardroom of hotel Homann on January the sixth 1942.

In these notes it is clearly stated that this officer in question was present by invitation of Colonel Arlen to a meeting in the boardroom of that same hotel on that day.

Colonel Arlen chaired the meeting. The topic of the meeting was to prevent the Regent's son and myself to get away to Australia, thereby contravening the wishes of the Governor-General. "First I should perhaps explain to the court, that Mas is the son of the Regent of West-Java, and is groomed to become the Sultan when the present one dies. The request who to succeed him, was made by the Sultan himself and the government through the Governor-General has agreed.

This was the reason that the Governor-General wanted to evacuate Mas, the Regent's son, to Australia. It was to prevent that the Japanese would capture him. The Governor-General foresaw that the Japanese for propaganda purposes would use him. I was also chosen, but only to accompany him.

Colonel Arlen wanted this meeting to be confidential and make it appear to me as though the Regent's son and myself were going to be given all the possible help he could give us in order to get away to Australia, as was the intention and wish of the Governor-General. I had asked Colonel Arlen this question specifically at the meeting, to which he had replied: "every possible help."

In fact the very opposite was planned. We were not to get away and encountered obstacle after obstacle in our attempt to reach Australia. Colonel Brink's notes are very specific in the details of the deceit that went on. He himself did not appear to agree whole-heartedly with this plan, I must add to his credit. Possibly because of this, did Colonel Brink make these notes, unaware of by Colonel Arlen. They are very explicit as I said and leave no doubt of the swindle planned against me and the nephew of the Sultan. Colonel Brink's widow has given me these notes, the handwriting can easily be verified," I held the papers up.

Colonel Arlen slumped down, shaken, his face ashen grey. His lies were now evident to the Judge and to all the others present in the courtroom. A deadly silence took over in the room after my last words. You could only hear the ticking of the clock on the wall. The Judge looked at Colonel Arlen.

"Have you any comments to make Colonel Arlen?" There was no reply. The Judge waited.

"Colonel Arlen, I asked you a question." Colonel Arlen shook his head.

The fool! All his scheming now turned against him.

"Do you wish to say something Colonel Arlen?" the Judge asked again; "you are not on trial," he added severely. "But I would like a clear answer please."

"No your Honour," Colonel Arlen said.

"Very well then," he turned to me. "We are calling a recess. You have brought up accusations, which only have a minor bearing on the case for which we are present here. Do you wish these accusations to be retained as a side issue? If so they will be."

"I do your Honour." He turned to the clerk of the court.

"You heard what the prosecution wishes?"

"I have your Honour," the clerk replied licking his pen.

"So far we have not made any progress with the real issue: the case against Major Cane," the Judge looking in my direction, continued.

"We have been side tracked the whole morning with irrelevancies from both sides. Nevertheless I also wish to read your book," he said to me with a wink unbecoming an impartial Judge.

"At a date to be specified later, we will start with your prosecution against Major Cane," he addressed me. "I am sure we will no longer be interrupted by having to deal with irrelevances." He closed his notes and hammered with his gavel on the table. I was sure that the Honourable Judge had enjoyed his morning.

Chapter 22

Aditripto sat at his desk; his feet on the table in front of him. He had just inspected his troops. It was only a small army. He wished it could have been very much larger than it was. He could then much sooner accomplish what he wanted, such as defeat the Dutch army and make himself the first President of the Republic of Indonesia by force.

Instead the Sultan was only interested in an army as a token of strength, keeping law and order in the small enclave, that consisted of the palace and surrounding area only. The army kept close liaison with the Dutch colonial army although the Sultan paid for the upkeep of his forces himself.

If he Aditripto would become the President, which was where his ambition lay, he would change all that. No more lip service to the Dutch. He opened his mouth wide. The yawn was not a sign of sleep but of boredom. Gambling was a pleasant pastime but it had its limitations. It was the same with cock fighting and the Sultan did not approve of that either.

His rank was of Major in the Sultan's army at last. He had waited a long time for this; trying to win this favour of the Sultan. Mas had agreed to be the successor to the Sultan 's position once his uncle died. Aditripto did not like that. That position he wanted for himself. By a quirk of nature if this was to be believed, he looked very much like Mas but Aditripto was declared to be no family. The Sultan had as much as possible made that plain. Aditripto was therefore nowhere in the line of succession. Yet he lived in the Kraton as a favour to him by the Sultan when he became a Major in his forces.

As children he and Mas had been very friendly posing for one another frequently. But at that time politics and power resulting from it, had not played a role as yet. That only came later.

Their resemblance in physical appearance amused them both. Different people often remarked upon it and Aditripto as well as Mas had often made use of it, to fool teachers at school. In elementary school when they were young, since they had been educated at different schools but still in the same town, Mas sometimes posed for Aditripto if the latter wanted to have a day off school, gambling. Even then he already enjoyed cock fighting. When they had become adults their different interests was the reason that they drifted apart. Mas had always been the studious scholar, but Aditripto was the practical one.

At last Aditripto's had thought up a scheme that had come off. He had waited a long time for it. He had needed cooperation from a spy from Mas' army. Ahmed had succeeded in putting the blame for the murders in Tjilan on Mas by dropping Mas' armband, torn and smeared with blood first, in the compound before he and Aditripto and his selected bunch of murderers withdrew. Before they left they murdered woman and children in camp Tjilan first. Ahmed had stolen Mas' armband when Mas was away in his other hide out in Bandoeng. Should Mas discover the theft, what of it? Anybody could have stolen it. Ahmed was well paid for doing it of course and Aditripto had to promise him a high post in his army if and when the time came.

By that time of course anything could happen to Ahmed, such as sudden heart failure for instance. For the time being he was very useful to Aditripto. Ahmed reported all Mas' movements and whereabout to him. Now that Ahmed had betrayed Mas, he was forever in Aditripto's service. Aditripto could always blackmail him from now on. Ahmed would never be free of him again. There were a few more jobs he wanted Ahmed to do for him. Ahmed always wanted to please him so much. And Aditripto made sure that Ahmed was paid well every time. He did not want to feel that he owed anybody a favour in return; especially not someone he considered inferior to himself. What of it? It did not cost him a cent. His Major's salary was sufficient for his needs and by blackmail he could acquire more. In any case, eventually it often came from the Dutch government.

Mas now featured in the bad books of the Sultan because Mas was now blamed as officially guilty for the murders at Tjilan. Eventually Aditripto would blacken Mas' reputation further so that the Sultan might appoint him Aditripto as his successor. So far so good! His scheming was paying dividends. There was more to come too! He would blacken Mas' character for good in the Sultan's opinion. How easily that could be done with the help of informers like Ahmed was even a surprise to him. He should have thought of it earlier.

Aditripto himself more and more believed from wishful thinking that the Sultan's position should be his. By his position through living in the Kraton it was assumed hy the noninformed that he was one of the many sons the Sultan had. Aditripto, always felt that he was: and even believed that he might be the eldest son although there never had been any reason to think so. A good thing was that the Sultan never knew that his two favourite wives were also Aditripto's mistresses. They might even have had children by him. He didn't care as long as nobody knew and the Sultan would never know. He was an old man already. Soon he would die and these two wives, who were pretty and young, would be his. The women would never give him away. They wouldn't dare! They would be banned if the Sultan found out about their infidelity. Their life was very comfortable as it was. They benefited from the situation as much as he did. An elegant solution Aditripto thought. It was called "live and let live."

Aditripto loved living in luxury and as long he didn't suffer for it in the sense that he had to pay for any of it, life was great!

The servant crawling on his knees brought him the card of the visitor he expected. Crawling on knees to approach a person of high birth was the way to show respect.

"Show the captain in," he ordered.

"Yes Sir," the servant replied in the court Javanese language, which a servant speaks to a superior. Aditripto had spoken low Javanese to the servant, a totally different language.

This was the way it should be. He pretended to be of noble birth and the servant; well, was only a servant! Again on his knees the man crawled backwards, never turning his back to Aditripto. Turning ones back in the proximity of a superior was the highest form of impudence. You would have been flogged immediately and then fired; that is if you survived the flogging!

A few moments later captain Hensen entered the room. He was dressed in full military uniform including wearing his sabre. It was the way it should be, Aditripto observed with satisfaction. The officer already treated him with the respect due to him. Aditripto got up. The captain saluted. Aditripto's rank was that of major, therefore he was the captain's superior. The Dutch forces and his forces wore almost the same uniform and the same rank insignia.

Aditripto extended his hand: "Welcome captain," he said "Sit down, I am glad to have this meeting." Captain Hensen sat down. He had looked forward to this talk with Adipripto. There must be bad feeling between this man sitting opposite him and Mas, because of the possible question of succession about which he had heard and if it was to be believed. He might be able to capitalise on it. Capturing Mas had been and still was high on his agenda. It had become an obsession with him. Mas operated just under his nose so to speak. But when he arrived on the scene, Mas had always just disappeared into thin air like a ghost, leaving no trace. It was uncanny. The difficulty was perhaps due to the fact that neither he, nor any of his men, knew what Mas looked like. Suppose that Mas at the last moment just ditched his military clothing and mingled with the natives around him. It would then be impossible for him to pick Mas out from the other native faces surrounding him. And the natives around him would not give him away.

But once he knew what Mas looked like, it would be different. He could then spot him and arrest him. He wanted to have a close look at Aditripto, study every detail of his face. He had been told that Aditripto and Mas looked very much alike. By studying Aditripto's face, he hoped that he could recognise Mas in a crowd later when the occasion arose. The killer of the women and children in Tjilan would not go unpunished! Apart from wanting to know what Aditripto looked like, there was another reason for coming to see Aditripto. The latter could easily be persuaded into believing that catching Mas was to Aditripto's advantage also! After all, the Sultan could change his mind again and favour Mas once again. Aditripto surely would help him to catch Mas to eliminate Mas from any possible succession.

"What did you come to see me for?" Aditripto wasted no time with preliminaries.

"Mas is a friend of yours?" Hensen started. Waste of time Adipripto thought to himself. The captain surely had already come by that information; otherwise he would not be here. He nodded.

"I have also been told that you look exactly like Mas." Again Aditripto wondered where this conversation was going. Both statements of Captain

Hensen were already an indication that he knew the two answers would be affirmative. Again he just nodded.

"What about your voices?"

Now this was something novel at least, Aditripto thought.

"Our voices?" he asked surprised by the question. "What about our voices?"

"Are they alike also? If you are speaking in a phone, could the person at the other end mistake you for Mas?"

"Oh I see what you mean; yes they are alike, very much alike." Aditripto suddenly smelled danger. Could it be that this officer was laying a trap for him? Aditripto had already impersonated Mas by phone. Did the captain know about that? The girl in intelligence, Lily Cane had given him all the information about the impending attack by the army on Tjilan camp to liberate the women and children which were kept hostage there.

He had impersonated Mas over the telephone then. He had been able to use the information, innocently given to him, by Lily, who thought that she was talking to Mas. He had capitalised on it by being just one step ahead of Captain Hensen. In the process he had murdered five women and three children and Ahmed had then left Mas'armband behind to be found by the army. Was that why Captain Hensen paid him a visit?

But Aditripto quickly decided that he had no reason to be suspicious. Hensen would not have asked that particular question if he suspected something like that. It would be too obvious a question if he thought along those lines.

Captain Hensen was very pleased with the reply he was given. As yet he did not know how to make use of this information, but it could become invaluable later.

"In fact," Adipripto confirmed, "we have impersonated for each other frequently as children and even as adults. If people don't see us, our voices can fool anybody. Our appearances are not that alike, but our voices are."

Hensen decided to tell Aditripto what he had in mind. But carefully! Only one thing at the time. It depended on the reaction he would get as he went on, whether to take Aditripto into his full confidence later on, or not. He had to assume that Mas was as much a thorn in Aditrpto's flesh as Mas was in his; irrespective of whether the man sitting opposite him wanted independence or not.

"I want to take you into my confidence," Hensen started. That is of course if you agree," he added. "I will lay my cards on the table. First a few questions: Do you agree with the tactics of your friend Mas?"

"Of course not; he is for Indonesian independence irrespective of the means. I am for independence too of course, but not as yet, and certainly not by force." He did not even blink when he said that. He could lie fluently in quite a few languages if the need arose.

"He is also guilty of murders," Aditripto resumed. "That is why the Sultan has now considered that he is unfit to follow in his footsteps." Captain Hensen could not have been happier with the answer. A scorpion till the moment of the sting can be thought of as harmless by a person not knowing anything about scorpions. And captain Hensen knew nothing about Aditripto. He moved over to Aditripto and he lowered his voice a little to indicate that what he was about to say next, was confidential.

"I think there is a spy informing Mas. I have laid several traps for him, but he seems forewarned every time. Every time I get near to him he seems to have disappeared."

"Informers," Aditripto said flatly. Of course, he thought to himself; was the captain not on to that yet?

"Yes but where?" Hensen continued.

"I know where to get that information," Adipripto said leaning back and folding his fingers together. He did not need a crystal ball to know what the next question from the captain was going to be. The captain himself was as clear as the crystal ball himself.

Did the captain not know who the spy was, spying for Mas? This was elementary stuff! He decided to play a little game with the captain. Pretend that he had an elaborate plan in his mind, which he would now enfold to the captain. He would put in a few lies here and there; he was good at that. The captain would not know the difference anyway. He would enjoy himself fooling this innocent captain.

"How can you find out?" Hensen in full anticipation innocently asked the question that Aditripto expected. He leaned forward so as not to miss one word from the lips of Aditripto.

"From Haroen Janoedi of course," the reply came.

"Haroen Janoedi, who is he?" Aditripto was amused. The captain was biting.

"He is a spy for Mas, but he is not the one who gets the information for him. He only passes it on."

"In that case he knows the other person who gives that information to him."

"What brilliant deduction," Aditripto thought to himself. No wonder Mas had always outsmarted this innocent captain.

"Of course captain," Aditripto said, cracking his knuckles loudly and omitting further information.

You needed to be brought up in the Indies not to know that every deal and every happening was accomplished by spying first. The opposition was doing the same. It was the way things went. He had grown up with this habit. It worked successfully for both parties.

"And how do we get to see Haroen?"

"If you approach him you alert Mas that you are on to him."

"Then how? What other means have you in mind?"

"There is only one way," Aditripto replied. "Unless you capture Hanoedi, then torture him to get the information out of him that you want, and then kill him without a trace, so that Mas doesn't know what has happened to him, you are wasting your time."

Captain Hensen was shocked.

"Torture him and then kill him?"

"What else?" Aditripto smiled. This was fun! "Have I shocked you captain? You are the one who wanted to capture Mas. I have merely suggested to you the means how to achieve it. Would you like a drink? Can I offer you tea, coffee, a lemon drink perhaps?"

Hensen's hand was shaking. The man smiling opposite him, had in his mind already tortured and killed Haroen and was now asking him coolly, if he wanted a drink. That Aditripto had in fact no intention to do what he said he was going to do with Hanoedi, was something the captain could not know. On the contrary; Aditripto had already decided long ago that Hanoedi could be useful to him, in many ways maybe later. He was a spy for Mas now, but later perhaps when he Aditripto became more powerful, he might work for him instead.

In any case he already knew who the spy was. It was not difficult at all to come by that information if you knew how and were brought up in the Indies! He did not need Hanoedi's help for something as easy as that to find out.

"Coffee please" Hensen replied, uncertain that he really wanted to go on with this kind of conversation.

"I know how to get Haroen," Aditripto went on in the same vein still enjoying himself, knowing that he was upsetting the captain.

"We abduct him, no problem. What is your plan after that captain?" Hensen felt like a fool. He had no plan as yet. Everything went too fast. He had to think of the next step but he needed a few moments to overcome his shock about the ease with which Aditripto had spoken of torture and murder of a human being. This fellow was no better than Mas. He felt that he should act to appear as though he agreed with Aditripto however, since he had approached him with regard to the matter of spying. Afterwards he would make his own plans. He regretted the encounter. He had enough of this cold-blooded killer. Hensen decided to remain as vague as possible as to the exact details. Aditripto saw through him and just studied his fingernails without saying a word. They agreed to have a meeting at a later date to discuss the plan fully.

"I have another better idea," Hensen said when they parted. He had no other idea but he wanted nothing further to do with this murderer Aditripto.

"I'll work on it and I'll tell you the details," Hensen said when they parted. He had no intention working out further details with this man. He certainly did not want Haroen whoever he was, tortured and killed even though he did not know the man.

Aditripto smiled. The captain was "chicken" when he came to grip with hard realities!

Although the meeting had not gone exactly as Captain Hensen had wished, nevertheless it had not been without value for him. Slowly another thought had taken hold of him. Of course he already knew that Aditripto looked like Mas. That was one of the reasons why he had come. But he had noticed something very important. Aditripto, he had noticed; whilst studying Aditripto's face intently, had a scar through his left eyebrow. Aditripto had taken care to mask it. Hensen had almost missed it and had only noticed it, because he had studied Aditripto's face in detail carefully, wanting to remember every part of it, so that he would be able to recognise Mas when the opportunity arose.

Why had Aditripto taken so much trouble to mask the scar? He must have known that Captain Hensen had freed camp Tjilan. All the women who had been freed by him had described 'Mas' as having a very marked scar through his left eyebrow. "We can easily identify him because of that scar," they had said.

Hensen now knew who had murdered the women and children in Tjilan. And the murderer was not Mas! It was a total revelation to him. He had been after the wrong man. The armband found in Tjilan belonged to Mas certainly. His best friend, the controller, had even identified it.

He knew that Lieutenant Searle had not liked to admit it, when he had been asked to identify the armband whether it belonged to Mas or not. Nevertheless he had been honest and indeed had said that the armband belonged to Mas. Of course it was Mas' armband but it had been stolen from him.

Aditripto had either done that himself but more likely someone nearer to Mas would have done that!

Captain Hensen long ago had decided that he would revenge the women and children of Tjilan. He had sworn that he would find the killer and now he had found him. But how could he carry out his revenge for those who had been murdered? Aditripto was Major in the equivalent forces of himself and perhaps even a son of the Sultan if gossip was to be believed. It might in any case be a diplomatic blunder if he shot him. He would have to think of another plan. He was determined to find it.

Two weeks later he received the call:

"Captain Hensen?"

"Yes," he answered.

"I know who the spy is." Hensen was puzzled.

"Who is speaking please?"

"Aditripto." A chill went up Hensen's spine.

"Oh hello, good morning major; I did not know what you said. Could you please repeat what you said?"

"Certainly: I know who the spy is."

The hairs on the back of Hensen's neck started to rise. To him that meant that Hanoedi was dead. He was murdered after being tortured first by this maniac!

"It took a long time," Aditripto continued his macabre game and speaking as though he was talking about the weather forecast. "He was quite stubborn I can tell you, but eventually he told me. We had to cut off all his fingers and also took his eyes out first before he told me," Aditripto continued, thoroughly enjoying himself, fooling this innocent captain who thought that he could capture Mas.

Hensen was horror struck. And he was partly to blame! He had brought up the question of the spy. But not that Haroen should die for it of course. All he could do now; was act as though he agreed with what he thought Aditripto had done to Hanoedi. Hanoedi was already dead in any case, he thought.

"Who is he," he asked. His icy voice would have frosted a good size refrigerator in an instant. He was furious with himself.

"It is not a he; it is a woman." Hensen sat upright.

"A woman," he exclaimed.

"Yes I thought you would be interested to hear that," Aditripto smiled to himself. "I don't know her name, but she is Mas' mistress.

Of course Aditripto knew Lily by name. But it would sound more true to life if Hensen believed that he didn't.

"She works for intelligence in the forces, the Dutch forces. She is at H.Q in Bandoeng."

Hensen was thunder struck. A spy in the middle of his forces and at headquarters of all things! He was now an accomplice of Aditripto, like it or not. He swore to himself. Then his thought processes took over. Mas could be impersonated over the phone. Aditripto could by impersonating Mas over the phone; instruct the woman spy to pass information to him. It could be done in such a way that he Hensen could listen in as well. He and Aditripto both would then have proof against her! She would be apprehended without difficulty, red-handed as they say. In that way Aditripto could be helpful. That Aditripto had already been one step ahead of him, he did not know.

Suddenly another thought occurred to him. Aditripto, also by mimicking Mas' voice, could instruct the women to come to a place where he could kill her, and do away with her altogether. He was just that kind of man. Proudly he would then ring again and say with that undertaker's tone of voice that he had just killed her. Sweat broke out from his pores. The woman would not get a fair chance and he was responsible if she were killed. Although she was a spy, she needed justice and needed a hearing before condemning her. Aditripto would not give her that.

That murderer might well be phoning her now! He must be one step ahead of Aditripto: phone Captain Hes of security quickly to prevent this. He knew that Hes had recently been put in charge of intelligence. In panic he dialled.

"Captain Hes is away for the weekend Sir."

"Where can he be reached, this is urgent."

"I don't know Sir." Hensen slumped in his chair. He was in a fix. If he wanted to speak to someone high up in intelligence now, he had to explain the situation to that someone he did not know. That person could well inform the woman spy and all would be lost. On the other hand if Aditripto killed the women he would never forgive himself. He realised that against his will he was put in a real dilemma.

"In that case I want to speak to the person who substitutes for him," he said. His mouth was getting very dry

"Hold the line please." Frantically Hensen tried to think what he was going to say next when Hes's substitute would come on the line. This was something on the spur of the moment. He had nothing planned for anything like this. A loud swear word passed his lips. He did not have long to wait. A women's voice came on the line. It was a pleasant voice his subconscience informed him.

"Miss Cane speaking."

"Oh God," Hensen thought, what was he to say now? She could well be the spy Aditripto had mentioned. "Miss Cane," he said, "this is Captain Hensen speaking from Semarang. I need to speak to Captain Hes rather urgently. Where can he be contacted?"

"I don't know sir," we never see him. He works in a different section.

What next? Hensen thought.

"Do you substitute for him when he is away?"

"He does not have a substitute. As I say he works in a completely different section."

Nothing worked. It was not his day. But maybe Aditripto had nothing further planned. He did not know the name of the spy in any case, and perhaps Aditripto was lying so maybe he was just suspicious for nothing. He decided to let things be.

"When will captain Hes be back?"

"Monday Sir."

"Very well. In that case will you inform the captain that I rang and if he could phone me back as soon as he returns please." He gave his name again, then his phone number and rang off.

Captain Hensen was not too far wrong as far as Aditripto was concerned. Where he was wrong as far as judging Aditripto's thinking was concerned however, was that it was always influenced by the fact that Aditripto wanted to know first, what was in it for him. Other than that, he had the perfect criminal mind that would make Al Capone's, an amateur by comparison. Lily's life was secure. She was of value to him alive. Aditripto only had one yardstick with regard to people. They were either of use to him or they were not. That was all that mattered. Lily already had served his purpose once.

What was in it for him to kill her? He had many more cunning plans in his mind for her than Hensen could imagine. He could now play Mas off against Lily. And he could get things done from her by threatening her that he would tell Mas' hide out to captain Hensen. And did she not know that Hensen would sell his soul to capture Mas? In the latter assumption he was totally wrong! Hensen had switched his murderous intentions from Mas to Aditripto, now that he knew who the true murderer of Tjilan was. Aditripto was not aware of that.

He stifled a yawn as he leaned back, then cracked his fingers loudly again. Life was great. He fully intended to enjoy himself!

Chapter 23

"We have specific instructions not to go into any deal with Mas and neither with any of these so called freedom fighters. They are murderers."

"Some of them yes," Colonel Xant had replied. "I still have no reason up to now to believe that Mas is one of those you refer to."

The words of the delegate were still ringing in my ears. Was Mas a murderer? I still didn't believe that. I had known him so well all these years. He had always been kind and sensitive to people worse off than himself. But what about the descriptions of him by reliable witnesses and what about his armband which was found in Tjilan? I had no explanation and it kept nagging my mind.

I got the message to see St Cyr. I had expected it. His chauffeur collected me again and drove me to his official residence. It would be the last time I sadly reflected.

"I am leaving by plane tomorrow," he greeted me. "Before I go I would like to speak to you."

"Your family has already left Sir?" I asked him.

"Yes, there is nothing more for me to do here. I have thought of your position here Richard. That is why I called you. You can still do valuable work here. I know no more of my successor than you do, but I would gladly write a letter of introduction to him on your behalf. He would be a fool, if he did not make use of your experience."

"That is very kind of you Sir, but under the present circumstances I am not too sure that I really want to; I have lost the appetite for it. Moreover I think that after Indonesian independence there will be no future for our kind of people. Independence, "Merdeka" as they call it excludes our position of governing."

"Well, I have something to tell you which may make you change your mind. Are you interested to listen?" I nodded; the Governor had something up his sleeve.

"What is it Sir?"

"Have you ever heard the name Aditripto?" I shook my head.

"Well he is rumoured to be the son of the Sultan although the Sultan himself has denied it. You know of course that Mas was to succeed the Sultan when he dies.

"Was you said?"

"Indeed, unfortunately the Sultan has changed his mind. He no longer wants Mas to succeed him when the time comes, but wants Aditripto to succeed him instead."

"What?" I was flabbergasted. "What has happened? How can this be? He has formally agreed with the Dutch government that it would be Mas."

"Indeed, but the Sultan is entitled to change his mind and has told me so. He wants to make it official."

"Does Mas know about this?"

"Presumably he has been informed."

"Why did the Sultan change his mind?"

"He told me the reason: he thinks that Mas is guilty of the murders in camp Tjilan. Moreover he thinks that Mas has attracted unwanted support; not the people the Sultan considers desirable. The Sultan wants a person with a clean slate; not someone with a dubious past such as Mas has"

"And what sort of a past does Aditripto have"

"Not a good one I have been informed as far as rumours go, unfortunately. He also is ruthless."

"What kind of a change is that and what proof does the Sultan have against Mas?"

"He does not need to have proof. Suspicion is enough to make one behave carefully."

"Have you something else in mind Sir?"

"I have and I'll put it to you. Have you never held any suspicions against your former fiancée?"

The question touched a tender nerve. I recalled what Mas had said to me when I spoke to him in restaurant Braga:

"Why is your loyalty not with us," he had asked me then. "Lily's loyalty is." I had then asked him, "in what way," to which he had not wanted to reply. Ever since I had wondered what Mas had referred to? Now the Governor brought it up.

"I don't know what you are referring to."

"I'll spell it out for you. Everywhere Mas appeared successful in his campaign, Lily had informed him of the strength and whereabouts of the Dutch troops."

"Are you serious? You mean to say that she is a spy?"

"Yes, her father talks to her about the plans the army makes and she passes that information on to Mas. It explains his success to a great extent. Also, that he has never been caught. There is more: she also works in intelligence. Draw your own conclusion." So that was it! Lily was a spy.

"How do you know all this?" I asked, I could hardly believe what I had just heard.

"Captain Hes came to see me. Did you know that he is in charge of intelligence? He is also in love with your former fiancée."

"In love with Lily? Yes I thought so. Not that he has said that to me in so many words. What do we do with this information about Lily?"

"Not what we do with the information is what counts, but what Captain Hes is going to do with it. He is an army officer and she is spying for the enemy. This is serious. Moreover she is the daughter of an army officer. That makes the charge even more serious. Of course you know what happened to Mata Hari don't you? She was executed by a firing squad. I don't want this to happen to

Lily any more than you do. She is doing this out of gratitude to Mas and he is using her."

"What about Aditripto? You mentioned him; is there any connection?"

"Something like that may well develop. He is very jealous of Mas. Quite understandable, since Mas through his charm has still got a large following albeit not under the elite the Sultan now approves of. He also looks like Mas I have heard. Of course you don't know this since you never met him. I pricked up my ears. If he looked like Mas, he could well be the one who was at camp Tjilan. Could it be?

"He is a danger to Lily", the Governor continued. "In what way is he a danger to Lily?"

"The story is rather complicated. What has happened is that the army captain called Hensen, whom you have met, visited Aditripto. Hensen was always surprised that he was never able to apprehend Mas and decided to speak to this man Aditripto about it. Whether that was a wise move is debatable.

"During the visit he was informed by Aditripto that Mas is fed secret information of the army's whereabouts and plans, by an informer in the army. Hensen's own plans and whereabouts included of course. Naturally Hensen was curious and asked who the informer was. Aditripto told him that it was a woman in the forces but didn't give her name. How Aditripto has found out, I don't know.

"In any case, he passed on the information that there is a woman spy in the army to Hensen. Hensen in turn notified Hes. Hensen still does not know that the spy is Lily but we do: don't we? Captain Hensen has always been convinced that Mas is guilty of the murders in camp Tjilan. If he finds out that Lily spies for him he will consider her an accomplice to these murders. You must warn her, you still love her don't you?"

I nodded. I had never stopped loving her, impossible though I knew, that due to circumstances, this was love without a future.

"Have I made you sufficiently curious to make you want to stay in the service as a liaison officer between the government and the army? I wish I could remain myself. The future should become very interesting. I hope the handling of the Indonesian independence is done with care. You can play a role in this. For instance your friendship with Mas is still very valuable. You grew up together.

"Apart from the fact that Mas has taken up arms against us, I do not believe that he is in any way connected with the massacre in camp Tjilan or in any other murder. He comes from a very peace loving family. You know them well yourself, having served with his father in Australia. The latter has been a loyal friend to me also. I very much regret that I have to abandon people like that. You may, by staying in your job be able to exonerate Mas some day. I sincerely hope you will be able to do that. And should Mas turn out to be an influential force to the benefit of the Indonesian cause one day in the future, he will need to have friends like you around him to help him."

Little did the Governor know how futile his words would prove to become. That evening I phoned Lily that I wanted to speak to her and Wong together. I wanted to bring up the spying affair. But when I visited them it was so unnatural that she possibly could be connected with anything like spying, that I left it to the last.

"How is your father?" I enquired innocently.

"He is very lonely since the death of mother. He looks very ill. He lives within the compound of the barracks. Fortunately he gets his meals there. I often visit him."

"And when you do visit him you get information about the movement of troops from him, isn't that right? Does he know what you do with that information?"

"What do you mean by that Richard?"

"What I mean by that is that you are spying for Mas and Mas wants you to do that for him. You are in great danger that you will be detected. Are you not aware of that?" She was taken aback.

"You know?" she stammered.

"Yes, and I am not the only one. The Governor told me to warn you. Hes came to see him. I don't know what Hes will do, now that he has found out. After all he is head of intelligence. He may already have evidence against you. On the other hand he may not and may only suspect so far.

"But he has spoken to the Governor which means that he must at least have strong suspicions. The greater danger is, that you may be caught out spying, for instance by Captain Hensen. He won't be lenient to you like Hes might be. You don't know who Captain Hensen is. I know him. He is determined to capture Mas because he holds Mas responsible for the murders in Tjilan. And it was Captain Hensen who informed Hes that there is a spy in intelligence and that the spy is a woman. That much he does know. He doesn't know your name though, which is fortunate. At least so the Governor told me."

"They can never prove it. All the information I give Mas is by word of mouth. I agreed with Mas that it should be this way."

"How naive you are Lily. Do you know who Adipripto is?"

"Yes he is Major in the Sultan's forces."

"Do you also know that the Sultan now wants Adipripto to be his successor when he dies?"

"No, it is the first time I hear it, but what has this all got to do with giving Mas information about the movements of troops?"

"I am not too sure about Adipripto, he is jealous of Mas and ruthless the Governor told me.

If you are caught with Mas, Adipripto may testify that you just brought Mas valuable information. He could even have stolen that information himself, just to implicate you and Mas. You are treading on thin ice. The important thing is that he will be believed and you won't be. The army, that is Captain Hensen, is frustrated that Mas seems to be one step ahead of him all the time. You will be declared guilty. There is nothing that neither I, nor Hes can do for you once you are accused! And there is another thing. You know Aditripto and you know his voice. Is his voice the same as Mas?" What I am coming to is this: he could well telephone you, pretending that he is Mas who is on the line, asking for secret information. You then thinking that it is Mas you are speaking to on the other side of the line, may give that information, innocently to Aditripto, thereby incriminating yourself.

Lily suddenly went white.

"What is it Lily? What have I said to upset you?" She did not reply immediately. After a while she said:

"That has already happened!"

"What do you mean Lily; what has already happened?"

"It has only dawned on me just now, since you have brought up this possibility. Oh I have been a fool. I thought that Mas had rung me. The person I thought was Mas, wanted to know the strength of the military garrison near camp Tjilan, Tjilan being the camp where women and children were held against their will by guerrilla fighters."

"You gave that information?" She nodded

"There is more." She stopped

"What?"

"I informed the person on the phone that the military would attack camp Tjilan to liberate the women and children."

"You did what?"

"You see Richard; my mistake was that I thought I was speaking to Mas. And I gave the information because I knew that Mas would never harm anybody in that camp. I was certain of that. And you may remember that I even gave Mas an alibi, which was a lie, when you came to visit us, myself and Wong together one day. I said that I was with him the day when the murders were committed. In fact I was at my mother's birthday party as Wong said. You suspected that he was guilty and I was certain that he was not. I also later informed Hanoedin that he should give Mas the same alibi if you approached him, which he did apparently. You see now that Mas is innocent of the murdered women and children in Tjilan?"

We were quiet and busy with our own thoughts. I realised now that my suspicions when I thought that Lily was lying that day in question had been correct. And I had believed Hanoedin because he also had said that Lily was with Mas the day in question. Haroen Janoedin had also on the same occasion told me that Lily was Mas' concubine. Was that also not correct? I didn't know what to think any more. Lily eventually broke the silence.

"That is why the guerrilla fighters withdrew and had plenty time to murder the women and children first before they did. I am responsible. Through my stupidity some women and children died." I said nothing because I didn't know what to say.

Of course she was not guilty of those murders. She had been tricked into giving that information. I knew now for certain that Mas had nothing to do with the murders in camp Tjilan and that it was Aditripto who was the guilty one. It was quite a burden off my mind, which had lingered there a considerable time. So Lily was spying for Mas. Why did Mas allow her to do that? Her life was in danger doing that. Did he not see that?

I remembered his words again. "If my father and mother are killed for the freedom of Indonesia, then so be it."

At the time that he said that to me, he meant it. He would condone it. Did he think the same way about Lily? Would he condone her death if it would be convenient for the Indonesian independence cause? She was obviously a supporter for Indonesian freedom no matter the cost, even if the cost she had to pay with was her own life.

Wong had said nothing so far.

"I know Adiptipto also," he now joined in the conversation. The Governor is correct. He is jealous of Mas. Mas has always been popular. He very much looks like Mas but he is bigger and fatter. Although from a distance you could take one for the other easily."

I did not realise at that time the truth of Wong's statement and the implication it held for Mas.

"You are right to warn Lily," Wong continued. And I condemn Mas for jeopardising Lily's life. He is no longer a friend."

When I got to my barracks that evening the thought of Lily getting into danger did not leave me. Adipripto had already used her services once. He had also used Mas' armband to implicate Mas. What next was he up to in relation to Mas? Unfortunately I was to find out.

Chapter 24

"Miss Cane," the voice behind her mentioned her name. She knew the voice but could not place it. Where had she heard it the last time? She turned round. Instantly she recognised him.

"Lieutenant Hes, she stammered. How are you? Oh, I am sorry, you have become a captain, forgive me."

"Don't bother with formalities Miss," he said. She still looked stunning he thought. He knew again that he was still very much in love with her. He would never be able to be free himself of her in his mind. But she was married.

"May I call you Lily?"

"Of course you may." She was very pleased to see him. He could tell, because she was spontaneous, not in the habit of concealing her feelings. She had always been an open book he remembered.

"How are you captain, you survived the war I see."

"Barely; do you remember me from our dancing days?"

"Of course; I have not danced since."

"And I probably can't dance any longer: I got a bullet through my thigh. I have some difficulty walking now.

But I came here wanting to speak about you Lily. I wanted to ask you how you are. You got married I heard. You were engaged the last time I met you, nearly five years ago."

"Has it been that long already? Yes I am married captain. My husband is ill. He is in bed, I am standing in for him at the moment but there is not much to do."

"That is what I want to talk with you about."

"Why, is Wong fired? Is that what you want to tell me?"

"Oh no, there is something else I want to talk about. Could we go somewhere quiet so that I can talk with you without being overheard? I wanted to invite you for a cup of coffee. The Braga all right?" She nodded. When they arrived, they went upstairs. He chose a table in the corner.

"Coffee, or would you rather have something else to drink?"

"I like a cup of coffee captain." He ordered a coffee for her and a whiskey for himself.

"How is your father Lily?"

"He is far from well, may I call you Carl?"

"Certainly; do. You called me that also in villa Isola I remember when you danced with me. I danced with you nearly every dance that night."

She nodded, recollecting the happy moments they had enjoyed together. She then continued speaking about her father.

"He was very ill as a POW. He has received many terrible beatings. The constant fear for his life every minute of the day! He also had malaria and dysentery. He is lucky to have survived. He has lost my brother his only son and now also his wife. My mother has been ill since the war. She was also beaten. My father was so upset to see her become the invalid she was lately and Richard Searle is taking him to court, a military court. He never told me exactly what the charge is: perhaps desertion. Has he not had enough! He won't survive, I feel it, and he was spitting blood recently. I fear so much for his life. It is so terrible for him."

"I know Lily," Hes said, patting her hand to console her. "Richard has asked me to be a witness at the trial. It will be terrible for your father. Richard is your former fiancée right?"

"He is and he still holds it against me, that I married Wong. He feels that I let him down, which of course I did. He is so hurt. I thought that he was dead. He was on the list of passengers of a plane that blew up in Tjilatjap. All passenger and crew were killed. Of course I did not know that he was not in that plane because I found out for certain that he was on the list.

"He escaped on a ship to Australia instead which I did not know. When he came back from Australia I was already married to his friend Wong.

Wong, Richard, Mas and I have always had a non-separable relationship. Richard himself says that he understands that due to circumstances I had no choice in the matter. Although he says that, he does not agree about that within himself, no not deep down.

"I would have felt the same, because the love between us was so intense. I therefore know exactly how he feels. In reality I had little choice. If I had not married Wong I would have been put in a Japanese women's prisoner camp or more likely killed. I found this out myself only recently, by putting two and two together. I think that Mas was blackmailed by the Japanese to say what they wanted him to say otherwise I would be killed. They had found out that he was a friend of mine and therefore cared for me. At the time I was not aware that he was being blackmailed. Even now I am not certain about which I am speaking. Mas never said anything. Wong also never said anything about this. They both don't want me to feel that I was in Mas' way. But it must have been something like that.

"And I did not care who I was married to. I was so broken hearted when I thought Richard was dead. I wished I were killed also. Mas persuaded Wong to marry me. I am sure about that. I did not love him, but he was a good friend. I can never forget that. I have a past and I will never be free of it. My past and the obligations as a result of that, keeps me prisoner. Obligation is even a stronger bond than love. Don't ever marry anyone if it isn't out of love no matter what the circumstances are!

"But why am I telling you all this? It must all be so unimportant to you. You wanted to talk to me about something else." She sighed.

Hes realised how sad and lonely she was. Otherwise she would not have opened up her feelings to him. It must be because she saw a good friend in him too. At least a person she could trust. Someone she felt affection for also.

Hes was quiet. What was it that he wanted to say to her? That he loved her with all his heart and that it would always be so? But he could not. It would be altogether out of place. All these years that he hadn't seen her, he had hoped to find her again one day. And now that he had, he might as well never have seen her again. She was married! Not to her former fiancée, but it made no difference: she was unattainable for him in any case. Yet he could see that she was very pleased to see him again. She was not good in hiding her emotions.

"There is something I want to talk with you about," he almost reluctantly said at last. You don't have to say anything till I have finished. You work in intelligence. I also know that you pass on information to Mas who is considered to be an enemy by the present law and order government. Whether you agree or don't agree with the government's opinion does not matter. The government is the law! Your privileged position enabled you to pass on information that should be kept secret. You are a spy Lily! Are you aware that you can be shot for passing information to the enemy?"

"I am guilty Carl. I admit it and you know it anyway. How have you found out?"

"I did not intend to tell you how I know exactly, because that is secret information, but since it was not difficult for the person who found out that you are a spy, there is every possibility that others also will know.

And since you may well be in danger, on second thought I have decided to tell you the source. The information came from a person Aditripto who is an officer in the Sultans forces. Do you know him?"

"Vaguely. I have met him once or twice. He looks like Mas, he is a year older but I never liked him. He was always jealous of Mas. How did Aditripto find out?"

"I cannot tell you more than that. How Aditripto found out is no longer important. The point is that you are in great danger. Aditripto can have you killed whenever it suits him. I shudder to think that you could have been murdered already, because Aditripto knows that you pass information to Mas and he is against Mas. Somehow I think that this does not suit him otherwise he would have killed you a long time ago."

"Carl, I have something to confess to you. I already knew since last night that you are aware that I have been spying for Mas. Richard told me. He came to tell me that you knew. I will now tell you something you did not know. And this is my fault entirely. One day, approximately two months ago, I received a call from a person whom I thought was Mas. Now I know that that person was Aditripto. His voice is indistinguishable from Mas over the phone. He pretended to be Mas and I fell for it. He wanted to know when Tjilan camp would be freed by the military. I gave that information which I happened to find out through my father." Lily fell silent for a while then continued.

"So now that you know what I did, what are you going to do with me? I am guilty of the death of those women and children who were murdered in Tjilan. I do not deserve clemency."

Hes did not speak. Thoughts raced through his head. He was determined that he would protect Lily. Her only guilt was that she was loyal to a friend. The consequence of that loyalty however was that it had resulted in the murder of women and children. That was not her fault. But the army would not see it that way if that leaked out. He would have to lie over her. Deny that she was a spy. Deny on his word of honour as an officer, that she had not passed any information to the enemy.

He knew instantly the implication that would hold for him. That however was for later consideration. First he had to protect her and protect her he would whatever the cost. The army would never be able to prove anything if he denied that she ever spied for the enemy.

After a long while he continued the conversation. Not even by one word did he refer to what she had told him and what lying for her would cost him.

"I do not know how to protect you against Aditripto." he said at last. Neither Hes nor Lily knew that it was Mas who needed protection against Aditripto; not Lily.

"It is perhaps wise when you and Wong move into the barracks with your father." Hes continued. "At least you will be safer there.

"Lily, I have to tell you something too. I have been looking for you ever since the war came to an end, but I could never find you. Your father until recently also did not know where you were and what had happened to you. I knew that you were a friend of Mas before the war. The only way to find you, it seemed to me, was to find Mas and indirectly through him find you. My informant traced Mas' whereabouts and reported to me that you were still in guerrilla held territory.

That was the nearest I could get to you. That was before Mas arranged your evacuation to Batavia. It wasn't till I met Richard at a reunion two weeks ago, that I heard about you again. Even then I did not realise that Richard had been your fiance.

You were engaged you told me when I first met you. That seems so long ago now. At that time I only knew that you were engaged but did not know who your fiancé was, although I knew Richard from Tjipatat of course. He recently asked me to be a witness in your father's trial and so it came about that I asked Richard if he knew what happened to the major's daughter.

Then for the first time I knew whom you had been engaged to. Through your father I then afterwards heard where you were; in intelligence of all things! I did not contact you before now, because I heard that you were married. But now I had to, because I cannot condone you spying for the enemy, when I am ultimately responsible for intelligence."

"I am glad that you found me," Lily said spontaneously. He looked at her. No, she was not putting on an act. She looked genuinely pleased.

"I am," she repeated. What was he going to say now? He had already opened his heart out to her as much as it was possible in the circumstances to do that. She was still a spy even though he loved her.

"It is now clear to me why Mas was always able to escape the traps laid for him. I discovered that on every occasion when that happened, you had taken over from Wong because he was ill. You always replace him when he is ill. And he is always ill when Mas asks you to do a job for him.

I know why you do it. You feel that you owe Mas. He protected you during the war. But now he is using you. He knows the danger you are running, still he asks you to do the job for him. Stop Lily! I can't protect you. Already an army captain knows, and more dangerous than that, Aditripto does."

"Now that you know that I have been spying, what are you going to do with me? Are you going to take me to a military court? I am guilty. Will I be shot?"

"You know better than that Lily. I would never betray you." Lily looked at him for a long time. She knew that Hes, speaking about trying to find her, had as near as he could have done, said that he loved her. He could not have said that to her in any other way. When he continued speaking he said:

"Tell Mas that I have warned you. If you don't stop giving him information, I'll have you fired and you will not be able to pass on any further information to Mas in any case."

"I am sorry for the deaths I have caused. All the Indonesians want is independence. Why do they need to fight for it? And Mas is my friend."

"He was your friend Lily; he has now used you and you could have been killed for it! Somebody using you can't be a friend. Don't you see that Lily?

And there is another thing; Mas is still under suspicion of having killed women and children in Camp Tjilan although you think that Aditripto is the guilty one. Captain Hensen who liberated the women's camp Tjilan firmly believes in Mas' guilt, or so he did until recently. Maybe no longer? I don't know. Mas' implication in those murders was never disproved. Can we now believe that he is not guilty, but that Aditripto is?

Until now even Richard Searle held him guilty, although he would never say so in public nor would he ever give Mas away."

"Carl I want to thank you, but you are wrong about Mas. I have known him a long time. Even from the time when we were only children. And you must know now in your own mind, that it isn't Mas who is guilty of the murder of women and children at camp Tjilan."

"I do not know Lily. I wish I could be certain of it. What I do know Lily is, that you hold Mas very dear. But people can change Lily. May be not deep down. About one thing however we can be certain; Mas is ambitious. He probably always has been. Now his ambition drives him on. His ambition to become what he wants to be, perhaps the President of a free Indonesia, may become too strong for him. He may forget all about the other things he at one time held dear. Those other things like friendship, loyalty to friends, honesty and that sort of thing may stand in the way of his ambition now. He has already abandoned some of those principles that he held dear at one time. He has used you. You could have been executed. He let you take risks which could have cost you your life."

"What about my father Carl? Can you not help him? Richard is working for the army. Can't you stop him? You will be higher in rank than he is because you are on the nomination to become a major I heard."

"I can't Lily. First of all he is the prosecutor, appointed officially. Rank doesn't apply. And although Richard is the prosecutor in the trial, there are other high-ranking officers who want to condemn your father for desertion and they will overrule Richard. They are also higher in rank than I am. I will be called to testify against your father. I of course will do everything to help him. Here I will say something that may surprise you. So will Richard although he is acting for the prosecution. I know it. You probably won't believe it but it is true. He is only against your father because he thinks that your father is responsible for the deaths of his army friends, which may not altogether be correct and I will point that out to him in court. He also has already changed his mind to some extent."

"Maybe he at last has forgiven me for marrying Wong."

"Maybe," Hes said thoughtfully.

Chapter 25

Lily seemed happy or was it just a facade? Was she really happy to have gone out with me for a ride? The plan to go out together was her idea. And Wong had also encouraged it.

"She is so often alone Richard. Why don't you take her? She would like it so much and we have always been such good friends."

Nevertheless I felt uneasy because I did not know any longer how Lily felt about me under these abnormal circumstances. She had been present in the courtroom at the initial hearing of the case against her father but nothing really damning against her father so far had come up. She knew however, that I would prosecute her father at a later stage, although she was not quite sure what it was about exactly.

"Do you ever think of our holiday in Pasir Poetih Lily?" I asked her while I absentmindedly drove the military jeep.

"Of course I do Richard; don't you? It is forever with me; that memory will never leave me. It will always be there," she said spontaneously.

"How about you?"

"Yes I often think of the promises we made to each other on the Ringgit Lily; everything seems so unreal now."

"We made a promise never to forget each other don't you remember Richard? And neither of us has ever broken that promise. But the demons of the isle of Bali were against us. Why were they, and what had we done to them and why did the Gods not interfere? Could they not have helped us? Surely Gods are more powerful than demons! So much has happened since Pasir poetih. All the wrong things that happened to us since were beyond our control. There hasn't been much happiness between us since, Richard," she sighed.

I knew all too well that she was right about that but I wanted to cheer her up a little.

"But Lily, the memories of Pasir Poetih with you there with me, are not the only beautiful memories I have of you. There are many many more happy moments that I spent with you for me to remember.

We were so very happy with each other, so much in love; that it seems absurd and doesn't seem right that we don't belong together. Does that not seem strange to you also?" She did not answer immediately; I could see a few tears arising in her eyes.

Softly almost in a whisper she said:

"Why do you have it in for my father Richard? Has he done something to you that I don't know about? Something personal to you I mean. Why don't you tell me what it is?"

"Oh Lily," I said, it is impossible to tell you everything. I am in this respect just a pawn of circumstances. And perhaps so is your father. Don't ask me more; I am already so confused myself."

At the court case she would hear that her father would be branded a deserter and possibly a coward also. That far the proceedings had not yet reached, but they would eventually. The military court would certainly come up with that verdict. It would be Colonel Arlen for the army who would still make that accusation.

He would not make that accusation in a direct way but still counted on the fact that I would do it for him, in an indirect way. Just giving the evidence I had collected against major Cane with regard to his role during the war in Tamarkan camp, should be enough to condemn him, so he reckoned.

But he was totally wrong by counting on me. Whatever the court in the end would decide, it would not be because I would condemn Major Cane for his behaviour in Tamarkan. The evidence that I was going to present as far as the accusations in Tamarkan camp were concerned would on the contrary exonerate him. It would be a factual account. I would tell the whole story as I had heard it from Yakumi.

Lily's father could not have behaved differently; not as far as the death of Marcus was concerned; take it or leave it. As far as slapping his men was concerned, about that I would keep quiet. About this I held no opinion. The total of what I had to say would not suit Colonel Arlen's purpose and he would be furious with me.

He was now on shaky grounds in his so-called function of "defending" Major Cane. And I didn't care any more. I would not back up the army's accusation of desertion through cowardice and subsequent misbehaviour, which was what the army wanted to hear from me. If the army wanted to proceed with accusations against major Cane along those lines, then I washed my hands off the affair.

What remained of my personal feeling and accusations against major Cane now rested only on the fact that he had abandoned my army comrades in Tjipatat. And that was my feeling only because I felt that my dead friends deserved a hearing.

Who was really responsible for their deaths? Was Major Cane guilty? I did not know any more. The army would eventually raise that point irrespective of me anyway. And that issue no matter how I personally thought about it, and which was different from the army's point of view, was still desertion, as far as a military court would see it. My other: also personal accusations about the fact that Mas and I were deceived, by Major Cane also, and not only by Colonel Arlen; I had already aired in court. It still angered me when I thought about it. His deceit and the consequences as a result, were still very much alive in my mind. I really could not forgive him, even though the main culprit was Colonel Arlen.

It would perhaps not be brought up again since I had agreed with the judge who had correctly decided that it was only a side issue

The army in spite of Colonel Arlen's so called "defence", had the accusation for desertion well prepared and would proceed even in spite of the mitigating evidences that I would present and was determined to bring up in court. I already knew that by army standards the evidence against Major Cane was too clear to ignore. Personally I now felt that Major Cane had good reasons for his refusal to follow his orders to proceed to Tjipatat.

I only hoped that I would be convincing enough when I would state that Major Cane, when the accusation of cowardice came up, could not help himself and that he should never have been put in command. The accusation of wrongdoing would then have to be shared between Major Cane and the army.

Of course the army would never accept that. But Colonel Arlen would be stuck with my point of view and that point of view would be of no help to him.

"Do you prosecute my father because you hate me for marrying Wong?" Lily said after a while.

"No Lily; initially I could have been inclined to think like that. And that would have been very wrong of me if I really thought that. Of course that would have been ridiculous. I was dead as far as you knew. I did not exist any longer when you married Wong. Actually you had no choice. I might have condemned you in my mind not knowing the circumstances. And I apologise! You perhaps will understand my motives with regard to your father when I tell you about my experience in Japan. Perhaps it will explain to you how I feel and may be you will see my side of the story. My motives have nothing to do with you and me and that you married Wong, I assure you. Just hear me out:

"I met a girl there. Her husband was killed in the war. He was a Kamikaze pilot. I realised what sacrifice her husband had made, knowing that he would never return to this lovely girl; that he would never see her again. It must have been awful for him to leave her. She helped me. But that was not the only reason that I thought her wonderful. She was lovely in many other ways. She was proud of her husband, that he gave his life for his country. She did not even see the futility of it. I did.

"It was as though I felt the awful pain and longing for her on his behalf. Through his own personal feelings transferred to me in other words. It sounds ridiculous, I know. It was a true feeling nevertheless: something I can never explain to anyone.

She worked in the police force and spoke English well. Without her I would have accomplished nothing. I gave her nothing in return. Not even friendship, maybe she knew why. It was a strong negative feeling I held against her. It was only artificial. I didn't want to give her anything of myself; money yes, that was different, that held nothing of myself, but not any of my feelings did I want to share with her. Those I purposely kept away from her, strange as it may sound to you, since I thought so much of her.

"The two feelings were mutually inconsistent and I knew it. When I was in Japan, I also heard first hand the story from the Japanese camp commander in Tamarkan in Siam, where Marcus, an army friend of mine, was executed for trying to escape. That is what I went to Japan for. To find evidence that would condemn your father. Your father, who was the senior POW officer in that camp, could have done nothing to save him. I know that now. I initially thought that he was scared to the extent that he didn't want to help my friend. I was wrong, very wrong!

The Japanese camp commander on purpose wanted Marcus to escape so that he could capture him later and could execute him as a deterrent. He wanted it done publicly so that nobody dared to escape afterwards. It was horrible. Brutally they cut off his head. Yakumi, that is the name of that Japanese camp commander, also planned it in such a way that your father would get a bad name and would be hated by his own men for not shielding my friend.

The reason for that was because the other POW's had found out that a suggestion had been made to your father by the Dutch camp doctor. That plan offered a possibility that my friend's life could be saved.

That possibility however would never have come off. Yakumi knew all about that plan and your father, by not following up the doctor's suggestion did the correct thing. I wrongly concluded that your father didn't want to help because he was a coward and didn't want to risk his neck. But your father foresaw that traitors in the camp would inform the Japanese. Your father undoubtedly was right about that. There were always informers. Yes, I went to Japan initially to get evidence, which would condemn your father in court. Did I do that out of revenge because you married Wong? Of course not, but I did wonder about my own motives before I went.

"In Japan and some time afterwards I discovered my own true feelings about you marrying Wong. I certainly don't hold it against you that you married Wong. I am satisfied that my feelings hold no hatred against you. It needed Japan to make me see that. To make me see sense. You must believe me when I say that what I hold against your father has nothing to do with you and I any longer and probably never did. It is true Lily!

"The plan by the Japanese camp commander so that your father would get a bad name succeeded; the men did blame him. I did too, but that was only until I heard the total story."

"About this girl, why are you telling me about her? Are you in love with her?"

"I felt attracted to her, yes: but not in the way that you perhaps think. Maybe I was attracted to her because her husband died in the war. I was so sorry for her. There was a strange connection there. I felt that we were both victims of the same war, the same circumstances about which neither she nor I could have done anything.

"She had lost her husband and I had lost you. It was as though there was a common bond by what had happened to us. The similarity if you like. I can't explain it to myself, and neither to you, but that was nevertheless how it felt. This is just by the way, not relevant. I told you about her because I like to explain to you the way I feel about your father. It would feel like betraying my friends if I did not take up their case. I have to! They died Lily. They were abandoned.

"Unfortunately in my mind it is your father who abandoned them. I hold your father responsible. At least that is what I believe up till now. Exactly the same applies to this girl in Japan. She belongs to the race that murdered my friends. I could not forgive her because she happens to be Japanese. They killed my friends. And the similarity holds. I equally think that your father is responsible that my friends were killed.

"Maybe I judge your father wrongly; maybe one day I will see things differently just as I do now about the execution of my friend in Siam. Maybe the army is to blame, maybe nobody. The war upset many of our feelings and our judgements too. When you make judgements, you should create all the original circumstances back again. Only then can you come to a correct decision and even then only "maybe."

How can one ever judge another person not knowing all the circumstances and especially personal circumstances, which were present at the time? How can you do it?"

"About this girl in Japan, perhaps you are in love with this girl and you don't admit it to yourself. What happened to your love life during the war Richard? Did you not have a girl? It would have been so easy for you being free and at the same time lonely. Will you not do something about this Japanese girl?"

"No Lily, I have already explained that to you; she belongs to the people who murdered my friends. I couldn't feel love for this girl. I just could not. It would feel like abandoning my friends if I did. As far as answering the other part of your question is concerned; yes I did go out with girls. I met them at dances and cocktail parties here and there while I was in Australia. It was never a serious affair. For that to happen you were too much in my heart."

"What you are doing to my father now is in contrast to what you said before. You are condemning my father not knowing exactly what the circumstances were at the time."

"I know that Lily. I am confused in my own mind. It is difficult to explain. I want my dead friends to get a hearing they deserve. Otherwise they died for nothing: I owe them. I am indebted to them. I am alive; I was spared. What for? I often ask myself that question. I was certainly not spared for you or for the two of us together. "You were already lost for me when I came back, so you were not the reason for whom I survived and came back. I don't know the answers to the questions that I so often ask myself. Sometimes I keep awake for hours at night, pondering the questions and I never get an answer. And may be there is no reason why I survived. I just happen by chance to be the "in between". I happen to stand between you and your father on the one side and my dead friends on the other.

"And you are the "in between" also. You are the innocent one in all this who gets hurt. Oh Lily I am so sorry for you, I am sorry for us. This will drive a wedge between you and I. Even a bigger wedge than already exists. And neither you nor I have wanted it. I wish I did not have to do this. Do you understand my motives now?" She thought for a while.

"I do Richard, you have always been true to your friends. You have drifted far away in your feelings for me Richard. And I don't blame you. Your heart is keeping me out because of the way you feel about my father. But maybe there are also other reasons, not only because of my father. Richard," she continued. "It is I who is responsible not you. I let you down. I left you. Yes I did. My decision to marry Wong closed the door between us. That door will always be there because I owe Wong. It is an irrevocable step that I took. Nothing will ever turn the clock back. What else can I do? Wong needs me now more than ever. He did everything for me when I needed him. Can you turn your back on that?"

"No you can't Lily, I understand that."

"You don't know what personal grief can make you do Richard. I was so sad and felt desperate when I myself saw your name on the passenger list of the aeroplane that crashed and there were no survivors. Nevertheless I should never have married Wong; it is as simple as that. I did not love him. You are right in your thinking which you nevertheless never voiced to me; why did I not wait till I was absolutely certain that you were not alive? True the circumstances were impossible, but until I had the certainty that you were dead should I not have married Wong. And even believing that you were dead, as I did, I still should not have married him. "The only real reason that you marry someone should be because you love that person and I didn't love Wong. I used him to forget you. I see that so clearly now. At the time I was so sad when I thought you were dead that I didn't care whom I was married to. Wong was so kind to me. There is a guilt feeling and an obligation I feel towards Wong. I didn't realise that at the time but because he was so good to me I feel a bond with him, which I will always feel. I owe him. He deserved better. I did not feel it then but I know it now. I can't leave him." Her beautiful eyes were again full of tears.

"I don't blame you Lily. No longer, honest! And you must never blame yourself.

"I will tell you something you perhaps never knew. You could not have waited for me Lily. The Japanese would have murdered you. Mas was forced to make the broadcasts that he made. They used him for their propaganda and he was forced to say what they wanted him to say, otherwise you would be killed. They had discovered that you were somebody special to him and this was how they had this hold on him: through you.

He never told you that they blackmailed him, lest you would not have wanted that and would have refused. You would then have been accused of treason and beheaded. He also realised that by making those broadcasts, he would lose his standing in the Indonesian community. He knew that he would be tarred a "Japanese puppet" in the eyes of influential Indonesians who may even think that he sided with the Japanese, which is not correct.

I know how Mas is. No one else, maybe with the exception of you, yourself, knows that he suffers under it. He is ambitious and can no longer be the peaceful arbiter, which is what he really had wanted to be. Therefore and instead, he has taken to force as the only other alternative open to him to play a role in the future of Indonesian independence. That is why he is fighting the Dutch now."

"And he sacrificed his good name and all the other things for me Richard?"

"He did; he told me so. He said he would have married you himself, but even believing that I was dead, he could not bring himself to do that to me. He decided that Wong, who was in love with you, should marry you for your own protection. It was a wise decision. I agree with that.

"It was also a sacrifice on his part because he loved you too. He also reasoned that you were perhaps safer married to Wong since he himself was watched by the Japanese constantly." Lily did not speak for a long time.

"I have guessed for some time what you just told me about Mas. The sacrifices he made for me. I have always felt that, but neither he nor Wong, ever wanted to tell me that, lest I would feel guilty about it. I always felt that he protected me against his own interest.

"Richard you never have tried to take me away from Wong. Why didn't you? I'll tell you why: Because he is your friend and friendship means everything to you. You and Mas are the same in that respect."

We were quiet for a while and I drove automatically letting my thoughts wander.

"Turn in here Richard we are near Lembang. I'll show you where Mas lives. I know that you would never betray his whereabouts so I will take you."

"How do you know where Mas lives and how do you know that he will be there at this time?"

"I have already told you that I often see him."

"Yes you did."

"Well I am his concubine." I was taken aback.

"How could you Lily? What about Wong, does he know? He will be very hurt."

"I don't know Richard. Sometimes I think he does, but he has never mentioned it: maybe not, I don't know. The only excuse I have is that I was so heartbroken when I saw you again at the station in Batavia. I felt that there could never be anything more between us. I was so heartbroken about you all over again. And I have since felt that you are far away from me; out of love with me.

"Deep down you will always feel that I betrayed you. I know it. Not only because I am a woman, but because I would have felt exactly the same if our roles had been reversed and you would have married someone else instead. I feel it perhaps also because I am a woman. Women feel these things differently Richard. They don't need to reason things out."

So Haroen Janoedi was speaking the truth when he told me that Lily was Mas' concubine. I felt a pang in my heart. But what was it to me after all? We were "washed up" as they say. She could do what she wanted.

"Did I hurt you Richard? Surely you must have guessed it already when I first told you that I was seeing Mas often." I nodded:

"I guessed it Lily. Moreover I have heard it from Haroen also. He never knew there had been anything between you and I, so he told me that in all innocence."

I drove along the road aimlessly. My mind was elsewhere; where it was more than four years ago back in the days when we were engaged and very much in love when everything was still perfect between Lily and me. I should be married to Lily now instead of Wong, had the war not interfered with our lives. So much had happened in those intervening four years. What was the point of looking back? Yet I could not help it.

"Richard I hope that you will forget me. You must! One day you will meet someone new, who will be like I was: a long time ago and who will love you deeply as I did. You will fall in love again. She will make you happy all over again just as I have wanted to do that. Oh, Richard I so much wanted to make you happy. I can't make you happy any longer. I have a past Richard and that past will always stand between us and will follow us. Fate did not want us to be together. The war did all that to us. We have passed each other by, but I will always love you. Remember that and always remember the happy moments we shared together. You are my only true love."

I drove on aimlessly, my thoughts were wondering all over the place and nowhere in particular.

Suddenly the road was blocked by a large tree; just after a bend. I woke from my reverie with a start. I put on the brakes, hard. People armed and in uniforms came out of the foliage bordering the road. They were soldiers, but not mine! Freedom fighters they were and Lily and I were trapped! These thoughts raced through my head. My attention had lapsed while talking to Lily and I would regret it. I reached for my Smith and Wesson fast, but Lily grabbed my arm.

"Don't," she shouted, "they are Mas' troops, and you have nothing to fear."

In spite of what she said, I had my revolver out before she had finished her sentence. She threw herself bodily at me and wrestled with me to get my revolver. The freedom fighters also wrestled with me to get the weapon. I was attacked by about four of them and eventually the mob managed to pin me down the moment I had just knocked out one of them. All this time Lily did nothing to help me and instead was trying to hold me down too.

"You have nothing to fear," she repeatedly shouted to me. "They won't harm you."

It took me a while during the scuffle before I realised that they had not attacked Lily. My revolver, which had dropped on the ground, was taken by one of the freedom fighters. What was all this? Lembang was supposed to be a "safe" district. Where was the military post? Our military post? I looked round. There were only guerrilla fighters around us, well armed. The one I had knocked to the ground was just scrambling to his feet again. My hands were securely tied behind my back. It was done efficiently but with care so as not to hurt me. All this time Lily did nothing to help me. Neither did she try to escape.

"They are Mas' troops," she had shouted to me repeatedly: "you have nothing to fear."

I now realised that ten strong and armed men surrounded us and that escape was impossible. We were led along a wild track normally followed by wild pigs and the track ended by a free flowing river. Lily followed unmolested. I had a rope tied round my neck so I could not run away. The headman indicated that I had to enter the water. I imagined that they were going to drown me and I refused. He then bent down and indicated that he would carry me across.

What was this all in aid of? So far they had not harmed me as Lily had said they wouldn't and now here was their leader offering me his back, so that by crossing the river not even my shoes would get wet! To test whether the man meant it I climbed on his back after they untied my hands. He nearly toppled under my weight but he succeeded in crossing the stream with me on his back without falling in the water. He was wet up to his waist and breathless by the time we reached the other side of the river. There my hands were securely tied behind my back again.

The situation was ridiculous. Lily was also carried across. Now what?

"We are not far from our destination and your troops will never find you here," she said. "So far so good, nobody got hurt."

"What is this all about? What destination?"

"You are a prisoner but no one will harm you."

"Why?"

"So that you can't testify further against my father in court."

Now I understood what it was all about.

Lily had led me into a trap so that I could not prosecute her father. I recalled that she had been present at the initial hearing

"It is no use Lily," I said. "The army wants your father condemned; they will take him to court even without me. The army has the case well prepared; believe me. I have the evidence that as far as Marcus in Tamarkan camp is concerned your father could not do anything different. That testimony of mine will go in his favour. Yet the charge about not turning up at Tjipatat will be serious; that is a charge of desertion. Holding me will not help your father's case believe me. Rather the reverse.

"Oh Lily how could I tell you all these things against your father? I went to Japan to find out about your father's behaviour for not having shielded Marcus who was my friend from the army. Now I know that he could not have helped my friend.

But the main charge against your father which the army condemns him for, is that he did not go to the post where he was ordered to go. That is for the army to decide. I don't want to go into that at this stage. May be some day you'll hear the total story. I only wish to bring up the fact that he abandoned my friends resulting in their deaths. Was he himself the only one responsible for that, or are there other people also involved and who are even guiltier than he is? My dead friends deserve a hearing; that is all I want. I hold no other grievance against your father.

By this time we had arrived. It was an old colonial house on poles constructed of teak. The living area was on one floor about six feet high to give protection against snakes, scorpions and centipedes The total living area was surrounded by a very wide covered verandah with a wooden railing all around.

Four staircases gave access to the living quarters above: One staircase at each end of the building. The house must have been some kind of hunting lodge. I also saw a few native atap houses nearby. They had probably been servant dwellings.

Mas came down one of the staircases to greet us. He untied me.

"I am sorry I had to do this to you. You are my guest."

"Nothing doing Mas, I don't want to be your guest and I request that you free me forthwith and tell your people to let me go."

"I am sorry Richard but I can't comply with your request."

"In that case I will escape if I possibly can and you then will have to shoot me to prevent it."

"I don't want to do that either."

"Then free me and I'll go on my way peacefully. I will tell no one what happened. On the other hand if you don't free me now, you will be guilty of kidnapping. Do you realise what you are doing; what the two of you are doing? This is serious. Your credibility, whatever is left of it, with the Governor-General or his successor, will evaporate. It is not worth it Mas. I won't tell on you; of course not, but it is bound to leak out that you kidnapped me. You are doing it for Lily, but it won't help, I know it. The army accuses Lily's father of desertion and that is the way the army sees it. Keeping me makes no difference. Mas have you never been back to Tjipatat? Have you not seen the war graves? Tjaden lies there; also Werbata, Prado, Perquin, Lavallette. Do you not remember them? They were your friends too. Shall I mention all the names of the others who lie buried there? Your friends and my friends they were; our comrade in arms!

"Do they not deserve a hearing? That is what it is all about Mas. Major Cane has deserted these friends in Tjipatat. I want to give them a hearing. They deserve at least that. I am the official prosecutor for the army and the army will proceed with the court case with or without me."

Mas had said nothing. His eyes were moist when I said all these things to him. His thoughts went back to where he was four years ago; to where his and my friends lay buried. Memories were flooding back to him also.

"Please Richard, please don't try to escape. It will be only for a few days, you will be treated well. Two weeks, a month at the most; till the court case is finished and then we let you go again."

"No deal, and when and if I am killed by trying to escape, on your head be it. I assure you that I will try to escape."

There was nothing more to say. I was taken to a room, which contained a toilet and bathroom. It was barricaded from the outside. I contemplated my position. I was annoyed with myself. How could I so easily have fallen in this trap set up by Lily in order to so-called "save" her father? And how short sighted on her part and also on the part of Mas to think that by kidnapping me and preventing me from testifying in court, they could turn the tide into Lily's father's favour.

I had to get out. How? I would be noticed absent in my quarters, but not till the following day. I also had left no note that I was going out for a drive with Lily. The absence of the jeep would also only be noticed the following day. And nobody would know where I had gone. The jeep I was sure would be well hidden by the freedom fighters.

Yet there was one person who would wonder where Lily and I had gone. Wong had wanted Lily and I to go out together. He had encouraged it.

"Why don't the two of you go out together? It is no good Lily you sitting here with me all the time," he had said to Lily. "You must have a lot to tell each other."

If Lily returned alone, Wong would ask for me since he knew that I would not let her return by herself. She would have to tell a lie. And if someone else would take her back, one of Mas' soldiers possibly, it would even be more suspicious that I wasn't with her.

My thoughts returned to how to escape. There was one window but the window was barred with iron railings from the outside. No use to try it in that direction. There was also a sky window; glass, but too high. I would never reach it and the walls were bare. I could not possibly scale these and there was no ladder. No use giving the sky window another thought. I saw nothing more of Mas neither of Lily.

I liked it that way. I had let them know that I did not want to speak to them. Through the door food and drinks were regularly served to me. Mas brought me a gramaphone and a few records also, so that I would have music. Each time the door was opened there were five Indonesian guards well armed in front of the door. I would have to fight my way out and quickly realised that I was indeed a prisoner. Yet I was determined to get out of here.

If and when I got out, there would not be another possibility for Mas to have a meeting with possibly the Governor's successor. That chance was now faded history. The news would go around that Mas had kidnapped me. His credibility already low; would become nil. How could he be so stupid as to kidnap me!

The thought of escape became stronger by the minute. The tricks of fighting bare-handed had been well taught to us by Sergeant Brig in Tjipatat. Now I would try that method of fighting: almost certainly leading to my being killed. Yet I was so furious with Mas and with Lily that even being killed was no deterrent to me any longer. Who did they think they were, keeping me prisoner against my will! Two days went by. My chance of escape depended on the door being opened, even if only ever so slightly to offer me food.

Just as I was thinking how to do it, the door opened to offer me drinks. Almost at the same time, there was loud automatic fire. Very nearby, now even inside the house. My troops! How did they get here?

I didn't think twice. I leapt at the door, with my two feet in heavy boots like a battering ram, aimed at the side of the door. My body, all the weight of thirteen stones plus, behind the ram, plus the speed of the run towards the door, splintered the half open door and I got into the corridor.

The attention of the guards was focussed in the direction where the shots came from. I grabbed the gun of the nearest guard to me who looked stunned to suddenly see me and I fired two shots. Two guerrilla fighters dropped. My sudden possession of a gun had surprised them. The sudden firing of the commando's inside the house taking their attention away, had certainly helped. Mas stood at the far end of the veranda, automatic rifle in his hand. The gun was aimed in my direction. I dived and aimed; two shots. He was still standing. I had missed!

He jumped over the veranda rails, a drop of six feet, but he made it and ran away as fast as he could. How could I have missed? I was the crack shot of the platoon in Tjipatat. Was I not that good of a shot after all? Or did the gun have an aberration? Maybe there was some other reason? I also jumped over the veranda rails but I was not as nimble as Mas was and I tumbled headlong forward. Before I was on my feet again, Mas had disappeared.

I remembered what a good sprinter he had been when we competed at high school. I turned back, there was no point pursuing him. I would never catch up with him.

The army soldiers were carrying a wounded person away on a stretcher. Lily was bending over him: Wong! He was bleeding internally from a gunshot wound in his abdomen.

How did Wong get here? His life was ebbing away fast. He was restless, yet smiled when he saw me. I held his hand in mine.

"How did you find me Wong my friend?" I said to him. "You have just saved my life." He kept smiling, but he didn't say anything. His face was already very pale due to lack of blood, the mask of the dying.

Later I understood what had happened; Wong did not know that army spies secretly followed him. Captain Hensen who was in charge was still after Mas who had escaped him so many times in the past. After Hensen came to know that Wong and Mas had been the best of friends, he took a gamble that by observing Wong's comings and goings and by simply following him, he would eventually know where Mas was hiding

Since Lily and I had not returned, Wong had gone to investigate the next day. That he innocently had led Captain Hensen to where Mas was hiding; he only realised when the shooting started.

Hensen was lucky. Wong indeed knew how to find Mas' hideout. Did that mean that he knew about Lily and Mas? I sincerely hope he didn't but I shall never know the truth.

Wong died soon afterwards. I kept holding his hand in mine and Lily stroked his forehead. He kept looking at her. I do not know who shot him and I still wonder about that. I knew that Mas would never on purpose have fired at Wong, his friend. Mas had been his friend, our friend. Mas had never fired the gun, which had been aimed in my direction either. We had all been friends from our young days: Lily, myself, Wong and Mas. And is there anything in this world more valuable than true friendship? At that moment I realised that there isn't.

Four guerrilla fighters were lying dead. Two had surrendered and one was left wounded. The rest escaped. Captain Hensen who had led the raid shook my hand.

"We meet again, I am glad you are safe. I am terribly sorry that this man Wong who eventually brought us to Mas' hide-out, although he did not know we were following him, died in this cross fire. Most unfortunate," he wiped his forehead. "The amazing thing is that I could have sworn that he wanted to protect the person who I think was Mas. He covered that person with his body and was thereby killed accidentally. Was he such a good friend of Mas?" I could see that he really felt sorry.

"To answer your question simply Captain Hensen; he was!" He shook his head.

"There must be much more to Mas than I thought, for him to have such friends. Because you are his friend also. I remember my first encounter with you. I had wanted to attack the camp where you had just met Mas. Near camp Tjilan that was. That was almost a year ago. You then stopped me from doing so and at the time we did not like each other very much. I warned you against Mas at that time, don't you remember?"

I thought that he was saying it, proud in his belief, that he had been correct about Mas after all, and that he had saved me from harm by Mas, but I was wrong.

"You told me then that he was your friend. I have since found out that the real killer of Tjilan was not your friend Mas. Initially I thought he was. Nevertheless he is still a guerrilla fighter but I respect him.

"The irony is that I have never seen him in reality, except for today perhaps. He has always escaped me. What is even stranger still is that I nevertheless know exactly what he looks like. How you wish to know? Because he exactly looks like a man called Aditripto, the real killer of the women and children of camp Tjilan. And even more ironic; I swore that I would bring the killer to justice and he gets off scot-free because he is a member of the Sultan's forces. I can't touch him. He may even become a highranking politician in Indonesia very soon, when Indonesia becomes independent. There is no justice in this world.

"Speaking about the devil; this fellow Aditripto is also a born liar. Would you believe it that he had me at one time convinced that there was a spy in the forces spying for Mas? He even told me that it was a woman. Of course he could not come up with a name, the liar! I know now that he has taken me for a ride. He pretended that he got this information out of a man called Haroen Janoedi. He pretended that he had captured him; afterwards by torturing him and finally killing him, he said he had obtained the information. None of which, I found out is true.

I have found this man: Haroen Janoedi and I have spoken to him. He is as alive as you and I. Aditripto has made up the whole story only to confuse me and put me off the scent. Why did I ever believe him that we have a spy in our forces, a woman at that? The liar!

But tell me, I am confused. You are Mas' friend. At least you were. Why then did he keep you prisoner here?" I could see that he was totally puzzled when he asked me the question.

"Don't break your head over it Captain Hensen. I thank you for liberating me. I might even have been killed but only if I had been stupid enough to fight my way out of here, which is just what I was about to do, not a minute before you arrived.

The truth you see; is that Mas is my friend and always will be. We were children together and would never harm one another. Only circumstances have changed our loyalties. You have been wrong about Mas from the very beginning. It isn't what you think it is that you are seeing here, but I owe you my life and my thanks. What happened is that Mas only kept me prisoner here so that I could not testify against her father in court. He did not mean to harm me, not in the slightest. I was perfectly safe here. He did it for her."

"Who is the person you are talking about and who is her father, I am still puzzled."

"Over there, you are looking at her. Her name is Lily Cane. You are wondering how she got here aren't you? That is a long story. She has her arms around her husband Wong, the one who was accidentally killed in the crossfire.

"Who is Lily? You might well ask; that is a much longer story still. You see Captain Hensen, the four of us; Mas, Lily, Wong and I grew up together. Each one of us, either Mas, Wong or I myself could have married Lily. Circumstances were such that she married Wong. One of these days when my emotions have died down, and I can think straight again, I'll write a book about her. It will be a long story and nobody will probably read it. Yet I owe this to myself, to her and to what was once our love. At least I will do that. Would you believe it: I was engaged to her once. We wanted to get married before the war. But that now seems almost centuries ago".....

Chapter 26

Aditripto in an open; chauffeur driven car, proceeded to the large central aloon-aloon (large open grassfield area) in the middle of Batavia the capital. Motor bicycle riders in military uniform, two on each side flanked the car and two drove in front of the car.

Their motor bicycles were carrying the red and white flag of Indonesia on their front mud guard. Aditripto's car was also carrying the red and white emblem next to the flag of the Sultan.

Aditripto was full of new plans once he would become president. To start with, the name of the capital was going to be changed to Jakarta, the name it had before the Dutch arrived more than three hundred and fifty years ago.

It had been no more than a fortress in those days; the early 1600. Now it would be the place where he Aditripto, was going to have his palace. He was also going to take down the statue of Jan Pieterszoon Coen, the Dutch founder of Jacatra. It was shortsighted of him. He didn't foresee that it later could have had a historic value for tourists visiting Indonesia.

He would develop the capital to become the biggest Capital in the world. He was not alone in this megalomania thinking! Nor was he original. Every ruler drunk with power before; had entertained similar idea's. Not everyone had succeeded, and many that had tried, had died a sudden premature death! It was not a healthy endeavour. There were always scores of others who felt jealous or who had been passed over roughly and wanted revenge for real or even only for imaginary injustices.

Even the most powerful potentate drunk with power had acquired someone or even more than just one person, lusting for his blood. And of course every powerful dictator had arrived where he was by dirty dealings.

Aditripto fulfilled all these criteria and more. He had aquired a score of enemies in the process. It didn't worry him unduly. He was used to having these!

The platform in the centre of the aloon-aloon from where he was going to make a speech; was built specially for this occasion. Today he gave not much thought to possible enemies, since he had already organised with careful planning, that Mas would receive the bullet if there was going to be any shooting.

This was going to be his triumph day. His inaugural speech was going to establish him as the most eligible candidate for the presidency of the newly created republic. Reluctantly the Sultan had given in and had made him a General in the Sultan's army. It was the position Aditripto needed. His chances to become the president would enormously increase thereby he thought. The Dutch government had bestowed the medals he wore on his chest. But for no other reason than that it was a gesture of respect to the Sultan honouring a high-ranking officer in his army. For good measure Aditripto had added a few more glittering ones to those already adorning his chest. They were made by the Chinese gold smith around the corner. The non-informed Indonesian would be impressed to see him in this uniform and would vote for him. They would see him as the liberator from Dutch colonial rule, although he had in fact done nothing to deserve that respect. Mas had. He had fought the Dutch and the Dutch forces respected him. For him, Aditripto, the Dutch only felt contempt. He knew that captain Hensen for instance, since their initial meeting, had cold-shouldered him.

It did not matter to him. He did not need respect. People needed to fear him. The Dutch influence would soon disappear anyway. He was looking forward to this speech. He had it well prepared. He knew of himself that he was a good orator.

Foreign correspondents from many different countries would be there. He had invited as many as he could find. The more newspapers wrote about him, the better his chances. The newspapers were already full of his photographs.

These never showed the scar through his left eyebrow. He had, sitting in front of a mirror, always carefully hidden the scar when pictures were taken. He looked more like Mas that way.

Ahmed would lead the procession of the troops. He had arranged this with Mas. First they would march into the aloon-aloon carrying their banners. Then the military band would open up. The band had studied and would play the national anthem of Indonesia first. Only after that would they play the Dutch national anthem. Aditripto would have liked to dispense with the latter altogether but the Sultan had insisted.

The latter did not want to offend the Dutch. The Dutch had always treated him with respect. He was going to return this respect.

The bandleader with the utmost care had practised the new national anthem. Aditripto had assured him of a big reward if he played it correctly, but the band leader also remembered the very clear hidden threat in Aditripto's voice when he had coolly said: "make no mistake, because if you do, I will be the laughing stock and there are many hired killers in my service who wouldn't like that."

Ahmed whom he had put in charge of the soldiers, but only for today, had approached him.

"Now that you are a general, you should reward me for my services. Have I not done everything you wanted me to do for you?"

"You have Ahmed and you did even more, but you must be patient. There are people who know that you were in Tjilan camp. If I rewarded you now, I will be seen to agree with the murders that have taken place there. Be patient, once Indonesia becomes a republic and I have become the president, you will get your reward, I assure you".

Ahmed was still valuable to him. He had to be watchful of Mas and Ahmed still had friends in Mas' freedom army. Surely Ahmed could, provided a big reward was offered of course, find a hired assassin among those "freedom" soldiers? And nobody would be able to connect him with that murder.

"You will not be forgotten, I assure you," he repeated the promise to Ahmed. Ahmed didn't know what to make of the last remark.

He knew the reputation of Aditripto all too well, so as not to be altogether at ease about this last assurance. He knew that Aditripto was clever and that he applied his cleverness especially in one direction: getting rid of his opponents.

"You were in camp Tjilan yourself also," he reminded Aditripto casually. Aditripto raised his eyebrow and almost spit out the words.

"How many times have I told you, that you are mistaken! It was Mas who was there! Did you hear me? It was Mas; get that into your head or you may lose yours one day."

A cold shiver went through Ahmed. He had gone too far. Aditripto was dangerous. Many times he regretted that he had betrayed Mas. Mas was dependable, he was an honest person. Ahmed being a crook could tell the difference. He vowed that he would never bring up the subject camp Tjilan again.

When Aditripto arrived, the aloon-aloon was packed with people who looked forward to hear what he had to say. Mas already stood on the platform, also dressed in full military uniform. Aditripto had also made him a General in the Sultan's forces; his equal in other words. Aditripto had done that for two good reasons:

Mas was an important figure; still influential, not to be ignored. He had fought the Dutch valiantly risking his life more than once. He still had a following not only from his troops but also from some influential Indonesians. And it was better to have Mas beholding unto him.

There was a second more ominous reason why he had appointed Mas as his equal. On large gatherings where he was to speak, such as this one, he wanted Mas to appear on the platform first. And Mas had to look like him, as much as possible, which of course included the uniform. People would be fooled to think that they were seeing Aditripto and possible assassins would shoot Mas instead of him.

Today was no exception. Mas would already have been on the platform shortly before he arrived! Mas had no reason to distrust him and considered that Aditripto had appointed him a General, as a reward for having fought a guerrilla war for the freedom of Indonesia. He should have been more careful. The only reason Aditripto had not got rid of Mas yet, was Mas' usefulness to him. On this particular occasion, Aditripto was very much aware that a group of dangerous Chinese held him responsible and knew, that he was guilty of the murdered women and children of Tjilan. These Chinese were the relatives of those that he had murdered in Tjilan. Aditripto counted on the fact that because he and Mas looked so much alike, that those people who expected him to appear, might easily be fooled to think that it was he, Aditripto, they saw, instead of Mas, especially so from a distance. And Mas was never suspicious why Aditripto wanted him to appear first at every public function that Aditripto attended.

He held no grudge that the Sultan had changed his mind about his successor. After all Aditripto held a high rank in his army and the Sultan had now become dependent on Aditripto!

The war against the Dutch had ended. At last an agreement between the Dutch and Indonesians through the influence of America had become effective. Indonesia was to become independent. The guerrilla war had at last ended. Mas could show himself in public now. He was no longer a "wanted" person.

Two hundred meters away from the platform, two male Chinese looked over the barrel of their guns. The guns were fitted with long-range telescopes. The two Chinese were father and son, forty and twenty years old respectively. They wore a black band around their upper left arm as a sign of bereavement. Their little daughter and two sisters had died at the hand of the murderer of Tjilan.

They had a photograph of him. As the Sultan's senior officer in the army he often appeared in many newspapers with large photographs. Neither father nor the son knew that another person existed who looked like Aditriptro: the Sultan's nephew Mas! Neither father nor son knew that they would aim at the wrong target.

The shots would not be fired at a difficult angle but the shots would have to be fired from a long distance; from the upstairs of an empty house bordering the large grass square where the platform stood on which Aditripto was going to give his speech.

The chances of hitting the target were not very good. The house had belonged to a family friend of theirs who had left to live in China. The family feared for their lives once the anti-Chinese resentment, which was already simmering under the surface, would be unleashed when the Dutch left. Father and son knew that their chances of escape were nil. It did not matter to them.

Since they were Chinese they knew that they would be killed by the mob. Justice they would not get anyway, because they were Chinese.

Siok Tiong and his son had practised shooting at the army range initially. They pretended to shoot for reasons of sport, wanting to have a reasonable chance in a forthcoming sport contest. So they made the Dutch sergeant who taught them believe. And by bribing the army sergeant who in the end had pronounced them "crack shots", they managed to buy two rifles fitted with long-range telescopes. They were German guns, from the best gun makers in the world.

The sergeant gave the ammunition free. He had made a handsome profit. Siok Tiong paid the extortionate price without blinking an eyelid. Neither he nor his son would need money any more. They were totally satisfied to die, once their mission was accomplished.

"You will easily win your contest," the army sergeant said, showing them the paper target they had been shooting at. "You see here the holes the bullets have made? They all are within a circle with a diameter of something less than ten centimeters! I have seen no better shooting than that."

"But what happens if we are asked to shoot at a target at two hundred meters?"

"Two hundred meters?" The sergeant was astonished. "What shooting contest is being organised to shoot at a target two hundred meters away? It can't be done." He spit at the floor.

"It has to be done," the older of the two Chinese insisted mysteriously.

The sergeant became interested. This was no ordinary request.

"I will tell you something," he said ticking his front teeth with his pencil. "Next sunday we go into the country. I know a spot on a hill. You can shoot down the hill from there. Two hundred meters it is. I will bring the ammunition free; but this time I'll bring differents bullets: for long range," he added. "Just give me a Chinese meal at the end of the day and I don't need to know who your target is.

I know that he, whoever he is, deserves to be killed because I know that I am dealing with two honest men." The father and son simply nodded.

Two days before the day of Aditripto's speech on the aloon-aloon, Siok Tiong and his son hid in the abandoned house. They had every item in the house arranged in such a way that from one upper window they had an unobstructed view on the platform where Aditripto was going to stand. All they had to do now was to wait.

The Chinese had been taught well. They had indeed become "crack shots" as the sergeant who had taught them had said.

Both bullets hit Mas. One entered his head, the other pierced his heart. The two Chinese were lynched by the mob. They never knew that they had shot the wrong man. Before they died they were satisfied that they had, as they thought, "succeeded" in revenging their murdered relatives. My best friend had died by their mistake!

I especially regretted that I had never been able to speak to Mas again since the day that I had been led into the trap, set up for me by Lily and Mas, to what they thought was to "save" Lily's father from prosecution by the army.

Mas must have wondered why, when he was standing on the verandah of the house where I was held prisoner, I had missed hitting him although I had fired my gun twice at short distance. He knew very well that I had been the best marksman in Tjipatat.

Every time I visit his grave, I find that fresh flowers have been put there. Among them there is always one red rose. It doesn't lie among the others but is placed separately. It overlies the area of his heart. I know why. True love is difficult to define. I realised that Lily had always held it, not only for me, but also for Mas and Wong equally also. Did that mean that she loved Mas more than I? I don't think so and I am not jealous. Nuances of love in life are determined by circumstances but the essence of love does not change.

Chapter 27

"There are a few things which I would like to be clear about and that is why I came to see you tonight," Hes was talking to major Cane. "I would like you to keep this talk between you and myself strictly confidential please.

"There is an important question in my mind which has never been answered to my satisfaction and I am looking for the truth. You must be aware that the guerrilla fighter Mas, who was recently killed: perhaps through mistaken identity, I understand, was always blamed for the massacre in camp Tjilan.

"I myself never knew what to believe since I have always been puzzled, that the women, who were liberated from Tjilan, mentioned that they can easily recognise the leader of the band of guerrillas who murdered the women and children in that camp, because "he had a marked scar over his left eyebrow". They have also described him as "extremely brutal." Mas never had a scar over his left eyebrow. That I have had confirmed already. But this fact alone; as far as I am concerned, is not enough to exonerate him.

"I have not seen Mas again since he was a military recruit, also stationed in Tjipatat where I was posted during the outbreak of the war as you know. However since you knew Mas from even before the war, when he was friendly with your daughter, you are the person I wanted to ask this question to. This is very important to me."

"What is the question you want to ask me captain Hes, and why is it so important to you?"

"I will explain later why. I very much would like to have your opinion first. Have you ever considered Mas capable of murder?"

"I don't think so, certainly not, I would say. A few months ago I would not have been so sure. At that time there were so many reports of his wrong doings that I began to wonder. It even occurred to me that there might be another person who commits the attrocities and that Mas is blamed. It has also been years since I saw him, before the war, not recently although he came to visit me one night but unseen by me. I will tell you the story later.

"Anything could have happened to a man since then of course. There has been a lot of violence and killing lately. Even the most gentle of men may have turned to become murderers in these abnormal conditions. It is possible that people under these circumstances become what they really are in essence, showing their true nature in other words and that living under the veneer of a normal society this true nature is hidden, who can tell? A sort of Jekyll and Hyde in other words.

"I have seen my own men become callous, unforgiving and extremely cruel. That is what war conditions can do to you. But as far as Mas is concerned, I have evidence that he has always protected my daughter throughout the war and afterwards. I also have a good memory of him myself. Very recently that was.

"One night I got a letter from him, delivered through a messenger boy. The message was; that Lily would be arriving by train the next day. He made sure that I received the message although taking a risk that he might be caught doing so. I have never forgotten this kind gesture on his part towards me. I have never been able to return his kindness to me. "My daughter is a good judge of character and has always defended Mas. If anybody knew Mas, she did. She and Richard both did. Richard has always been his best friend. You could ask him that question also. But why do you ask me this question about Mas? He is dead now. I personally very much regret that he was killed. In spite of the fact that he fought the Dutch, deep down he felt friendship for the Dutch. He also was a clean fighter. He would have been a good statesman for Indonesia had he lived. No, he was certainly no murderer. I cannot be wrong about him. But Lily will be able to tell you about him best. Why don't you ask her?"

"I have been on the point of asking her that question but did not do so outright. The reason that I didn't is because she already holds herself guilty for what happened, namely the murders in Tjilan. I don't want to make her feel more guilty than she already does, by asking her any further questions about Mas."

"Why should she feel guilty about those murders?"

"She shouldn't but she does and that is why it is so important that I know who the person was she spoke to. I'll now explain this to you.

What you may not know is that Lily has been spying for Mas."

"What? I hardly believe it."

"Just hear me out major. I am not here to condemn Lily. Rather I want to find out about one incident when Lily was rung by someone who either was Mas himself or somebody posing as Mas. What happened I think went something like this: Lily herself thinks that it went this way and I tend to agree with her point of view. Accept that she was spying for Mas, wrong of course but she considered him her saviour in the Japanese period, which is undoubtedly true. Accept that she was telephoned by a person she thought was Mas but in fact was Aditripto and not Mas. What you don't know is, who Aditripto is. He is an officer in the Sultan's army. He uncannily looks like Mas. His voice and that of Mas are indistinguishable, especially over the phone, I am told. Aditripto himself mentioned this in a conversation he had with Captain Hensen. Although very likely, that this is the way it happened, it is still not absolutely certain that it was Aditripto she spoke to, pretending that he was Mas or that the person in fact was Mas himself. I wish that I could be certain about that. The person she spoke to over the phone asked Lily the plans the army had, with regard to the liberation of camp Tjilan. You did discuss this with Lily didn't you?"

"I did, and I remember that she asked me specific questions about that. I was especially surprised about her interest at the time; that is why I remember it so well. I did give the order for Hensen to move in and free the camp. Of course: that must have been the way it went. Innocently she passed the information on to someone whom she thought was Mas and instead was this other man you mentioned, whatever his name is. This must fit the description by the women of camp Tjialan of a "Mas with a scar through the left eyebrow" Does your man have a scar through his left eyebrow?"

"He does."

"Then there is no doubt in my mind and neither should it be in yours that this was the man she spoke to on the phone.

Does that not answer the question you asked me about Mas? This is terrible! Lily a spy and she is my daughter. She is responsible for those deaths."

"No Sir, I don't think so. She would need to have given the information deliberately knowing that it was Aditripto she spoke to, for that accusation to hold true, and she did not. She was as much a victim of circumstances as were the victims of Tjilan. I don't want to saddle her with this guilt. That is not fair. I have pointed this out to her.

"Why I so much wanted your opinion about Mas is because I know the way Lily feels about him. If he had really been the killer in Tjilan I would tell Lily that she feels obligated to a killer and I would have tried to find more damning evidence against Mas; in fact as much as I could find, so as to topple Mas from his pedestal as far as Lily is concerned. You have relieved me from that burden.

"Lily has told me also that Mas has sacrificed his good name for her as far as his standing in the moderate Indonesian community is concerned. No, hear me out: Mas never said this to her to make her feel indebted to him. Richard told her that and that is how she found out. Knowing this to be the case has made her feel doubly indebted to him. It explains why she was willing to spy for Mas. Nevertheless as far as the army is concerned, I am ultimately responsible as head of intelligence that she was able to spy for Mas; officially an enemy of ours, although he is now dead.

"In that capacity I may be questioned by my superiors because Hensen was told by Aditripto that there is a woman spy in intelligence and the news went round. Fortunately he wasn't given the name. Why I don't know but it is a stroke of luck. Perhaps he did not want Hensen to know everything.

"Also fortunately, it is known that Aditripto is a born liar. We can deny whatever he says. Nobody will believe him; not even Hensen believes that any longer. And Hensen is out for his blood, which is also fortunate. I am relieved that I no longer need to have doubts about Mas and that I now am convinced it was Aditripto and not Mas who committed the murders. For Lily it is necessary to have a good memory of the person Mas, who was so special to her. This also puts me in a better frame of mind when I think about the spying aspect. At least she gave the information to a clean fighter apart from this one exception, when she gave the information to Aditripto by mistake, which was unfortunate but not her fault."

"Captain Hes, may I call you Carl?"

"Of course you may Sir."

"I would like to ask you a confidential question. I hesitate to ask you that question but I will tell you later why I am nevertheless asking it."

"Feel free to ask major Cane, we are having a confidential talk, which shall always be between you and me only."

"Are you in love with my daughter Carl?"

"That is not difficult for me to answer major. I have been in love with your daughter from the first time I saw her, which is when we were dancing in villa Isola five years ago. She was engaged then and after the war she was already married. Her husband Wong has since been killed accidentally. He has deeply loved her and sacrificed his health trying to protect her, to the extent that he became an invalid.

"I know that his memory will always stand between Lily and me. The trauma she has sustained seeing him become the invalid that he was, has resulted in a feeling of being so sorry for him, that she will never be able to forget him, and that she will never marry someone else again. She more or less told me that unintentionally.

"Although Wong is now dead she still has a guilt feeling towards Wong for having used him instead of having married him for love. If she marries again, this will compound her guilt feeling. She told me that there is bonding for love but also bonding for obligation and that the latter is the stronger of the two.

When you think of it, this is perfectly understandable and at the same time also so immensely tragic.

Love is a complicated human feeling and guilt feelings associated with love are never far away."

Major Cane looked out from the window of his living room. There was a long pause. Hes realised that what was coming was very important for major Cane and difficult for him to say.

At last he spoke slowly:

"Carl, I will tell you something in confidence. It is why I asked you the question before. I will only have a few more months to live, if that. The doctors have told me that I have lung cancer. The disease is in the last stages. There is no hope for me. The rot has already spread in my bones also. Lily does not know it. I haven't told her yet.

"I know that the army will dismiss me dishonourably. The case is coming up soon, but I won't be there. The humiliation would have killed me in any case. I have a request to make. It will be asking very much of you: will you look after Lily? She will have no relative left. We were a happy family once Carl.

"My son died in the battle of the Java Sea and I think my wife died from grief over his loss. She never talked about him till the day she herself died. It was strange that she talked about him on that day for the first time and also for the last time ever since his death. It was as though the will to live died for her when she heard the news about his death. My will to live has also died with her. Soon Lily will be alone. I struggle to keep alive meantime, as long as I can, only for Lily. There is nothing else to live for: my army career is a thing of the past.

"There is one thing which I did and which I regret more than any other thing I may be guilty of in my life. What is worse is that I will never be able to undo the damage it has caused. Richard rightly holds me in contempt. I let him down; worse: in the end I deceived him when he trusted me. That was despicable of me. I was not happy with the way he felt about the timing of Indonesian independence. I wasn't the only one. But I was wrong, very wrong to make him suffer for my belief. He cannot possibly forgive me. He will never trust me again.

"In my defence I can say that I never foresaw the implication of what I did. Somehow already too late, I sent him to Tjilatjap in the hope that he would manage to escape to Australia. I knew that since he was a good sailor; that he would try to get away by the means well known to him; by boat of course. And Tjilatjap was the best jumping off point from which to escape by those means. He indeed managed to reach Australia but he easily could have drowned. I can never explain this to him; he would never believe me because he found out that I deceived him once."

"Richard? He was to become your son in law. Why have you not tried to explain? He is a reasonable man, but since you are talking about him, what about Richard and Lily?"

"Yes, she loved Richard deeply. They wanted to get married on her twenty-second birthday but the war interfered with all that. There was a deep feeling between them. It was real love. But it was not only between Lily and Richard. There was a strange friendship between all four of them. I can't put it in any other way. It went very deep: Lily, Richard, Wong and Mas. They were willing to die for each other, I sometimes think. The friendship was as though they had a common soul, if something like that exists. And that I know, at the same time, is also the reason that Richard and Lily will never marry. The memory of Wong and Mas stands like an insurmountable wall between them and will always be there.

But it is different with you and Lily. You were not a part of them, so therefore there may be hope for you."

"About Lily," Hes resumed, "I know it perhaps sounds trite, but I love your daughter deeply. She means everything to me. I will always look after her: if she will only let me. I could not ask her to marry me. I know for certain that she will turn me down for the reason I told you. And yet I know that she holds me dear too."

"I know; that is why I dared to ask you the question. Carl; don't give up hope. You and Lily are both still young although you have lost many years of your lives as a result of the upheaval of the war and its consequences. Lily is fond of you. That I know. And moreover you both have an experience of life, due to this war and this extraordinary period afterwards, which other people in normal circumstances only acquire in a lifetime if ever.

"No one knows what lies ahead for both of you. Lily's feelings may change with time. She will need someone to love I am sure. My life lies behind me. The ending was not good but I have known a good life too. I was happy with my family."

Captain Hes shook major Cane's hand when he left. He had not said much, but major Cane knew that his handshake was as good as a promise given to him by an officer of his army who was an officer in the true sense of the word. Hes never saw major Cane again. The last time I saw Hes was at major Cane's funeral. He had his arm around Lily then to comfort her. He never married her. I never knew if he ever asked her the question and if he did, what she then would have said to him.

All I know is that Captain Hes left the army soon thereafter. Nobody could understand why, but I do. Knowing that Lily had been a spy for the guerrilla forces of Mas and not reporting that fact in order to shield Lily, made it unacceptable for him to remain an officer in the forces he respected.

Will Lily ever find out the sacrifice he made for her, to cover up her spy activity? I hope she never does. Everybody said that Hes had such a brilliant future ahead of him.

Lily never married again. Was it really because of the memory of Wong and Mas? She also never confided in me again. Somehow her father's death has estranged her from me. I had foreseen that this was to happen. It was inevitable. I was the wedge between the love to honour my friends who were lying in an already forgotten and lonely graveyard on the one hand and my love for Lily and Lily's love for her father on the other. I could not escape the consequences of this dilemma. She never knew that I had forgiven her father long ago for what I once felt was his wrong doings against my comrade in arms and myself.

She has become an attaché to the ambassador for the Netherlands in a foreign country. I have never questioned my love for her. It has never died. Maybe one day I will meet her again. We both have grown older living separate lives.

Could the story of Lily and me have ended differently, I often ask myself?

Not very likely; our lives took place in a time predicted by Djojo Bojo as being tumultuous. How could we have escaped its destructive influence without the help of the benevolent Gods in the island of Bali? From the outset they had not wanted to help us. That is why I think it ended the way it did for Lily and me. Some people would call it Karma. And Karma seldom ends on a happy note.

Aditripto never became president of Indonesia. The Indonesian elite chose someone else. Even the Sultanate of Indonesia has become unimportant now. The prediction of Djojo Bojo had come true in every detail. Even today the Chinese who live in Indonesia are always blamed if anything goes wrong in Indonesia. Their misfortune is that they are successful in an economic sense and out of jealousy they have often been murdered by Indonesian mobs, looking for a scapegoat. The Chinese are also discriminated against when it comes to applying for a job, and they have been forced to change their Chinese names to Indonesian names.

The prediction of Djojo Bojo has passed none of us by lightly. Maybe that is why Doel had told me about it. He wanted to warn me. His story about the prediction had an inner meaning but I could not grasp it at the time when he told me the story.

The prediction never mentioned who would become the first president of Indonesia after the white buffalo returned to its stable. Did the wise man not know, or did he on purpose remain silent about that? He wasn't a person chosen by the Dutch. I knew that in any case it would not have been Mas even if he had stayed alive. My memory of him is very strong and always will be. I know that he will live on in Lily's heart forever

Chapter 28

He was thirty-four he said, but his hair at the temples was getting grey already, she observed. He rarely smiled and he showed deep grooves in his forehead. The uniform he wore was neatly pressed, showing up the one medal on his chest. He must have travelled to Probolinggo very early by train she thought, to be on time for this bus now heading for Panaroekan. There was this particular something about him she couldn't fathom and which had stirred her interest in him. What was he doing here? There was a restlessness she could tell, but it was also combined with a certain degree of sadness in his features.

"What is it that you are looking for in Panaroekan soldier?" she asked wanting to resume her conversation with him, which had come to a halt.

"Not Panaroekan but Pasir Poetih." I replied not offering any further explanation.

"Why Pasir Poetih? There is nothing there," she tried keeping up the dialogue.

"Oh but there is; there is a memory, a long story. It happened before the war."

"Not a pleasant one I think?" she tried again.

She got no reply.

"I am sorry," she said.

"No it's allright, I am just going back to see if I have forgotten something which is perhaps still there," I said.

"Is it something bad? Something you want to forget?"

Again he didn't reply. It was beautiful, but time has changed all that, I thought. The girl went silent; then she wanted to speak again to make him talk. It would perhaps help him to do so.

"Pasir Poetih has changed you know," she tried once more. "It is no longer the beautiful place it once was. You won't recognise it," she volunteered.

I thought of Blommesteyn.

"Do you know Pasir Poetih well?" I asked.

"Yes, I was a child fourteen years old when the war broke out. I sometimes worked there in my school holidays."

"Does the name Blommesteyn mean anything to you?" I asked.

"He died; the Japanese took him away. He never came back. The bungalow park is still there though. It is being run by Dr. Schoppel now."

"Run by Dr. Schoppel? It's impossible. That cannot be. He is dead; he died in a sea transport to Ceylon before the Japanese invaded the Dutch East Indies. The ship was torpedoed and he was missing. He must have drowned."

"This Dr Schoppel is very much alive. He is very well thought of. You know him then?"

"Yes he was a good friend of the family; especially my brother's friend."

"You obviously did not come back for him; was there a girl for whom you are coming back?"

The moist in her eyes betrayed that she sensed something: woman's intuition. She guessed that there had to be a sad story. Perhaps he wanted to forget. It was embarrassing. I looked out from the window pretending that I had not seen the tears in her eyes.

"You stayed away too long." How true, I thought. Her remark did not upset me, but I wondered why she had said it. She was not inquisitive, only kind. I noticed her hair clean smelling. Jasmine flowers. Why did she remind me of what happened years ago? It must have been the jasmine flower smell that had triggered it off.

She pointed to the decoration medal.

"Yes," I said, but volunteered no further information. I remembered the friends I had lost. The medal was for bravery and services to the forces. I had never deserved it. My dead friends had, but they had only received a marble slab to cover their graves for their bravery. They had been more than friends. They had been comrades in arms, not to be forgotten. Yes we had lost the war all right.

I wondered how I could have slept last night because the following day would be full of emotion. The emotion showed through when I asked the next question. "Damn," she had noticed. Why was it so easy for her to see through me? I had asked the question nonchalantly. At least I thought I had: obviously not.

"Did you know a girl called Lily Cane?" I had questioned her. "She stayed at the bungalow park before the war, just before the war."

"I do and now I remember you too. You and she used to go sailing with a Madurese fisherman. He also died. He became blind did you know?" I shook my head.

"No, I didn't know."

To see Doel again was one of the reasons for my returning to Pasir Poetih. The girl had been right: I had stayed away too long. I had wanted to sail with him once more and had hoped that I would find him. Hoping that through him, I perhaps would find what I was looking for. Something that I wanted to find; only I did not know what exactly: perhaps peace of mind?

"He was an interesting man," the girl continued. He used to tell me stories. They sounded like fairy stories to me at the time, but I have since found out that they came true. It was as though he could tell the future. Maybe because he was blind that he could foresee things. Do you believe that it is possible for some people to foresee things which are still to come?"

She did not wait for my answer but continued.

"What I don't know is how one particular story of his will end. It was quite different from other stories as far as it went. Will it have a happy ending like many of his other stories before, did? I would very much have liked to know the outcome of this one because this one was unusual; it was a love story. What was remarkable; was the fact that it was the only love story he ever told me. And the sad thing is; that he died before he could tell me the ending. There was also something about the story even though I never got to know the ending of it, which made me think that he intimately knew the people or at least some of them, who were involved.

Also this story had some quality of sadness in it. Because of this quality in it, it kept haunting me all these years."

"How romantic," I remarked. "You hope that there will be a happy ending of course? There usually is, so this one will be no different."

"No; not necessarily so with this story. I was very uncertain how the ending of this one would be. I'll tell you why.

The girl in this story by mistake, married a friend of her's who was not her sweetheart. She married this man because she thought that her true sweetheart had died and was very sad about that. She thought that he had flown away to a far distant land with a big bird. And because the big bird was killed in the sky, hit by an arrow and fell down from the heavens, she concluded that her lover and the big bird must have died together. That sadly is what she thought. But she was mistaken to think that.

Her lover never flew away with the bird so her lover didn't die with the bird. He had gone to this far distant land by boat instead.

When her lover returned from this distant land, he naturally was very distressed to find that his true love, the one who had promised to marry him, was already married.

What happened next was, that the man she was married to, the husband in other words, subsequently was killed in a fight in which her lover was also involved.

You may perhaps think that it was the sweetheart who, because he was jealous, killed her husband. But no, that isn't what happened. The husband was not killed by the one she loved but by someone else. The interesting thing is that the husband was killed in an attempt by him to find his wife and the sweetheart she truly loved. The two of them had gone out together and had not returned. He was not only concerned about his wife's safety, but also about the safety of her lover. Which husband would ever have such considerations! It did not fit. It surely is not normal that any husband would worry about the safety of his wife's sweetheart!

I mentioned this anomaly to Doel and he explained why it was nevertheless correct. You see the husband, the girl and the sweetheart; had known each other well. They had grown up together. There had always been a very strong bond of friendship between them. It was because of this friendship that she married the man who became her husband when she thought that her lover was dead. I told you already that the lover did not kill the husband because he and the husband would never hurt each other. Moreover her husband was trying to prevent that anything harmful would happen to her lover as I already said before."

"Then the question remains: who killed the husband?"

"I don't now for sure but it certainly was not the lover. No, it appears that another man killed the husband. What I would like to know of course is, if the girl and the lover will ever come together again, now that her husband was dead anyway.

"It would only be natural to expect that the girl and her sweetheart would now be able to marry, since they were both free to do so after the husband's death. Don't you think so? Now I will never know, because Doel died before he could finish this story. And now I also will never know who the man is who killed the husband."

"I can tell you the ending of the story if you wish to know it. This love story unlike most love stories did not have a happy ending. They never came together again."

"That cannot be true. You are a cynic; why don't you believe in happy endings?"

"As far as who the man is, who killed the husband is concerned," I continued, ignoring her remark, "I like to think that the husband got killed by accident; not by any particular person, certainly not on purpose."

"No, I don't think that that is all there is to it; not the way Doel told me. There was this other person, I am sure about that. The story went further.

"Yet another man was involved. This other man was a friend of the husband also, but he particularly was a good friend of the lover. He probably was the killer."

"Why should that be, since you just said that he was not only a friend of the lover but also of the husband? It becomes very complicated."

"His stories were sometimes complicated but not this one. I have to think what he said. Oh, I have got it now.

"The killer; if he was that, kept the lover prisoner in a large house. Yes that is what it was, I remember. Why his best friend kept the lover prisoner, Doel didn't say, but armed people stormed the large house in which he was kept prisoner and freed the lover. It was in that fight that the husband got killed. I now remember that detail. The man whom I thought initially was the killer had aimed his gun at the lover in the fight, but never pulled the trigger. It was impossible for him to do so."

"Are you certain that the man; whom you at first believed to be the killer, never fired his gun?"

"I am absolutely certain, because I am very inquisitive as you have noticed, and I wanted to get it water tight correct. I questioned Doel thoroughly about this particular point and about this last man.

"That part of the story did not seem correct to me and I therefore wanted to get it absolutely right because it was confusing.

"First this man kept the lover, who was also his best friend prisoner, but when the prisoner was forcibly freed by the armed people and this man had to fight for his life, he preferred to chance losing his life, rather than kill the lover whom he had kept a prisoner in the first place. That was what was really remarkable. There was such a friendship he felt for the girl's lover, that even in spite of the fact that the lover who now was free, had a gun in his hand and fired at him not only once, but Doel said twice, he nevertheless never returned the fire.

"And he easily could have done that, Doel said. Don't you think that is very remarkable? Doel was very specific in his stories. The killer if he was that, must have had a good reason, not to fire his gun, would you not think so?"

"Perhaps for old time sake, since you said that the lover was truly his best friend.

And do you know; maybe the lover missed him twice for the same reason; he also did not want to hurt his best friend, the man whom you at first believed to be the killer. It could be like that couldn't it?"

"Yes, that must be it. I never thought that it could be like that."

"Maybe it will help you to know that I myself don't believe that the man you held to be the killer, was in fact the killer of the husband. It can't be. They were good friends. You yourself were told by Doel that the husband and the man you suspect were very good friends." "That is true. It could not be him then, who killed the husband. But if he didn't, then tell me who did?"

"Don't ask yourself that question. I have been thinking about that question myself for a long time. I can't answer that for you either, as much as I would like to, even if only to know it for myself and my own peace of mind." She looked at me puzzled.

Things started to become clearer in her head. How did I know so much of the story?

"There is still another point I don't understand," she continued. "What was the reason for keeping the lover a prisoner? And that was by his best friend? That doesn't fit either. It must have been for a girl; the girl in the story don't you agree?"

"No, not exactly like that, but you are very close. Leave the exact reason be. A story is more interesting if some secrets remain. It is the same with people. You must not want to know everything there is to know about someone. You must leave them their inner secret."

"From the way you spoke it seems as though you know the story also. How do you know all this? Did Doel also tell you the same story and told you the ending?" I didn't reply and let her think for herself.

Then she understood:

"It is about you and the girl. Oh I am so sorry. I shouldn't have spoken"

"It is all right. Probably things have to work out as they were meant to happen. You believe in Karma don't you?"

"No, not altogether; it seems to me, that you sometimes, but maybe only sometimes, can escape, or rather can change your destiny, who knows? There are many mysteries in this world of ours.

Maybe we will discover the secrets one day. In any case, you have reached your present destination for today soldier. I am sure that coming back this way was your destiny and that we were to meet in this life, in this journey in the bus.

"I am glad you finished the story of Doel for me, although I am sad about the ending so far and maybe you can still change your Karma."

I got out of the bus and she embraced me.

"Good luck captain, I hope things will turn out well in the end. Doel once said to me: "the tide always turns." Let us hope for the good this time."

I waved her goodbye as the bus tuned the corner. I was alone again with my thoughts. What was this story Doel had told her about? Had Doel meant me to hear it through the girl also?

The story could apply to Lily, myself, Wong and even Mas. Did it? Who was the one who had fired the bullet that day which had killed Wong? I had fired four shots altogether, two of which had found their targets. What about the other two? Was Wong killed by one of my stray bullets? I was not in the mood to solve any more riddles.

I had come back. Why? I did not know precisely. The girl in the bus had said that it was in my Karma that I should return. What for?

Lily and I had promised each other that we would spend our honeymoon here. Blommesteyn also had promised that he would keep a bungalow for us.

Something must still be lingering here; a spiritual remnant of the past in some form or other perhaps? Was it the longing in my heart to make sense of all the turmoil that had happened to me in the last ten years of my life perhaps, which had made me come back? What other thing could there be?

But I knew all too well deep down that the awful unrealised longing for Lily, which would haunt me the rest of my life, was the reason for which I had come back.

The walk to the bungalow park was only a short distance. But everything had changed as the girl in the bus had warned me. The beautiful wide beach was now very narrow, altogether different from how I remembered it had been, when Lily and I spent our holiday here. And the sand was no longer white but had turned grey. I knew what that meant.

The coral reef that had protected Pasir Poetih, "White Sands" had died and the beautiful white sand was covered and mixed with decaying coral debris. The beach would never recover.

The foliage had also changed. The goenoeng Ringgit had once been covered by dense beautiful jungle, offering shelter to deer, panthers, monkeys and a great variety of birds including peacocks.

I had seen and heard the wild peacocks in front of my bungalow.

Nothing like that could be expected any longer; the goenoeng Ringgit was bare. Only the top still held some large trees. The scene depressed me.

Lily and I had been so happy here.

I passed the fisherman's hut where Doel had told me the prediction of Djojo Bojo. It had turned into a garbage dump. The eerie shadows dancing against the billik matting when he told me the story so many years ago; would never be there again. They had packed their bags and had left for good.

At the bungalow where Blommesteyn had lived, I squinted against the bright light. No, he was no longer lying in his lazy chair as he used to do at midday, before taking a nap. And he would no longer be there in the early morning, glued to the radio to listen to the news from Batavia.

Would there still be lizards at the verandah, like the one that had nestled against my foot looking up at me in all confidence that I would never hurt it?

I knocked on the door. The sign said: "Surgery and office."

A man about forty years old opened the door. He was bent, no longer the way I had remembered him, strong and erect, but he was Schoppel all right. It took a while before he recognised me.

"Richard," he exclaimed. "How good to see you. What are you doing here? You survived the war and you are a captain. But you studied to become a controller."

"That was a long time ago Schoppel. Indonesia will be independent very soon. Nobody needs controllers any more. We are a "dying breed". Moreover I was too long in the army. The war has changed my future drastically for me I am here only on a short visit."

"I can see that you have changed Richard. You have that searching look about you that some people have when there is unfinished business in their lives. I hope that you will find here, what you came back for."

"You look well Schoppel. But how can you be alive? I heard that you drowned."

"No, the ship was torpedoed in the sea between Sumatra and Malaysia, you got that right, but I was picked up by a Dutch Navy patrol boat and taken to Pulau Wei, North Sumatra. We, the survivors were put ashore. The Japanese found us and because we were supposed to be Germans, so the Dutch had claimed, we were their Allies and were free the rest of the war.

"Shortly afterwards, after studying another year, I qualified and I have been practicing medicine here. I knew Blommesteyn from before the war too. He encouraged me to settle here and when I heard that he had died in a Japanese prison camp, I asked his daughter if she would sell me the bungalow park. She knew that her father had wanted me to run it. So that is why I am here. There is still the odd tourist in season that comes. Some can pay well. This income provides me with the means to treat the poor free and I have no financial worries.

"Tell me what brings you here? You are staying with me are you not; we have a lot to tell one another. Are you married, have you got a fiancée? Fill me in with the latest."

"I can only stay a short time Schoppel. I want to climb the Ringgit. I have to. She is still in my mind. I have to get rid of the memory."

"Someone from before the war; am I right? Did she die? " I shook my head.

"What about you Schoppel, are you not married?"

"I haven't got the time. Apart from my practice, I also still run this bungalow park for the odd guests also.

"The place is no longer as it was though. Nature seems to have given up. It died with Blommesteyn I sometimes think. Once in a while I am sure that he is still here. I almost see him but when I look closely he is gone. And I also dream about him. Vivid dreams, I can't explain. He loved this place.

"You can stay here as long as you like as my guest but please yourself, you can leave whenever it suits you. You can stay with me here in this bungalow, but you can also have a bungalow to yourself."

I thanked him, "but preferred to be by myself."

"Tell me Schoppel; panthers used to roam into this bungalow park at night sometimes, when I stayed here last." He started to laugh.

"That was before the war, ten years ago Richard. Time moves on. The last panther must have been shot years ago. There is no more wild life, the goenoeng Ringgit is bare."

"I still want to climb to the top."

"I know," he said, "but you will be disappointed. I know the legend also."

"One more thing Schoppel; did you ever meet a Madurese fisherman named Doel?"

"Yes I knew him but he died unfortunately. Before he died, when he was already blind, he said that a man would come back one day and ask for him.

"He said the man would be a captain and the captain would remember him well, because he told the captain a story about a prediction. Strange that you asked for him and that you are a captain, just as he said. Did he have you in mind Richard?"

"Difficult to say," I lied. I had said to Doel when I parted from him, that I would come back one day. He then had wished me luck. That was not extraordinary, but he had also said "farewell" to me. Did he know then already that he would not be here any longer when I would come back? The thought had upset my mind at the time, I now remembered.

The following morning I rose early. Climbing the Ringgit was best before the heat of the sun made the low mist evaporate. If that happened; it would then rise in the air and change into cloud higher up obscuring the view. I hoped that I could see the island of Bali once more. Just this once!

Exactly the way it had been when Lily and I had climbed the Ringgit for the last time. There were no more panthers, Schoppel had said, but I took the Smith and Wesson revolver with me all the same.

There was hardly a path to follow and only because I knew where it used to be did I find it.

There were no more spotted butterflies; no more hoof marks of wild deer; no more gibbons calling to each other from valley to valley. Why had I wanted to come back? Just to find a broken dream? No: I had wanted to get the feel once more. At least that is what I told myself. Something must still be there; something extraordinary. The magic had been here once. Maybe something of that magic had remained?

Lily appeared from behind every block of lava, only to evaporate into thin air as I closely looked. My eyes played tricks with me.

I reached the spot where Lily and I had sat together on the block of lava. She had draped her hair around my face then and we had promised never to forget each other. The loneliness of the place haunted me. The sky was already overcast and I could hardly see the sea.

I did not even try to look for the island of Bali; the sky was too cloudy. It would be impossible to see it. A few sails could be seen in a haze only. The nearest one reminded me of Doel's but of course that could not be his sail. He was no longer there. My imagination filled in the voids.

I closed my eyes: Lily was suddenly here. Was this the magic I had come back for? She draped her hair around my head again. I distinctly felt her. So strong was her presence that I felt her arms around my neck. Her presence became even stronger; the jasmine smell filled my nostrils. I knew that she was here. This wasn't imagination. This was real. I wanted to embrace her too.

But when I opened my eyes to do that, it was only the breeze that had touched me, and I had mistakenly thought that it was Lily caressing me. The spell or whatever it was; was broken.

At last I got up. Schoppel had warned me that I would be disappointed, but I would not give up. No, not yet. Not until I reached the grave. I surely would find something there. There just had to be something there, there had to be!

It became hot. The murky sky trying to keep away the sun so far was losing out and the sun took over with a vengeance. I could do with some shade but there wasn't any. Somehow even the remains of the jungle were giving up further.

So far I had not yet encountered a snake. They probably had left also. I was not interested any longer. I had not come back to make a wish. I just wanted to get the feel of the place. Just once more! At last I reached my destination.

The grave ought to be here. Instead I saw a deep chasm produced by the rain or perhaps another earthquake? Maybe I was at the wrong place. I looked around.

There should also be a wooden railing all round the grave. But a few slates already partly eaten by white ants, was all I could find. Was this really the place? Then I remembered: the Cambodja tree: of course! The tree must still be there. That would give me a clue.

Frantically I looked round. It should be at the head of the grave. Then I found it. The charred remains only. The tree was dead! Lightning had struck it.

This was the place all right. There was no more. The last traces of our love lay buried here.

I stayed half an hour. I had come to find something; at least something, but there was nothing. Was the hadji a fraud? Was his promise, which assured a mortal that a wish made, upon reaching the grave would come true, a fraud? Why had I ever believed in the promise?

But then I remembered that the Holy man had made no promise: neither to me nor to Lily that day so long ago. We had not been able to make our wish expecting that the wish would come true; because we did meet a snake on our way up, even though only just before our last few steps to the grave.

The one requirement, before one could make a wish and which then would be guaranteed to come true, had been very clear. No snake was to be met before reaching the grave in order that the wish could be guaranteed. That one requirement had not been met: neither by Lily, nor by me. The hadji was not to blame. Only we had not understood his silent message to us that the fervent wish, which had been in our hearts, was not to be fullfilled.

The next morning I shook hands with Schoppel to say goodbye to him.

"I am sorry Richard that you did not find what you hoped to find, by coming back. It is never easy to accept your fate. And I have no medicine for you. There is no cure; neither by pills nor by concoction for what ails you. It is not as easy as that. But you will heal in time. I know it. Come back when you are well again. You don't need to forget. You even must not do that! The events that have upset you deeply will in the course of time, become "bitter sweet". The sharp edges eventually will go and your memories will become valuable to you.

"Memories are like roses in December didn't you know? They are necessary ingredients for living."

Perhaps he was right. Lily a long time ago had in a philosophical mood said to me:

"Beautiful moments you only get on loan. They pass as time passes. You will never be able to hold on to them. We are mortals and tied to time. It is only the memories of those beautiful moments, which will always indisputably be your own possession. Those even the Gods can't take away."

What it amounted to was, that I needed to treasure my memories and should learn to bury my beloved ones of the past. The war had upset my mind in a big way and Schoppel had understood. We had lost the war.

My comrades of the war were dead and so were Wong and Mas my dearest friends of my youth.

And Lily, dear Lily who still comes back to me in my dreams when the long evenings have been lonely? Does she sometimes think of Wong her devoted husband who died so tragically and of Mas our dear friend who looked after her during the war against his own interest; maybe of myself also, once in a while?

When the bus for Probolingo rounded the corner, I did not look back as I did the time when Lily waved me goodbye, waiting and hoping for my return to her.

I have left my tears and my memories at the Ringgit and at the dream paradise Pasir Poetih, "White Sands" at the foot of the Ringgit, as it was when I knew it once, now so long ago. At last I said goodbye to my beloved ones of the past. I never returned to Pasir Poetih.